WICKED LOVELY
DESERT TALES
CHALLENGE

Wicked Lovely: Desert Tales
Volume 2: Challenge
Story by Melissa Marr
Art by Xian Nu Studio: Irene Diaz & Laura Moreno

Visual Storytelling Consultant - Barbara Randall Kesel

Lettering - John Hunt
Cover Design - Al-Insan Lashley

Senior Editor - Lillian Diaz-Przybyl
Pre-Production Supervisor - Vicente Rivera, Jr.
Pre-Production Specialist - Lucas Rivera
Managing Editor - Vy Nguyen
Senior Designer - Louis Csontos
Senior Designer - James Lee
Senior Editor - Bryce P. Coleman
Associate Publisher - Marco F. Pavia
President and C.O.O. - John Parker
C.E.O. and Chief Creative Officer - Stu Levy

A **TOKYOPOP**® Manga

TOKYOPOP and ⊚ are trademarks or registered trademarks of TOKYOPOP Inc.

TOKYOPOP Inc.
5900 Wilshire Blvd. Suite 2000
Los Angeles, CA 90036

E-mail: info@TOKYOPOP.com
Come visit us online at www.TOKYOPOP.com

For information address HarperCollins Children's Books, a division of HarperCollins Publishers,
10 East 53rd Street, New York, NY 10022.
www.harperteen.com

Library of Congress catalog card number: 2010920502
ISBN 978-0-06-149349-2

10 11 12 13 14   LP/BV   10 9 8 7 6 5 4 3 2 1
❖
First Edition

WICKED LOVELY
DESERT TALES
CHALLENGE

STORY BY
MELISSA MARR

ART BY
XIAN NU STUDIO

TOKYOPOP®

HAMBURG // LONDON // LOS ANGELES // TOKYO

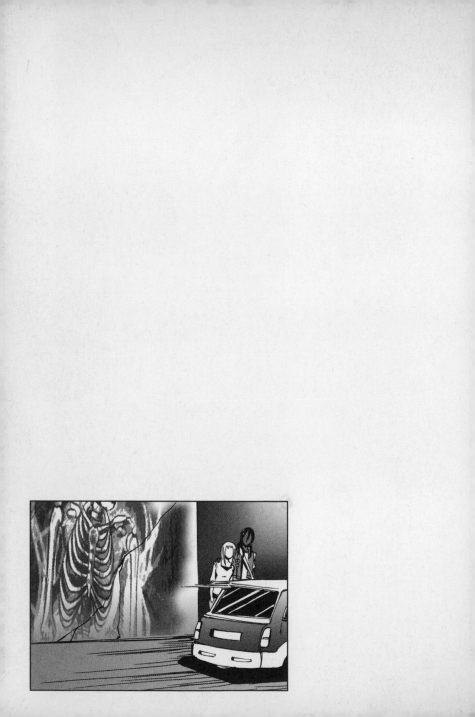

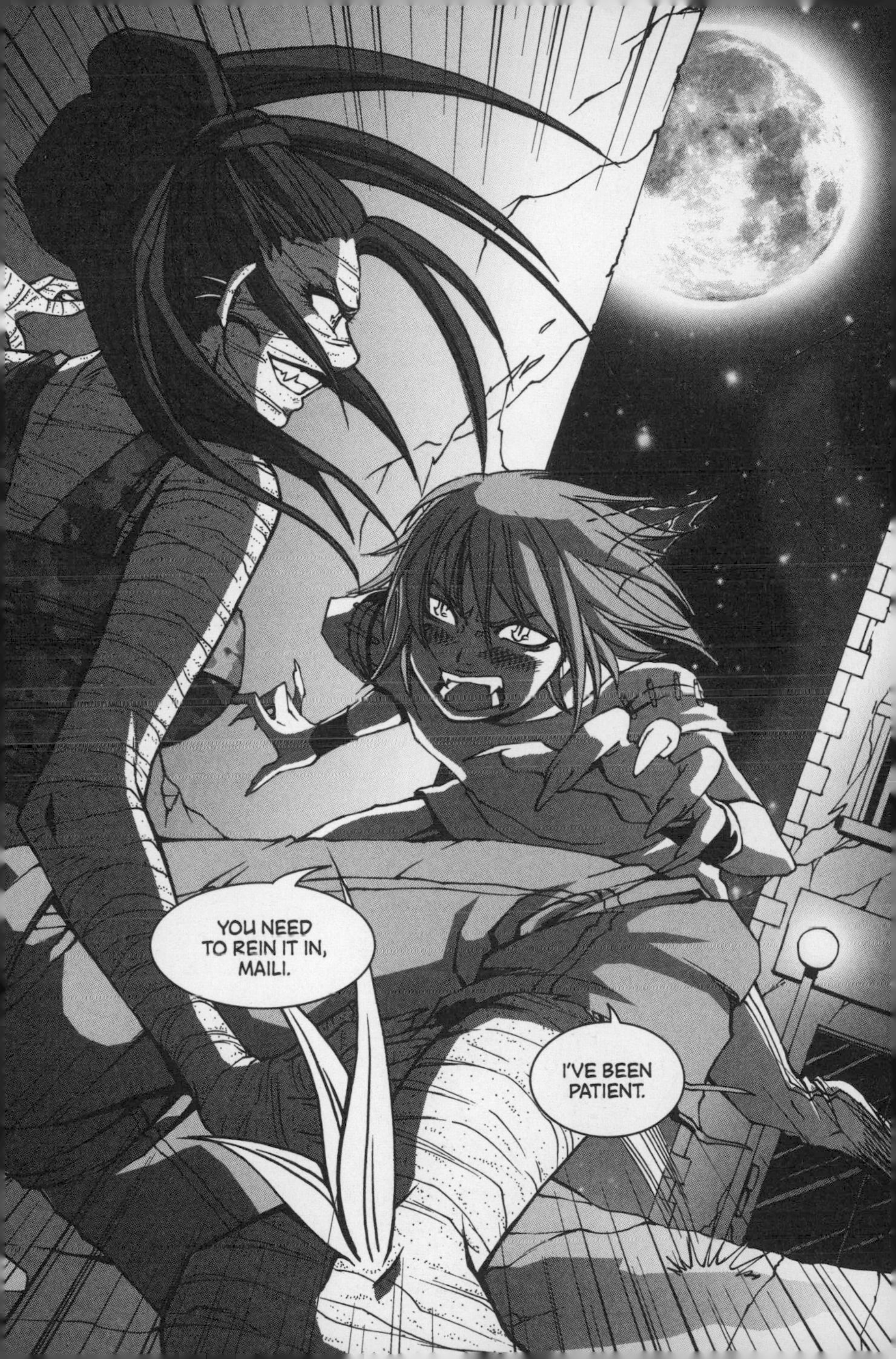
YOU NEED TO REIN IT IN, MAILI.
I'VE BEEN PATIENT.

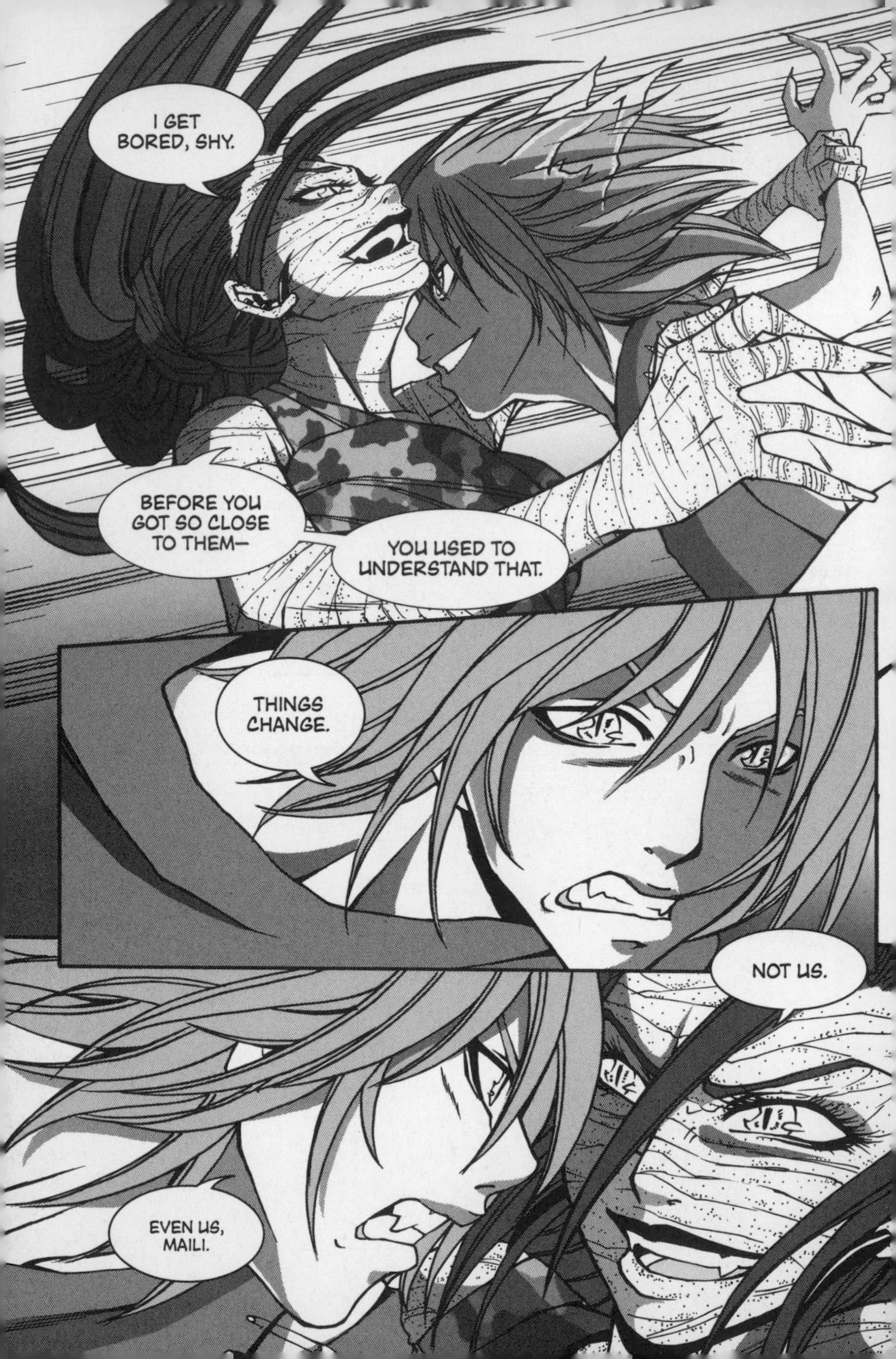
I GET BORED, SHY.
BEFORE YOU GOT SO CLOSE TO THEM—
YOU USED TO UNDERSTAND THAT.
THINGS CHANGE.
EVEN US, MAILI.
NOT US.

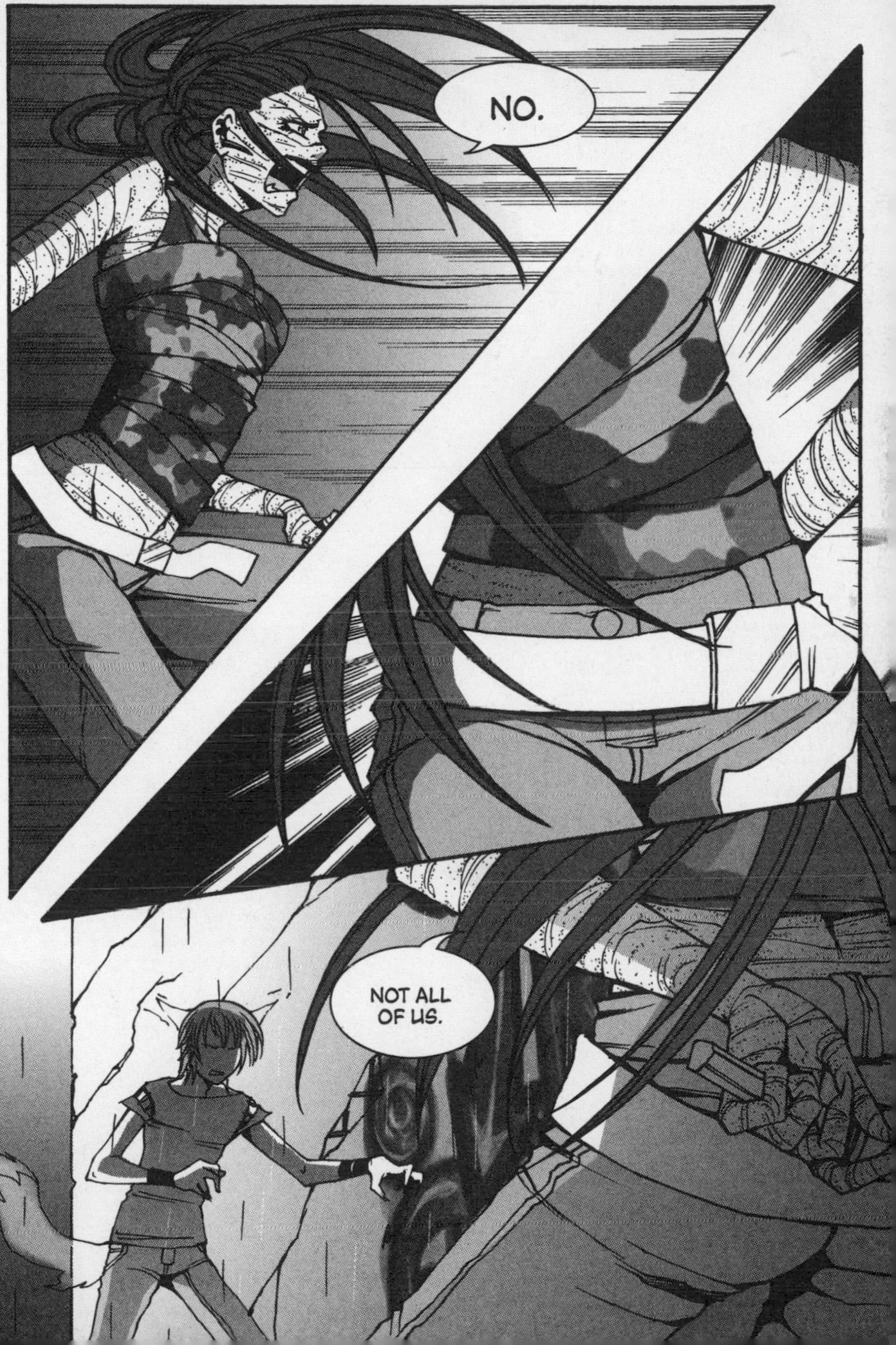
NO.
NOT ALL
OF US.

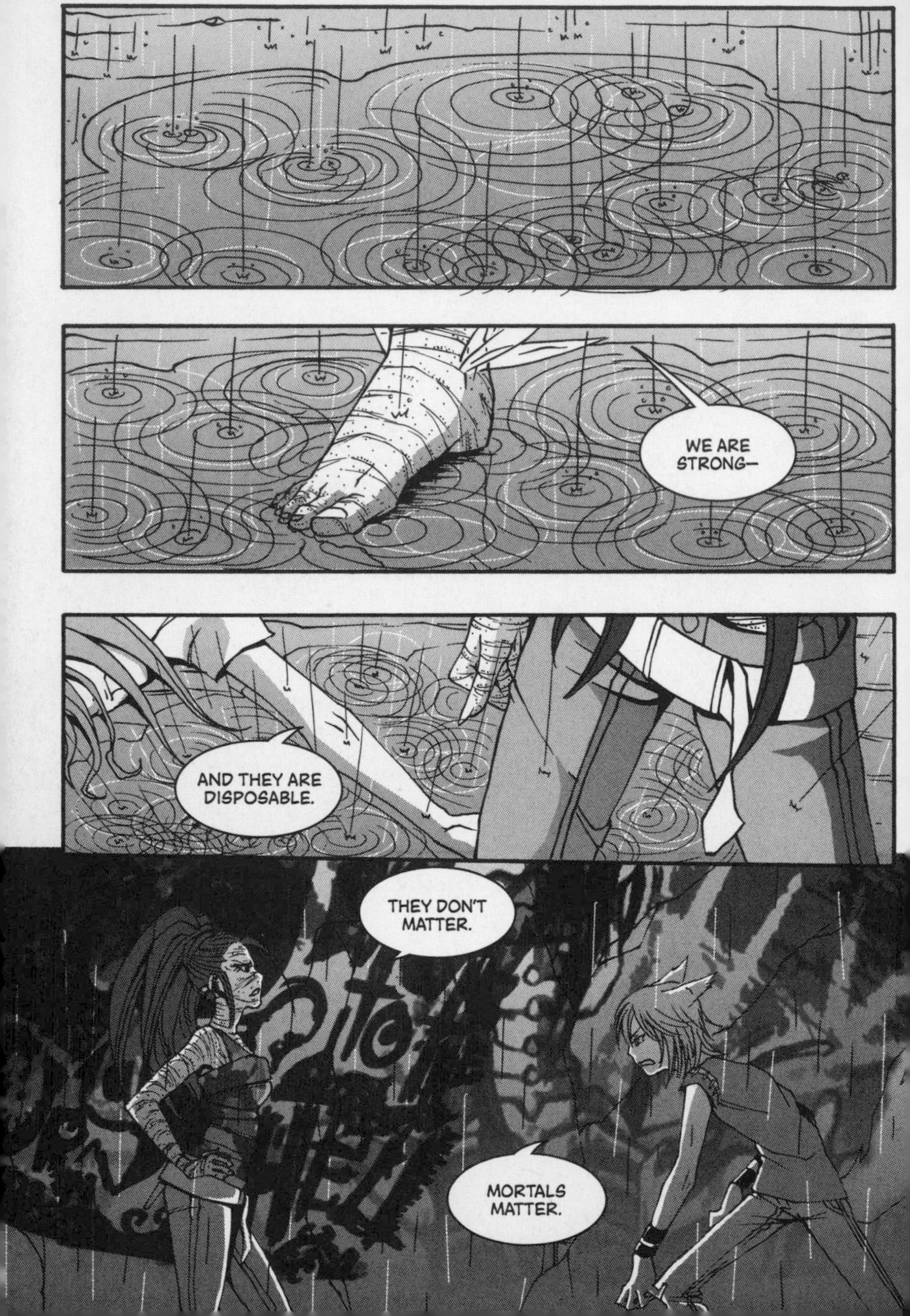
WE ARE STRONG—
AND THEY ARE DISPOSABLE.
THEY DON'T MATTER.
MORTALS MATTER.

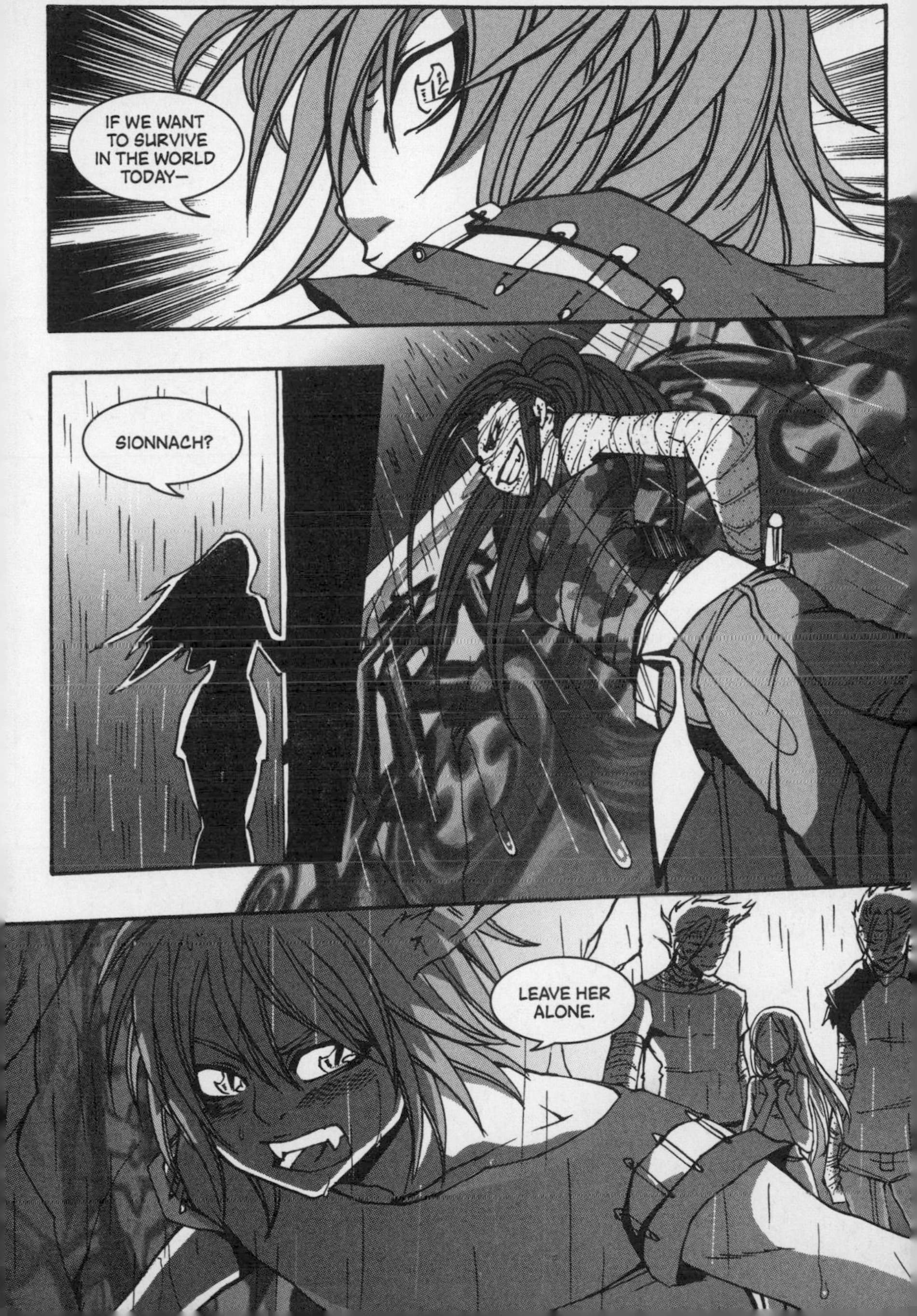
IF WE WANT TO SURVIVE IN THE WORLD TODAY—
SIONNACH?
LEAVE HER ALONE.

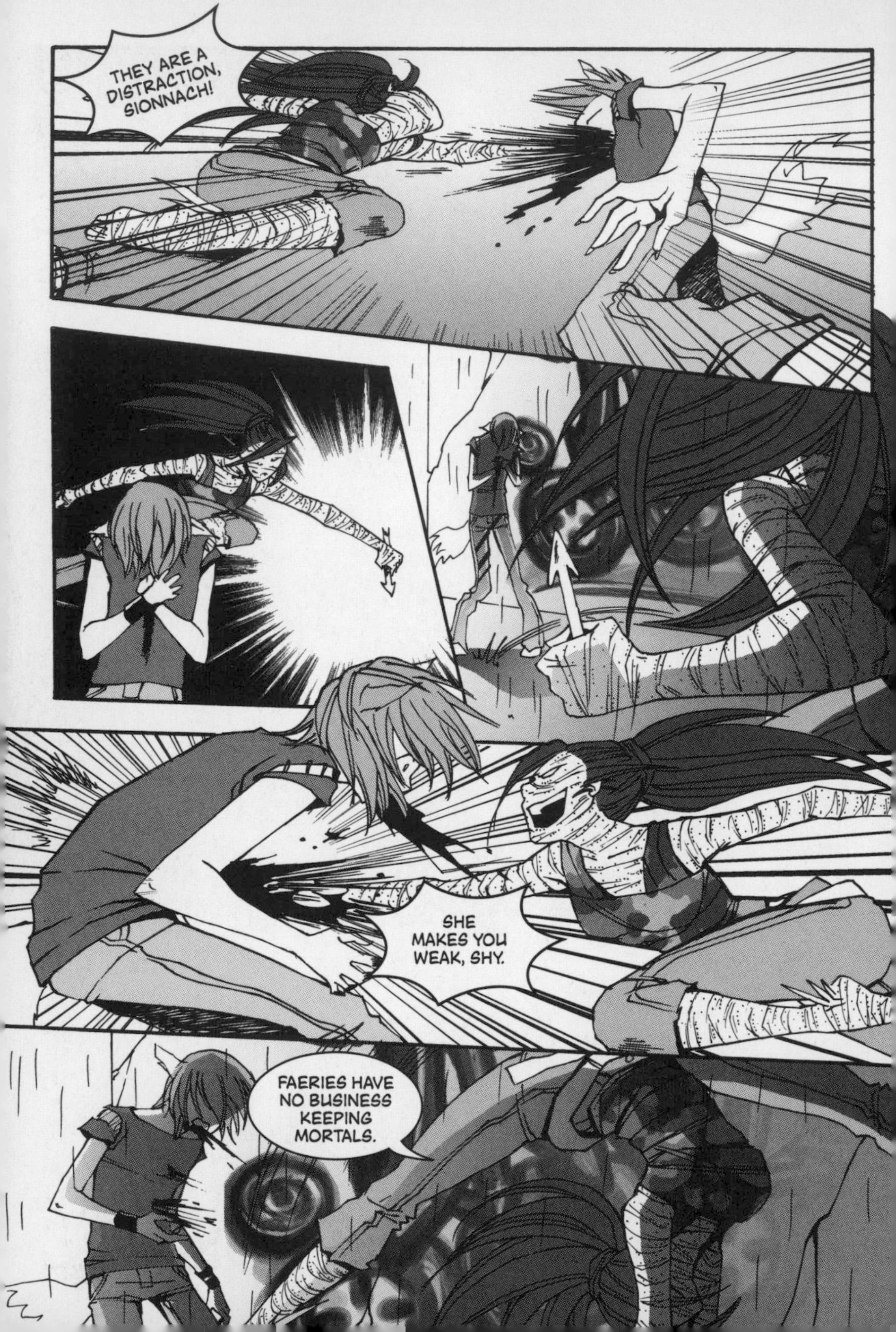
THEY ARE A DISTRACTION, SIONNACH!
SHE MAKES YOU WEAK, SHY.
FAERIES HAVE NO BUSINESS KEEPING MORTALS.

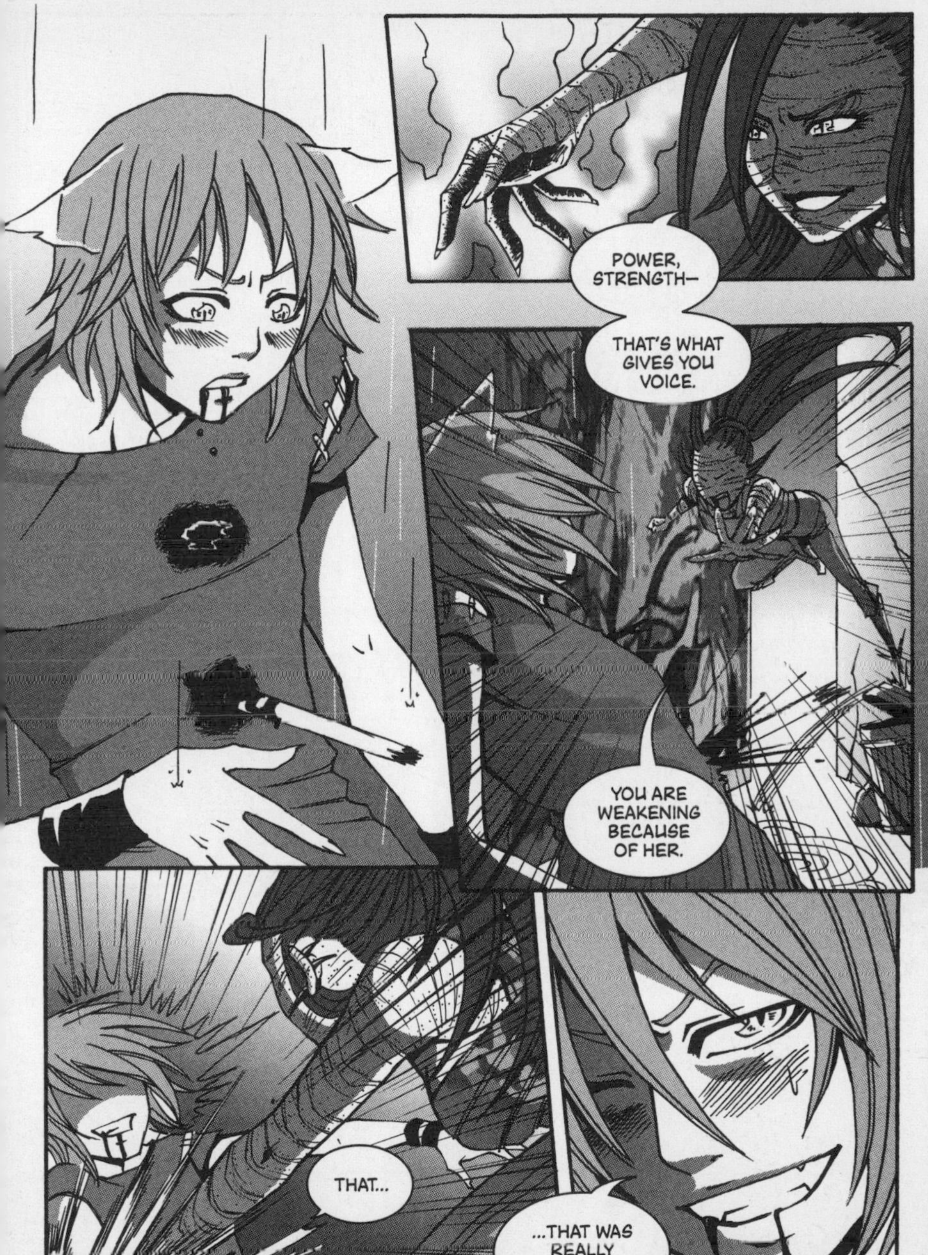
POWER, STRENGTH—
THAT'S WHAT GIVES YOU VOICE.
YOU ARE WEAKENING BECAUSE OF HER.
THAT...
...THAT WAS REALLY FOOLISH, MAL.

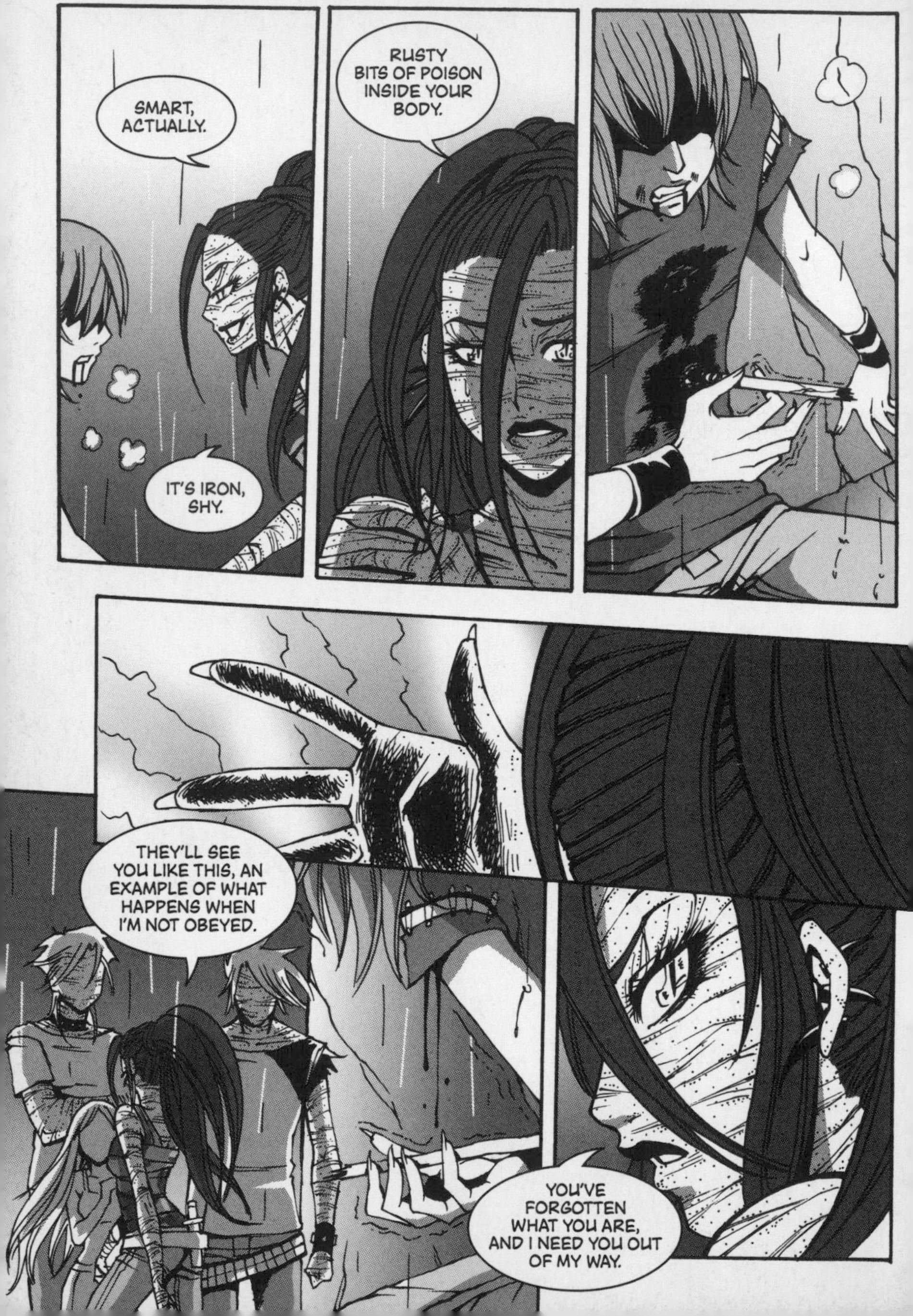
SMART, ACTUALLY.
IT'S IRON, SHY.
RUSTY BITS OF POISON INSIDE YOUR BODY.
THEY'LL SEE YOU LIKE THIS, AN EXAMPLE OF WHAT HAPPENS WHEN I'M NOT OBEYED.
YOU'VE FORGOTTEN WHAT YOU ARE, AND I NEED YOU OUT OF MY WAY.

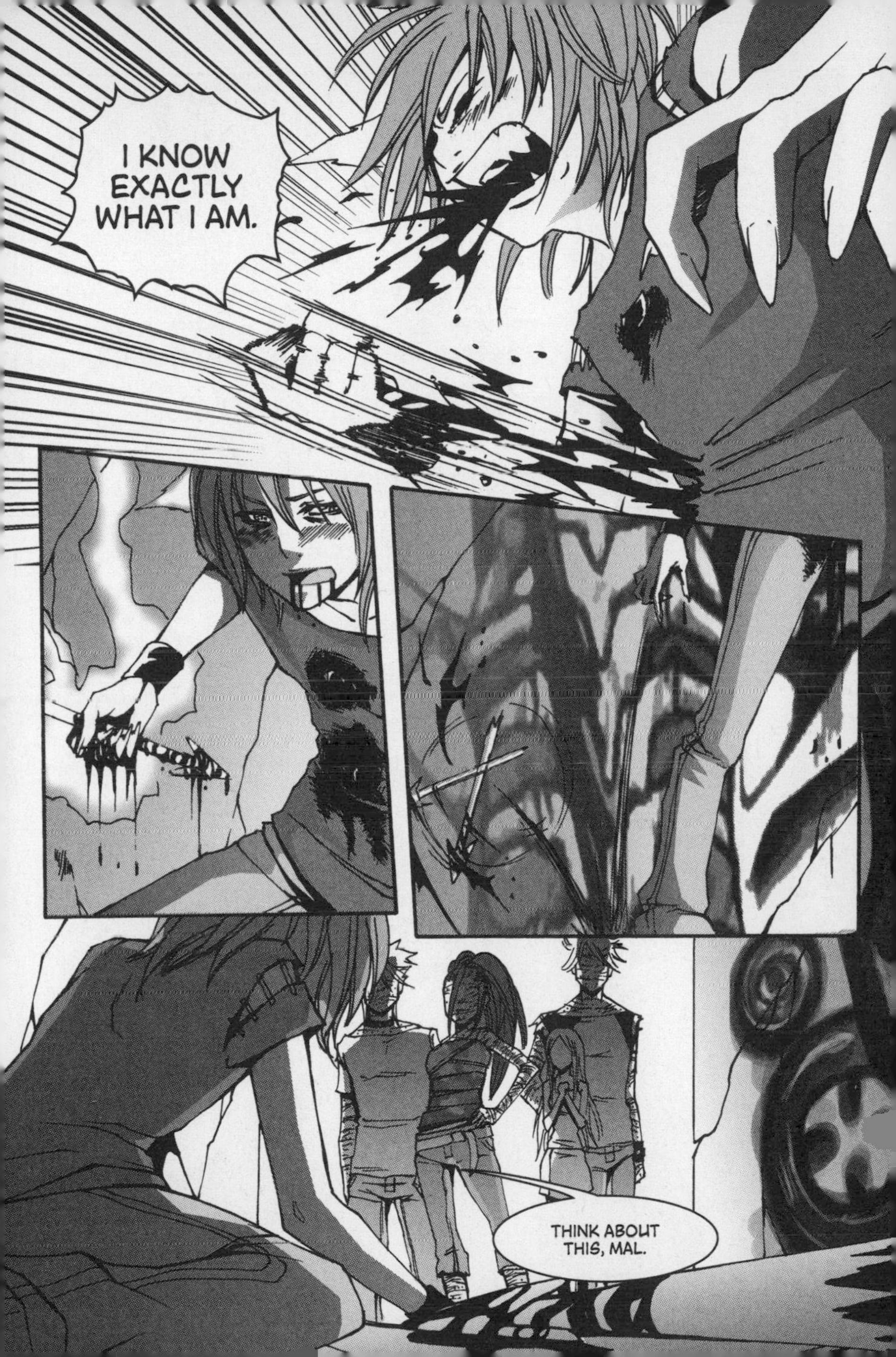
I KNOW EXACTLY WHAT I AM.
THINK ABOUT THIS, MAL.

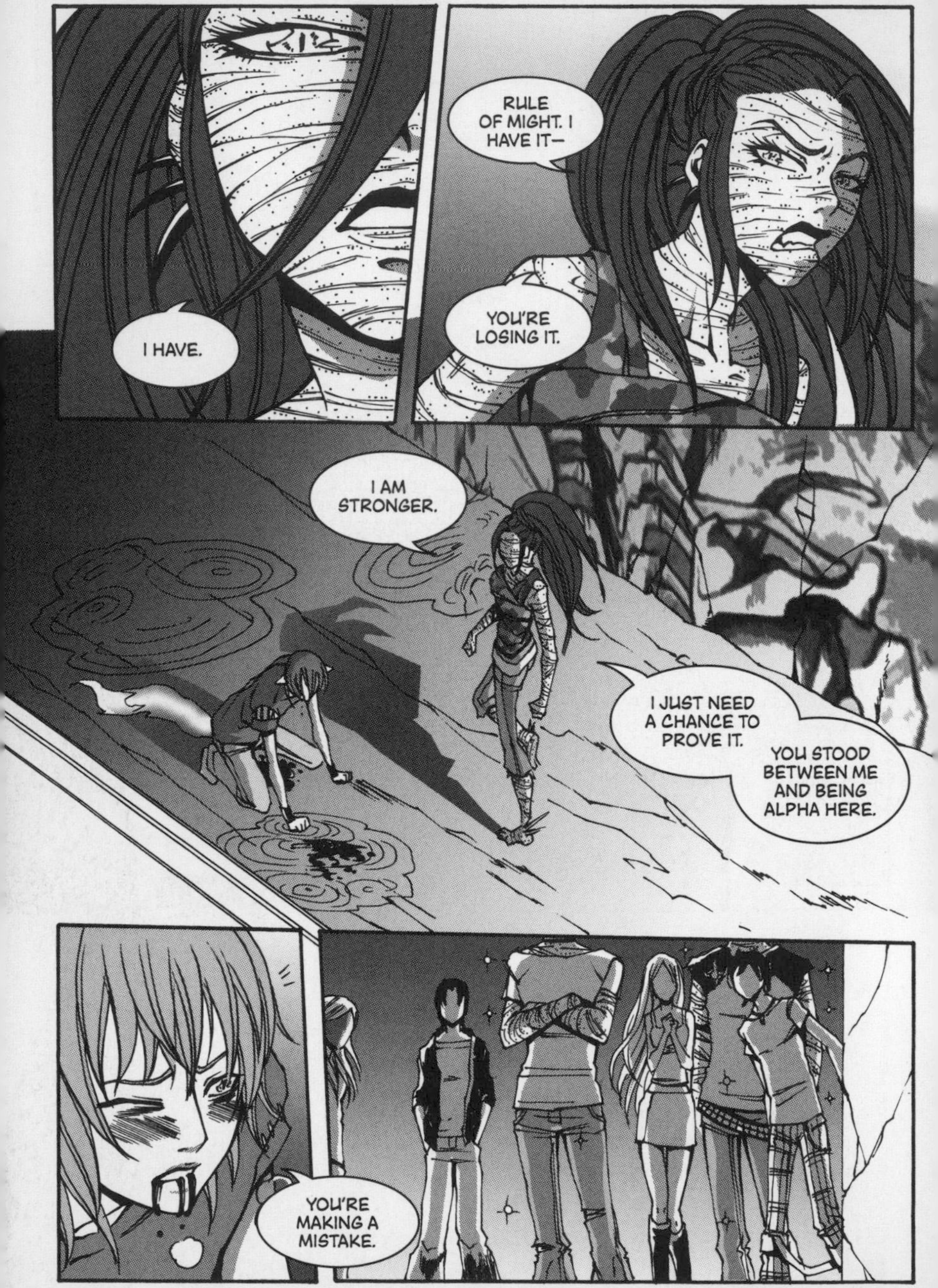
I HAVE.
RULE OF MIGHT. I HAVE IT—
YOU'RE LOSING IT.
I AM STRONGER.
I JUST NEED A CHANCE TO PROVE IT.
YOU STOOD BETWEEN ME AND BEING ALPHA HERE.
YOU'RE MAKING A MISTAKE.

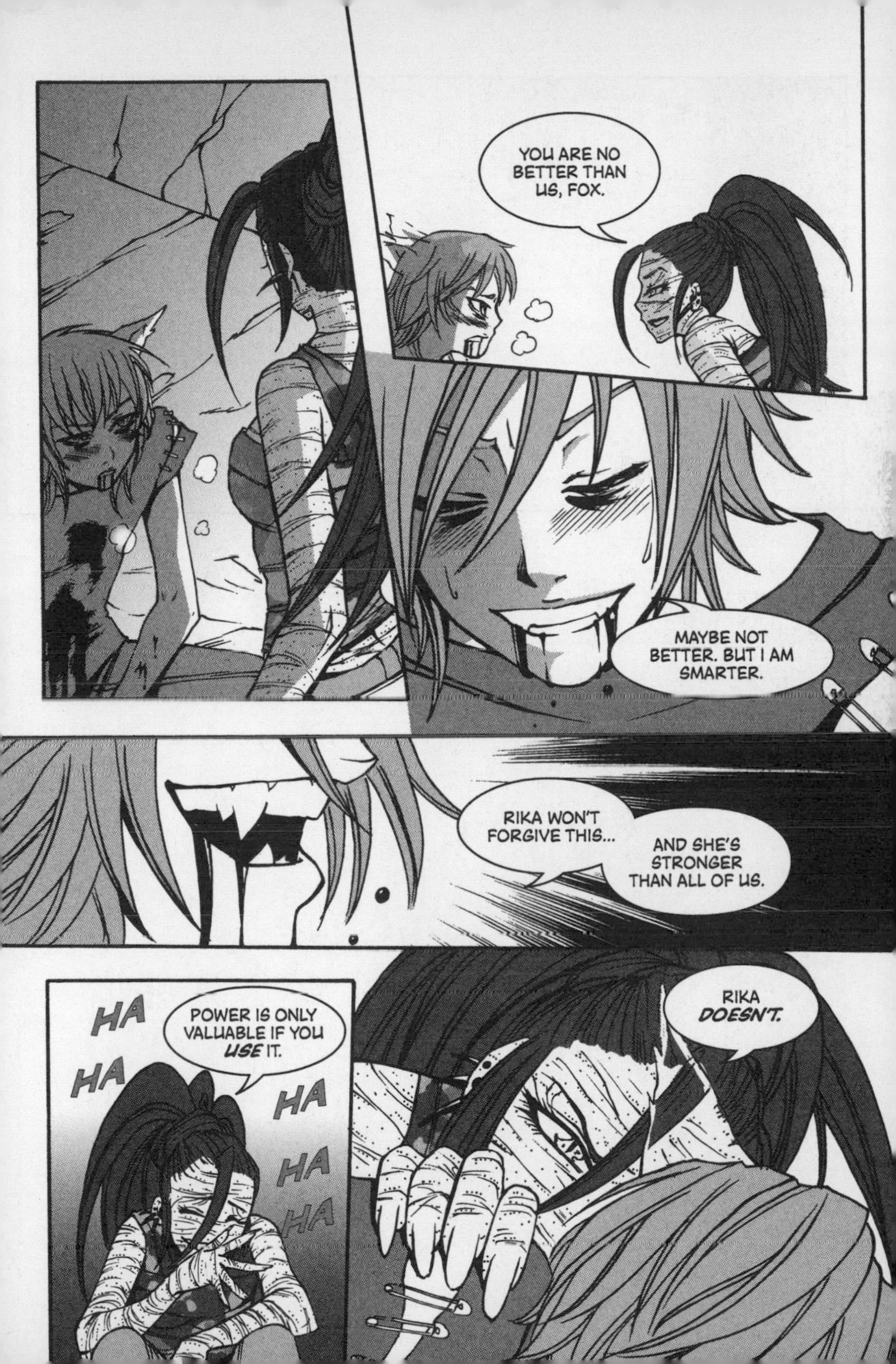
YOU ARE NO BETTER THAN US, FOX.
MAYBE NOT BETTER. BUT I AM SMARTER.
RIKA WON'T FORGIVE THIS...
AND SHE'S STRONGER THAN ALL OF US.
HA
HA
POWER IS ONLY VALUABLE IF YOU *USE* IT.
HA
HA
HA
RIKA *DOESN'T.*

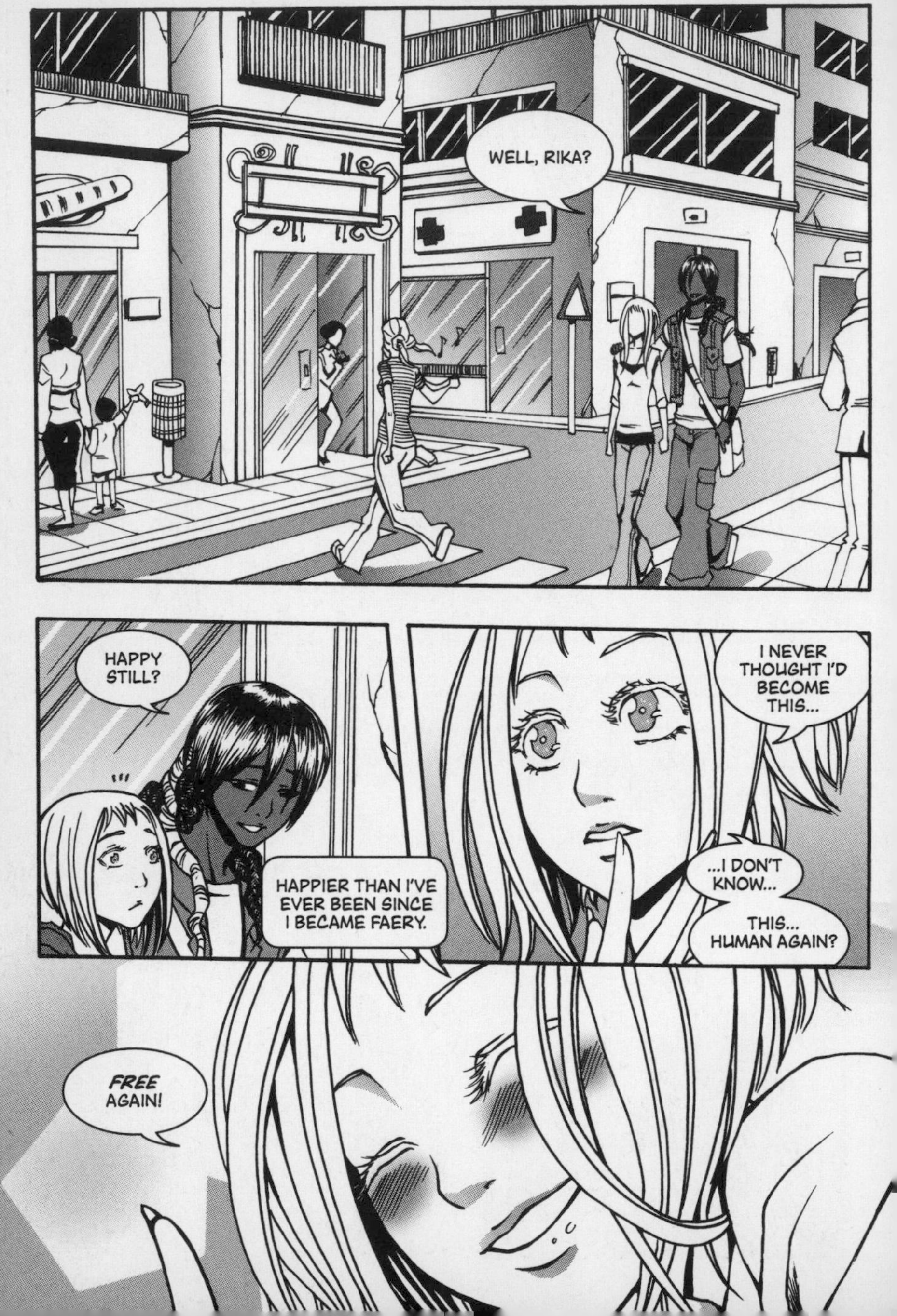
WELL, RIKA?
HAPPY STILL?
HAPPIER THAN I'VE EVER BEEN SINCE I BECAME FAERY.
I NEVER THOUGHT I'D BECOME THIS...
...I DON'T KNOW...
THIS... HUMAN AGAIN?
FREE AGAIN!

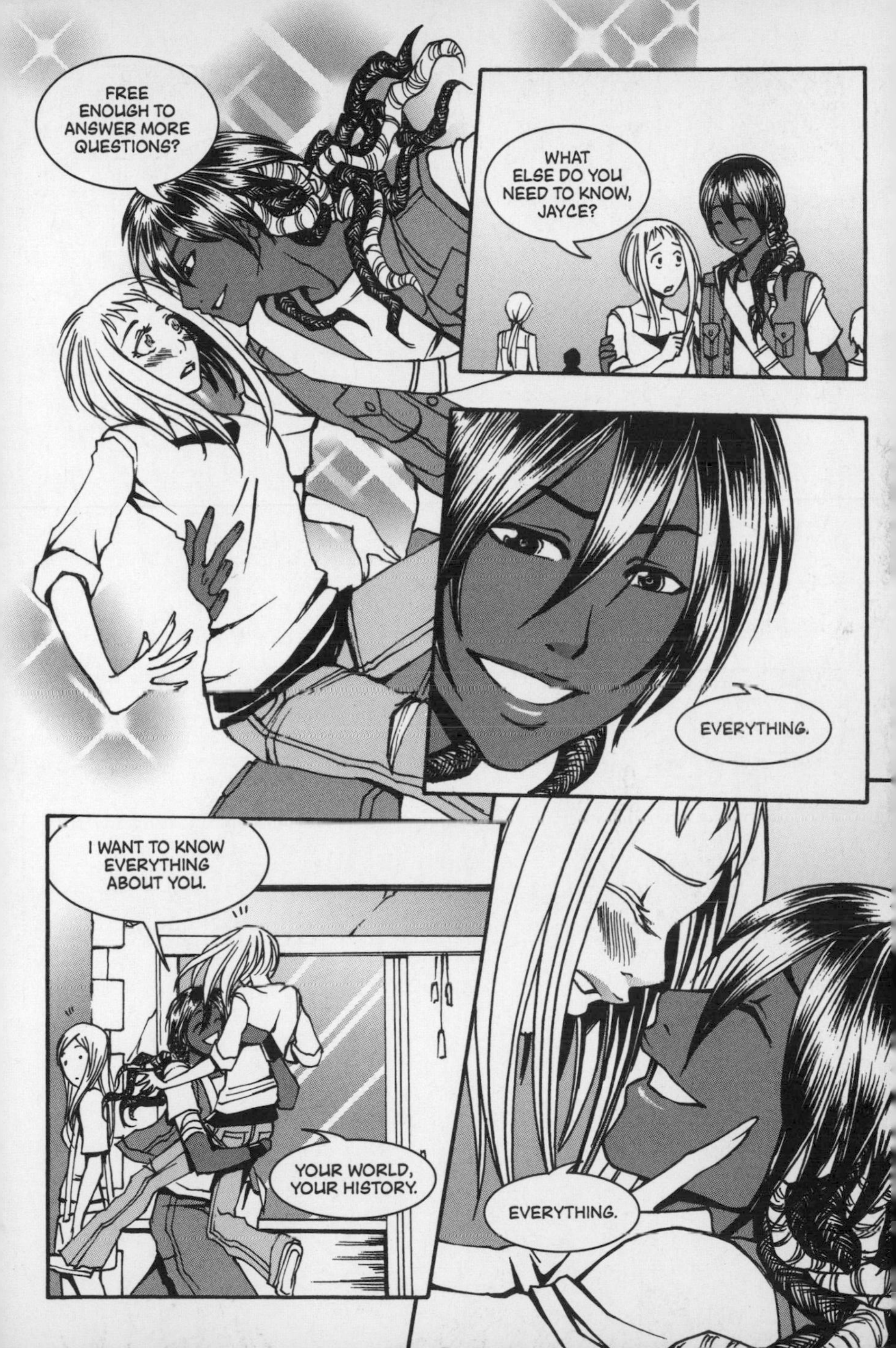
FREE ENOUGH TO ANSWER MORE QUESTIONS?
WHAT ELSE DO YOU NEED TO KNOW, JAYCE?
EVERYTHING.
I WANT TO KNOW EVERYTHING ABOUT YOU.
YOUR WORLD, YOUR HISTORY.
EVERYTHING.

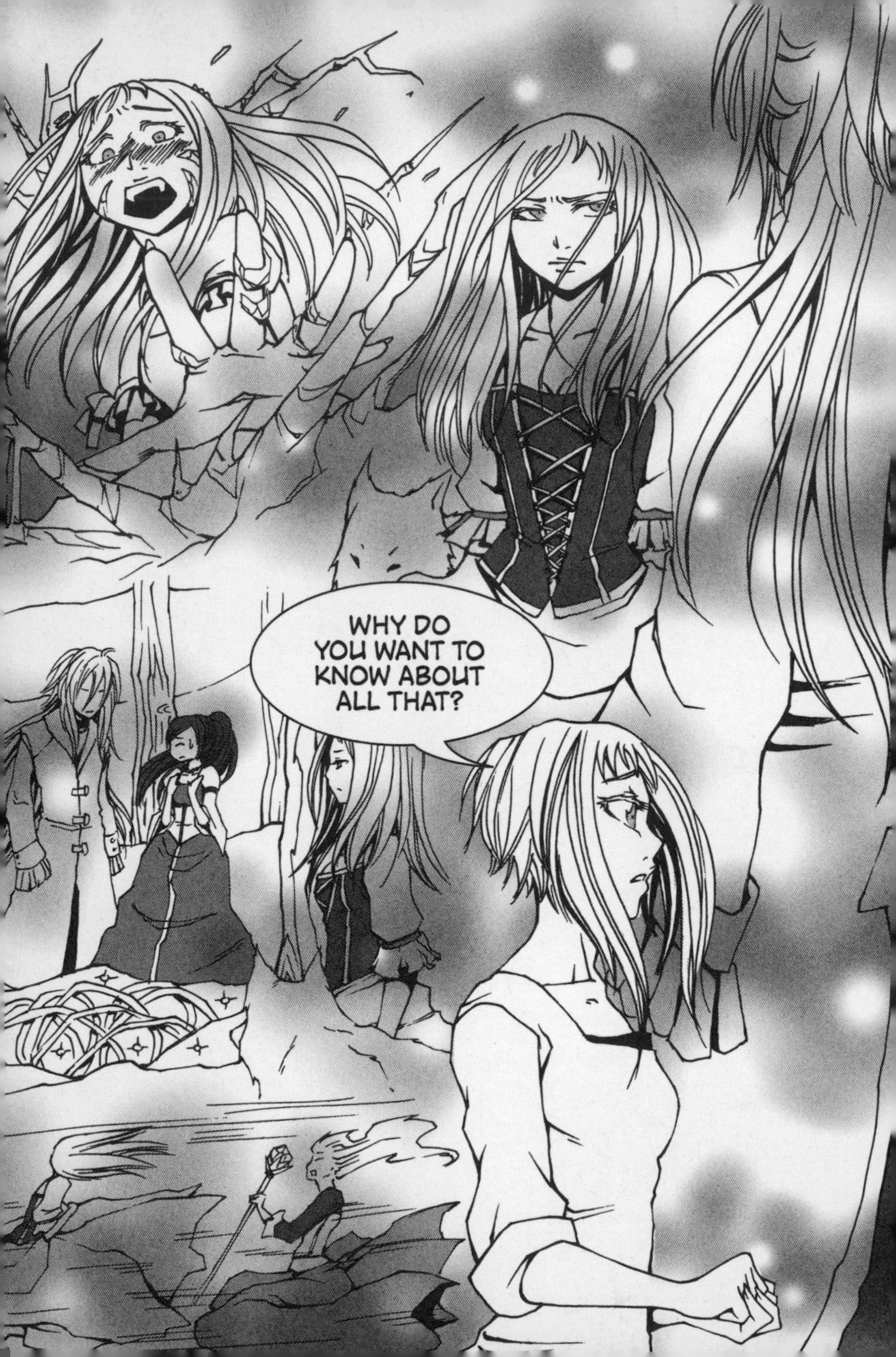
WHY DO YOU WANT TO KNOW ABOUT ALL THAT?

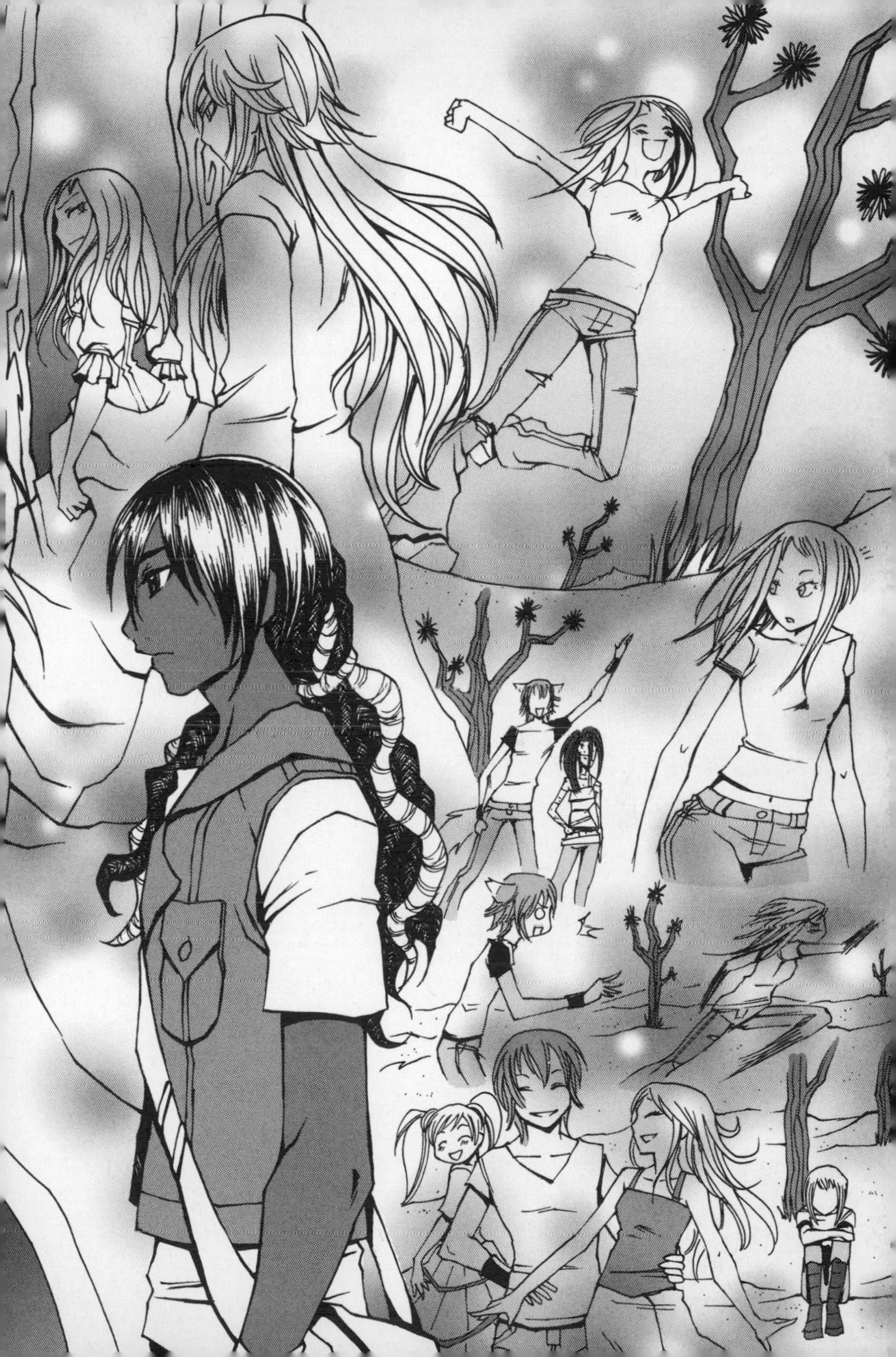

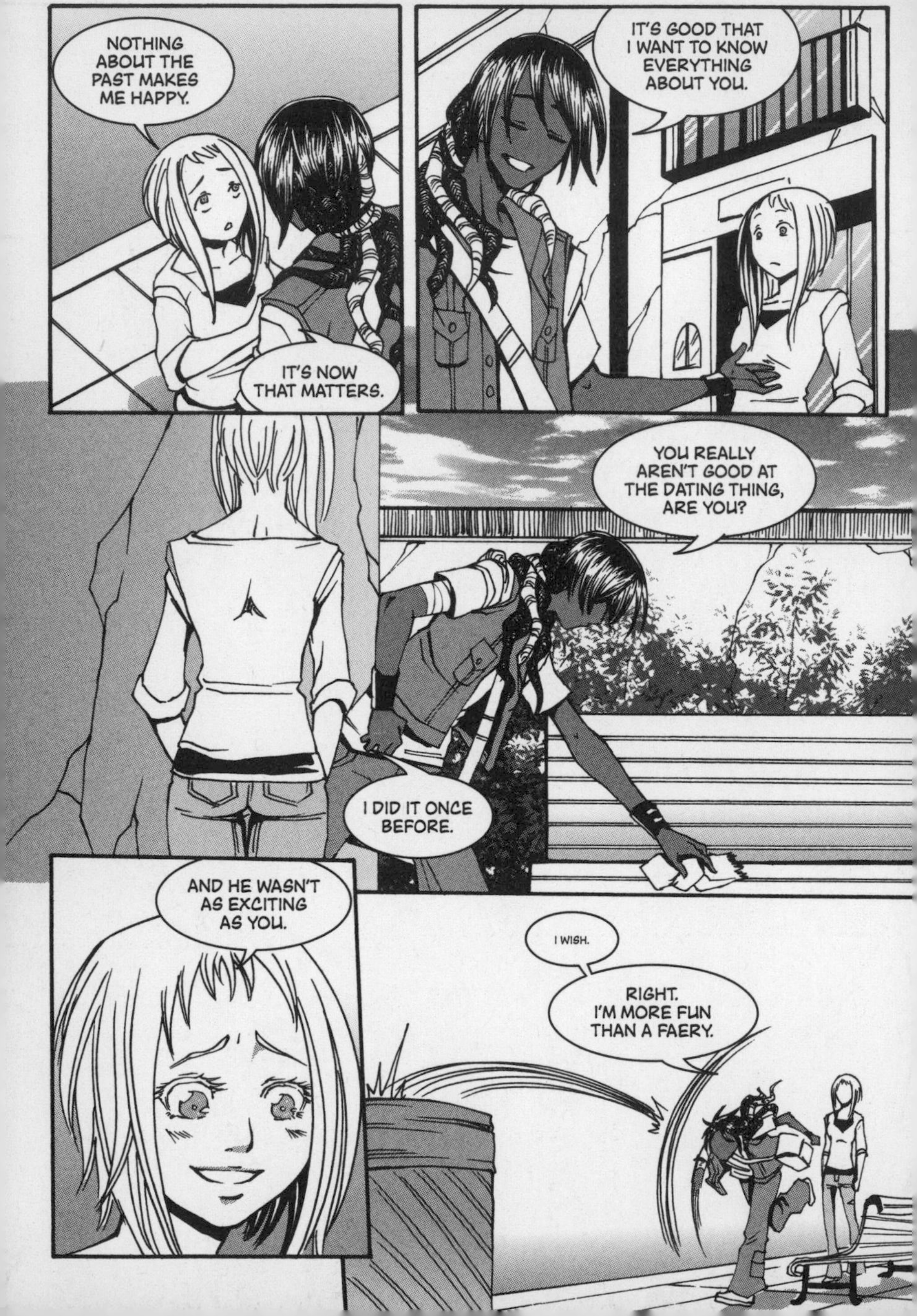
NOTHING ABOUT THE PAST MAKES ME HAPPY.
IT'S NOW THAT MATTERS.
IT'S GOOD THAT I WANT TO KNOW EVERYTHING ABOUT YOU.
YOU REALLY AREN'T GOOD AT THE DATING THING, ARE YOU?
I DID IT ONCE BEFORE.
AND HE WASN'T AS EXCITING AS YOU.
I WISH.
RIGHT. I'M MORE FUN THAN A FAERY.

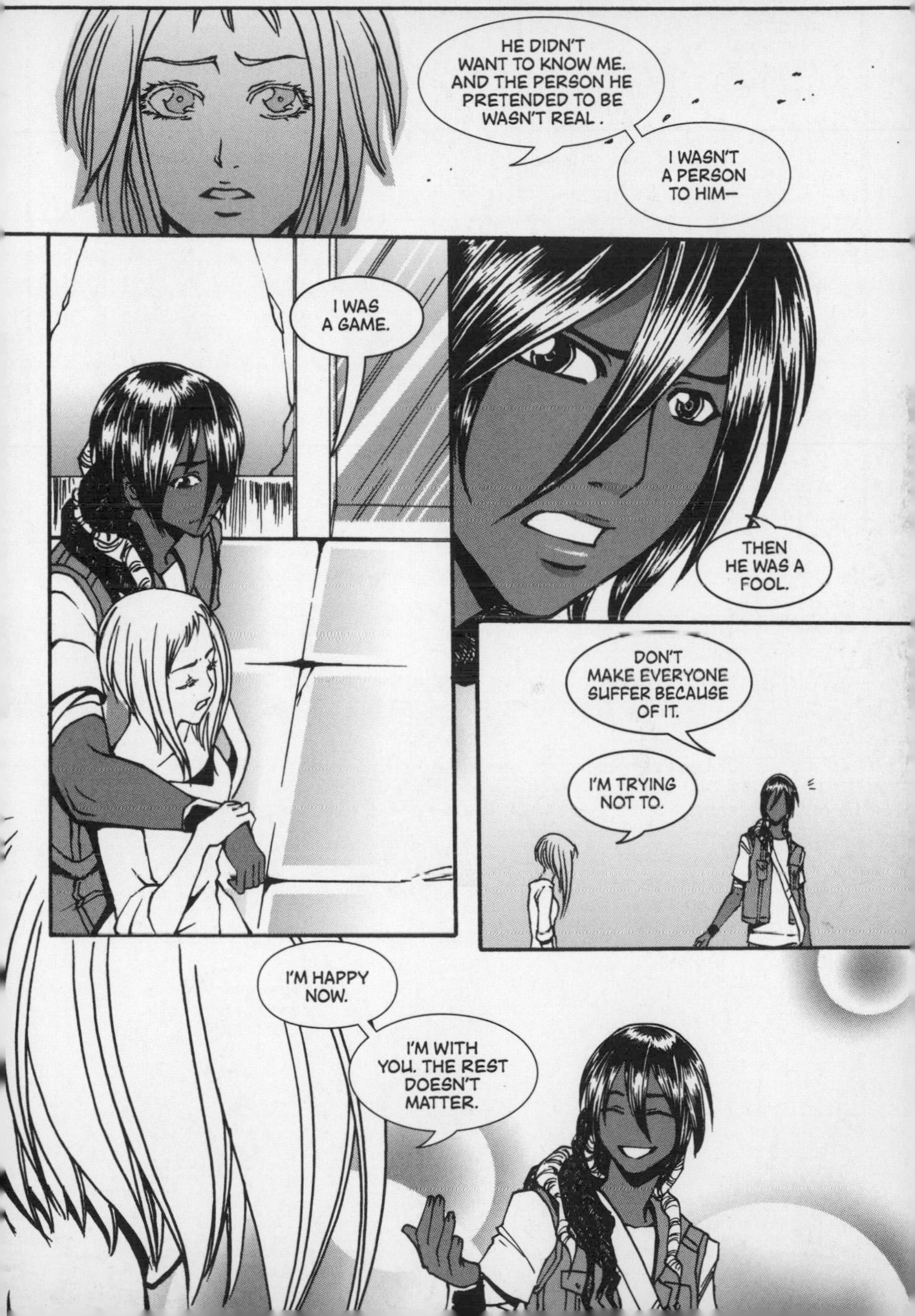
HE DIDN'T WANT TO KNOW ME. AND THE PERSON HE PRETENDED TO BE WASN'T REAL .
I WASN'T A PERSON TO HIM—
I WAS A GAME.
THEN HE WAS A FOOL.
DON'T MAKE EVERYONE SUFFER BECAUSE OF IT.
I'M TRYING NOT TO.
I'M HAPPY NOW.
I'M WITH YOU. THE REST DOESN'T MATTER.

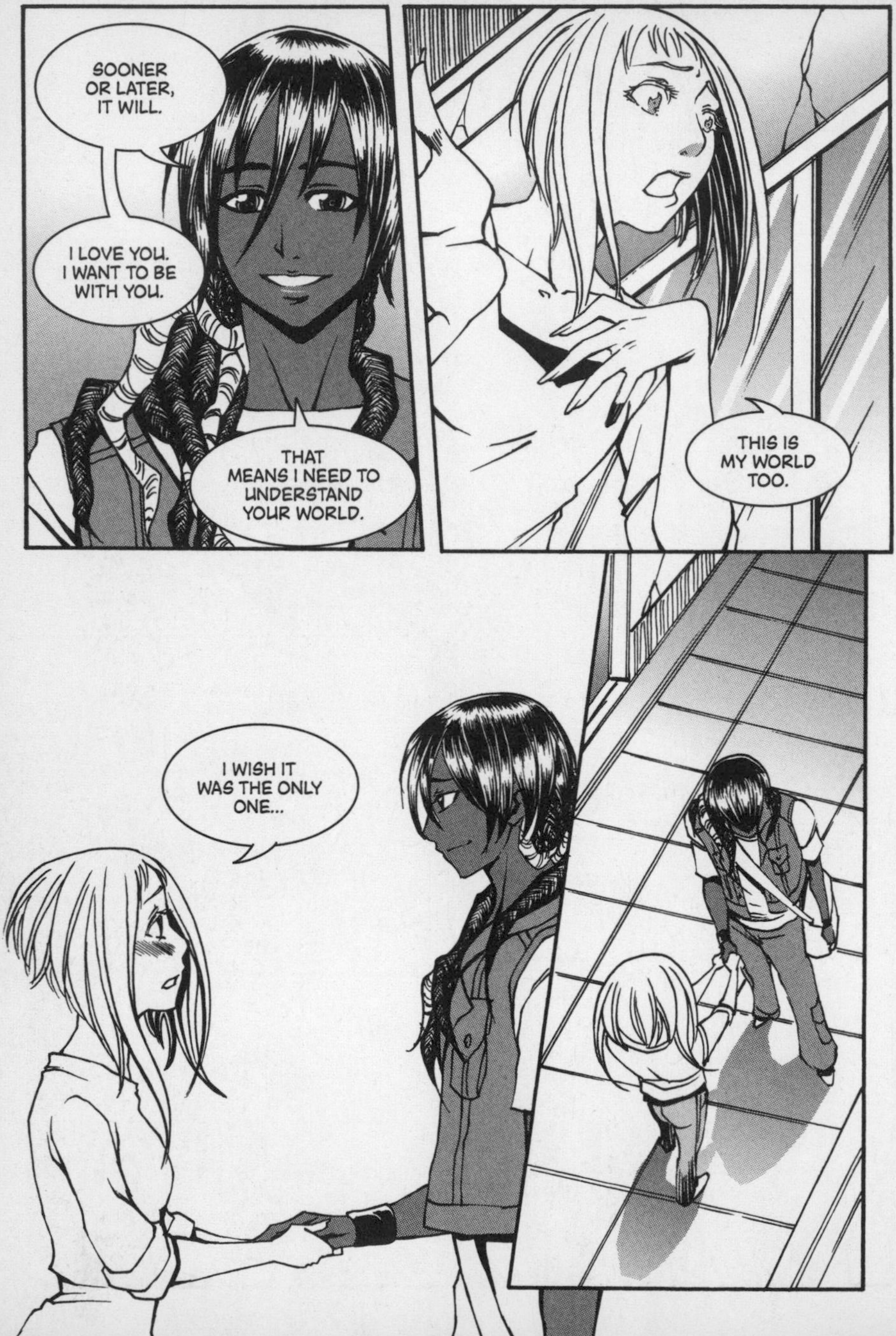
SOONER OR LATER, IT WILL.
I LOVE YOU. I WANT TO BE WITH YOU.
THAT MEANS I NEED TO UNDERSTAND YOUR WORLD.
THIS IS MY WORLD TOO.
I WISH IT WAS THE ONLY ONE...

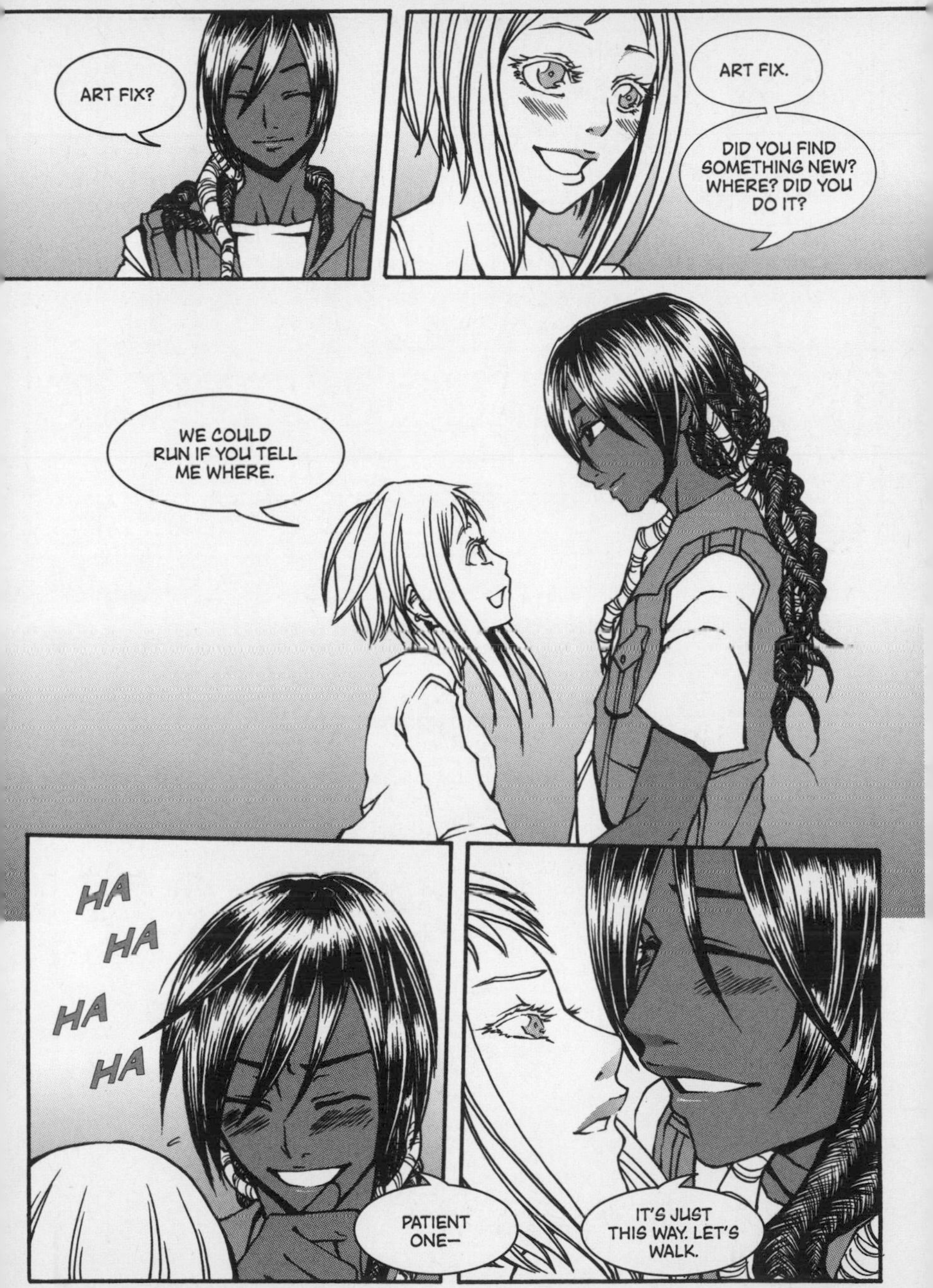
ART FIX?
ART FIX.
DID YOU FIND SOMETHING NEW? WHERE? DID YOU DO IT?
WE COULD RUN IF YOU TELL ME WHERE.
HA HA HA HA
PATIENT ONE—
IT'S JUST THIS WAY. LET'S WALK.

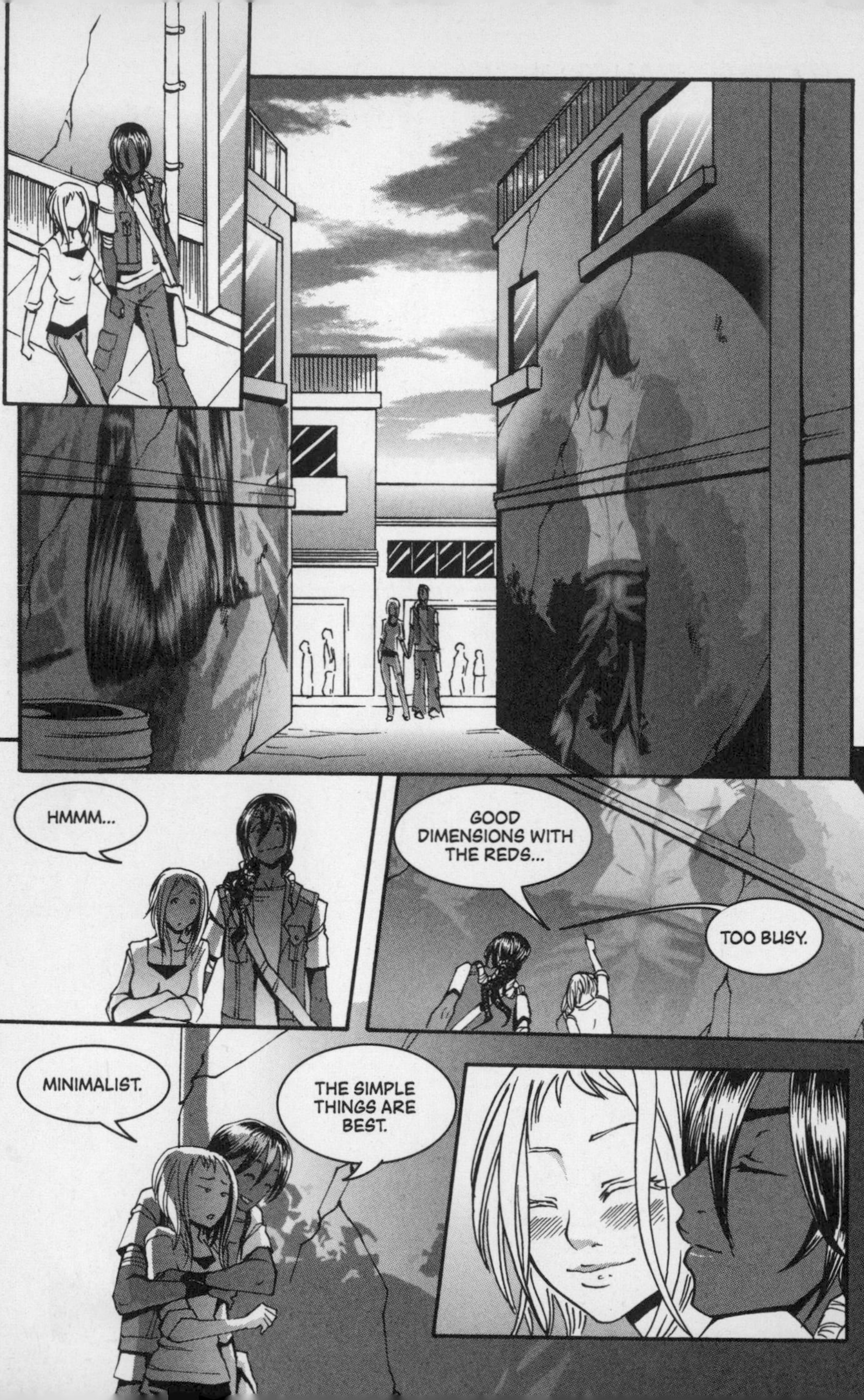
HMMM...
GOOD DIMENSIONS WITH THE REDS...
TOO BUSY.
MINIMALIST.
THE SIMPLE THINGS ARE BEST.

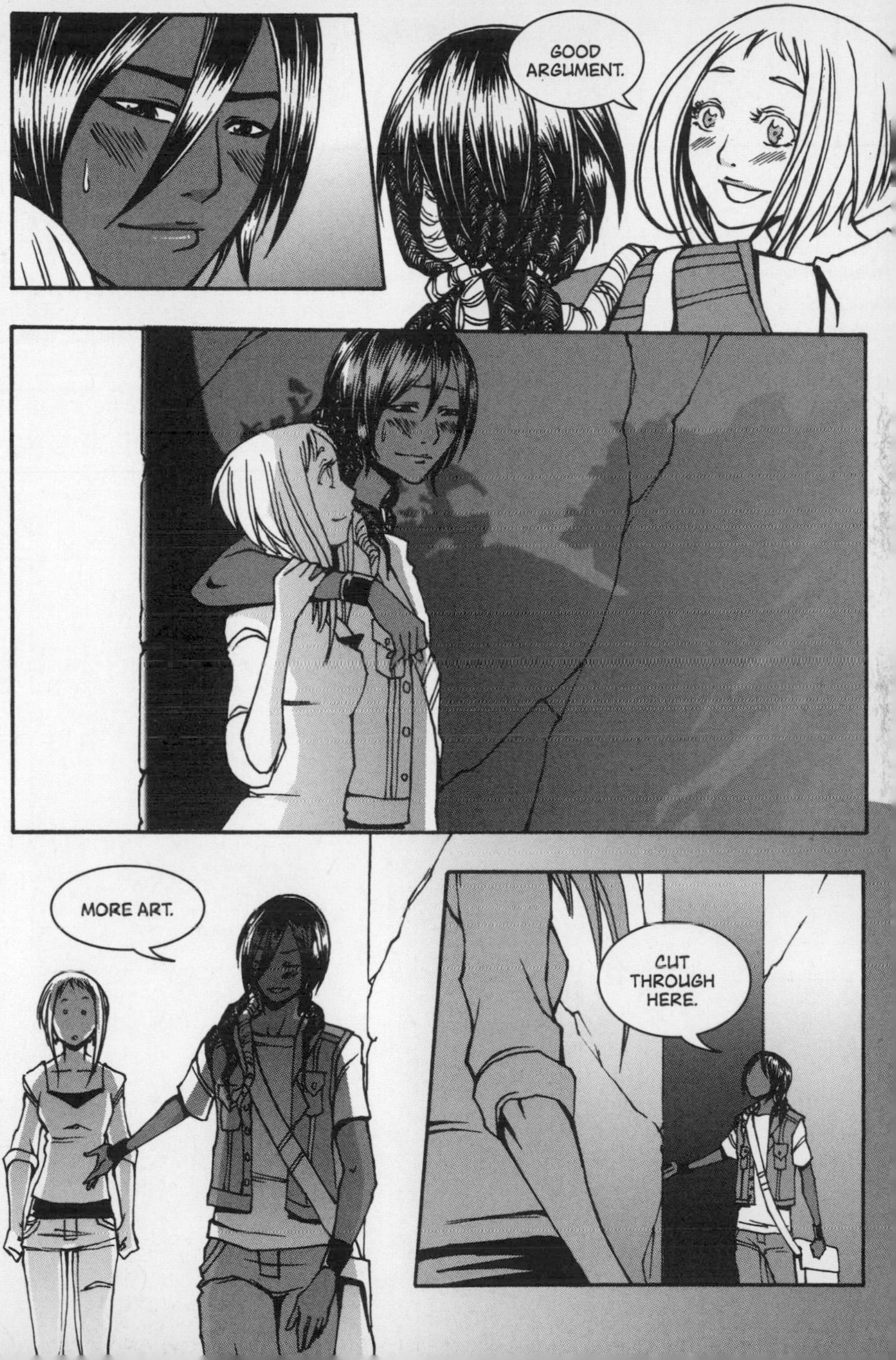
GOOD ARGUMENT.
MORE ART.
CUT THROUGH HERE.

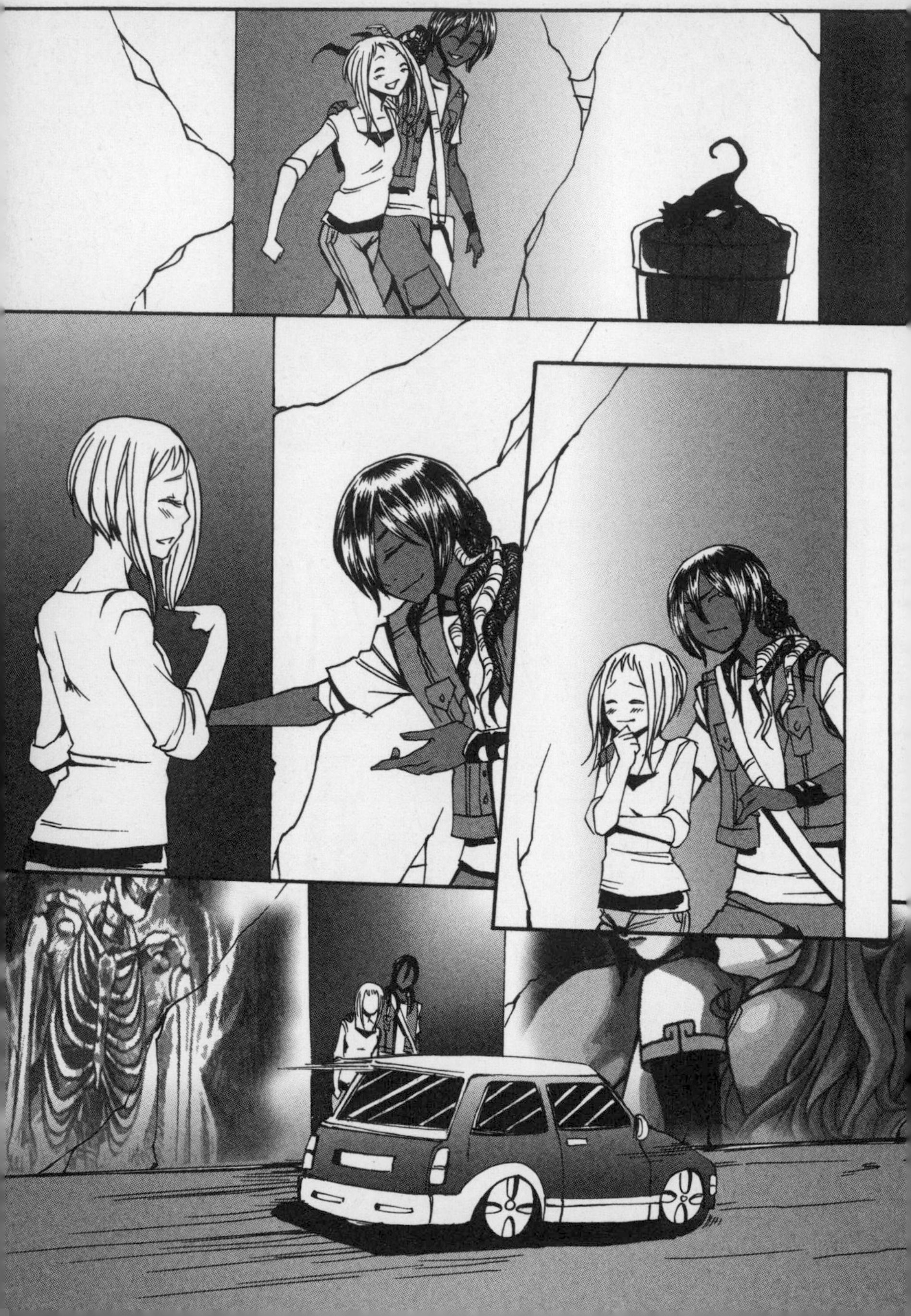

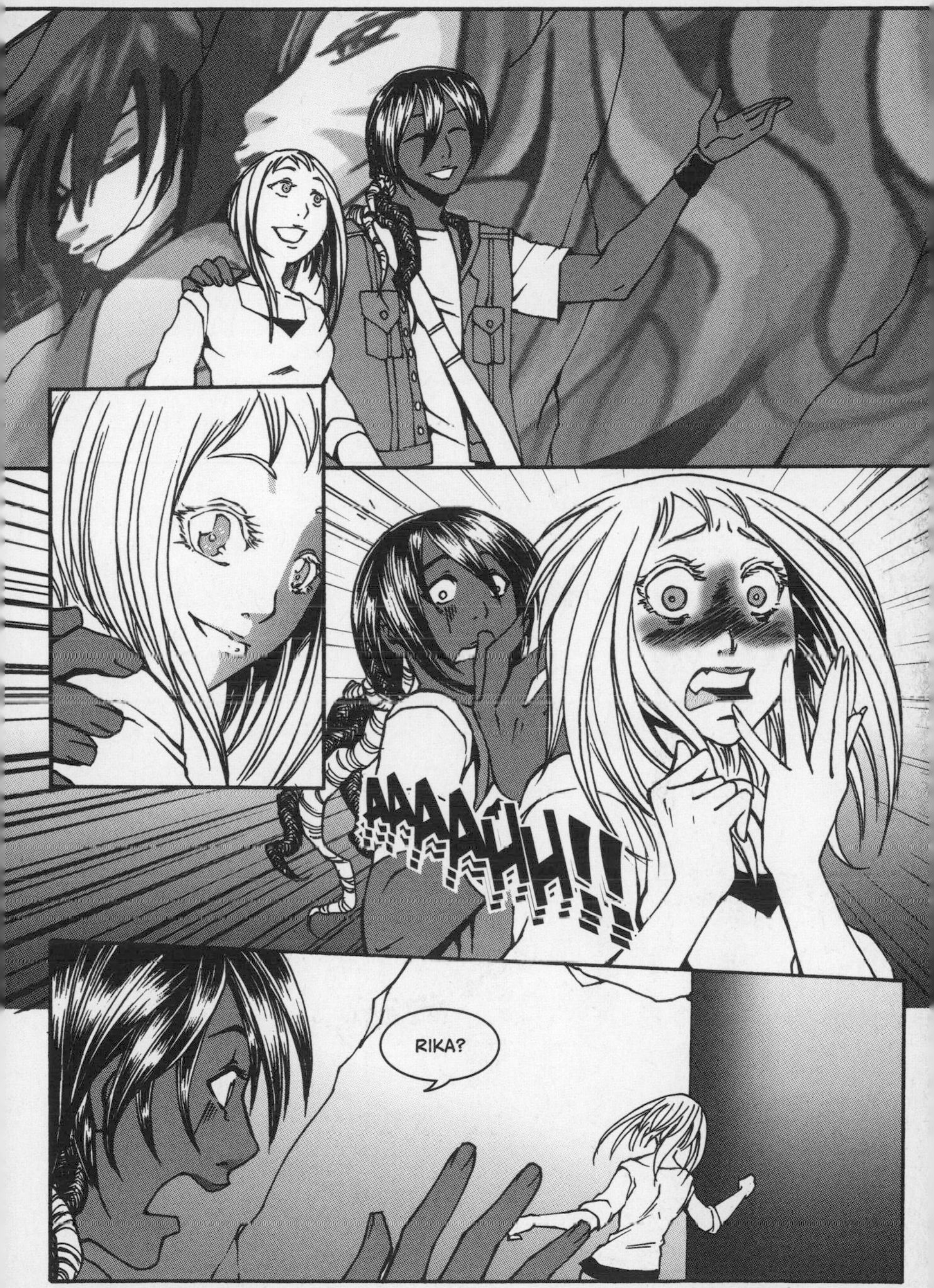
AAAAAHH!!
RIKA?

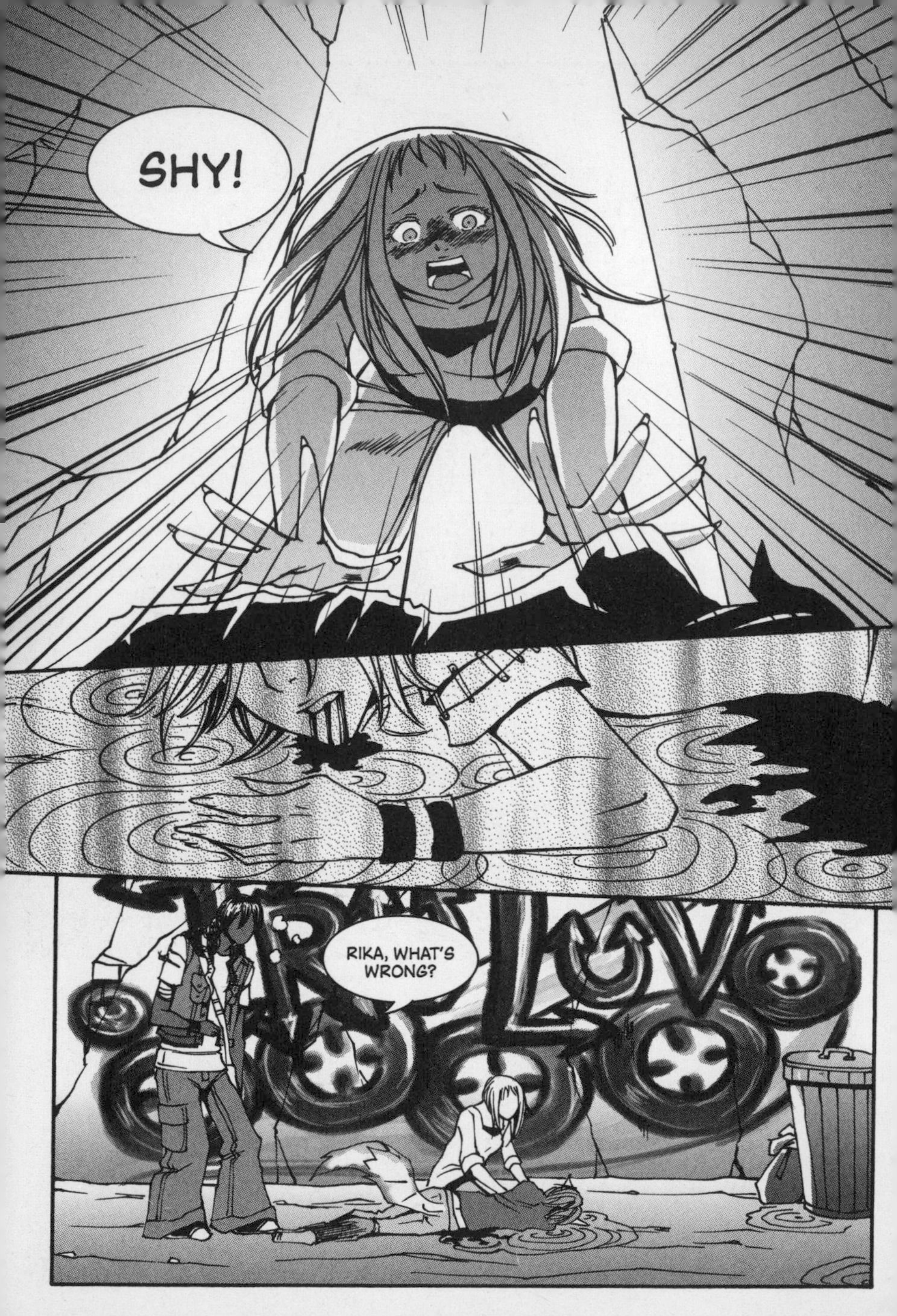
SHY!
RIKA, WHAT'S WRONG?

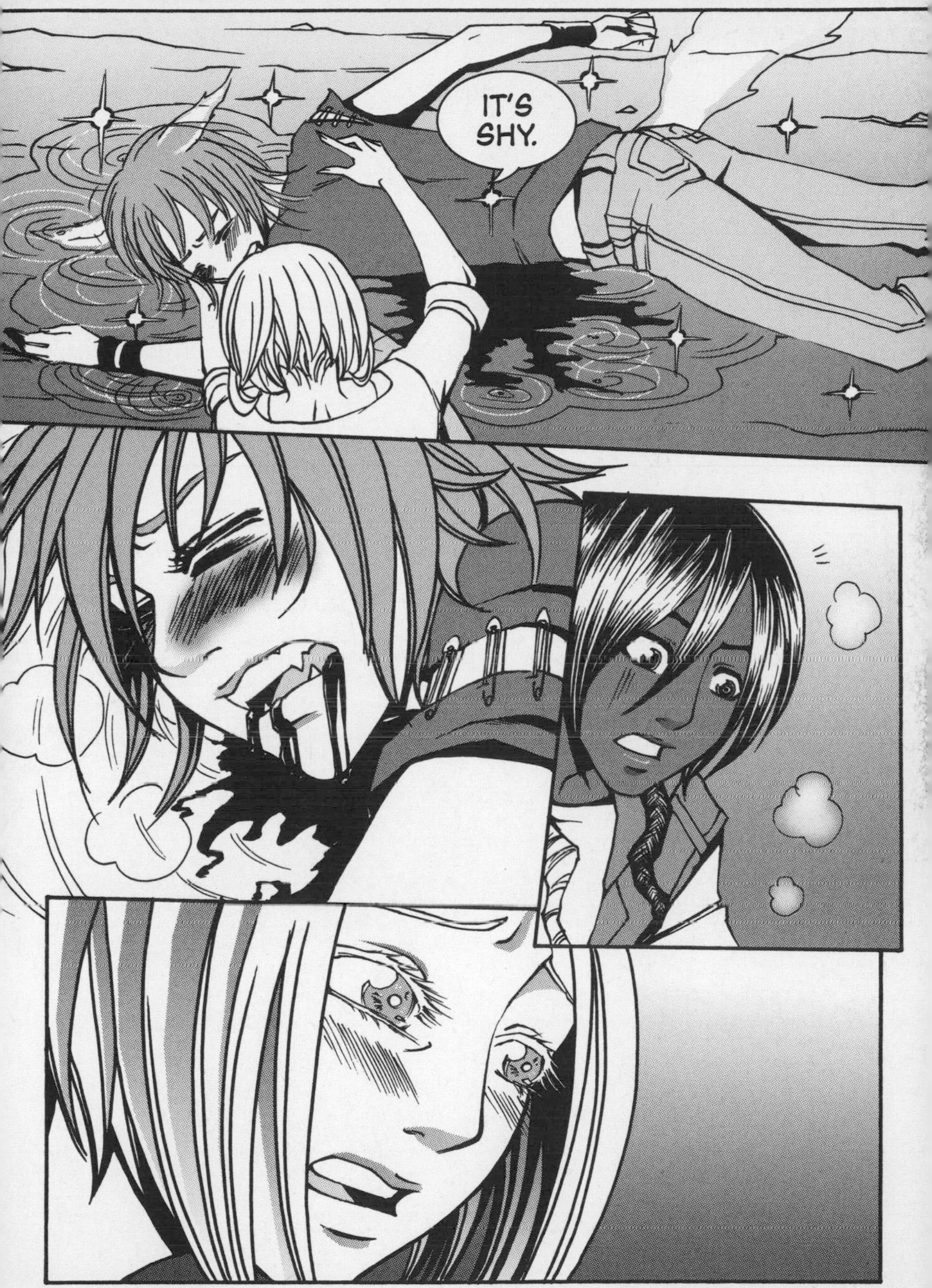
IT'S SHY.

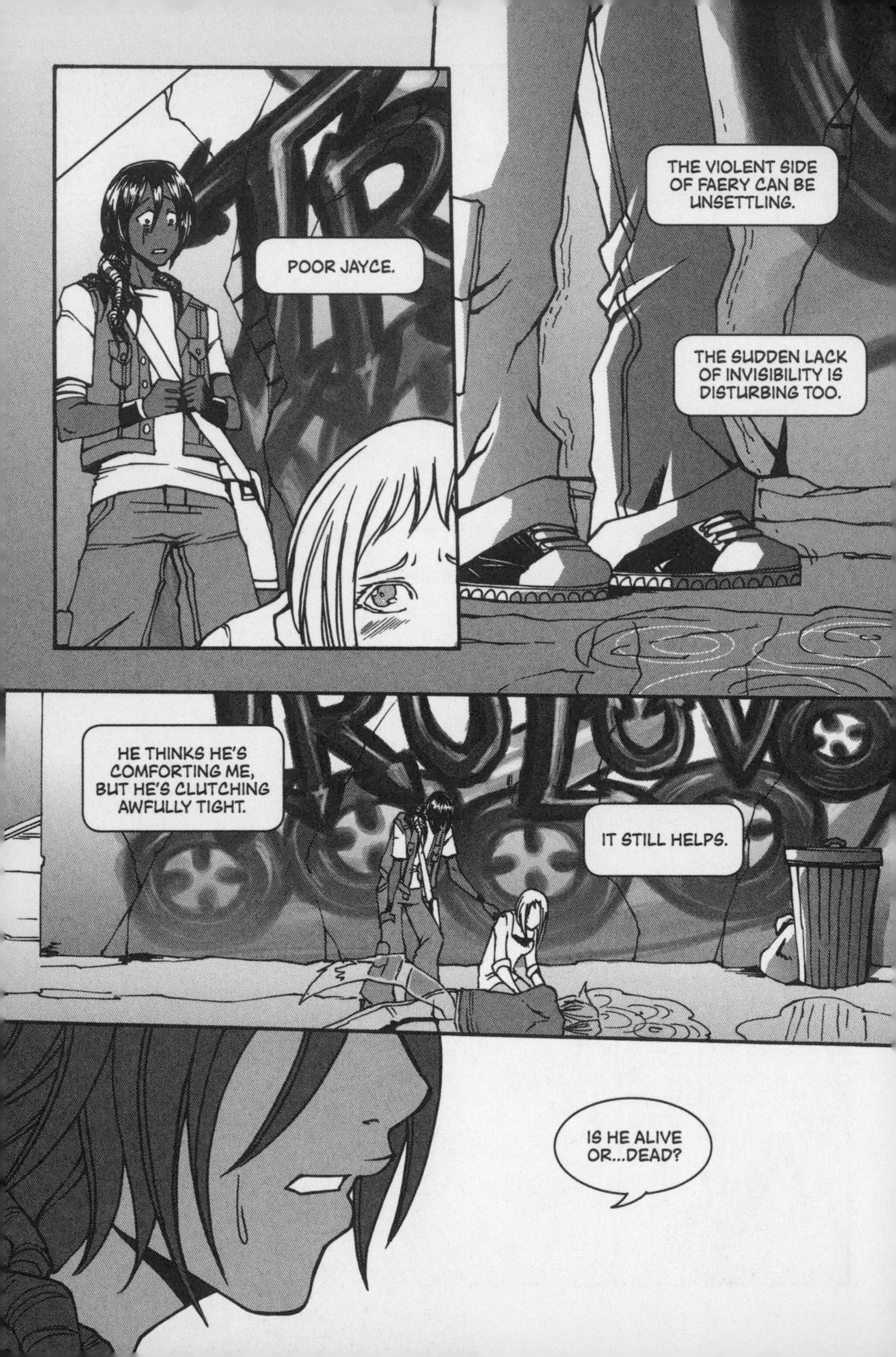
POOR JAYCE.
THE VIOLENT SIDE OF FAERY CAN BE UNSETTLING.
THE SUDDEN LACK OF INVISIBILITY IS DISTURBING TOO.
HE THINKS HE'S COMFORTING ME, BUT HE'S CLUTCHING AWFULLY TIGHT.
IT STILL HELPS.
IS HE ALIVE OR...DEAD?

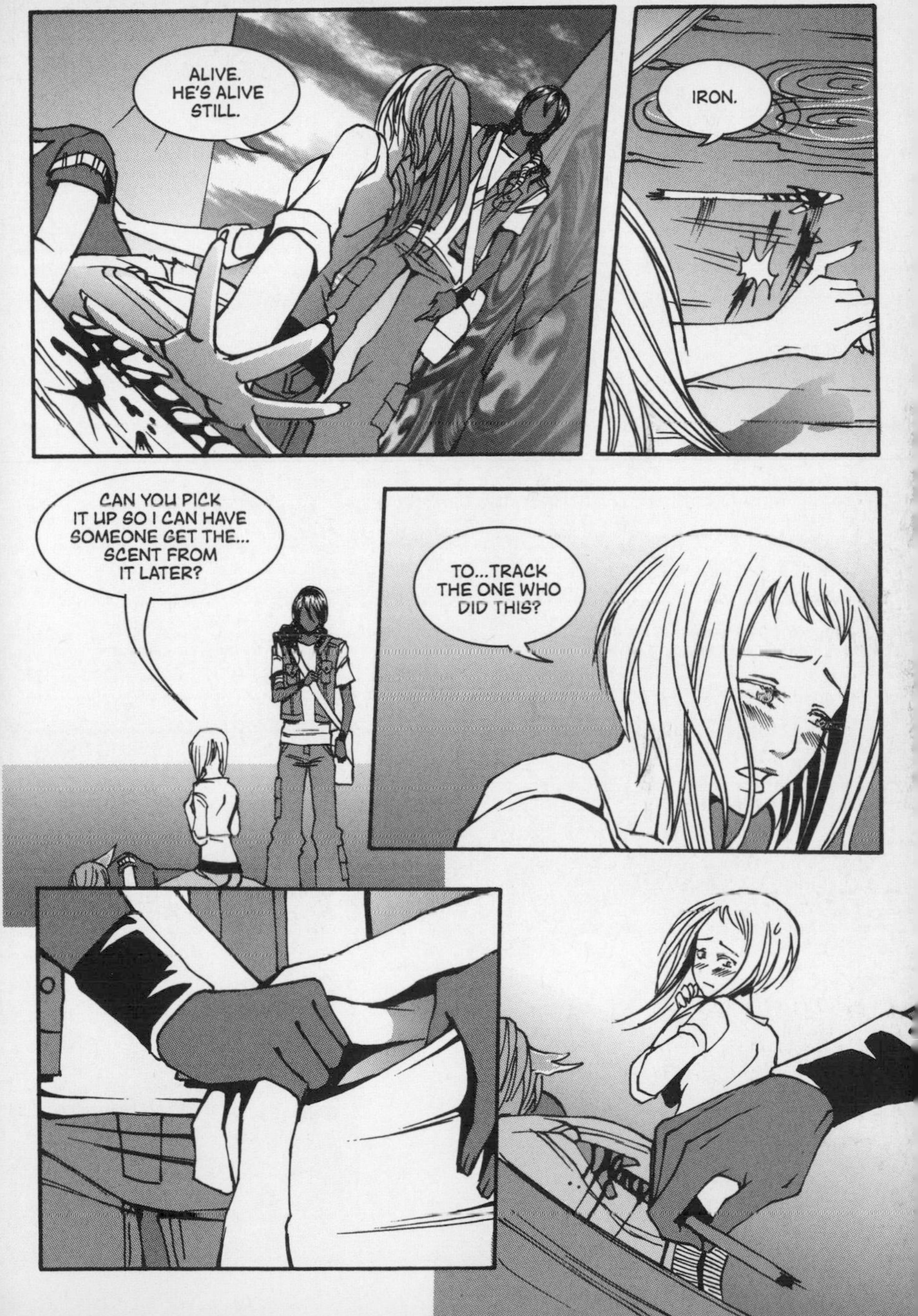
ALIVE. HE'S ALIVE STILL.
IRON.
CAN YOU PICK IT UP SO I CAN HAVE SOMEONE GET THE... SCENT FROM IT LATER?
TO...TRACK THE ONE WHO DID THIS?

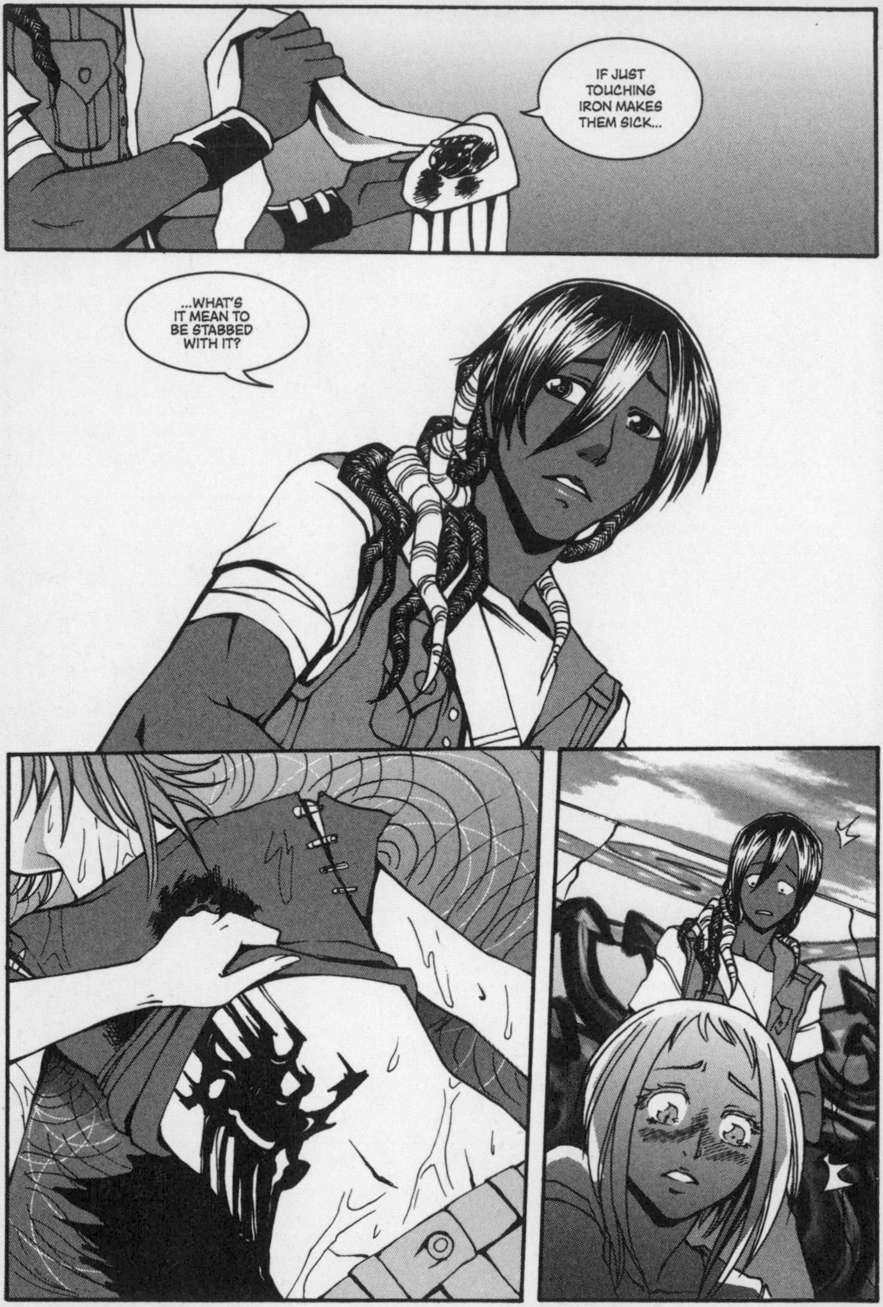
IF JUST TOUCHING IRON MAKES THEM SICK...
...WHAT'S IT MEAN TO BE STABBED WITH IT?

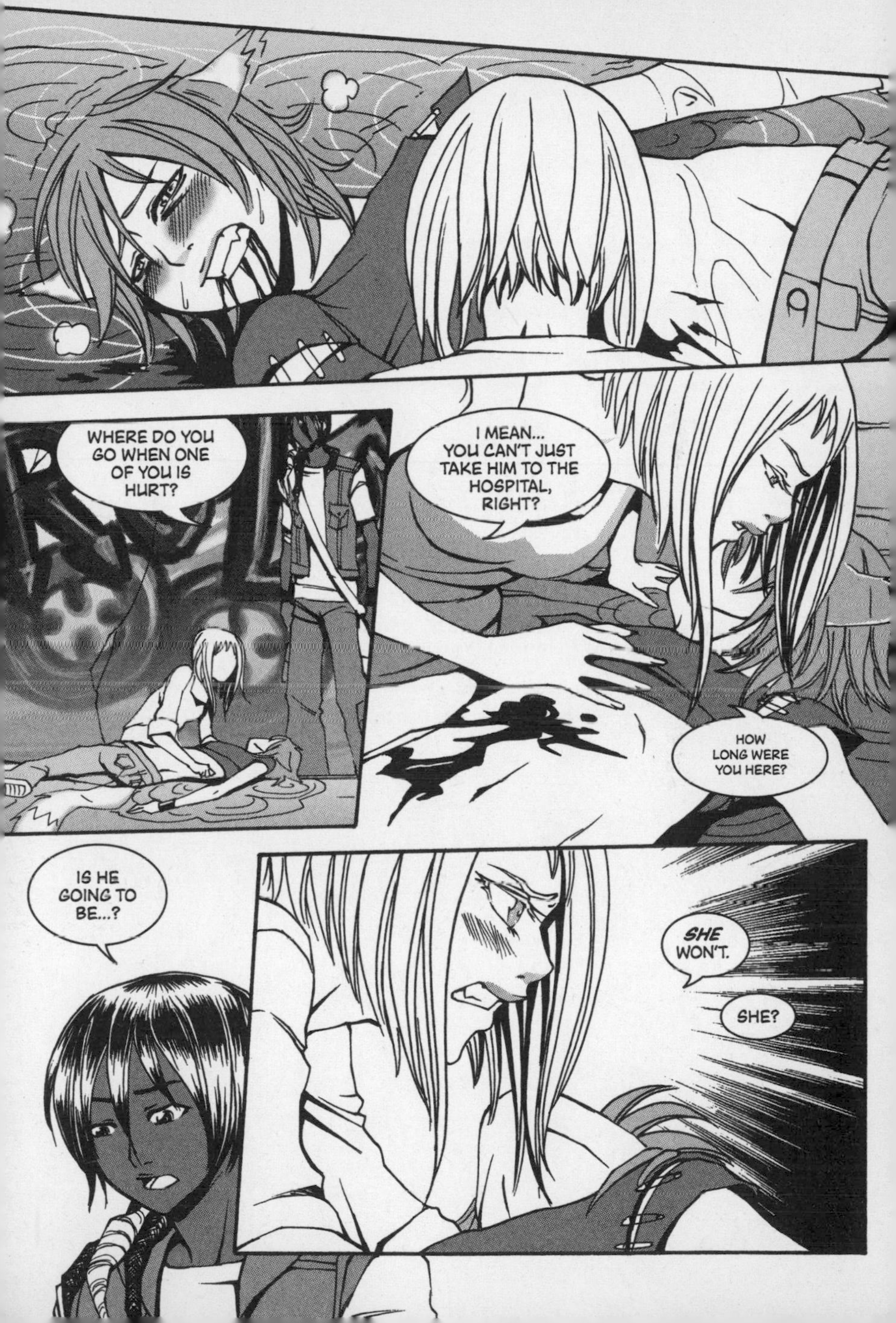
WHERE DO YOU GO WHEN ONE OF YOU IS HURT?
I MEAN... YOU CAN'T JUST TAKE HIM TO THE HOSPITAL, RIGHT?
HOW LONG WERE YOU HERE?
IS HE GOING TO BE...?
SHE WON'T.
SHE?

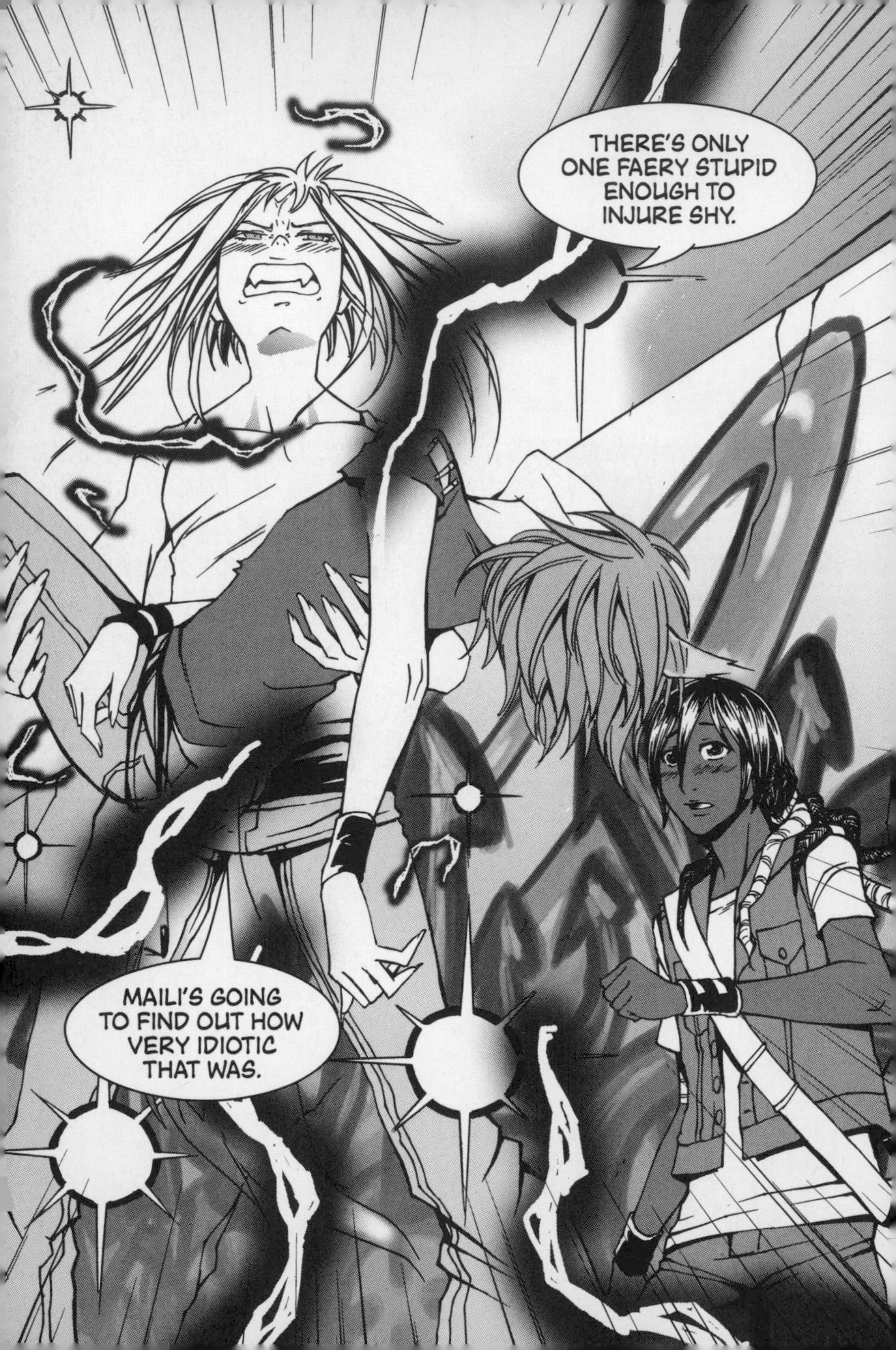
THERE'S ONLY ONE FAERY STUPID ENOUGH TO INJURE SHY.
MAILI'S GOING TO FIND OUT HOW VERY IDIOTIC THAT WAS.

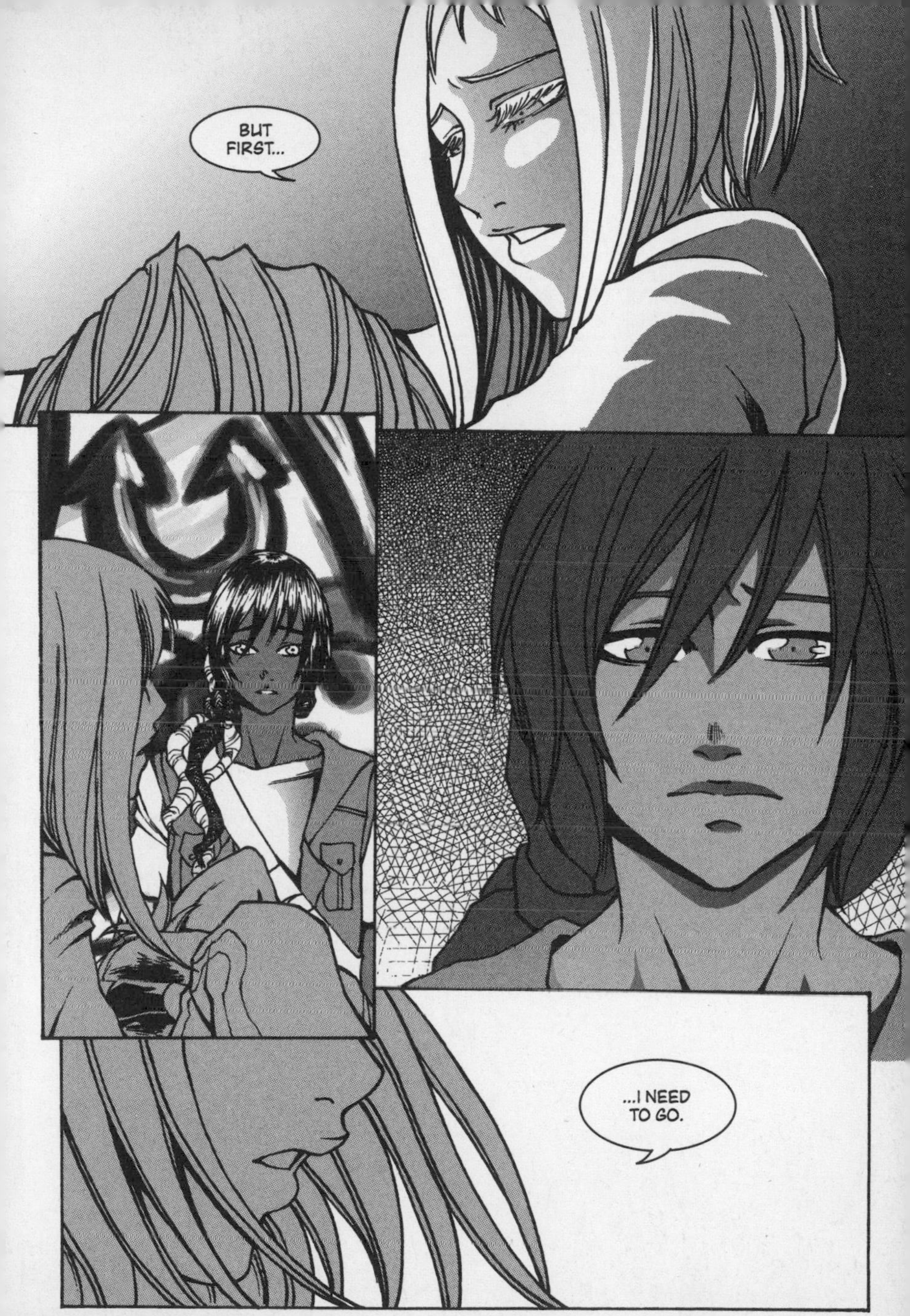
BUT FIRST...
...I NEED TO GO.

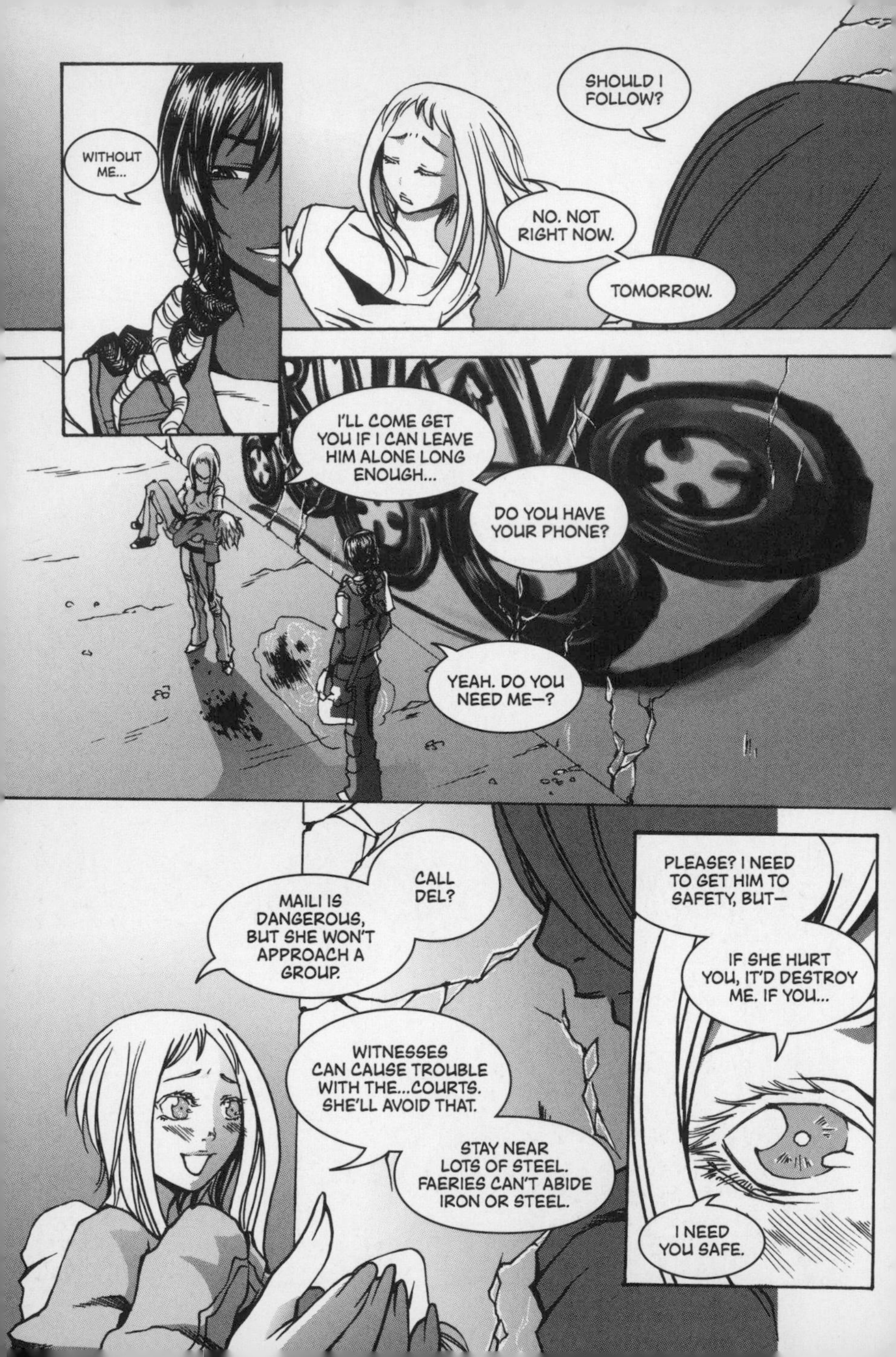
WITHOUT ME...
SHOULD I FOLLOW?
NO. NOT RIGHT NOW.
TOMORROW.
I'LL COME GET YOU IF I CAN LEAVE HIM ALONE LONG ENOUGH...
DO YOU HAVE YOUR PHONE?
YEAH. DO YOU NEED ME—?
CALL DEL?
MAILI IS DANGEROUS, BUT SHE WON'T APPROACH A GROUP.
WITNESSES CAN CAUSE TROUBLE WITH THE...COURTS. SHE'LL AVOID THAT.
STAY NEAR LOTS OF STEEL. FAERIES CAN'T ABIDE IRON OR STEEL.
PLEASE? I NEED TO GET HIM TO SAFETY, BUT—
IF SHE HURT YOU, IT'D DESTROY ME. IF YOU...
I NEED YOU SAFE.

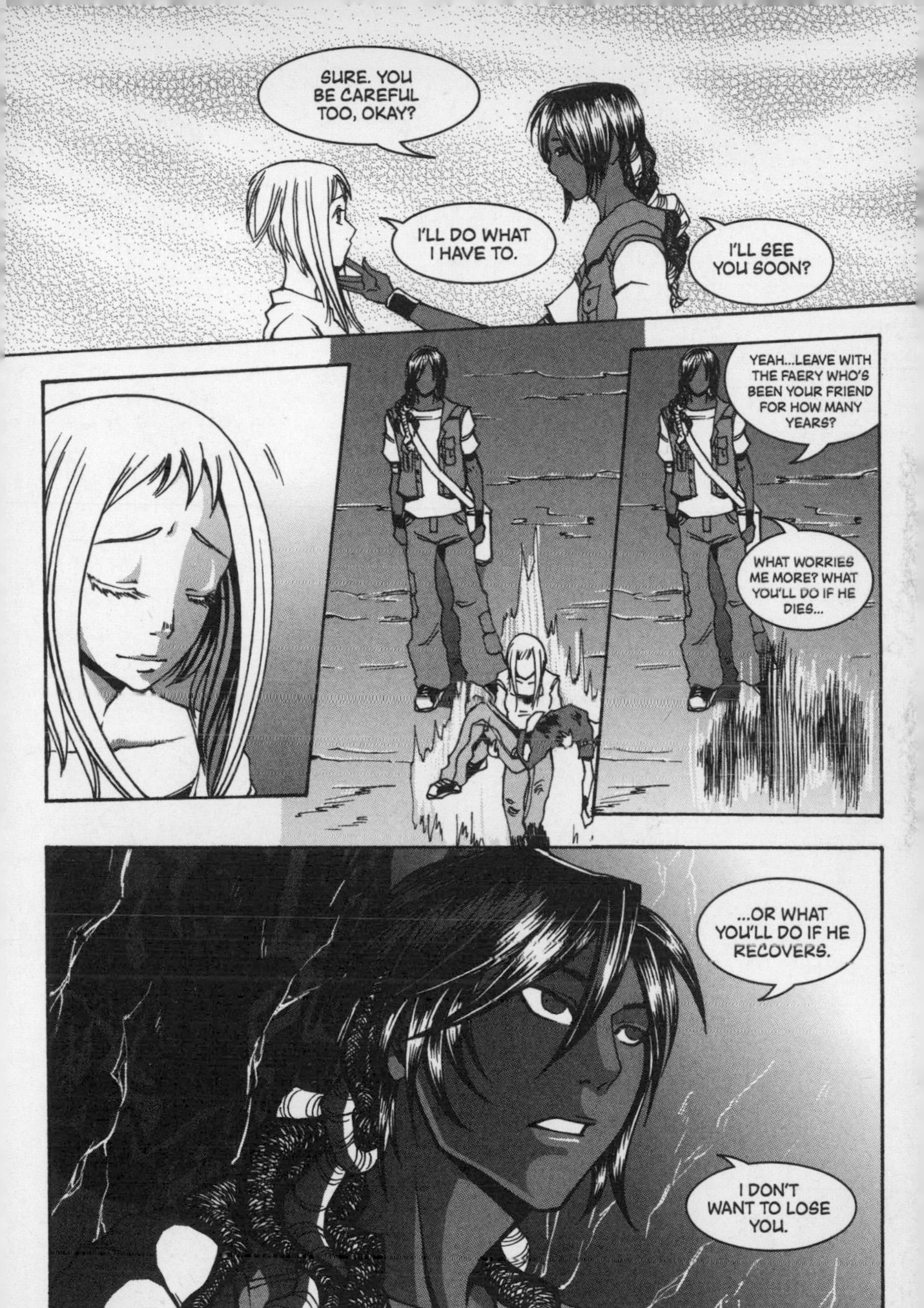
SURE. YOU BE CAREFUL TOO, OKAY?
I'LL DO WHAT I HAVE TO.
I'LL SEE YOU SOON?
YEAH...LEAVE WITH THE FAERY WHO'S BEEN YOUR FRIEND FOR HOW MANY YEARS?
WHAT WORRIES ME MORE? WHAT YOU'LL DO IF HE DIES...
...OR WHAT YOU'LL DO IF HE RECOVERS.
I DON'T WANT TO LOSE YOU.

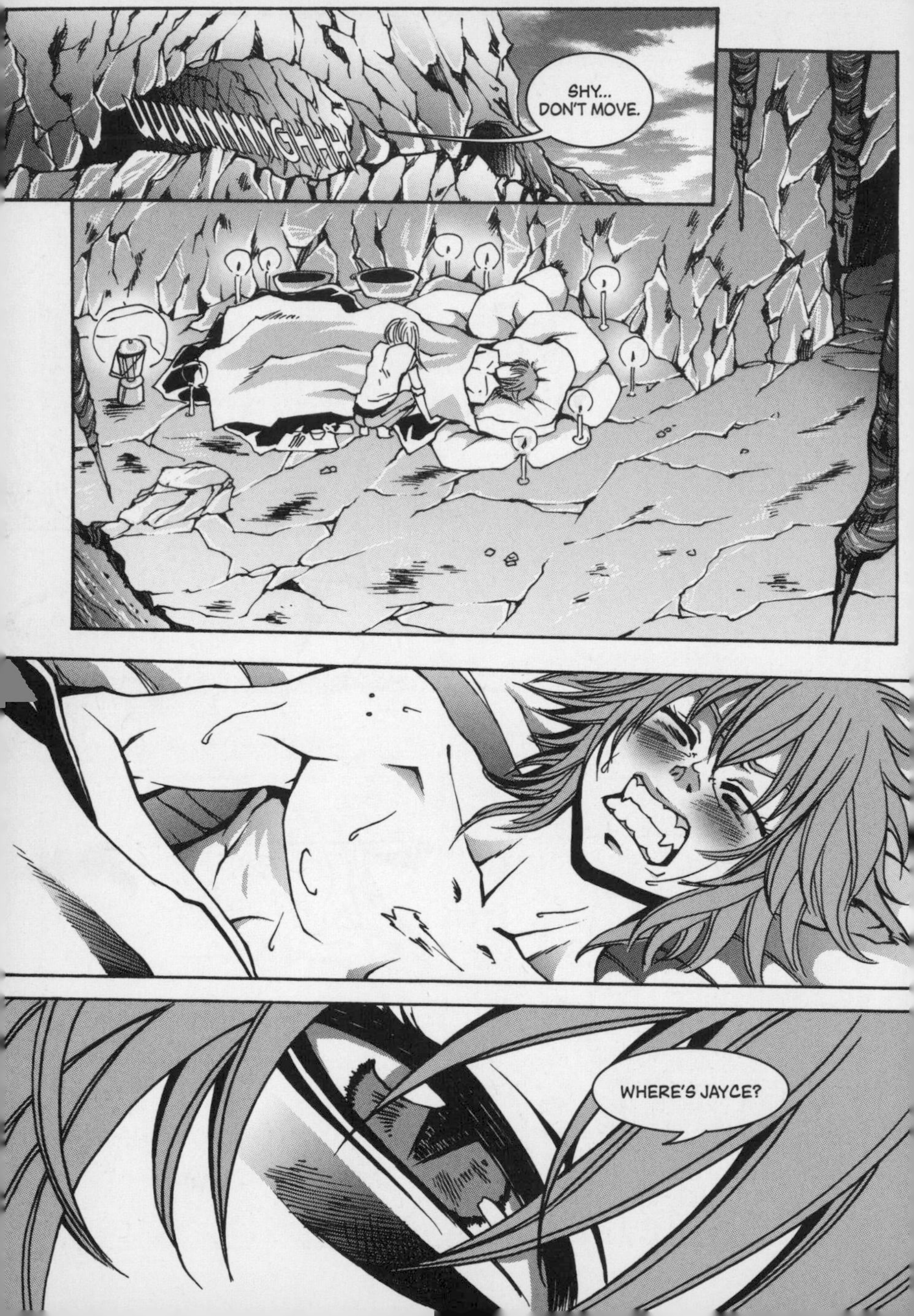
UUUNNNNNGHHHH
SHY... DON'T MOVE.
WHERE'S JAYCE?

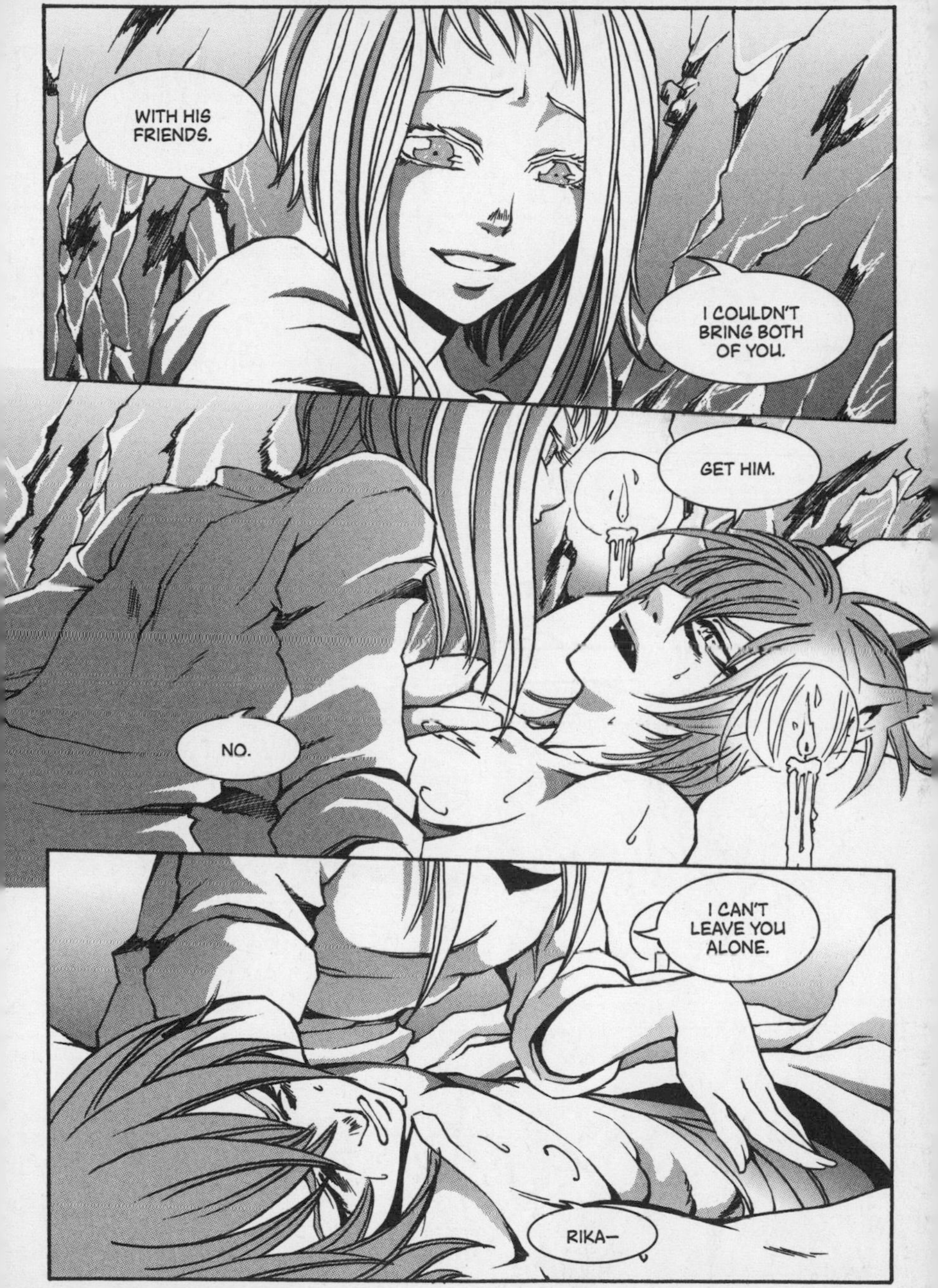
WITH HIS FRIENDS.
I COULDN'T BRING BOTH OF YOU.
GET HIM.
NO.
I CAN'T LEAVE YOU ALONE.
RIKA—

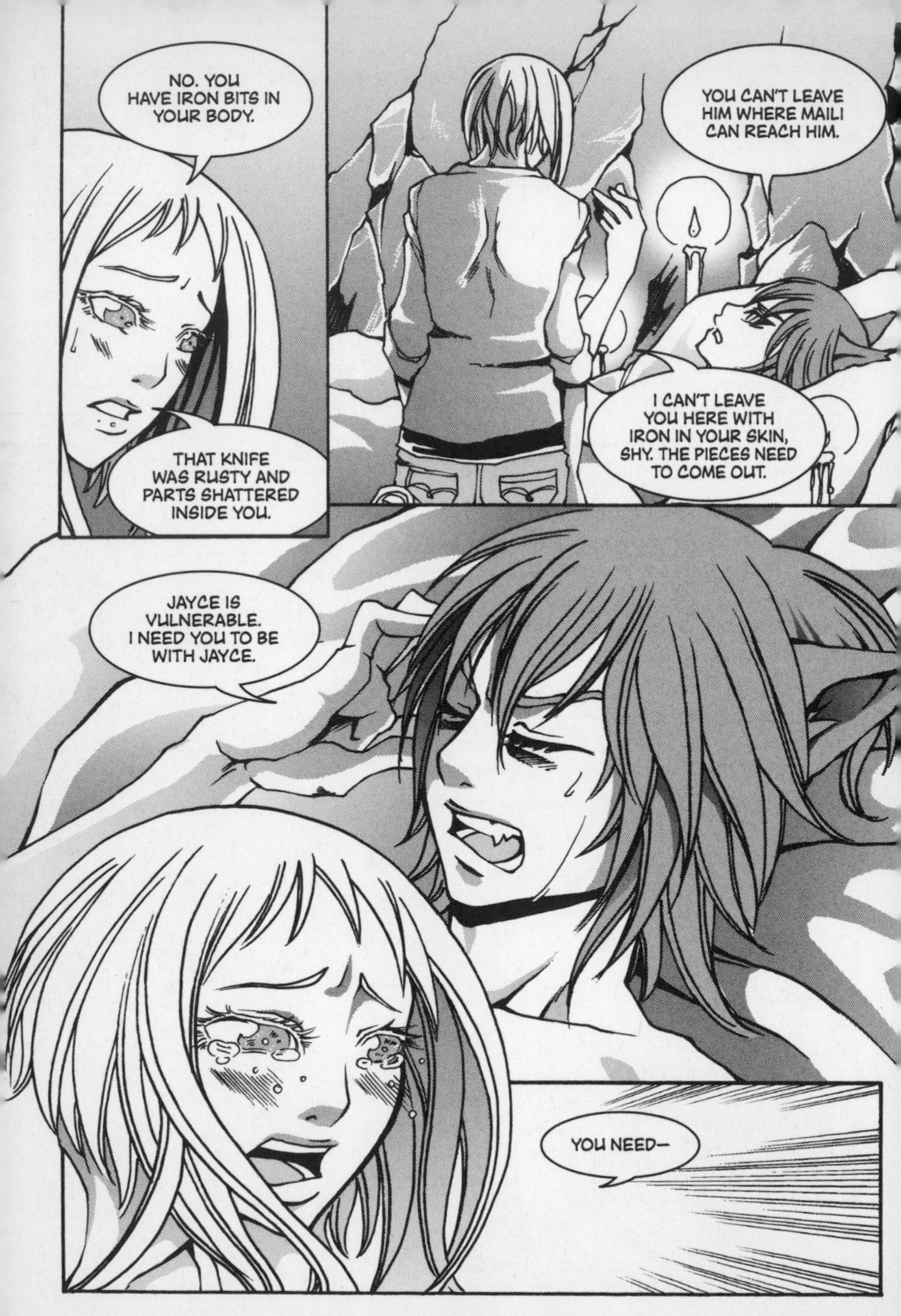
NO. YOU HAVE IRON BITS IN YOUR BODY.
THAT KNIFE WAS RUSTY AND PARTS SHATTERED INSIDE YOU.
YOU CAN'T LEAVE HIM WHERE MAILI CAN REACH HIM.
I CAN'T LEAVE YOU HERE WITH IRON IN YOUR SKIN, SHY. THE PIECES NEED TO COME OUT.
JAYCE IS VULNERABLE. I NEED YOU TO BE WITH JAYCE.
YOU NEED—

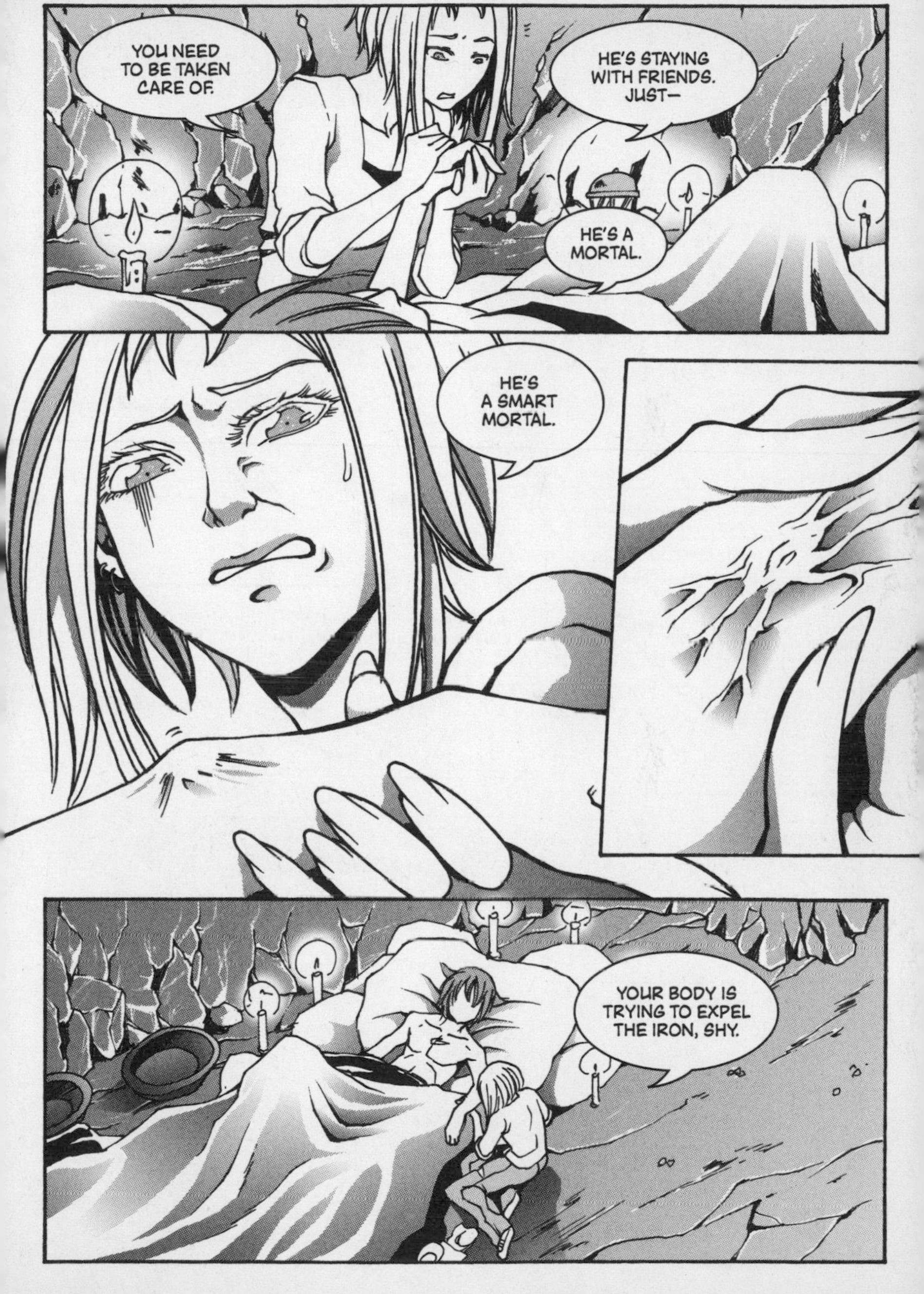
YOU NEED TO BE TAKEN CARE OF.
HE'S STAYING WITH FRIENDS. JUST—
HE'S A MORTAL.
HE'S A SMART MORTAL.
YOUR BODY IS TRYING TO EXPEL THE IRON, SHY.

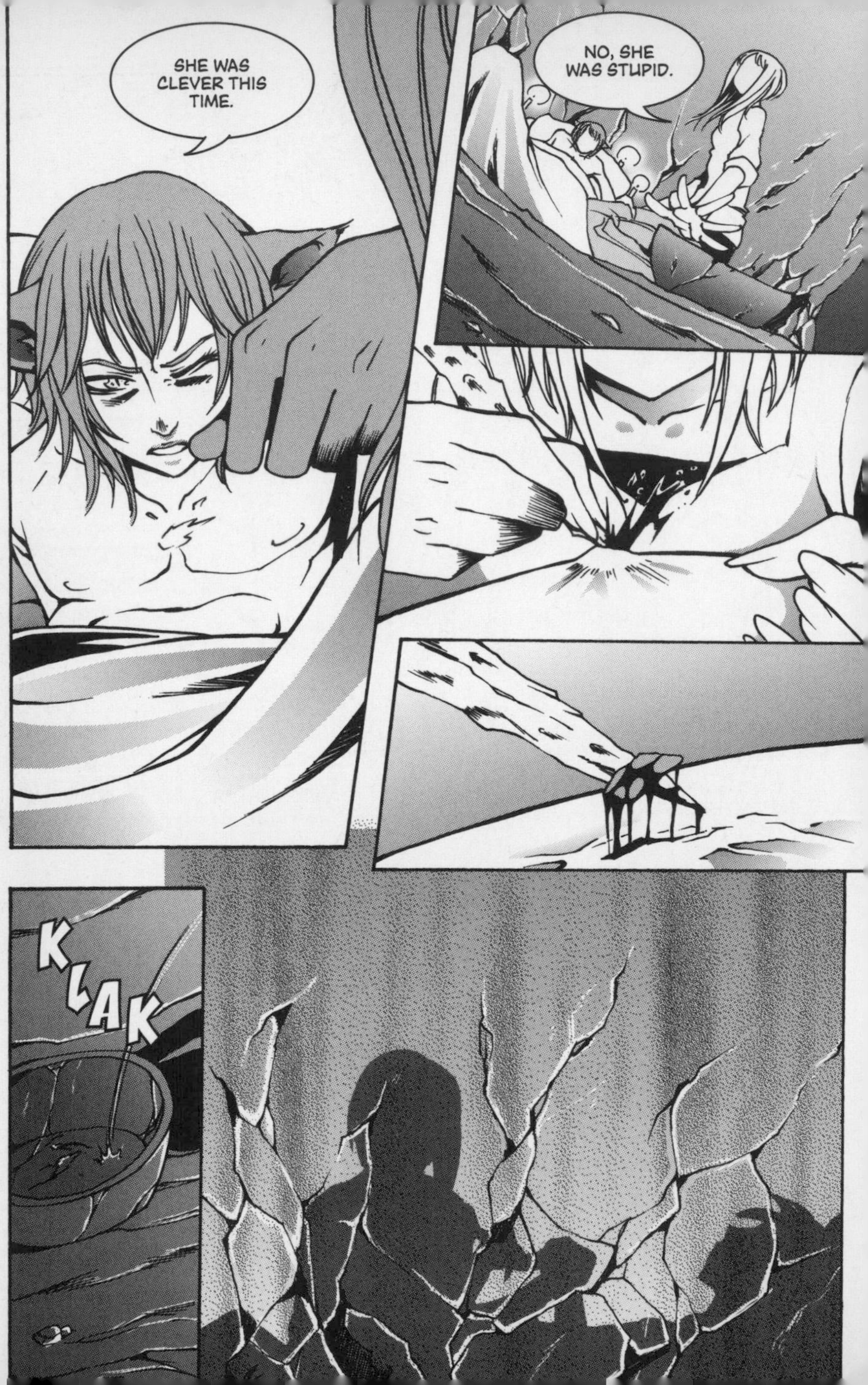
SHE WAS CLEVER THIS TIME.
NO, SHE WAS STUPID.
KLAK

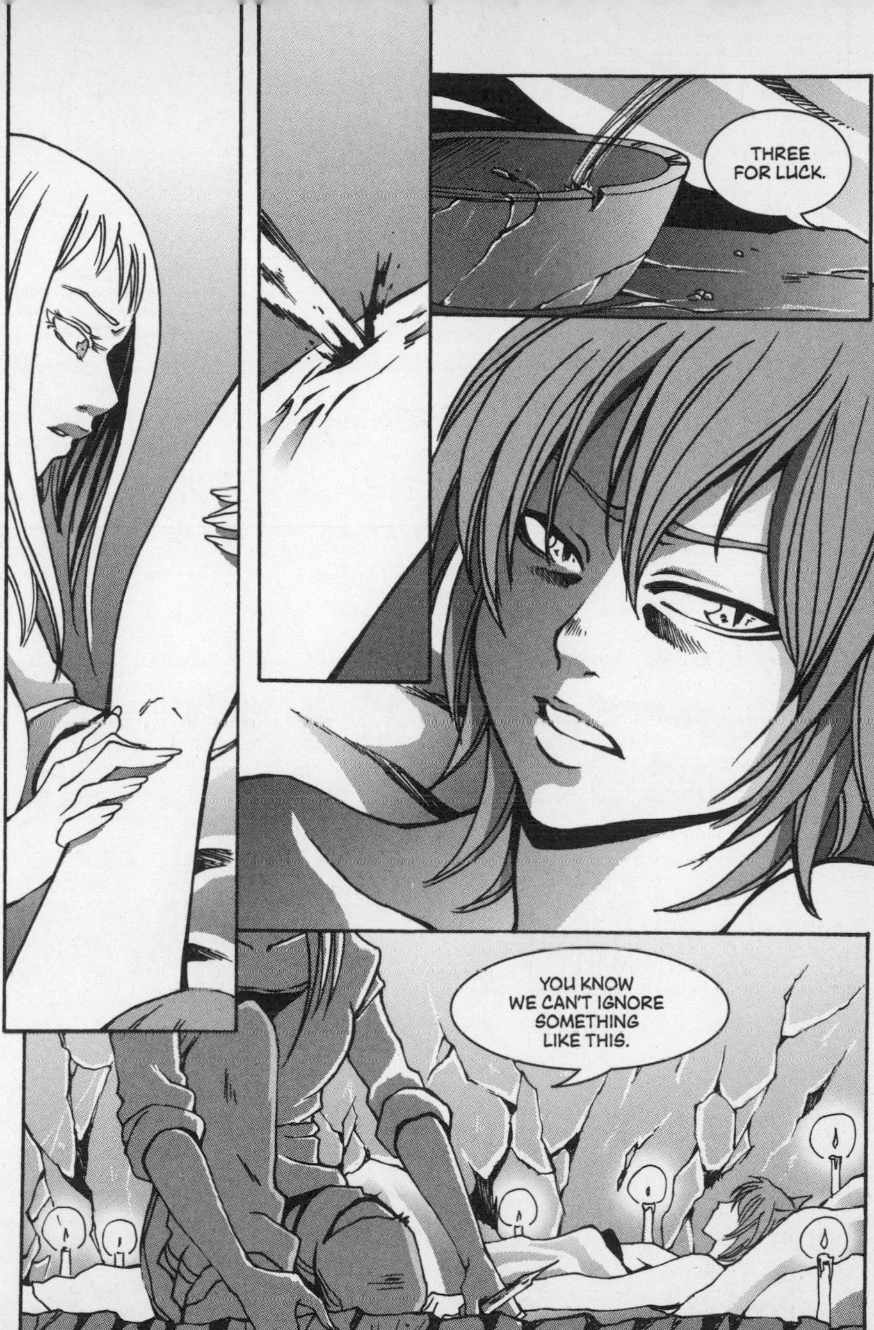
THREE FOR LUCK.
YOU KNOW WE CAN'T IGNORE SOMETHING LIKE THIS.

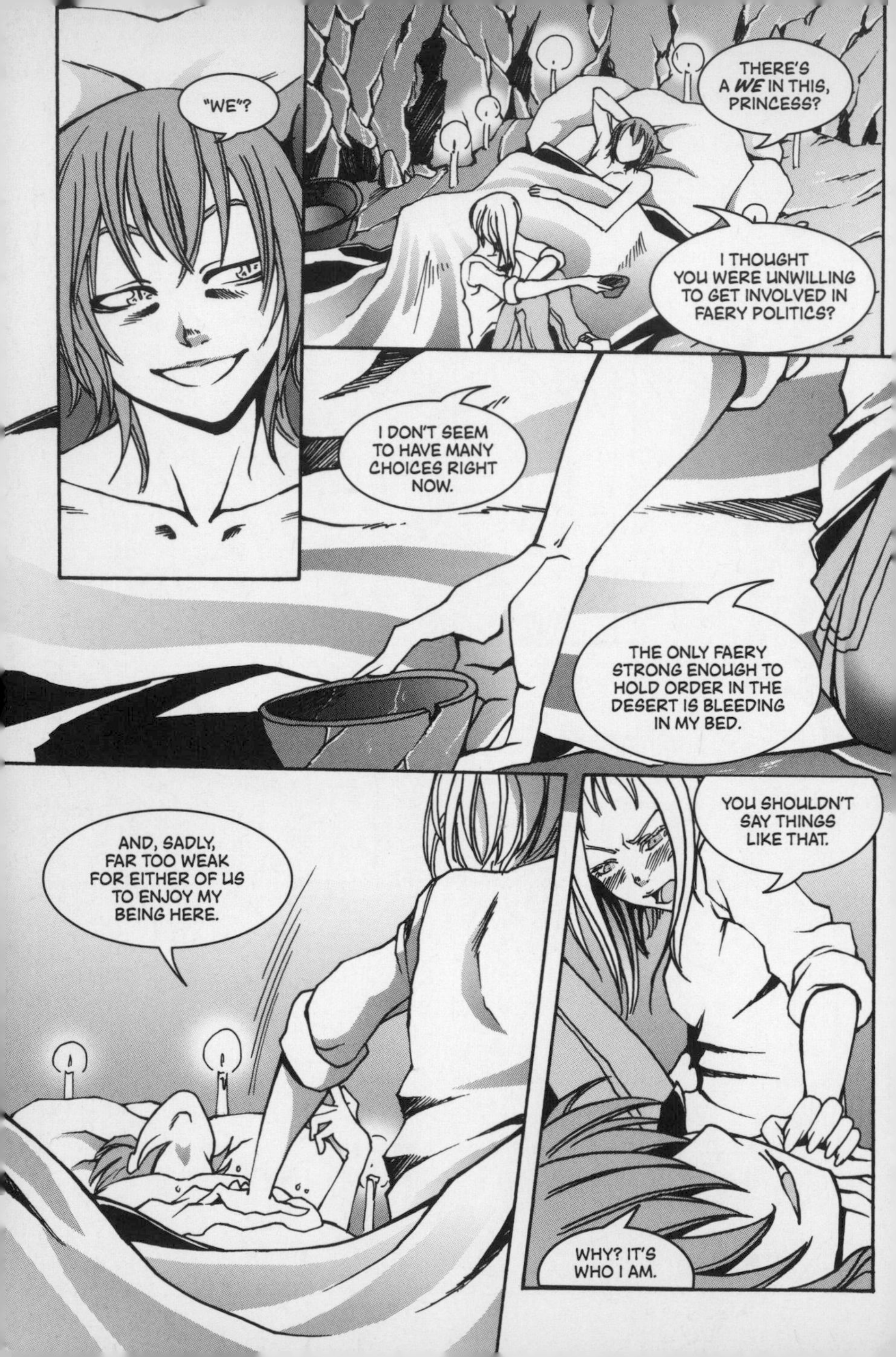
"WE"?
THERE'S A *WE* IN THIS, PRINCESS?
I THOUGHT YOU WERE UNWILLING TO GET INVOLVED IN FAERY POLITICS?
I DON'T SEEM TO HAVE MANY CHOICES RIGHT NOW.
THE ONLY FAERY STRONG ENOUGH TO HOLD ORDER IN THE DESERT IS BLEEDING IN MY BED.
AND, SADLY, FAR TOO WEAK FOR EITHER OF US TO ENJOY MY BEING HERE.
YOU SHOULDN'T SAY THINGS LIKE THAT.
WHY? IT'S WHO I AM.

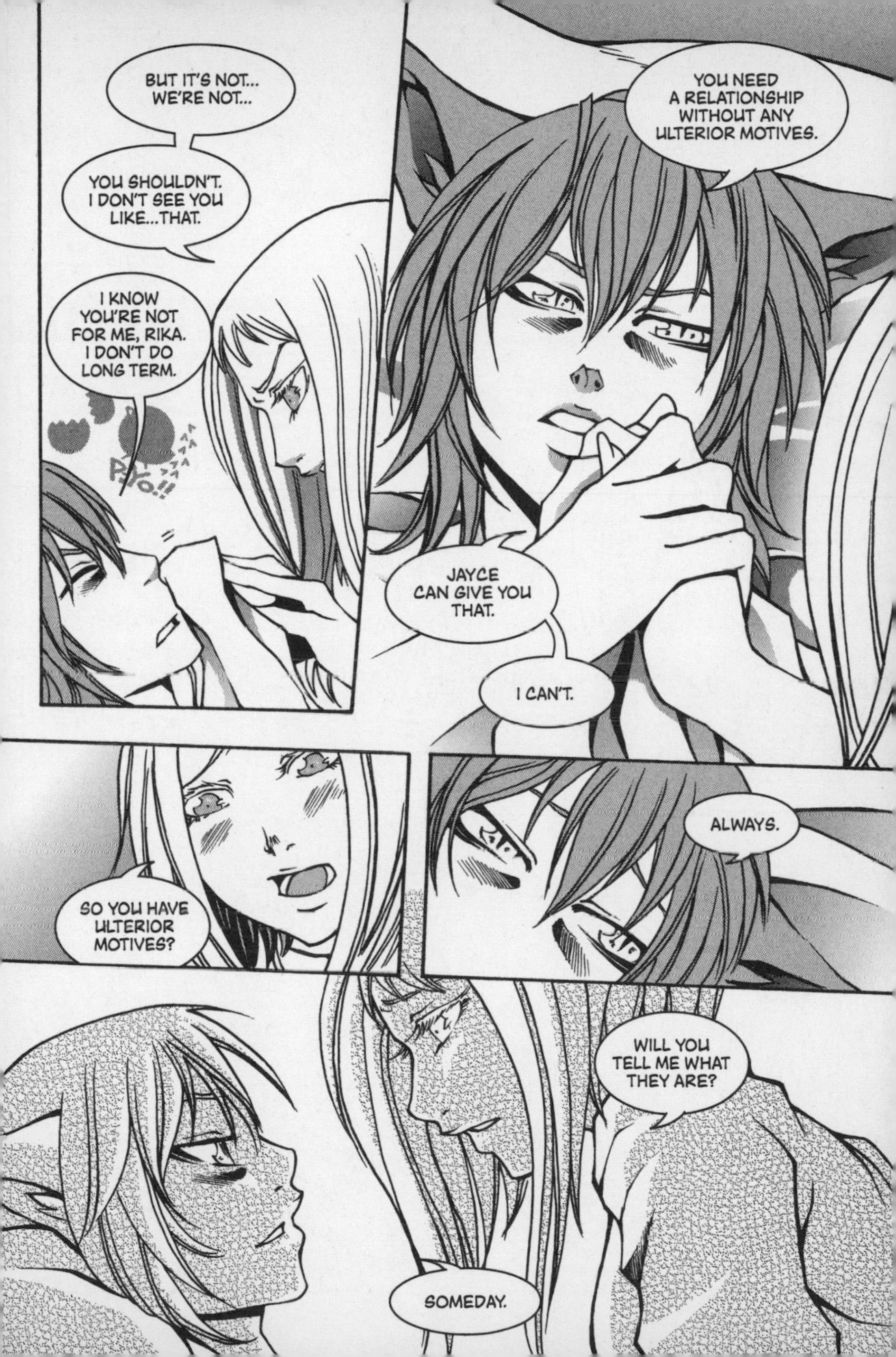
BUT IT'S NOT... WE'RE NOT...
YOU SHOULDN'T. I DON'T SEE YOU LIKE...THAT.
I KNOW YOU'RE NOT FOR ME, RIKA. I DON'T DO LONG TERM.
PYO!!
YOU NEED A RELATIONSHIP WITHOUT ANY ULTERIOR MOTIVES.
JAYCE CAN GIVE YOU THAT.
I CAN'T.
SO YOU HAVE ULTERIOR MOTIVES?
ALWAYS.
WILL YOU TELL ME WHAT THEY ARE?
SOMEDAY.

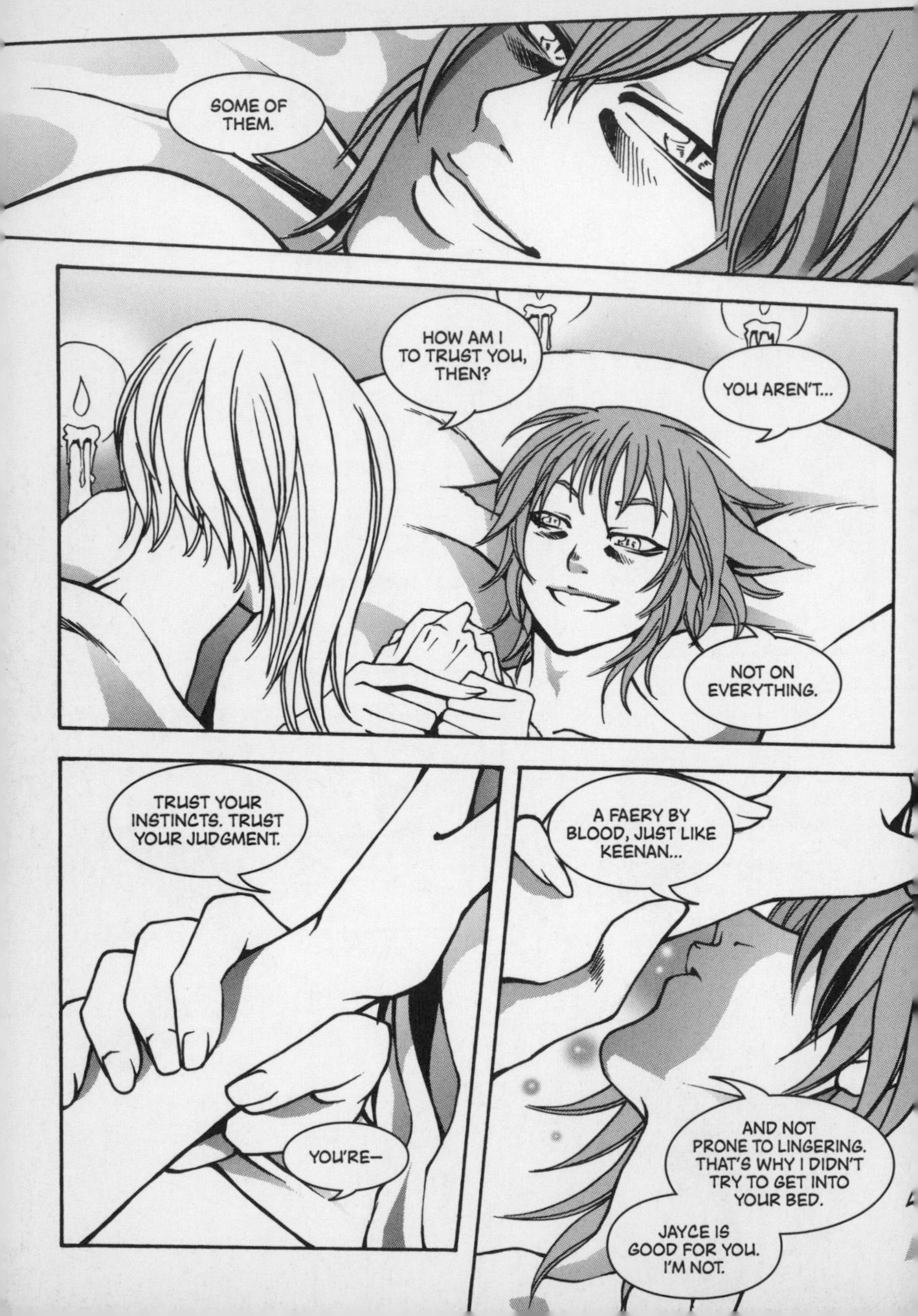
SOME OF THEM.
HOW AM I TO TRUST YOU, THEN?
YOU AREN'T...
NOT ON EVERYTHING.
TRUST YOUR INSTINCTS. TRUST YOUR JUDGMENT.
YOU'RE—
A FAERY BY BLOOD, JUST LIKE KEENAN...
AND NOT PRONE TO LINGERING. THAT'S WHY I DIDN'T TRY TO GET INTO YOUR BED.
JAYCE IS GOOD FOR YOU. I'M NOT.

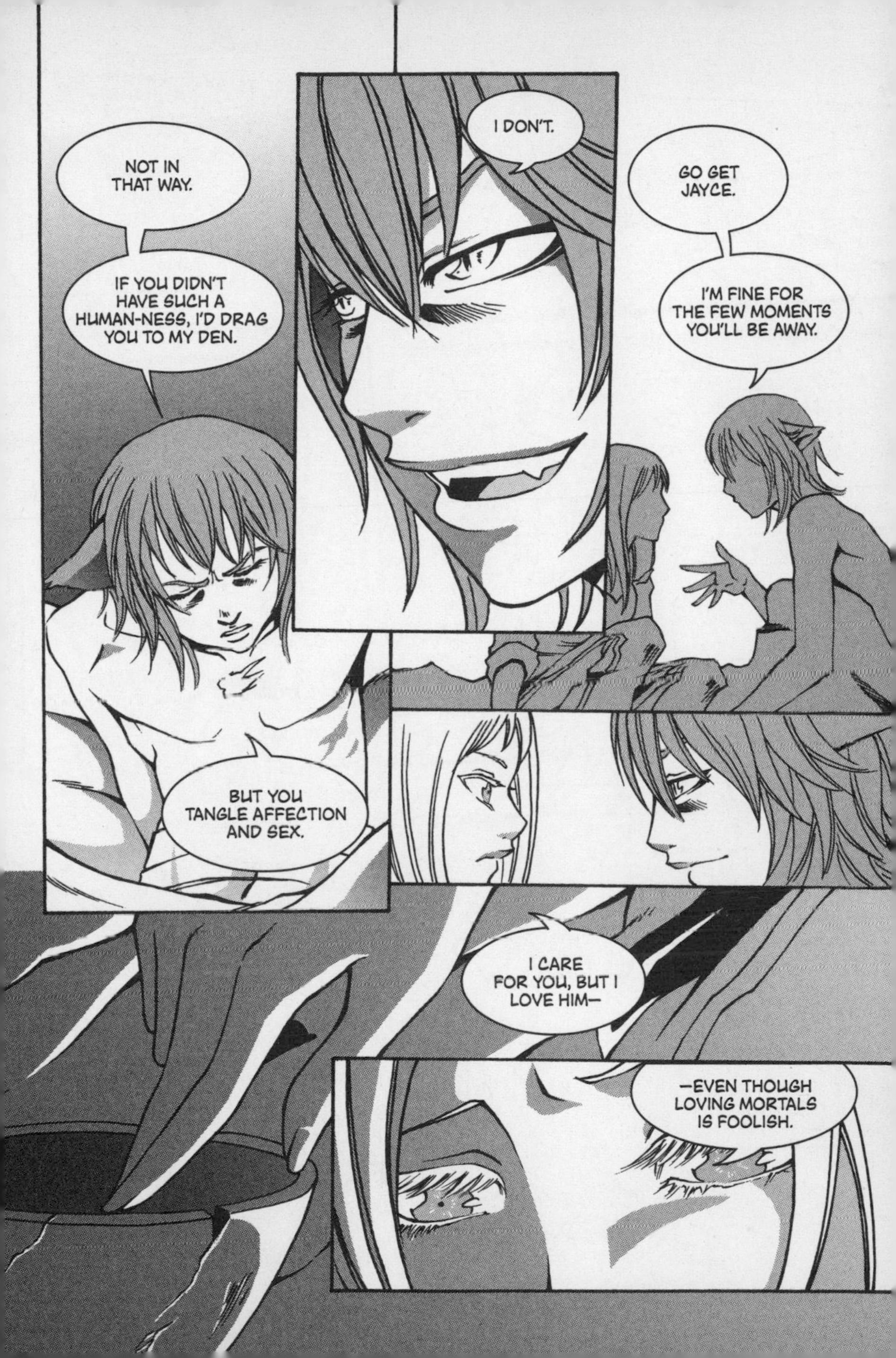
NOT IN THAT WAY.
IF YOU DIDN'T HAVE SUCH A HUMAN-NESS, I'D DRAG YOU TO MY DEN.
BUT YOU TANGLE AFFECTION AND SEX.
I DON'T.
GO GET JAYCE.
I'M FINE FOR THE FEW MOMENTS YOU'LL BE AWAY.
I CARE FOR YOU, BUT I LOVE HIM—
—EVEN THOUGH LOVING MORTALS IS FOOLISH.

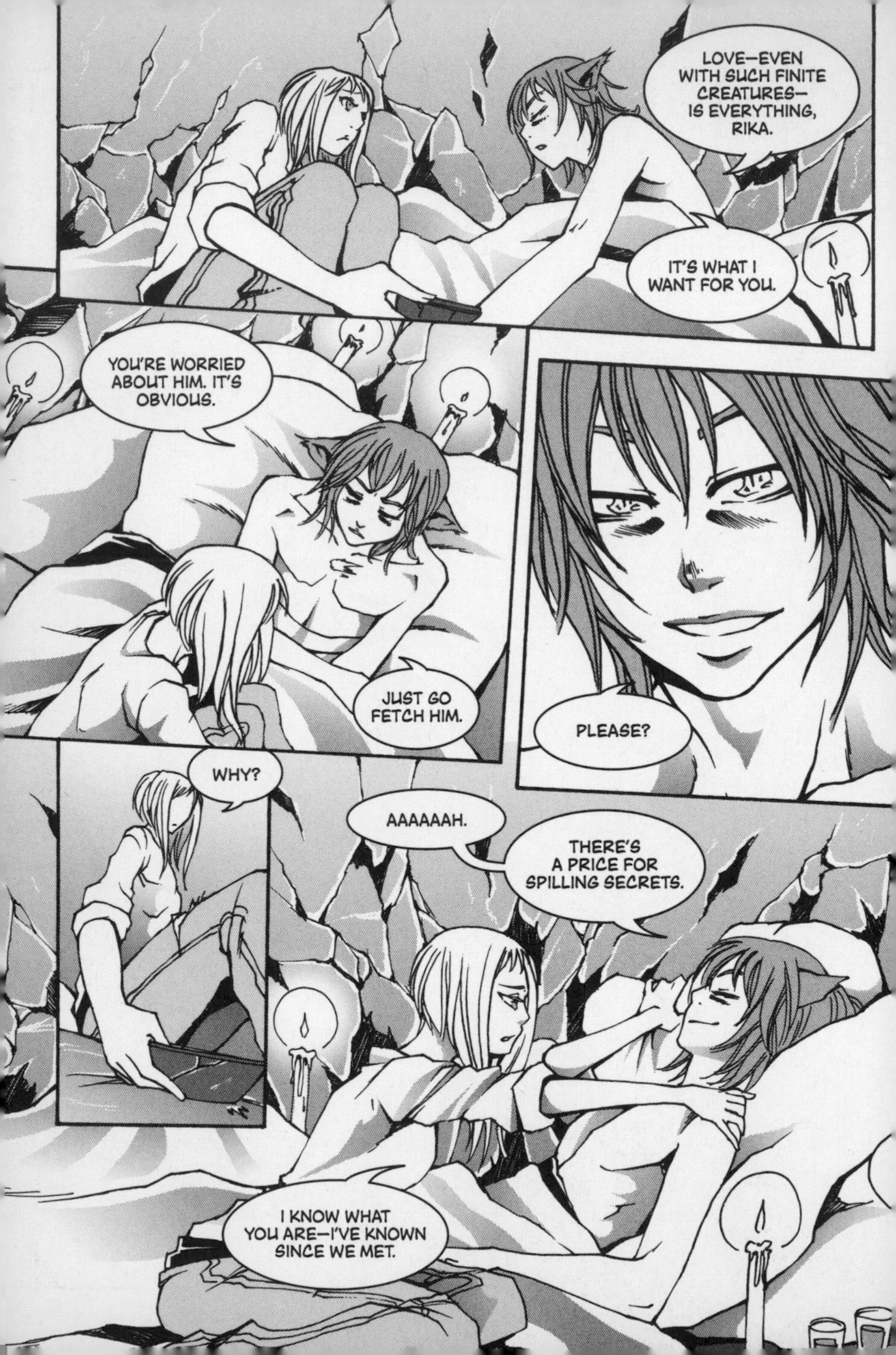
LOVE—EVEN WITH SUCH FINITE CREATURES—IS EVERYTHING, RIKA.
IT'S WHAT I WANT FOR YOU.
YOU'RE WORRIED ABOUT HIM. IT'S OBVIOUS.
JUST GO FETCH HIM.
PLEASE?
WHY?
AAAAAAH.
THERE'S A PRICE FOR SPILLING SECRETS.
I KNOW WHAT YOU ARE—I'VE KNOWN SINCE WE MET.

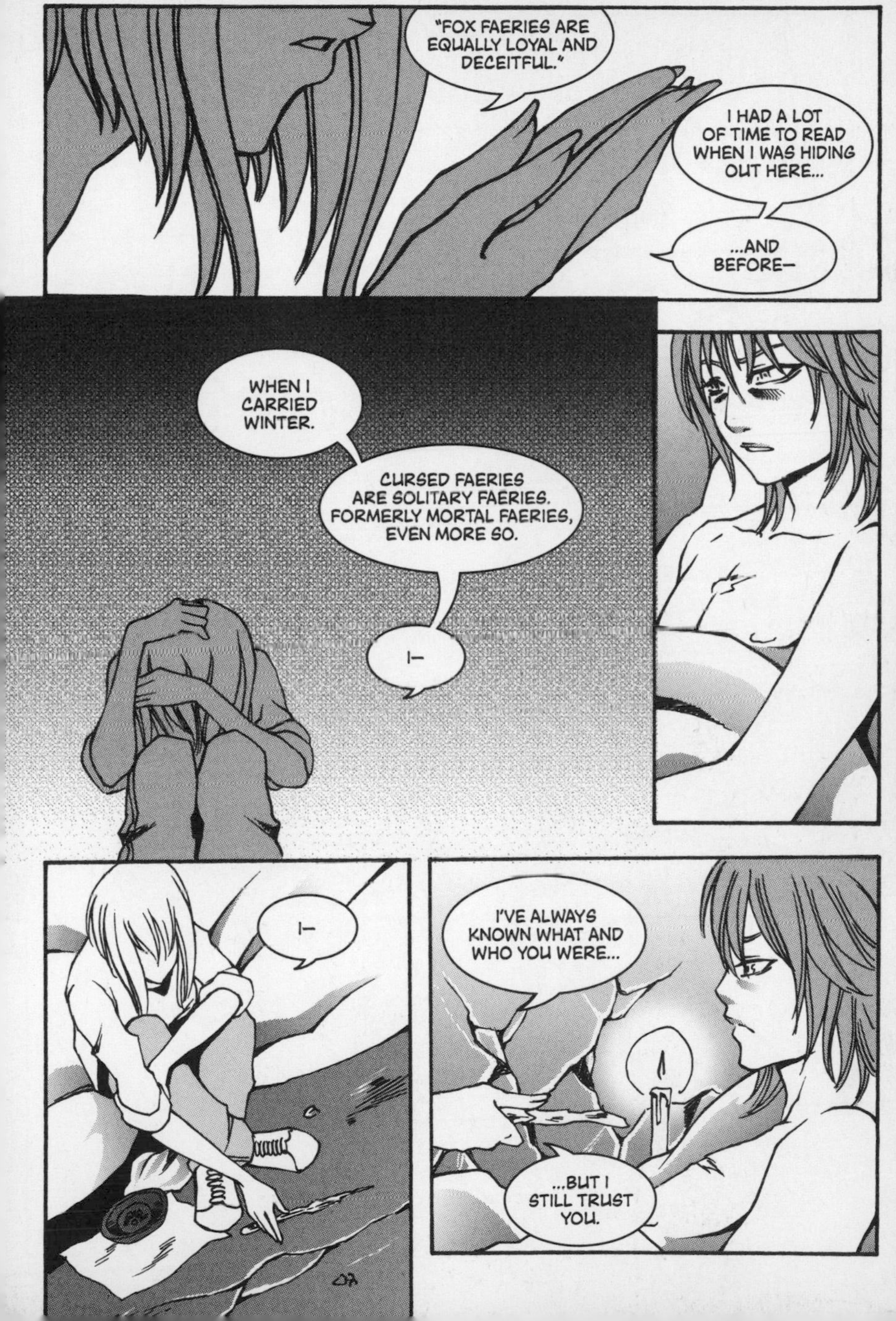
"FOX FAERIES ARE EQUALLY LOYAL AND DECEITFUL."
I HAD A LOT OF TIME TO READ WHEN I WAS HIDING OUT HERE...
...AND BEFORE—
WHEN I CARRIED WINTER.
CURSED FAERIES ARE SOLITARY FAERIES. FORMERLY MORTAL FAERIES, EVEN MORE SO.
I—
I—
I'VE ALWAYS KNOWN WHAT AND WHO YOU WERE...
...BUT I STILL TRUST YOU.

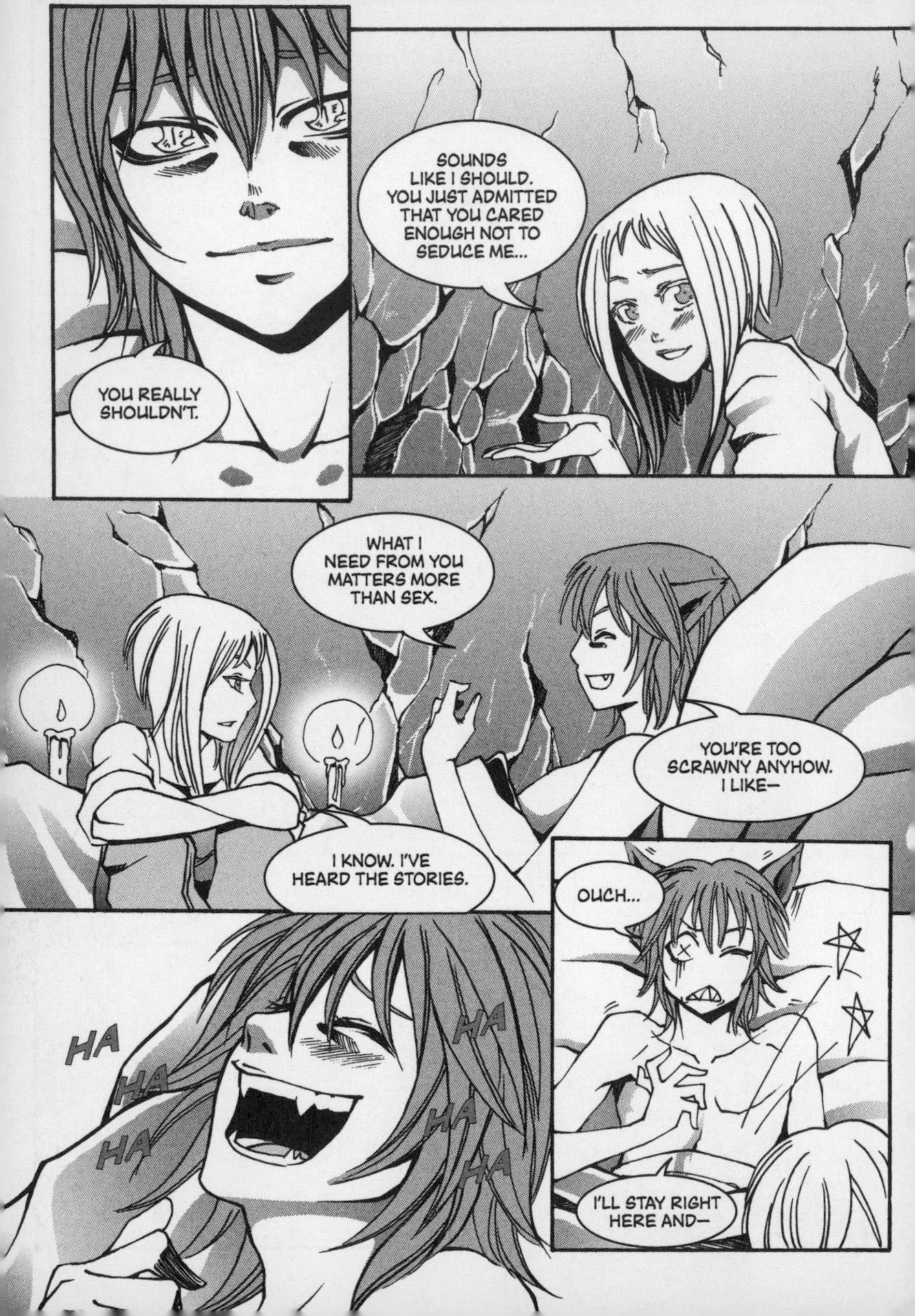
YOU REALLY SHOULDN'T.
SOUNDS LIKE I SHOULD. YOU JUST ADMITTED THAT YOU CARED ENOUGH NOT TO SEDUCE ME...
WHAT I NEED FROM YOU MATTERS MORE THAN SEX.
YOU'RE TOO SCRAWNY ANYHOW. I LIKE—
I KNOW. I'VE HEARD THE STORIES.
HA
HA
HA
HA
HA
HA
OUCH...
I'LL STAY RIGHT HERE AND—

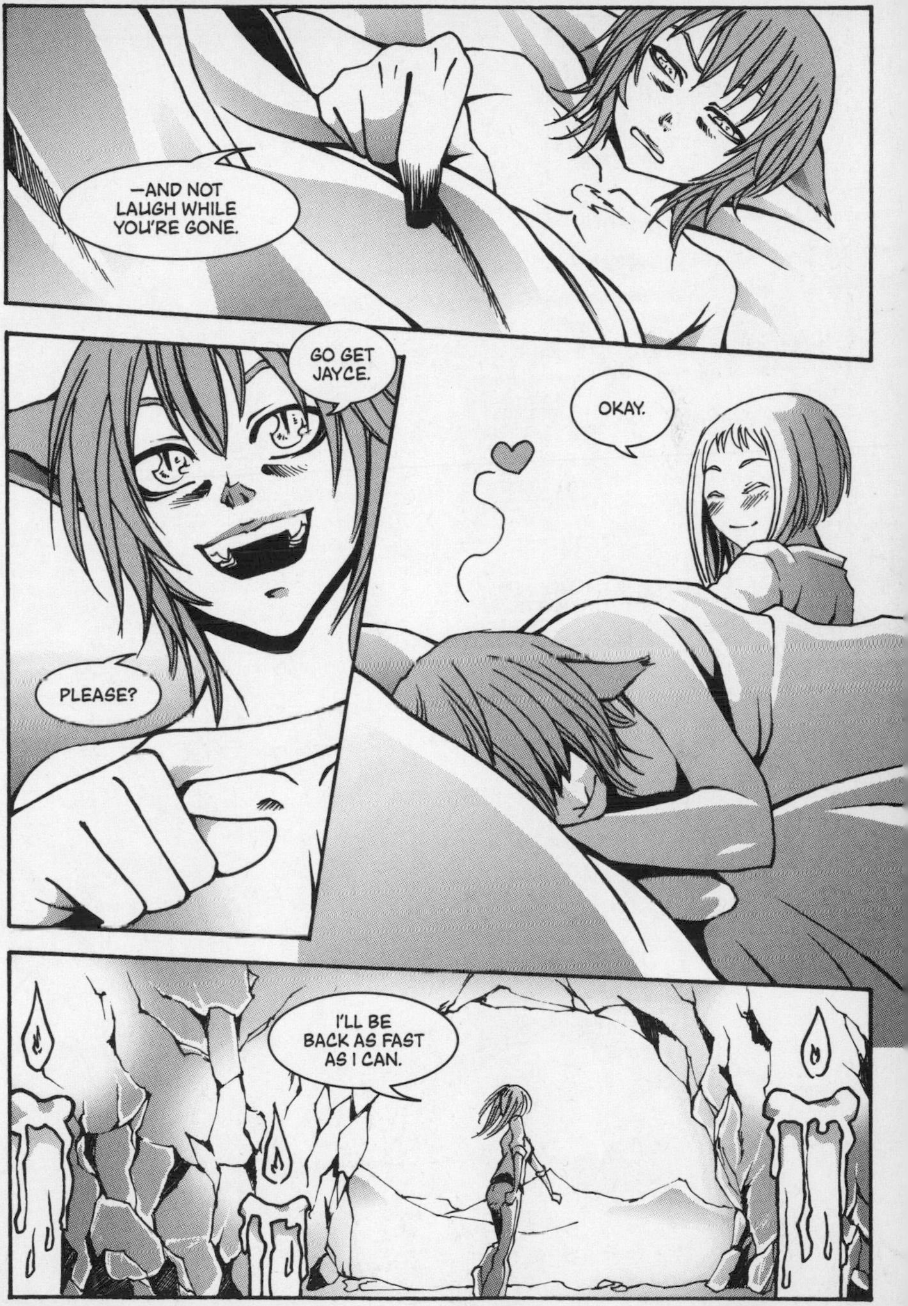
—AND NOT LAUGH WHILE YOU'RE GONE.
GO GET JAYCE.
PLEASE?
OKAY.
I'LL BE BACK AS FAST AS I CAN.

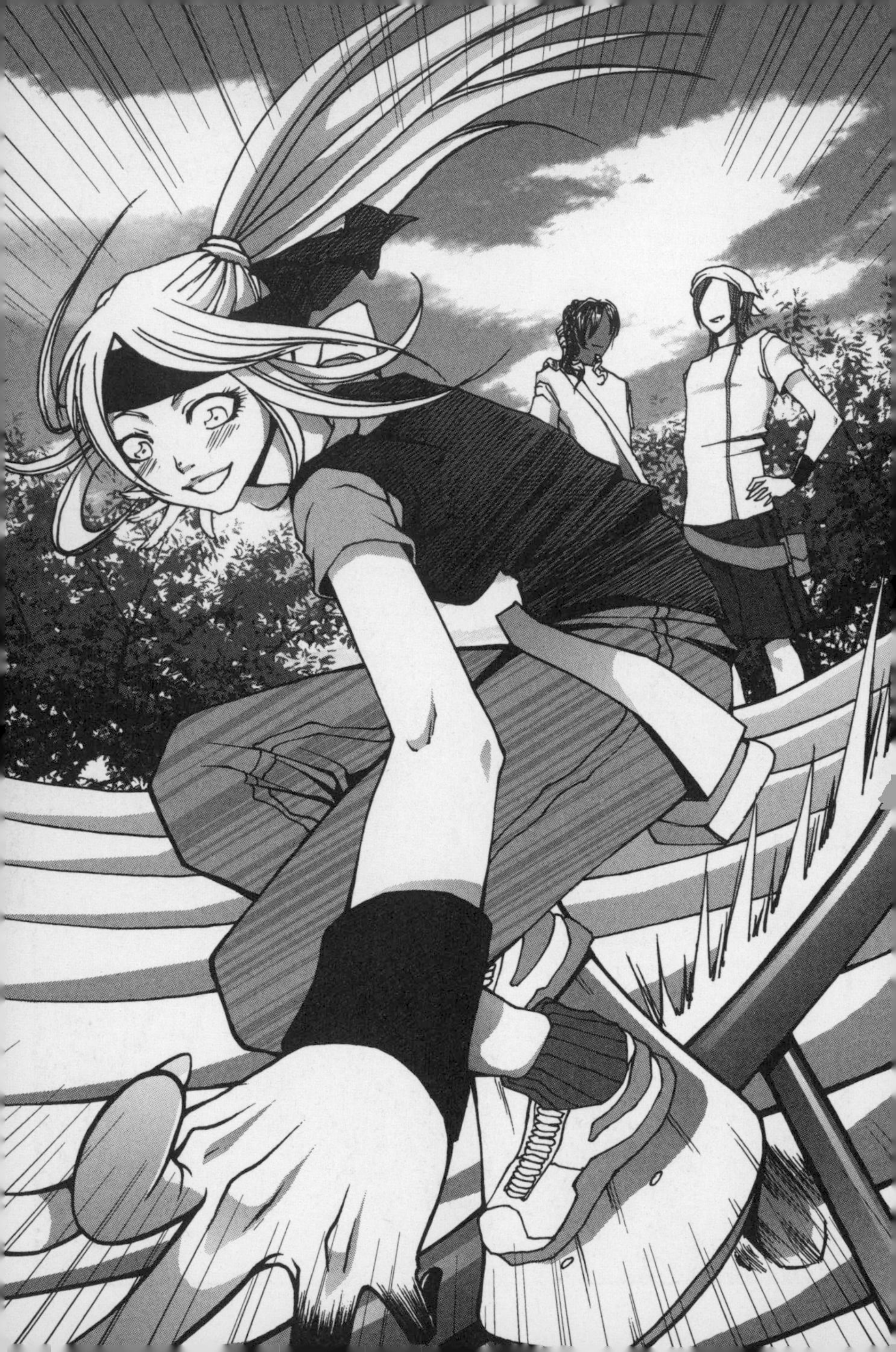

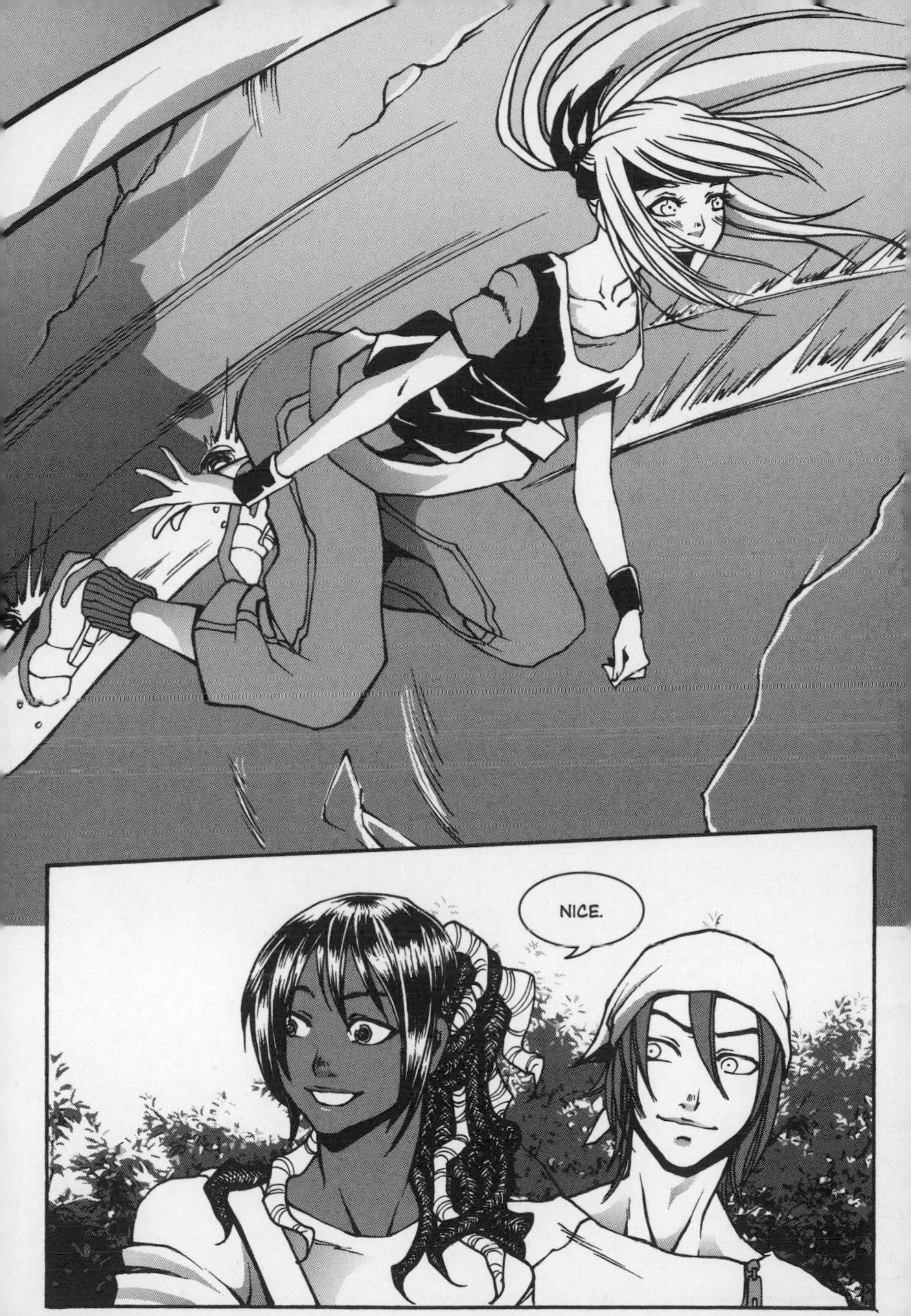
NICE.

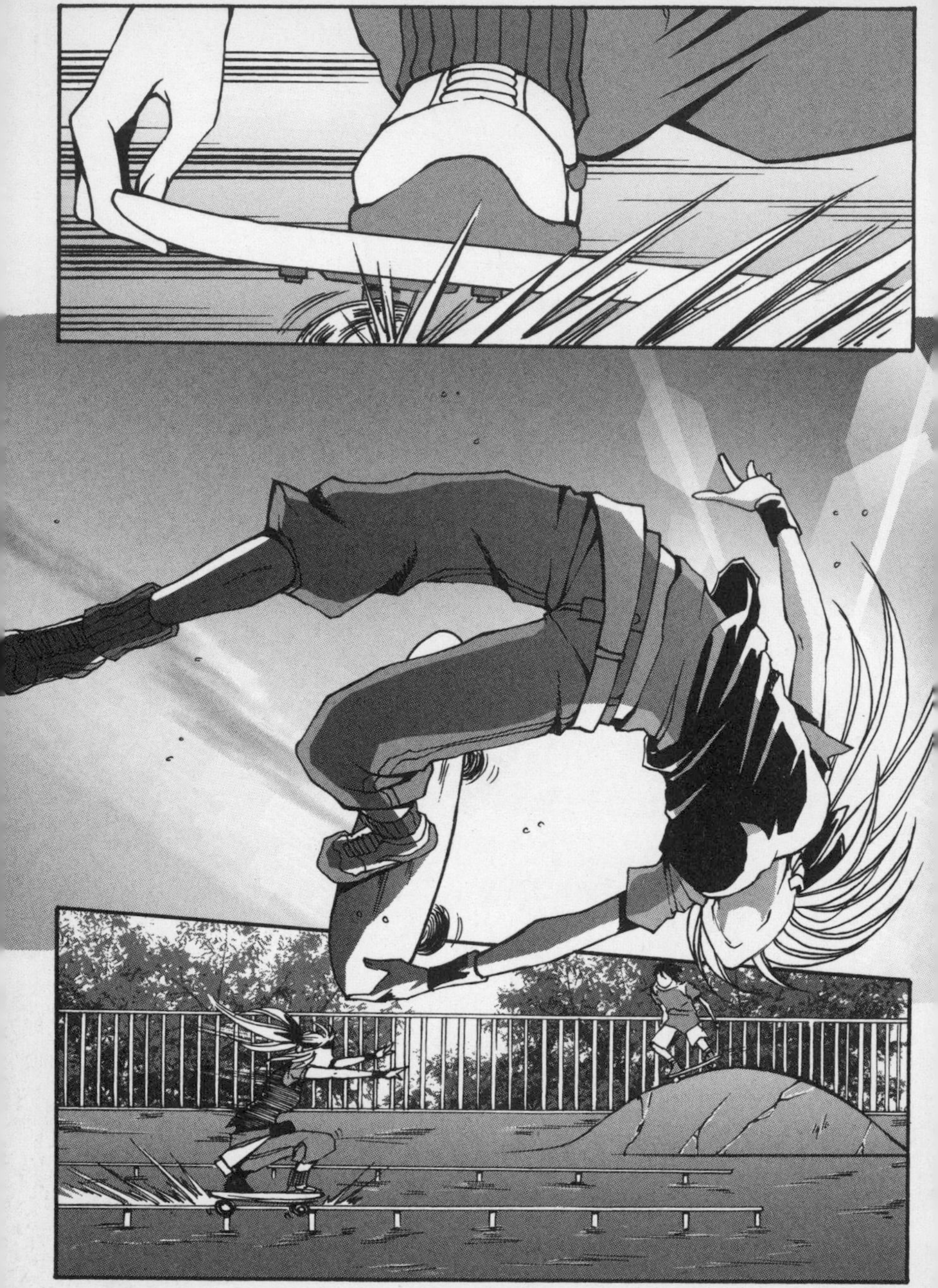

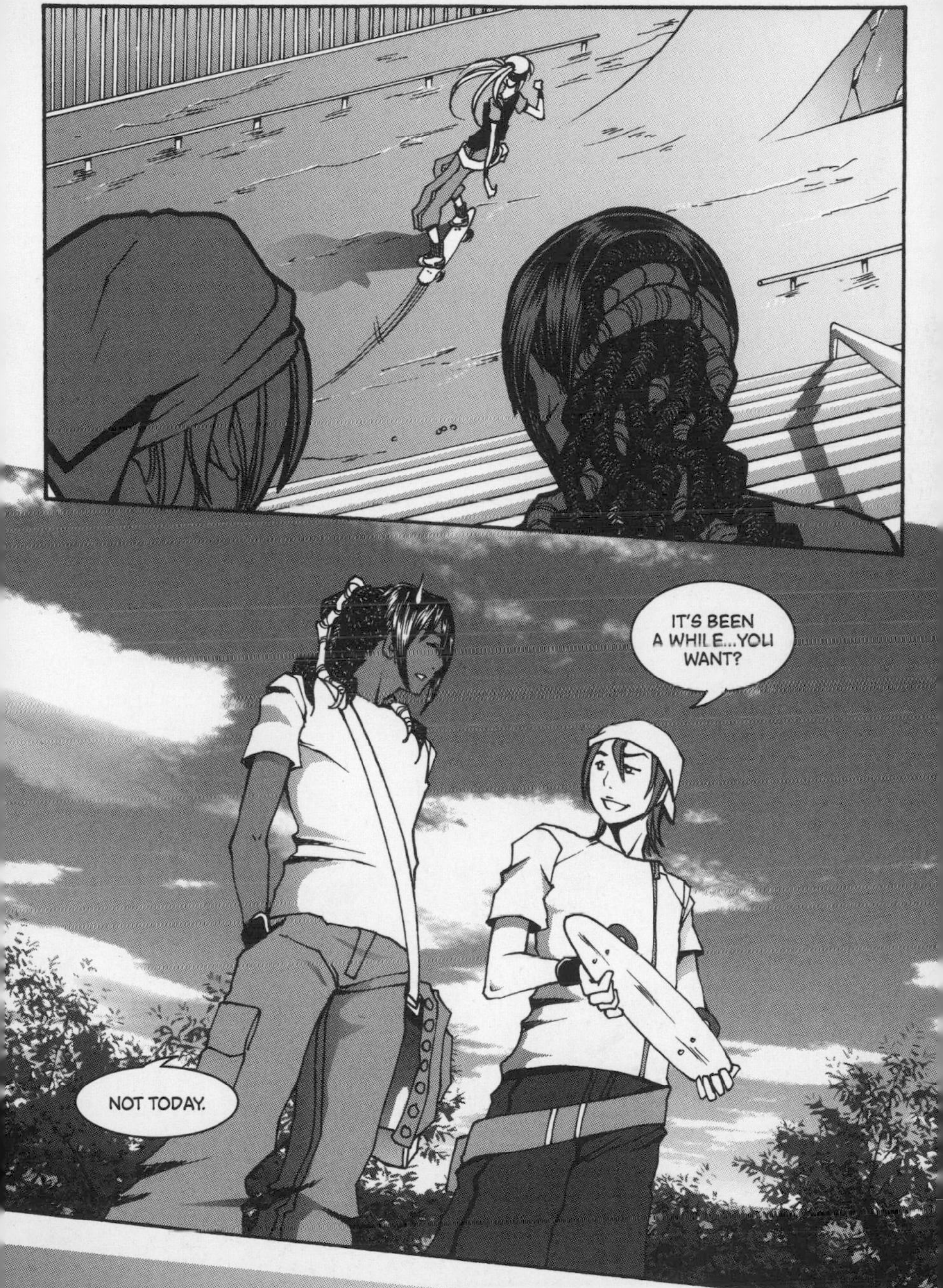
IT'S BEEN
A WHILE...YOU
WANT?
NOT TODAY.

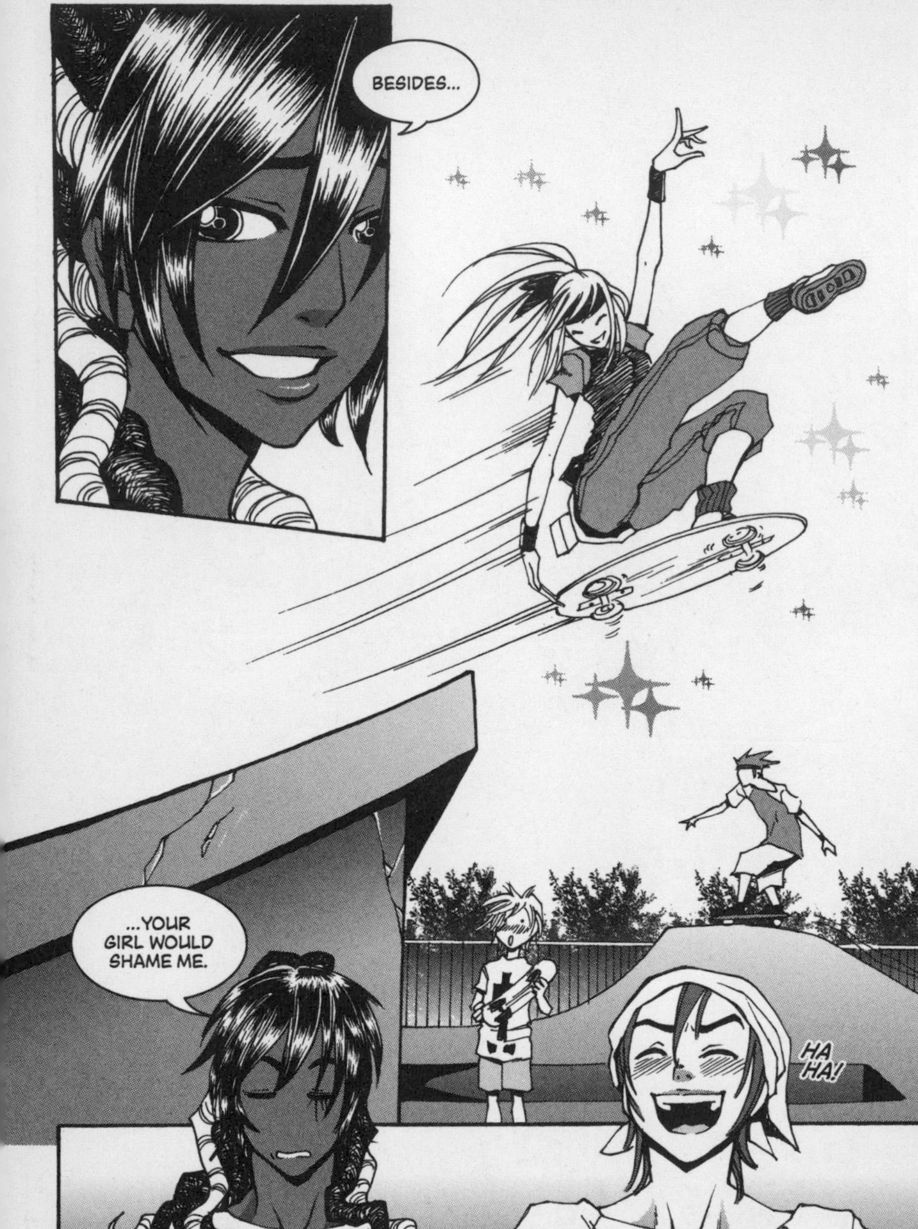
BESIDES...
...YOUR GIRL WOULD SHAME ME.
HA HA!

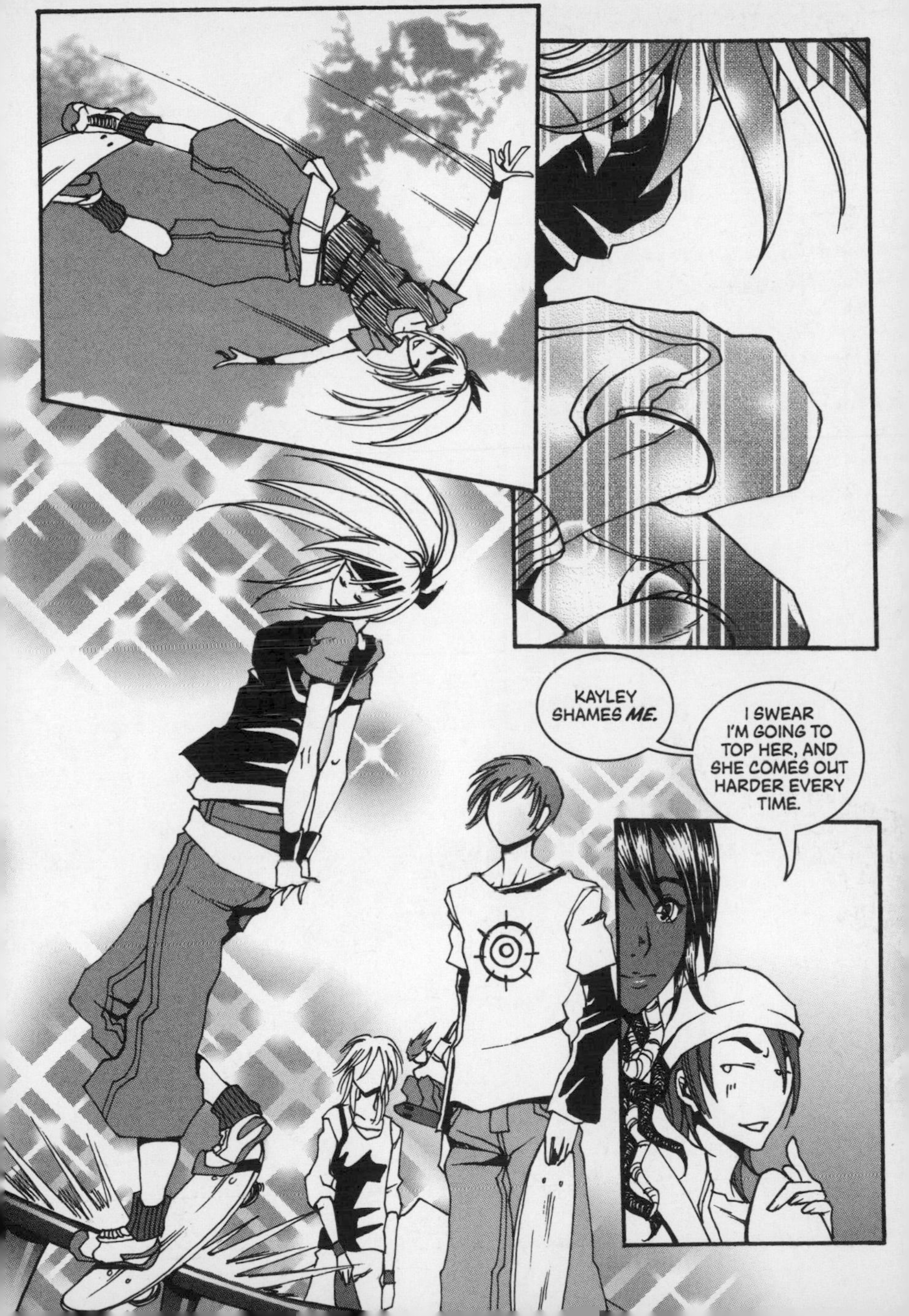
KAYLEY SHAMES *ME.*
I SWEAR I'M GOING TO TOP HER, AND SHE COMES OUT HARDER EVERY TIME.

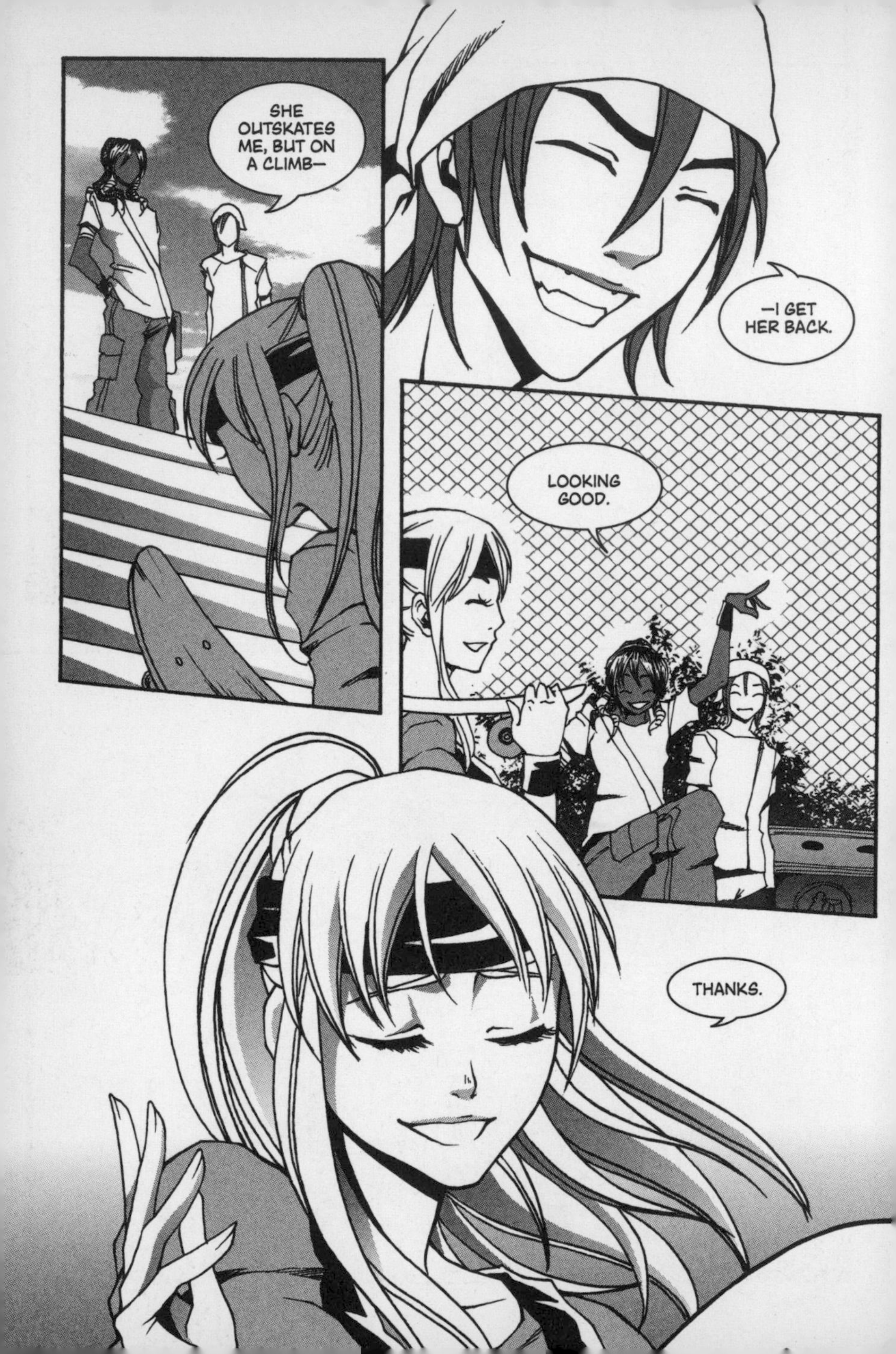
SHE OUTSKATES ME, BUT ON A CLIMB—
—I GET HER BACK.
LOOKING GOOD.
THANKS.

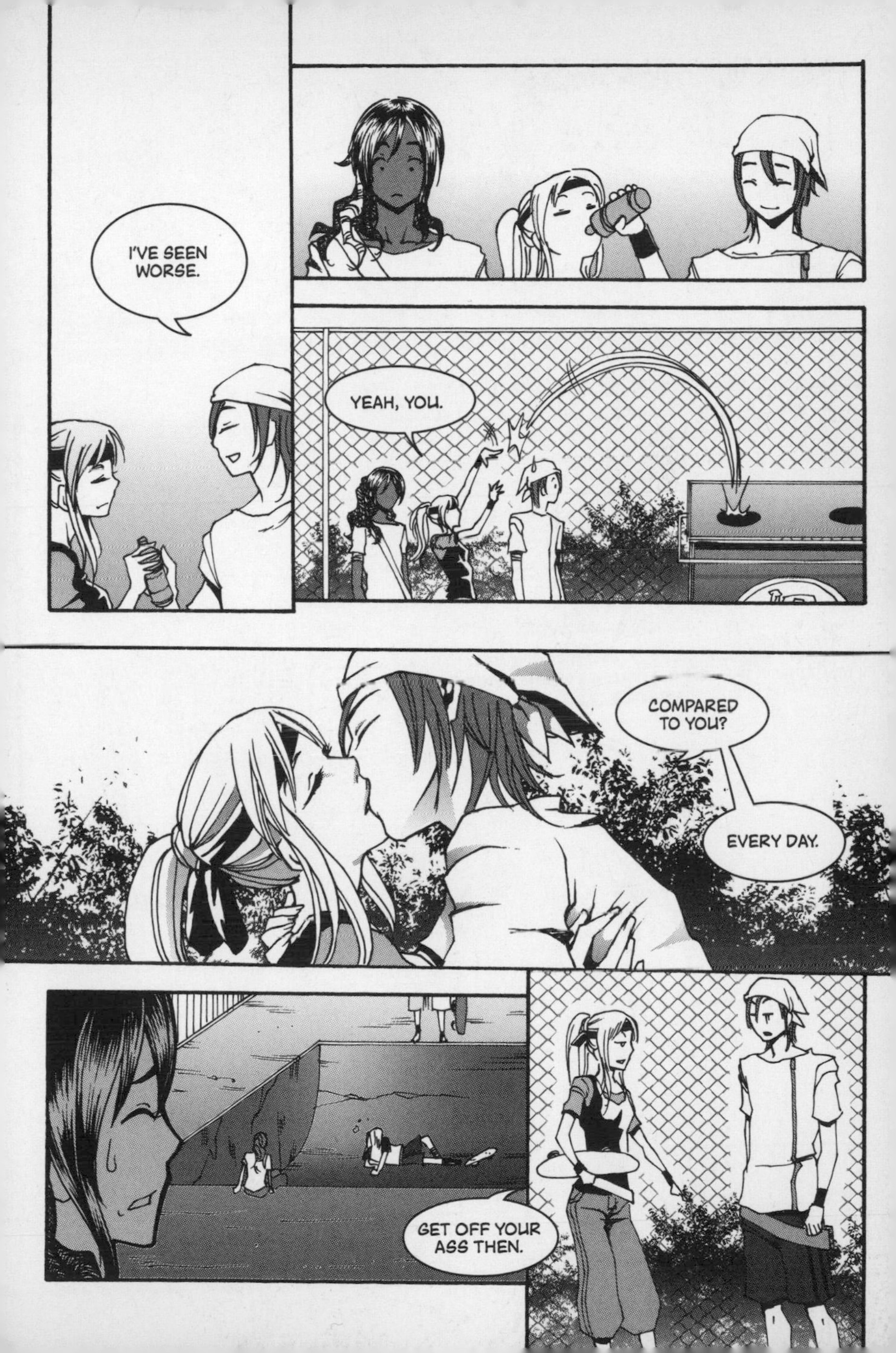
I'VE SEEN WORSE.
YEAH, YOU.
COMPARED TO YOU?
EVERY DAY.
GET OFF YOUR ASS THEN.

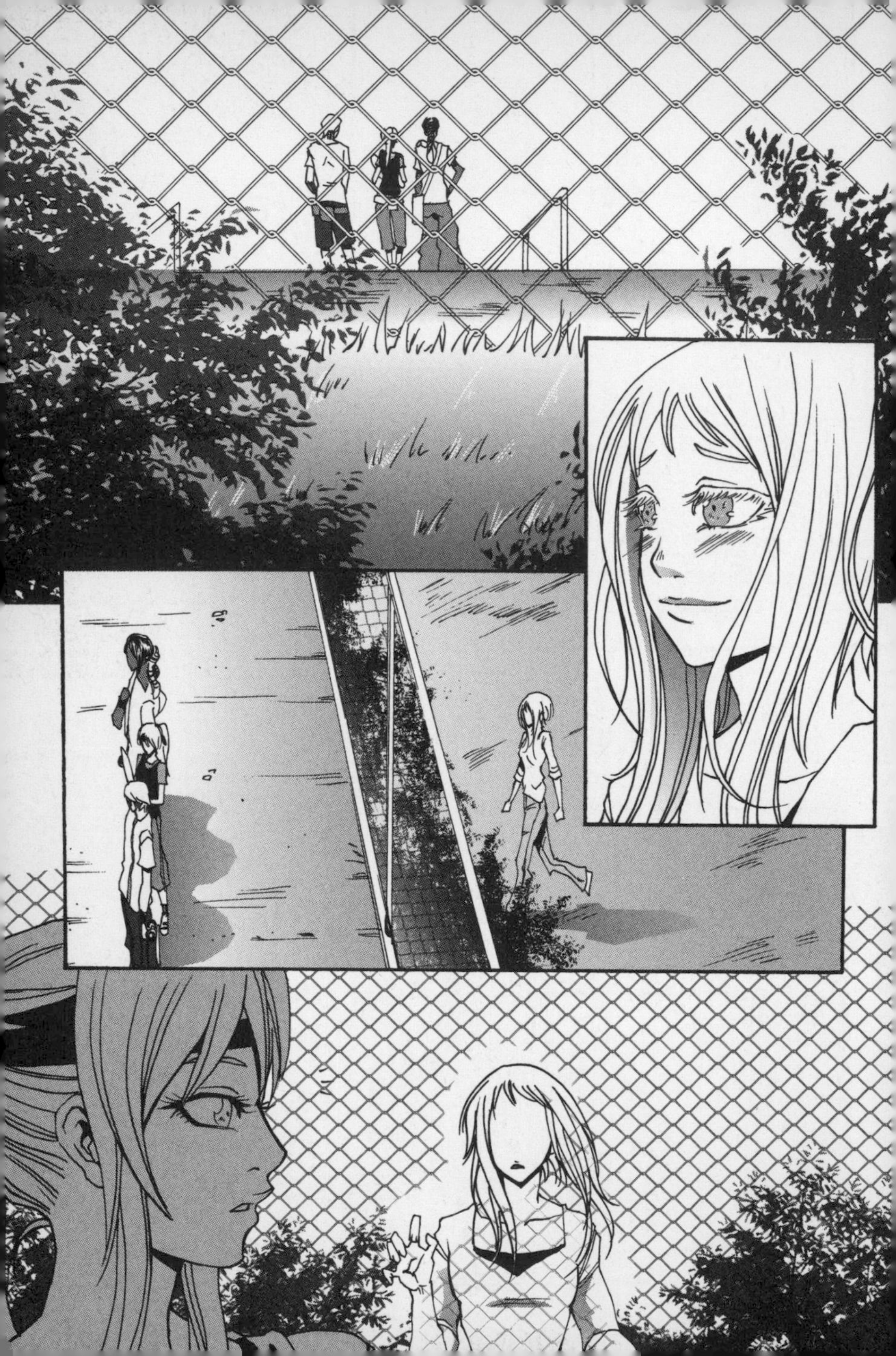

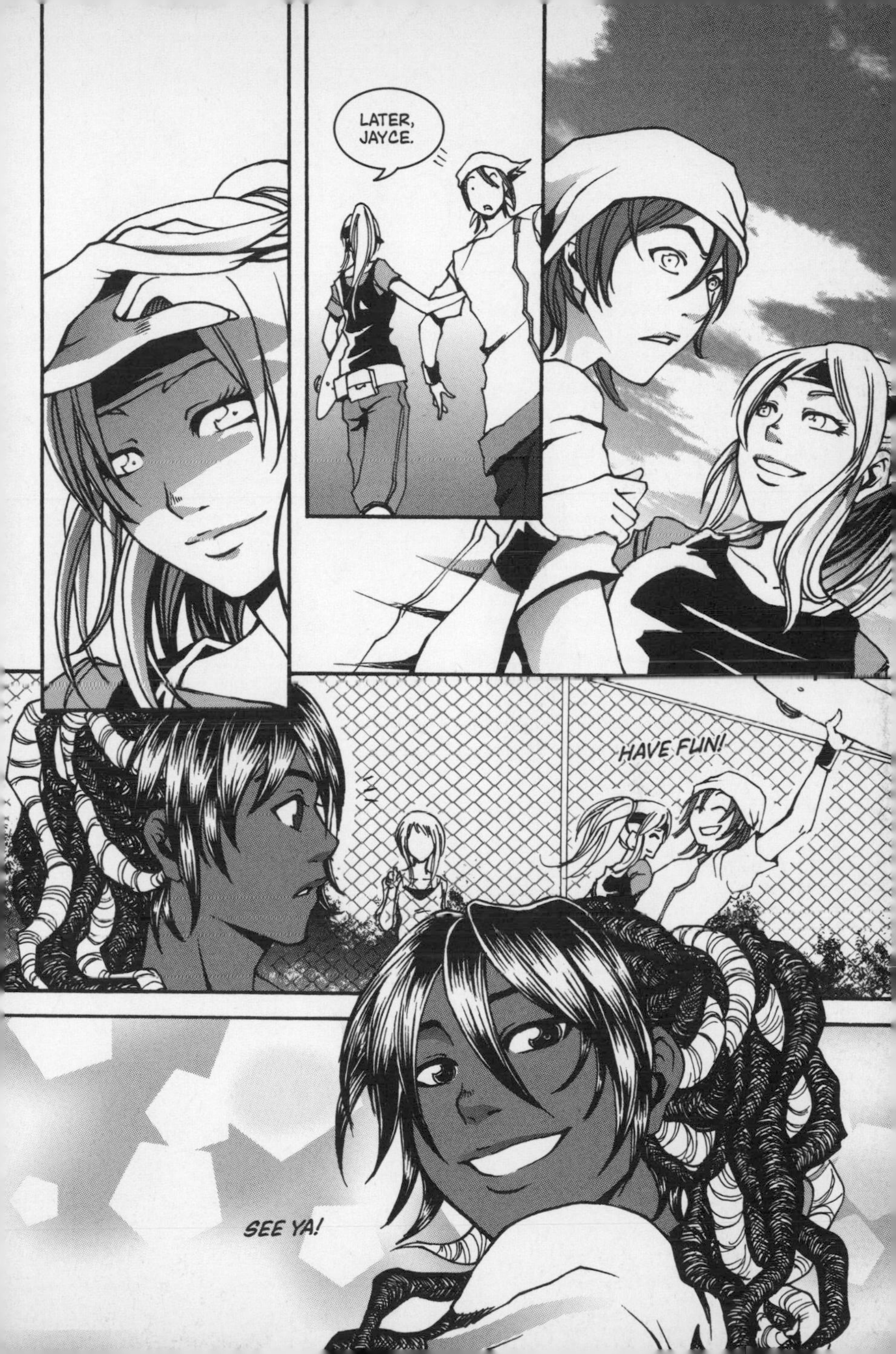
LATER, JAYCE.
HAVE FUN!
SEE YA!

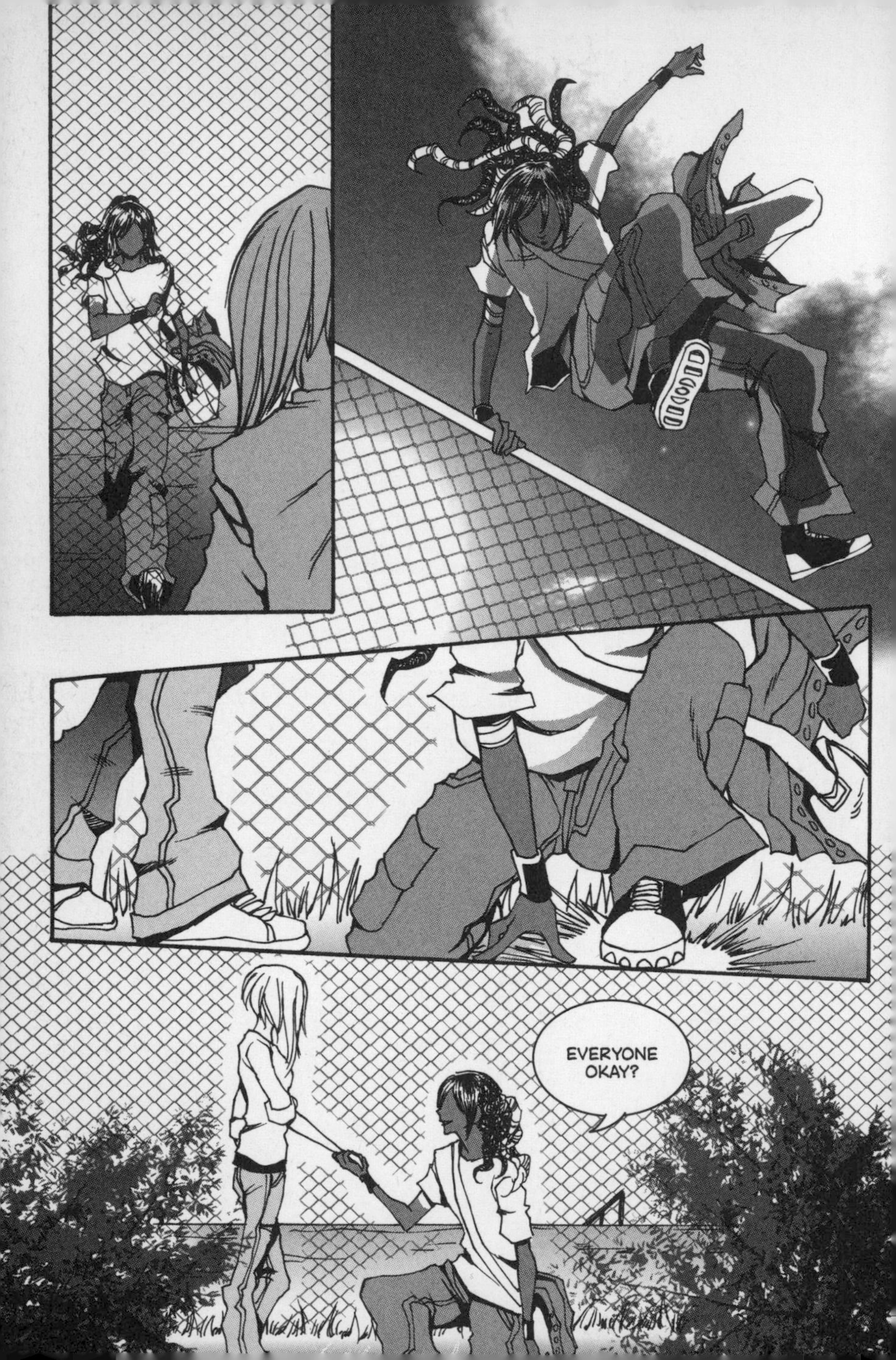
EVERYONE OKAY?

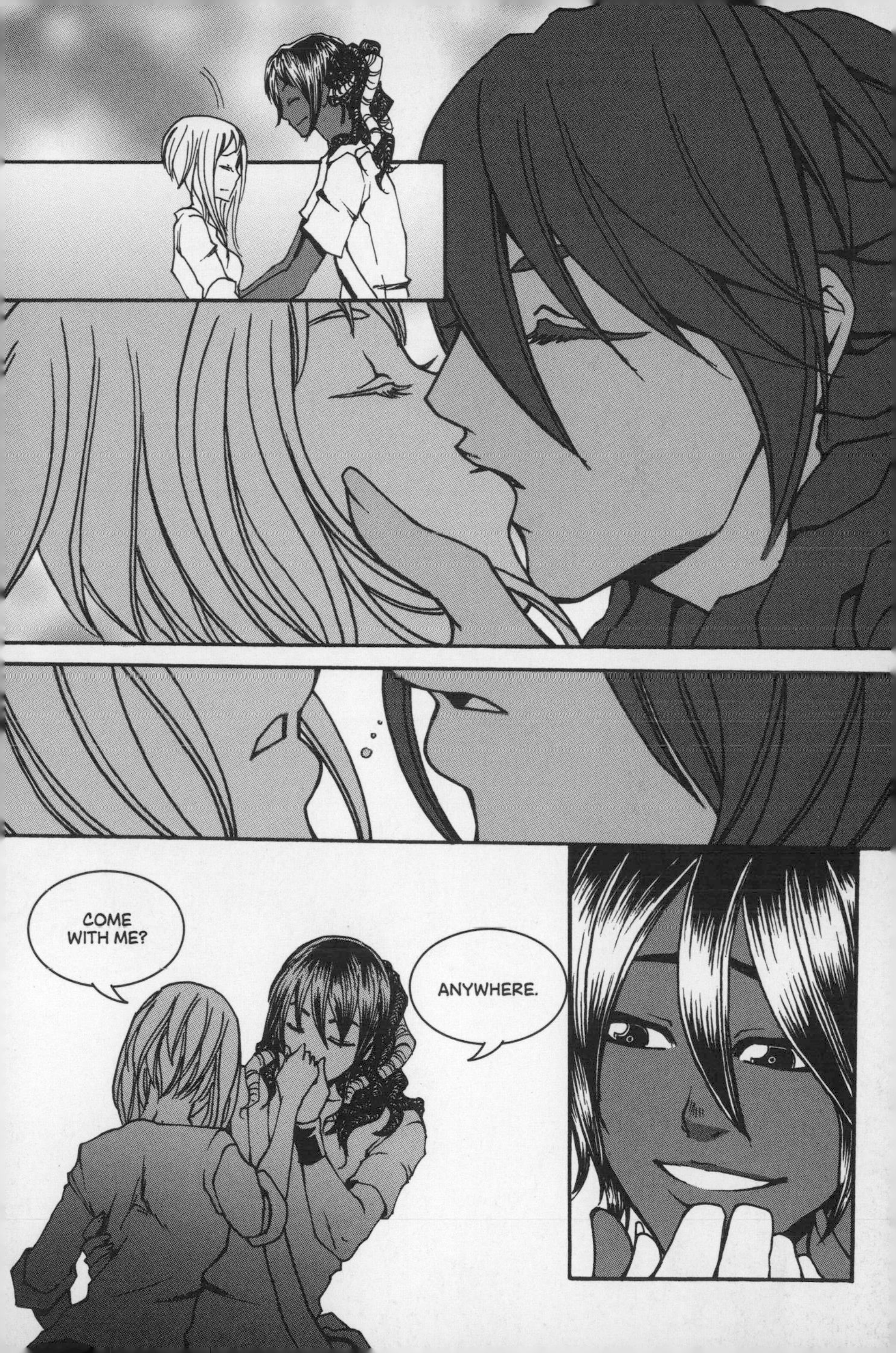
COME WITH ME?
ANYWHERE.

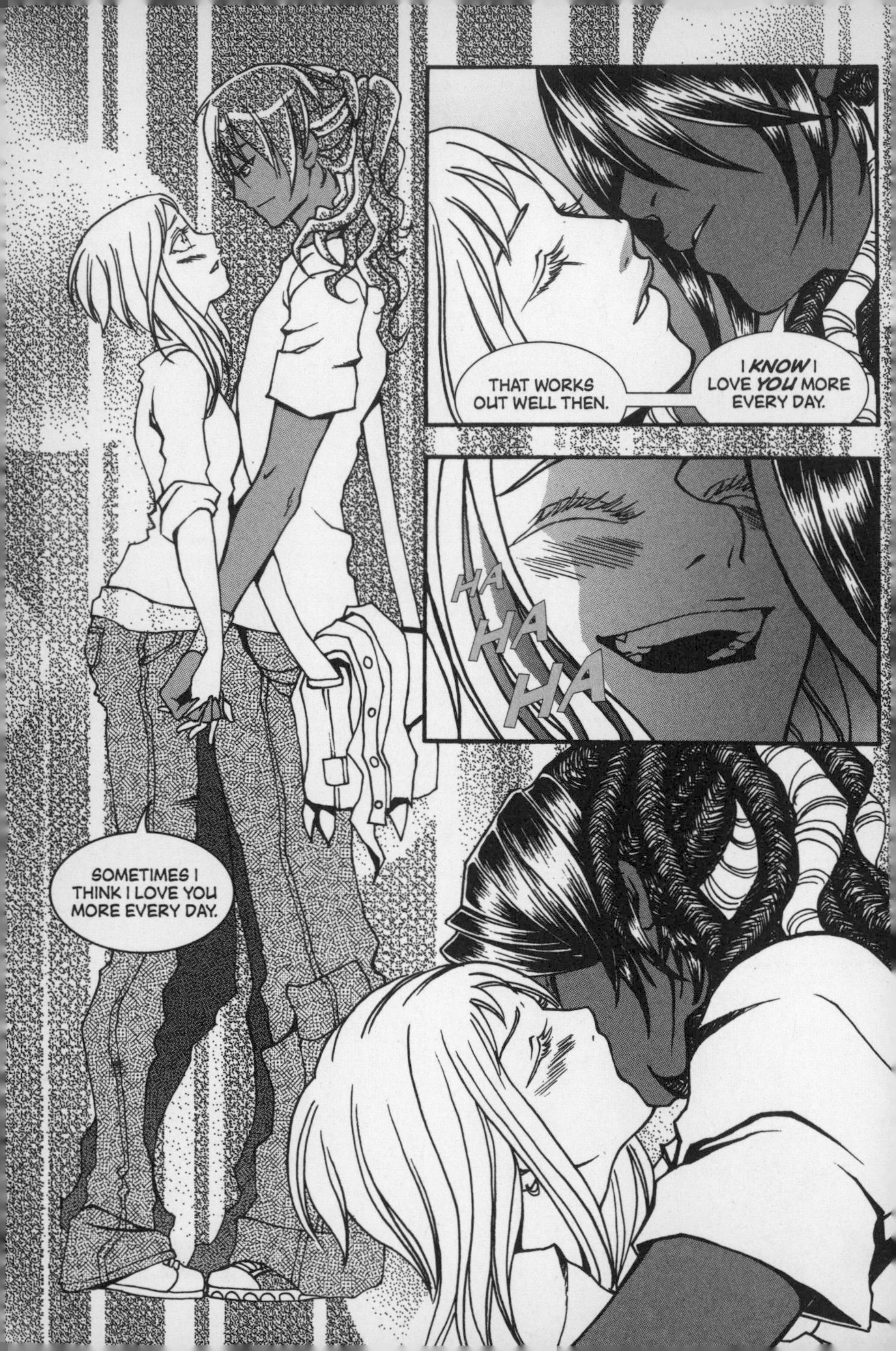
SOMETIMES I THINK I LOVE YOU MORE EVERY DAY.
I ***KNOW*** I LOVE ***YOU*** MORE EVERY DAY.
THAT WORKS OUT WELL THEN.
HA HA HA

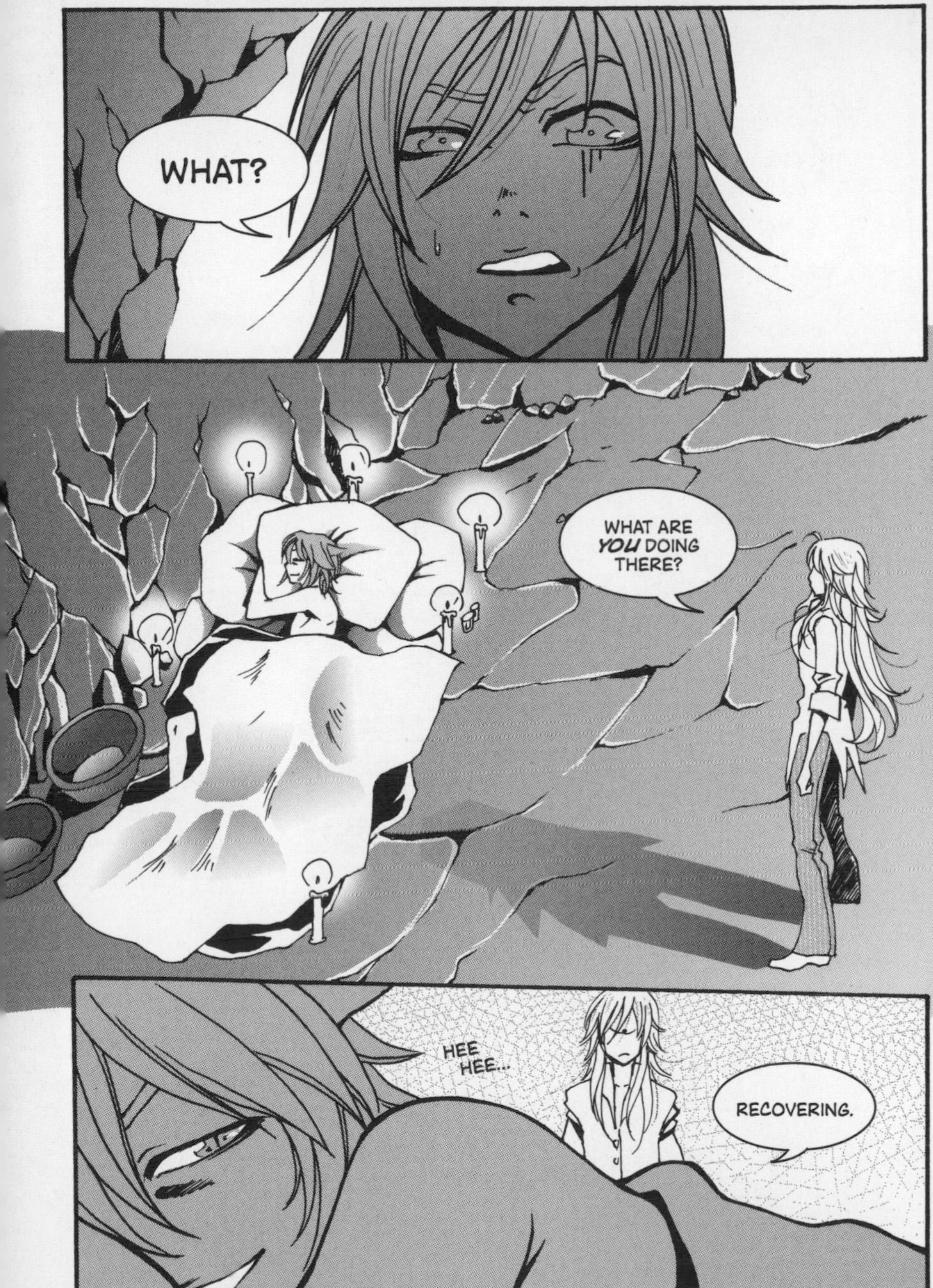
WHAT?
WHAT ARE YOU DOING THERE?
HEE HEE...
RECOVERING.

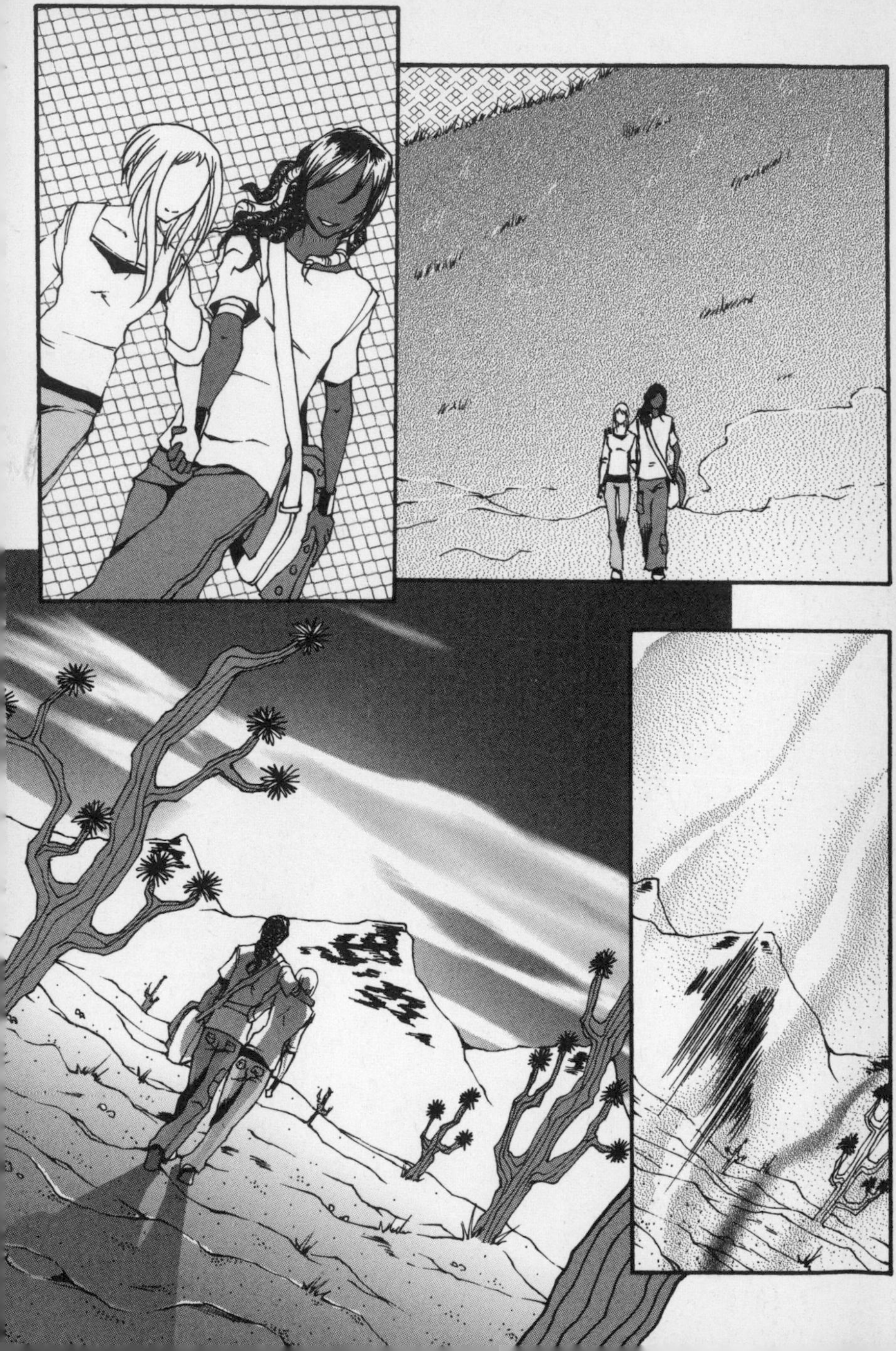

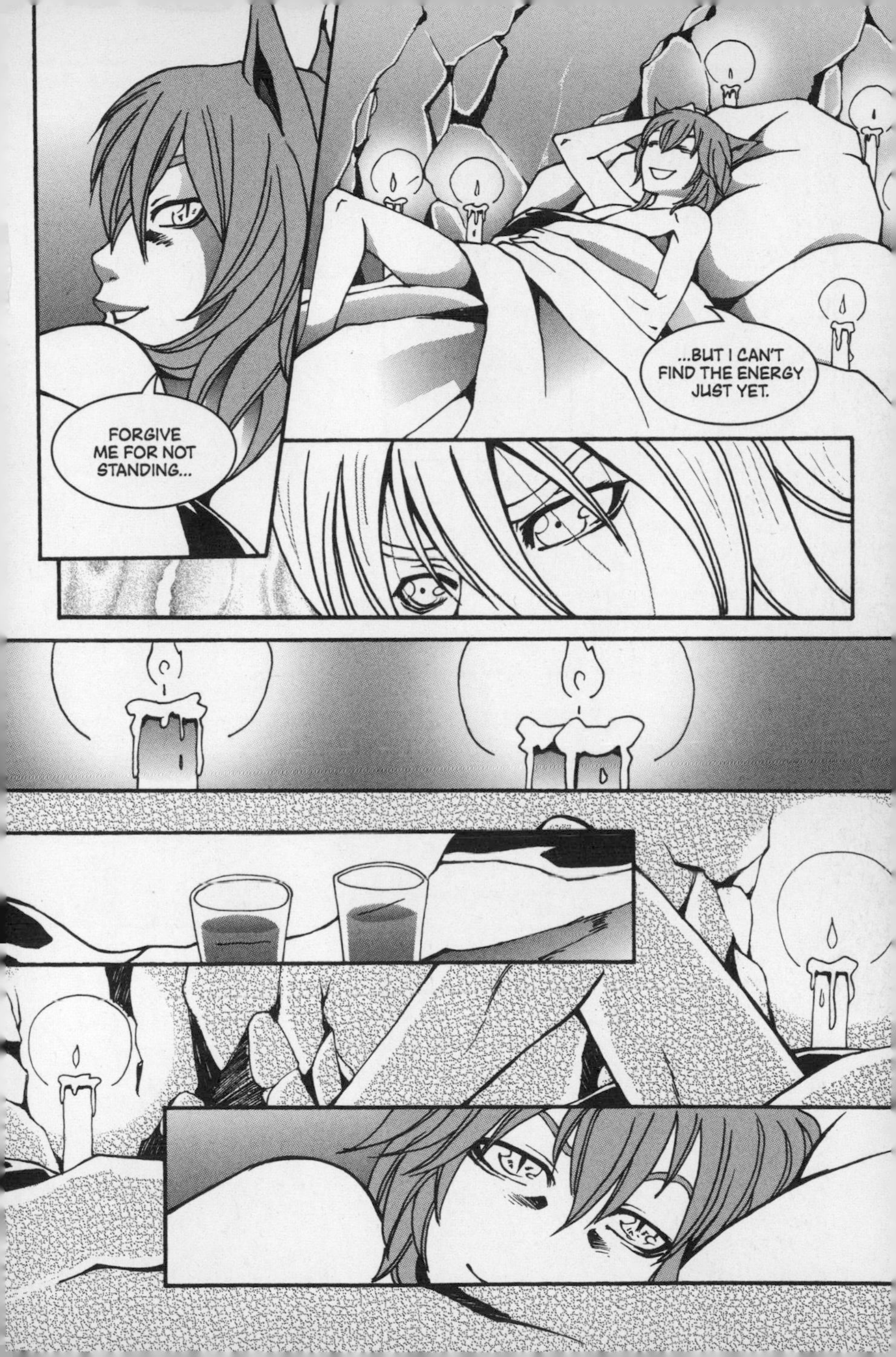
FORGIVE ME FOR NOT STANDING...
...BUT I CAN'T FIND THE ENERGY JUST YET.

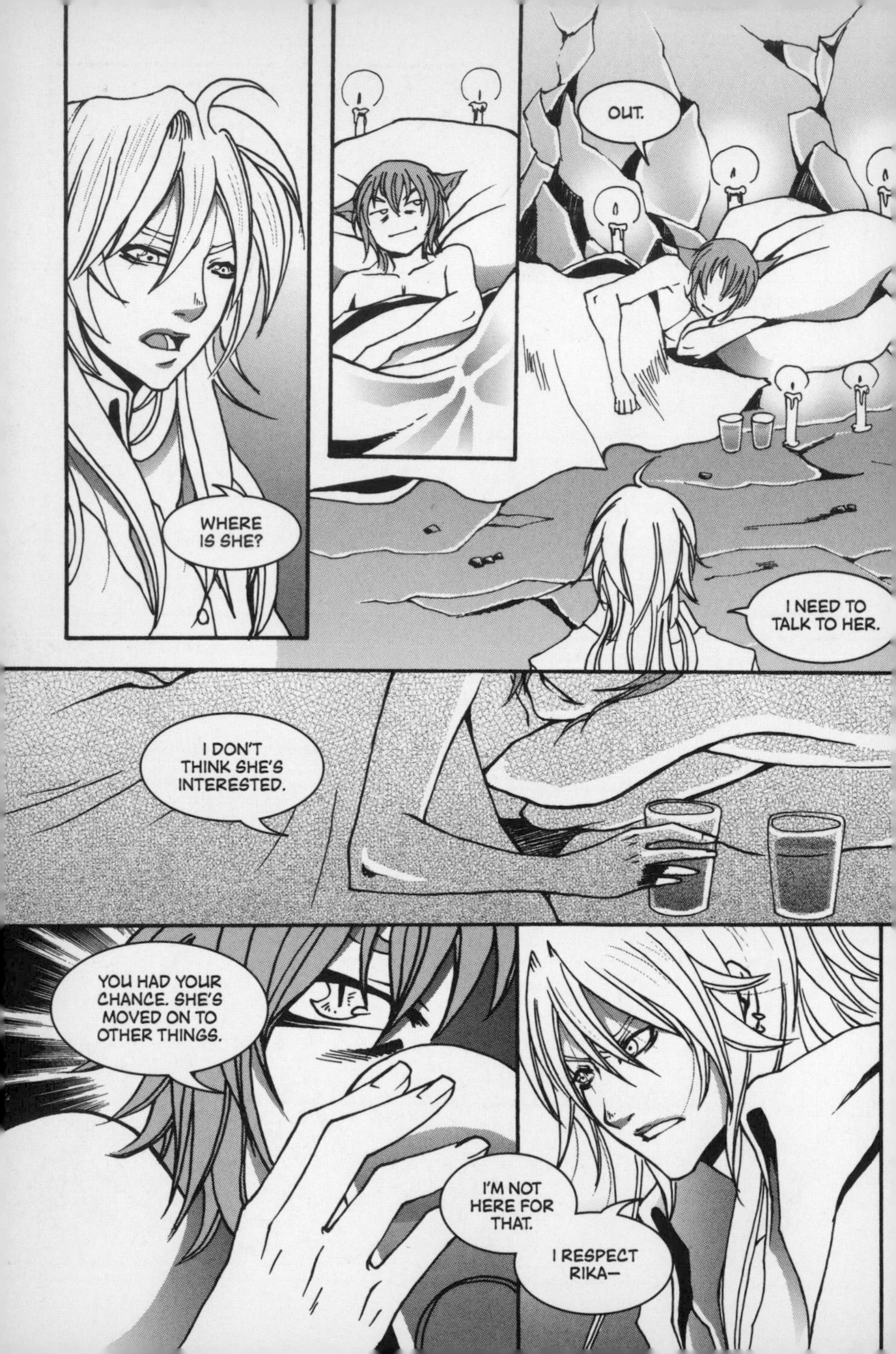
WHERE IS SHE?
OUT.
I NEED TO TALK TO HER.
I DON'T THINK SHE'S INTERESTED.
YOU HAD YOUR CHANCE. SHE'S MOVED ON TO OTHER THINGS.
I'M NOT HERE FOR THAT.
I RESPECT RIKA—

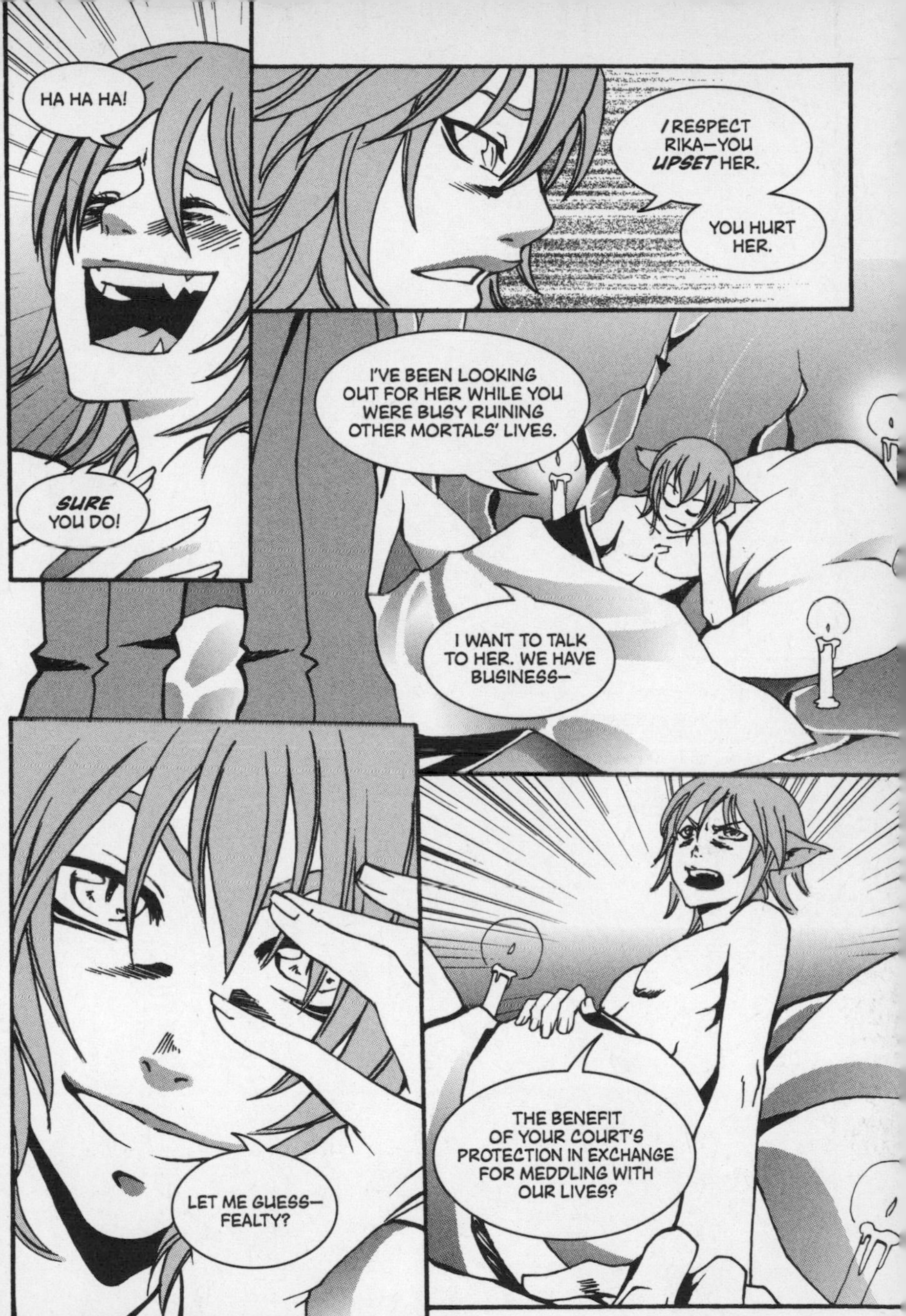
HA HA HA!
I RESPECT RIKA—YOU *UPSET* HER.
YOU HURT HER.
SURE YOU DO!
I'VE BEEN LOOKING OUT FOR HER WHILE YOU WERE BUSY RUINING OTHER MORTALS' LIVES.
I WANT TO TALK TO HER. WE HAVE BUSINESS—
LET ME GUESS—FEALTY?
THE BENEFIT OF YOUR COURT'S PROTECTION IN EXCHANGE FOR MEDDLING WITH OUR LIVES?

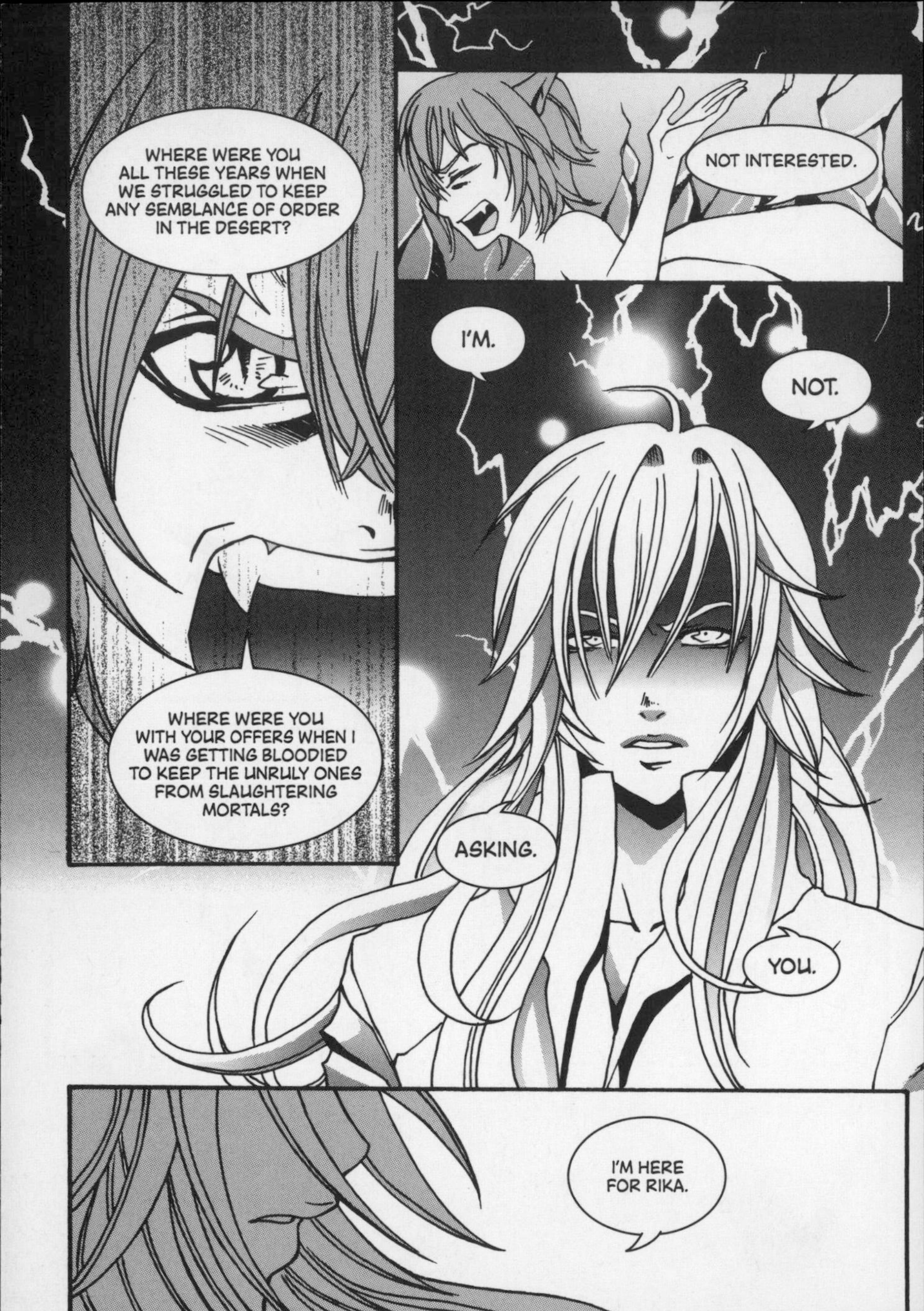
WHERE WERE YOU ALL THESE YEARS WHEN WE STRUGGLED TO KEEP ANY SEMBLANCE OF ORDER IN THE DESERT?
WHERE WERE YOU WITH YOUR OFFERS WHEN I WAS GETTING BLOODIED TO KEEP THE UNRULY ONES FROM SLAUGHTERING MORTALS?
NOT INTERESTED.
I'M.
NOT.
ASKING.
YOU.
I'M HERE FOR RIKA.

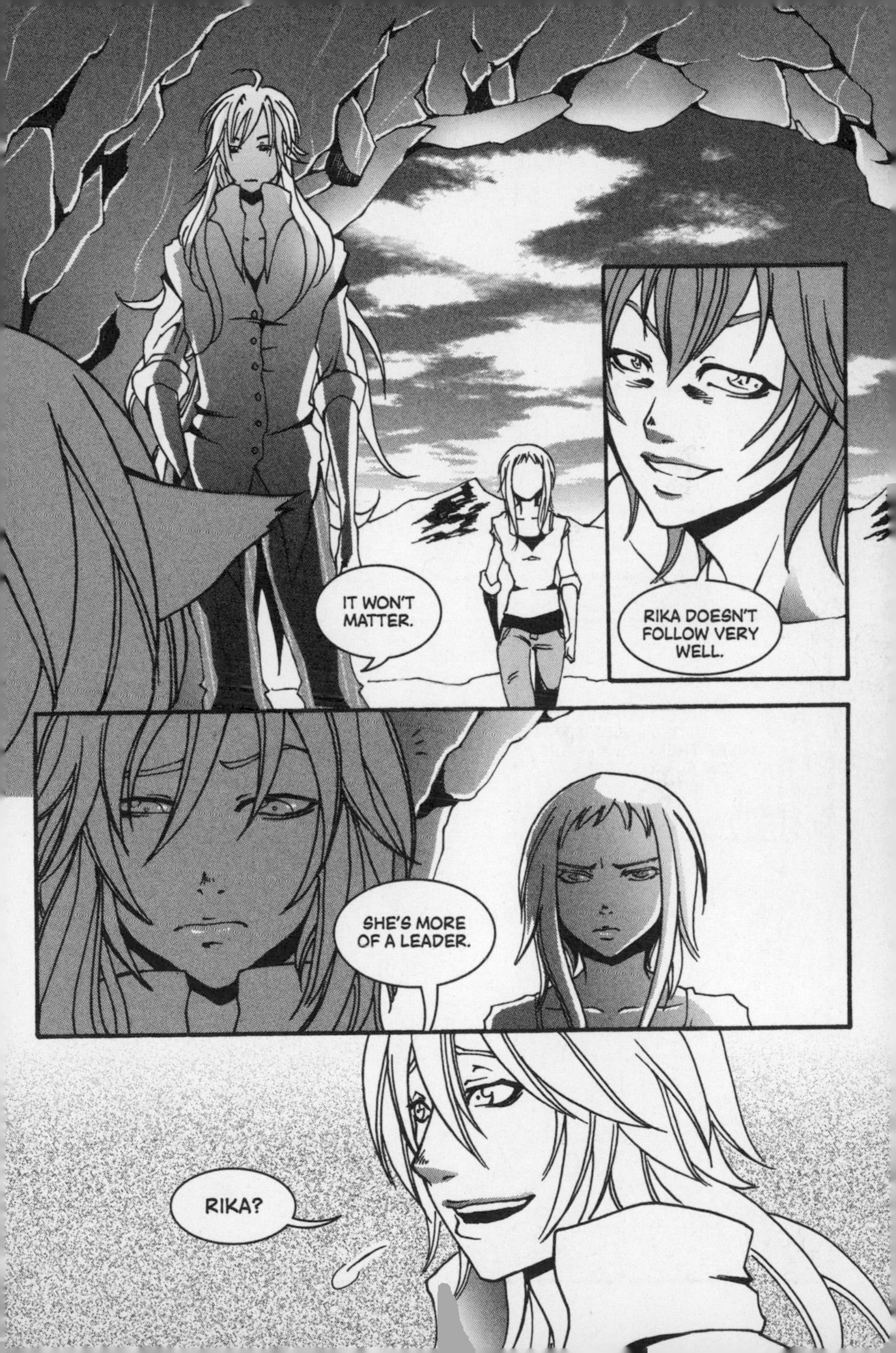
IT WON'T MATTER.
RIKA DOESN'T FOLLOW VERY WELL.
SHE'S MORE OF A LEADER.
RIKA?

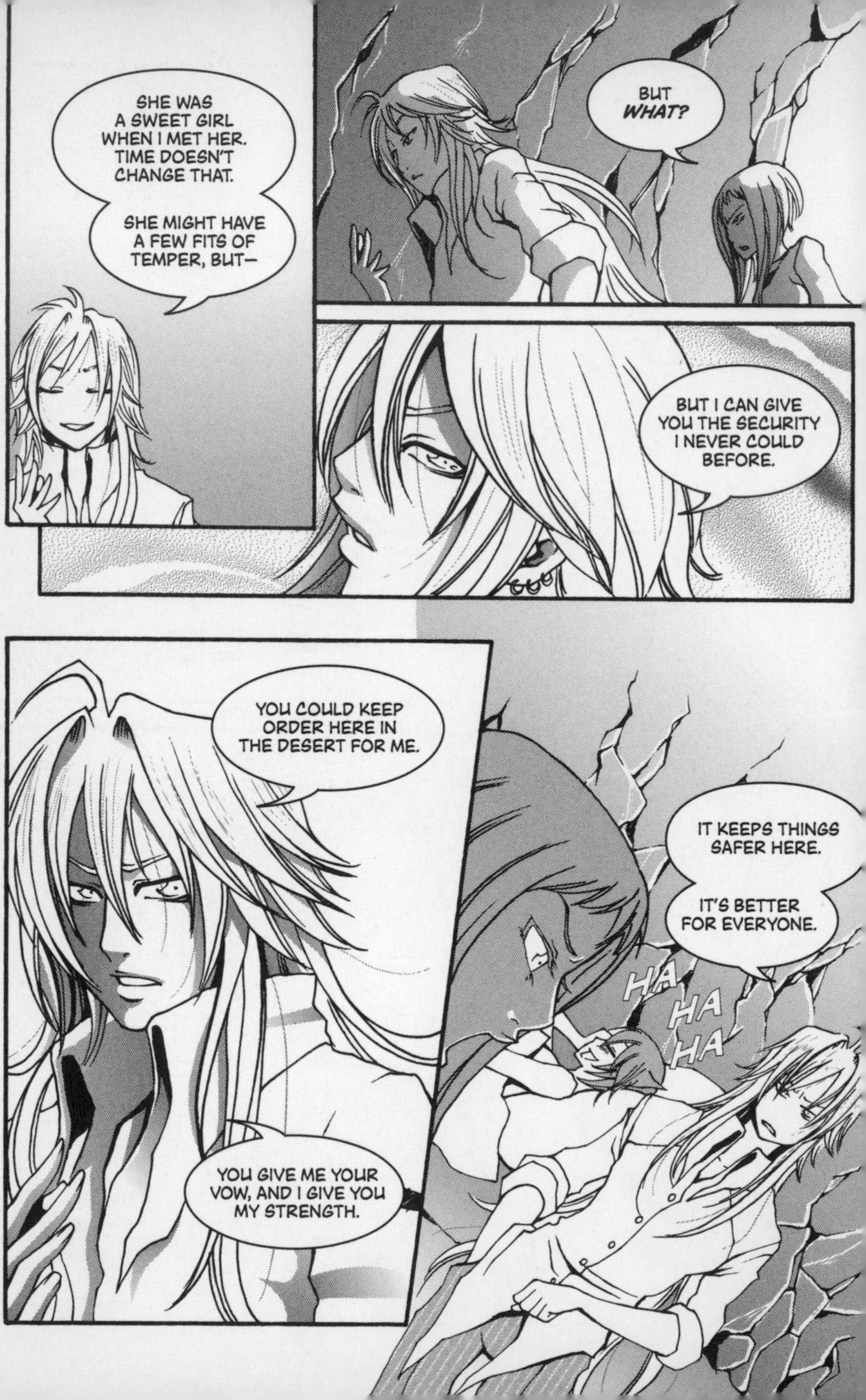
SHE WAS A SWEET GIRL WHEN I MET HER. TIME DOESN'T CHANGE THAT.
SHE MIGHT HAVE A FEW FITS OF TEMPER, BUT—
BUT *WHAT?*
BUT I CAN GIVE YOU THE SECURITY I NEVER COULD BEFORE.
YOU COULD KEEP ORDER HERE IN THE DESERT FOR ME.
YOU GIVE ME YOUR VOW, AND I GIVE YOU MY STRENGTH.
IT KEEPS THINGS SAFER HERE.
IT'S BETTER FOR EVERYONE.
HA HA HA HA

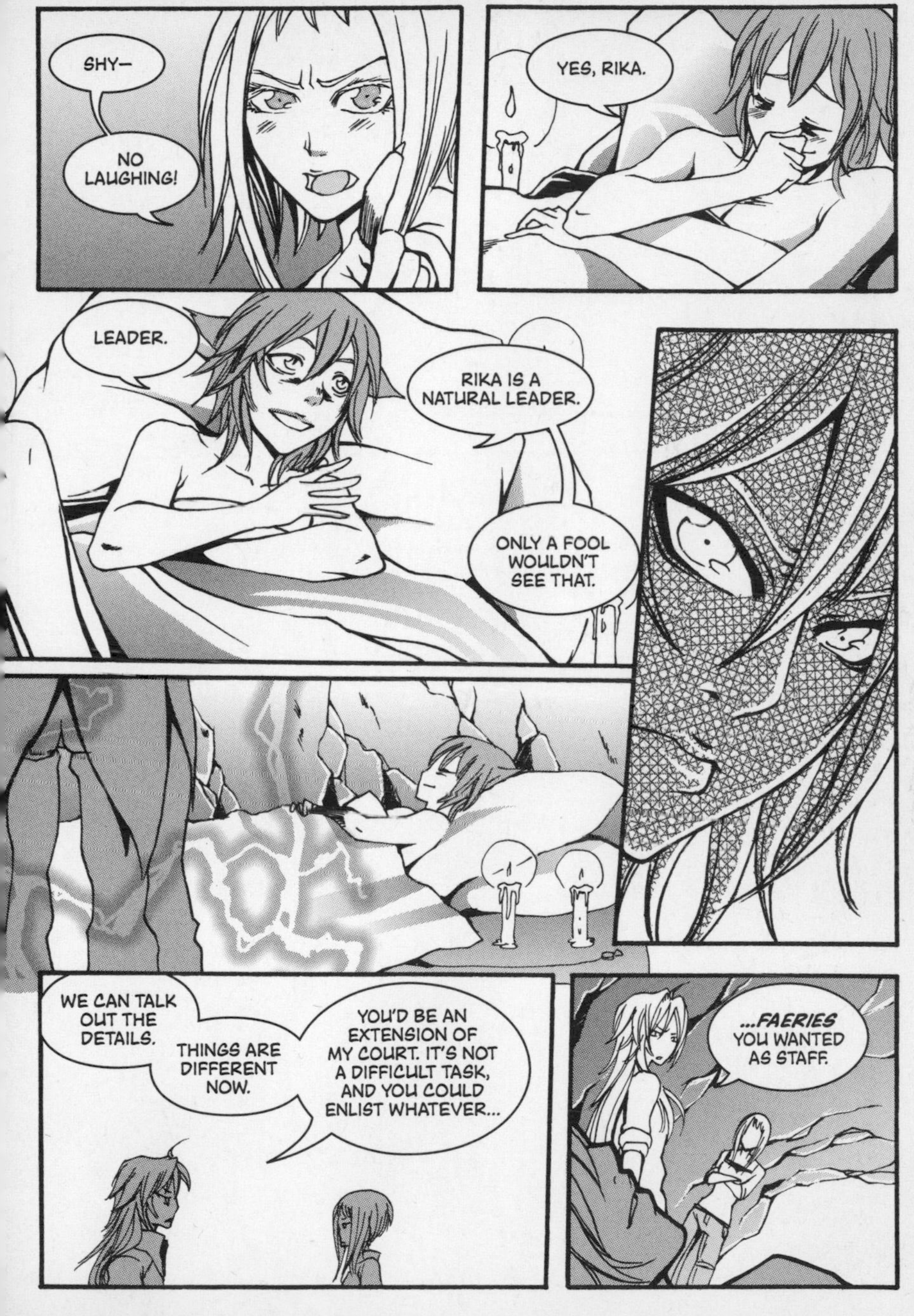
SHY—
NO LAUGHING!
YES, RIKA.
LEADER.
RIKA IS A NATURAL LEADER.
ONLY A FOOL WOULDN'T SEE THAT.
WE CAN TALK OUT THE DETAILS.
THINGS ARE DIFFERENT NOW.
YOU'D BE AN EXTENSION OF MY COURT. IT'S NOT A DIFFICULT TASK, AND YOU COULD ENLIST WHATEVER...
...*FAERIES* YOU WANTED AS STAFF.

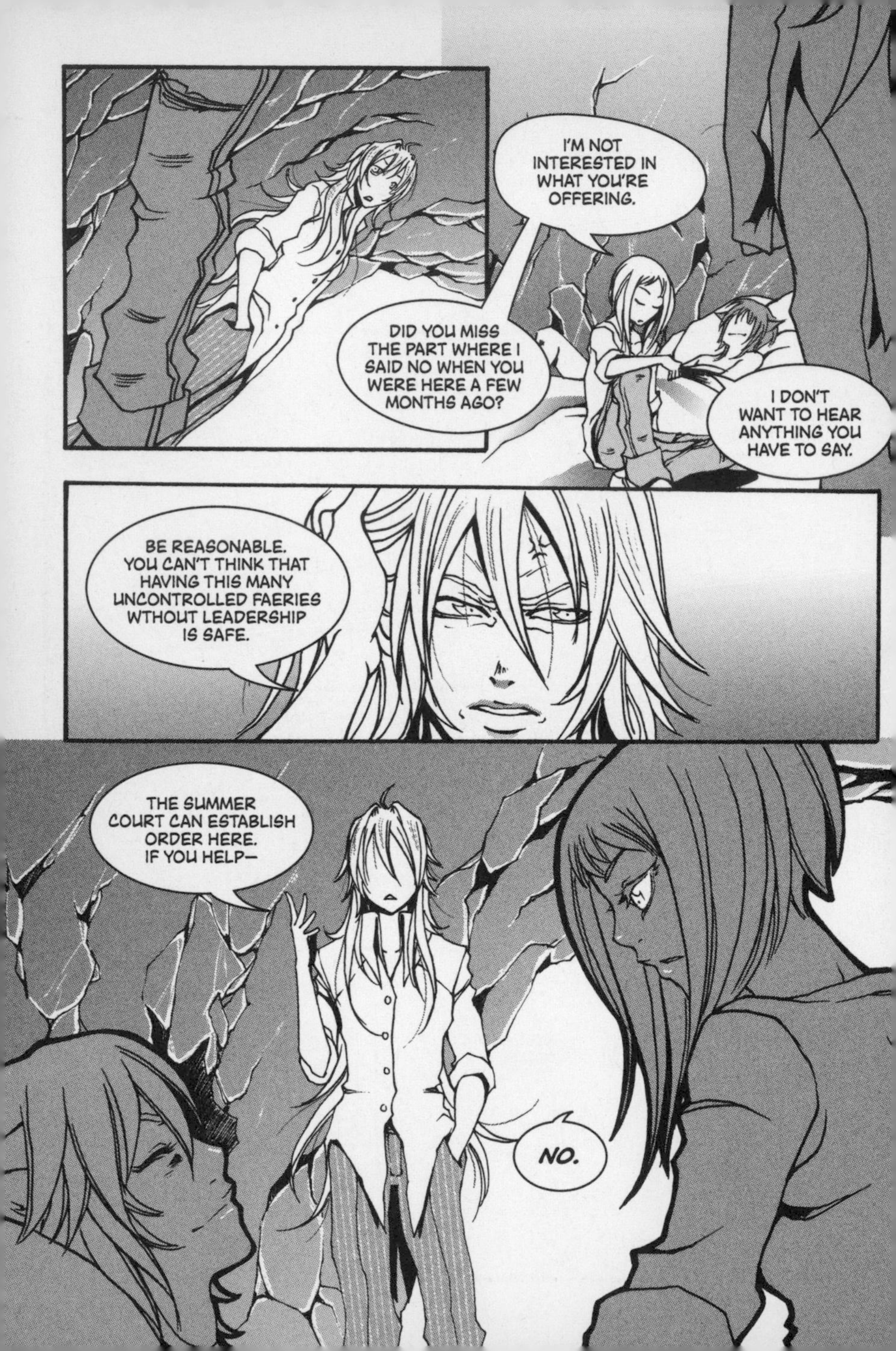
I'M NOT INTERESTED IN WHAT YOU'RE OFFERING.
DID YOU MISS THE PART WHERE I SAID NO WHEN YOU WERE HERE A FEW MONTHS AGO?
I DON'T WANT TO HEAR ANYTHING YOU HAVE TO SAY.
BE REASONABLE. YOU CAN'T THINK THAT HAVING THIS MANY UNCONTROLLED FAERIES WTHOUT LEADERSHIP IS SAFE.
THE SUMMER COURT CAN ESTABLISH ORDER HERE. IF YOU HELP—
NO.

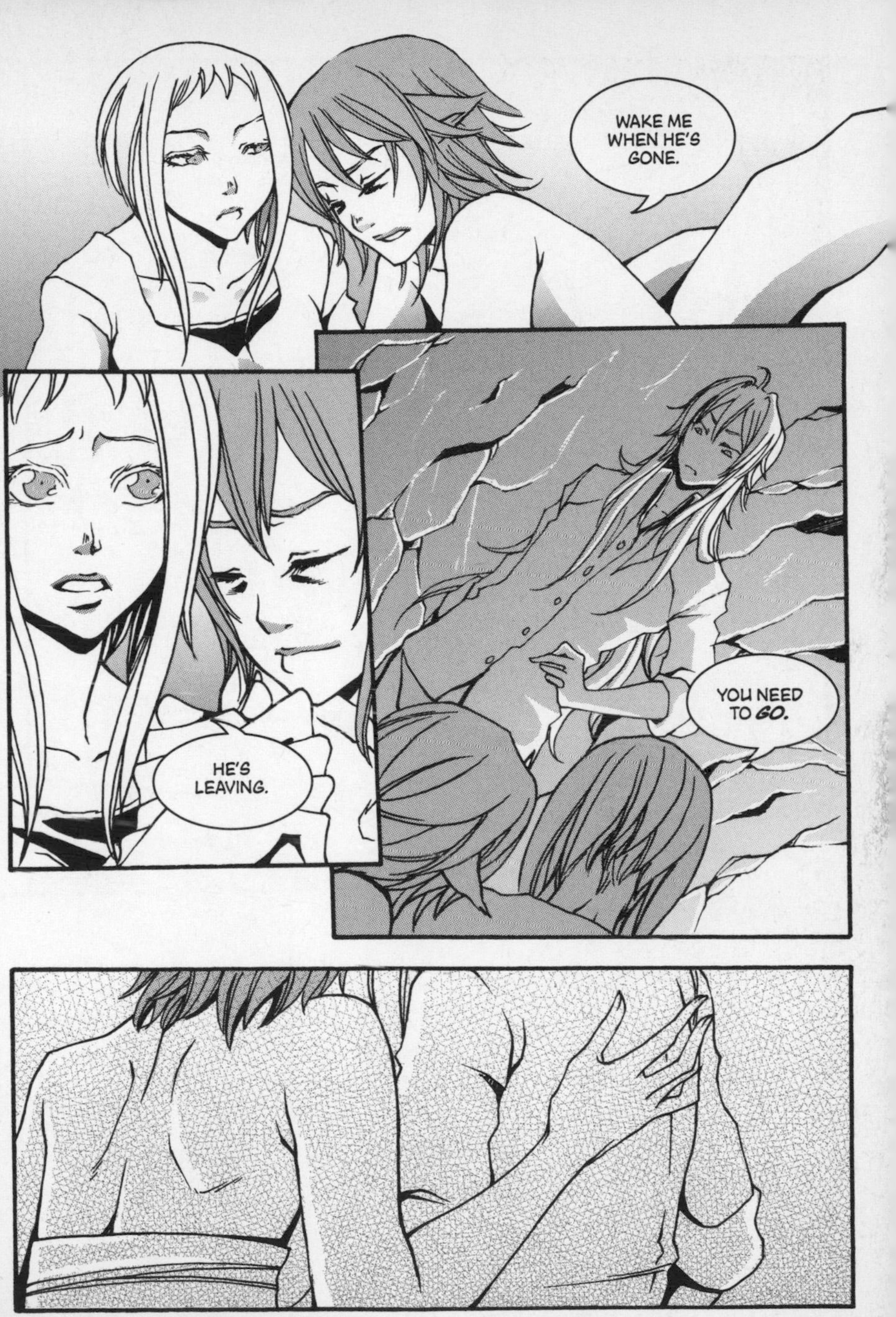
WAKE ME WHEN HE'S GONE.
HE'S LEAVING.
YOU NEED TO *GO.*

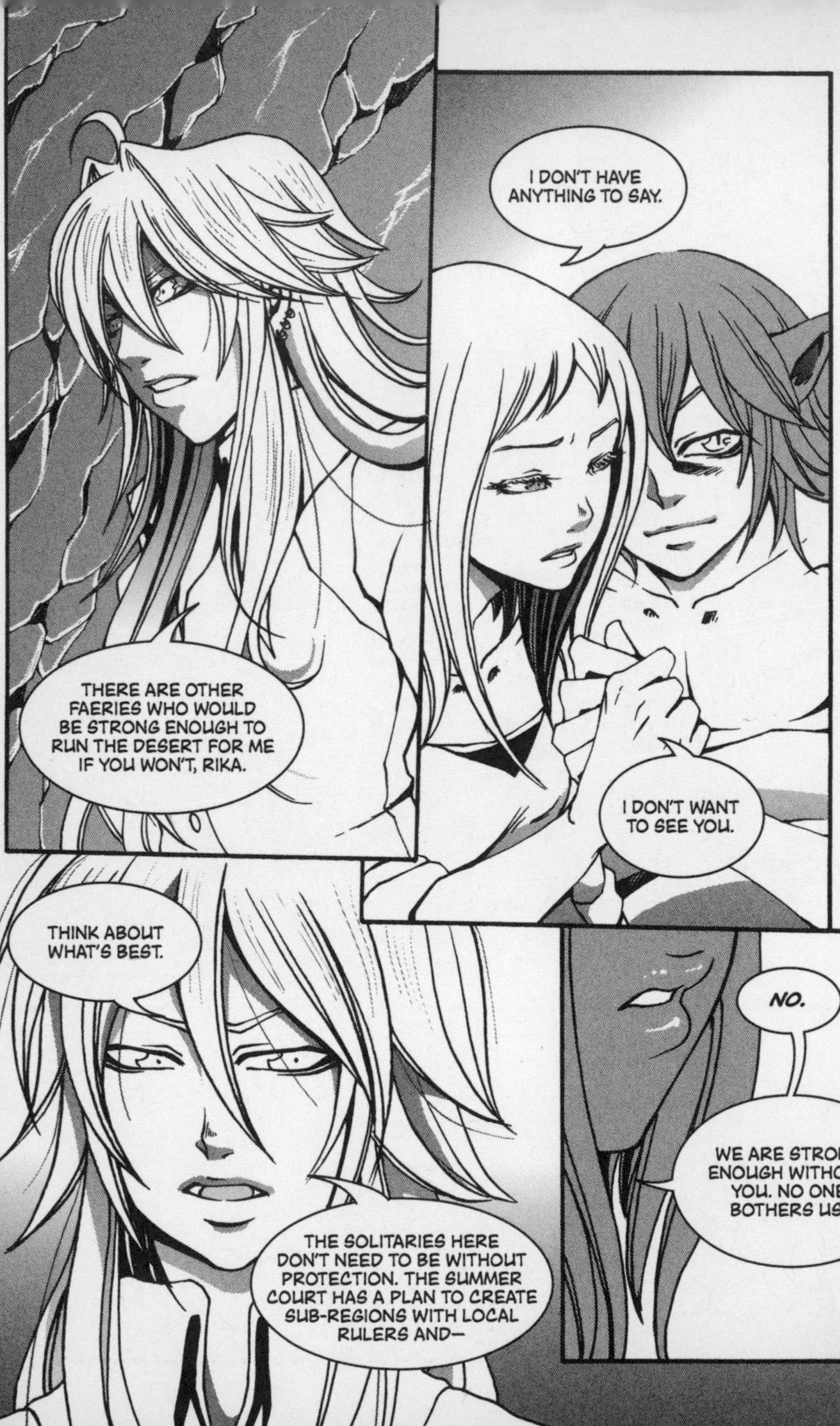
THERE ARE OTHER FAERIES WHO WOULD BE STRONG ENOUGH TO RUN THE DESERT FOR ME IF YOU WON'T, RIKA.
I DON'T HAVE ANYTHING TO SAY.
I DON'T WANT TO SEE YOU.
THINK ABOUT WHAT'S BEST.
THE SOLITARIES HERE DON'T NEED TO BE WITHOUT PROTECTION. THE SUMMER COURT HAS A PLAN TO CREATE SUB-REGIONS WITH LOCAL RULERS AND—
NO.
WE ARE STRONG ENOUGH WITHOUT YOU. NO ONE BOTHERS US.

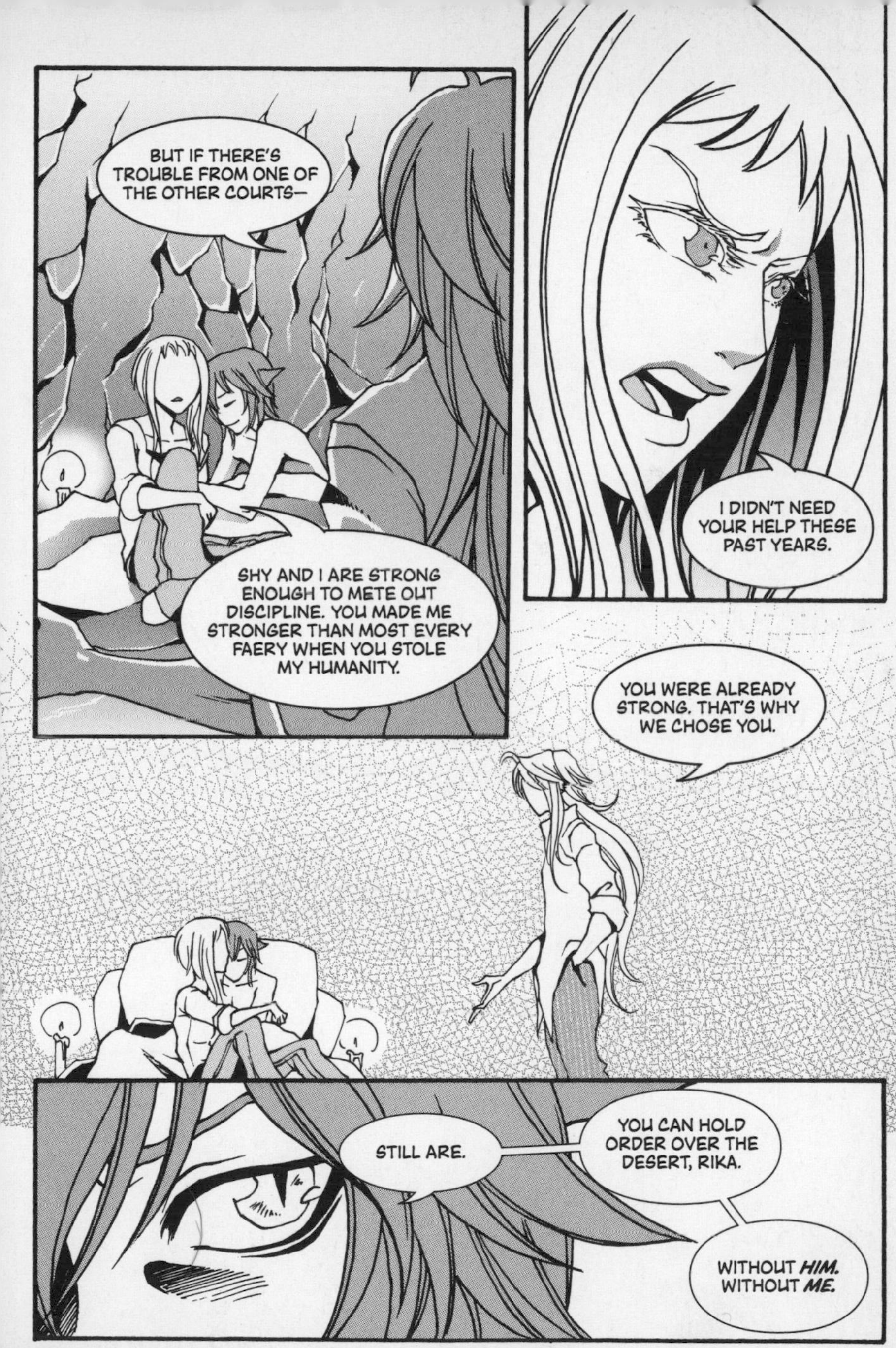
BUT IF THERE'S TROUBLE FROM ONE OF THE OTHER COURTS—
SHY AND I ARE STRONG ENOUGH TO METE OUT DISCIPLINE. YOU MADE ME STRONGER THAN MOST EVERY FAERY WHEN YOU STOLE MY HUMANITY.
I DIDN'T NEED YOUR HELP THESE PAST YEARS.
YOU WERE ALREADY STRONG. THAT'S WHY WE CHOSE YOU.
STILL ARE.
YOU CAN HOLD ORDER OVER THE DESERT, RIKA.
WITHOUT *HIM.* WITHOUT *ME.*

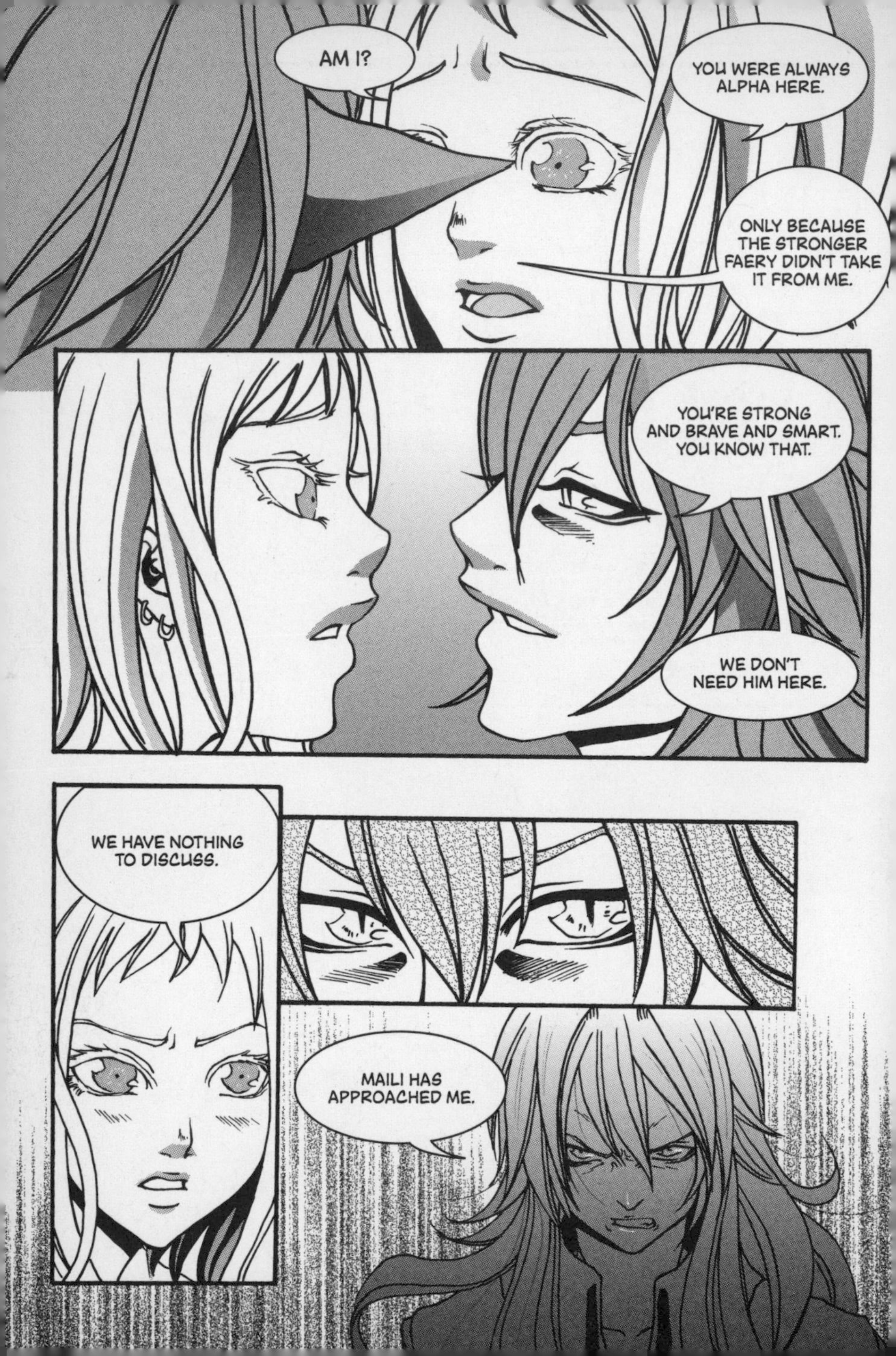
AM I?
YOU WERE ALWAYS ALPHA HERE.
ONLY BECAUSE THE STRONGER FAERY DIDN'T TAKE IT FROM ME.
YOU'RE STRONG AND BRAVE AND SMART. YOU KNOW THAT.
WE DON'T NEED HIM HERE.
WE HAVE NOTHING TO DISCUSS.
MAILI HAS APPROACHED ME.

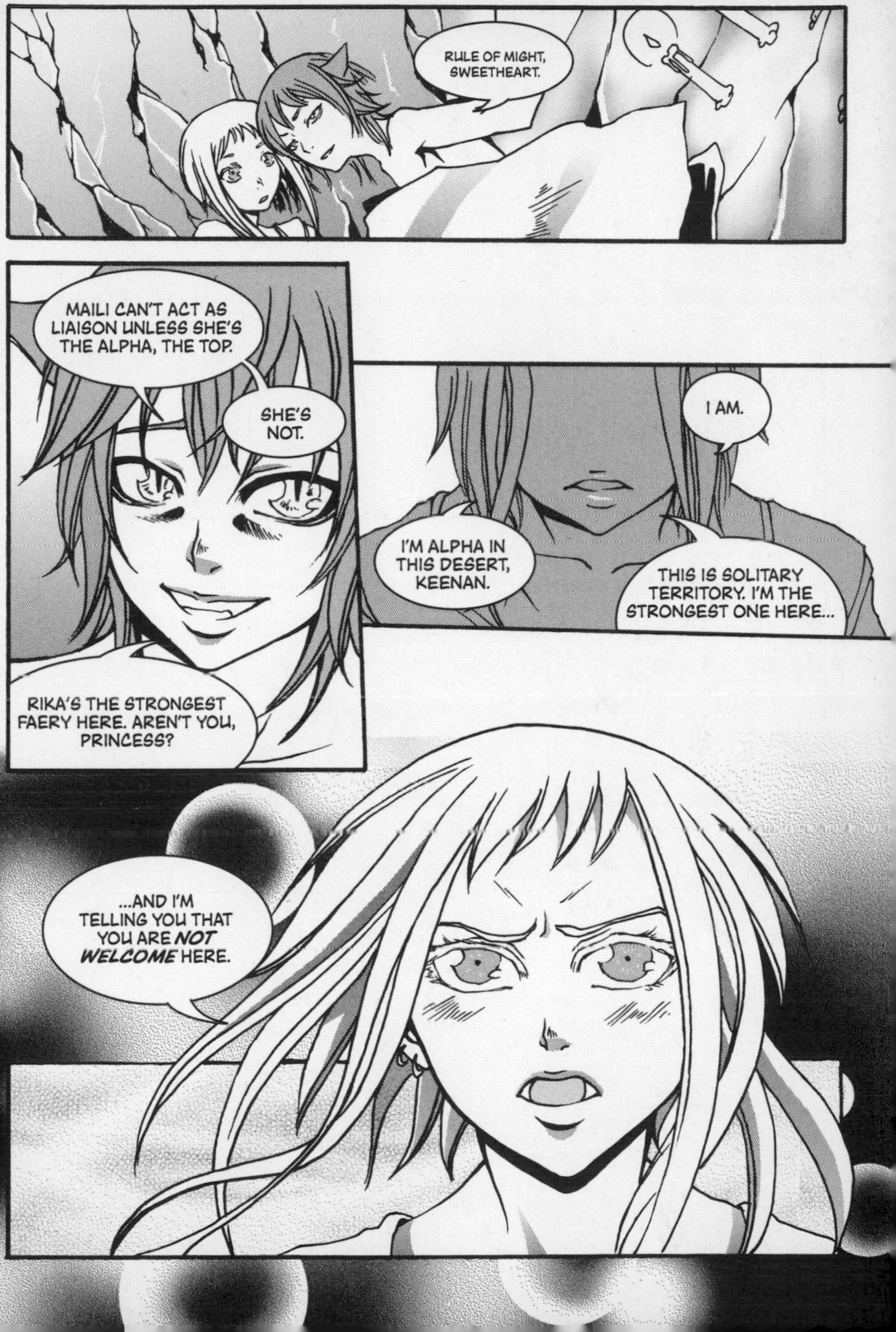
RULE OF MIGHT, SWEETHEART.
MAILI CAN'T ACT AS LIAISON UNLESS SHE'S THE ALPHA, THE TOP.
SHE'S NOT.
RIKA'S THE STRONGEST FAERY HERE. AREN'T YOU, PRINCESS?
I AM.
I'M ALPHA IN THIS DESERT, KEENAN.
THIS IS SOLITARY TERRITORY. I'M THE STRONGEST ONE HERE...
...AND I'M TELLING YOU THAT YOU ARE ***NOT WELCOME*** HERE.

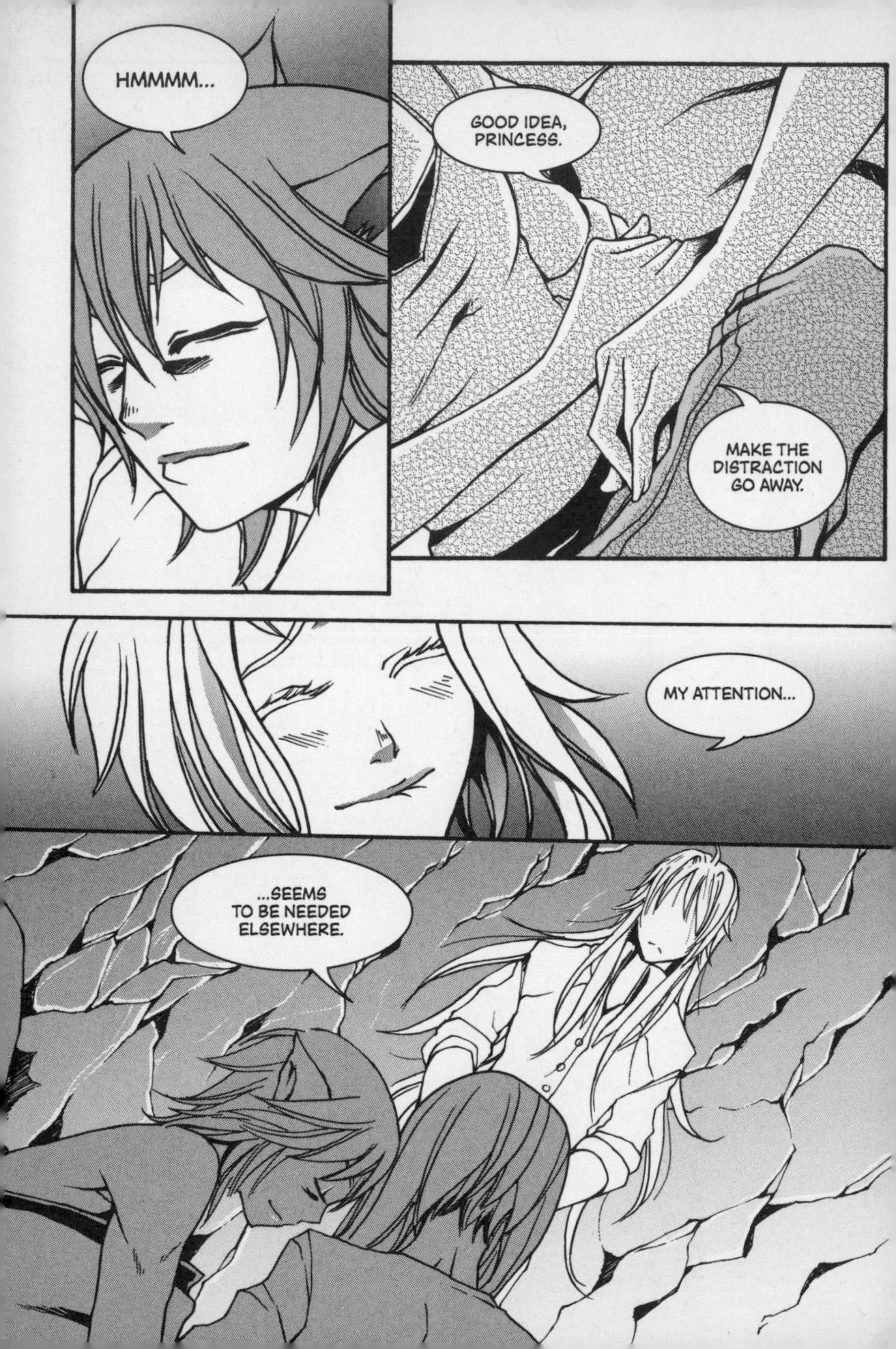
HMMMM...
GOOD IDEA, PRINCESS.
MAKE THE DISTRACTION GO AWAY.
MY ATTENTION...
...SEEMS TO BE NEEDED ELSEWHERE.

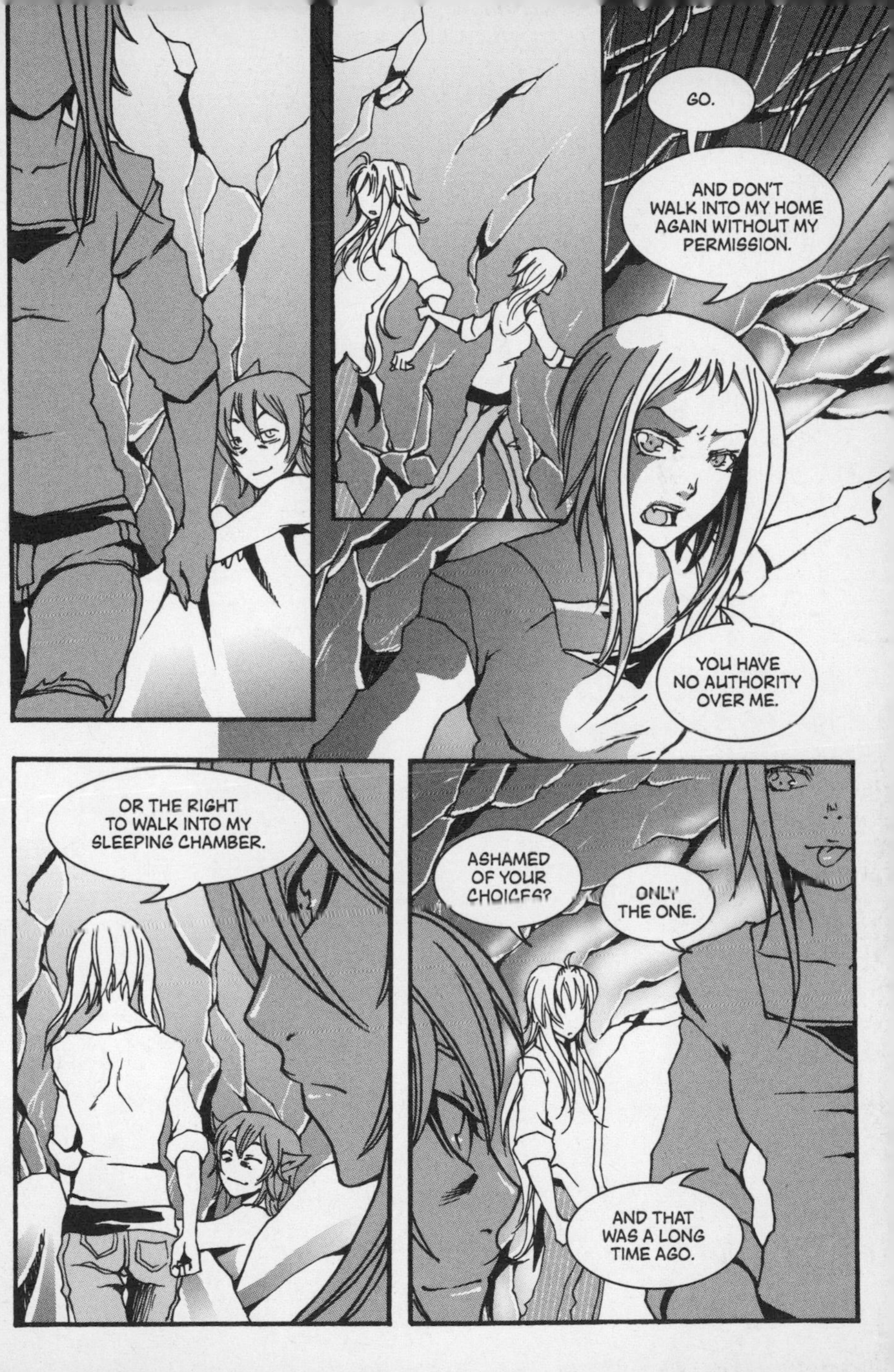
GO.
AND DON'T WALK INTO MY HOME AGAIN WITHOUT MY PERMISSION.
YOU HAVE NO AUTHORITY OVER ME.
OR THE RIGHT TO WALK INTO MY SLEEPING CHAMBER.
ASHAMED OF YOUR CHOICES?
ONLY THE ONE.
AND THAT WAS A LONG TIME AGO.

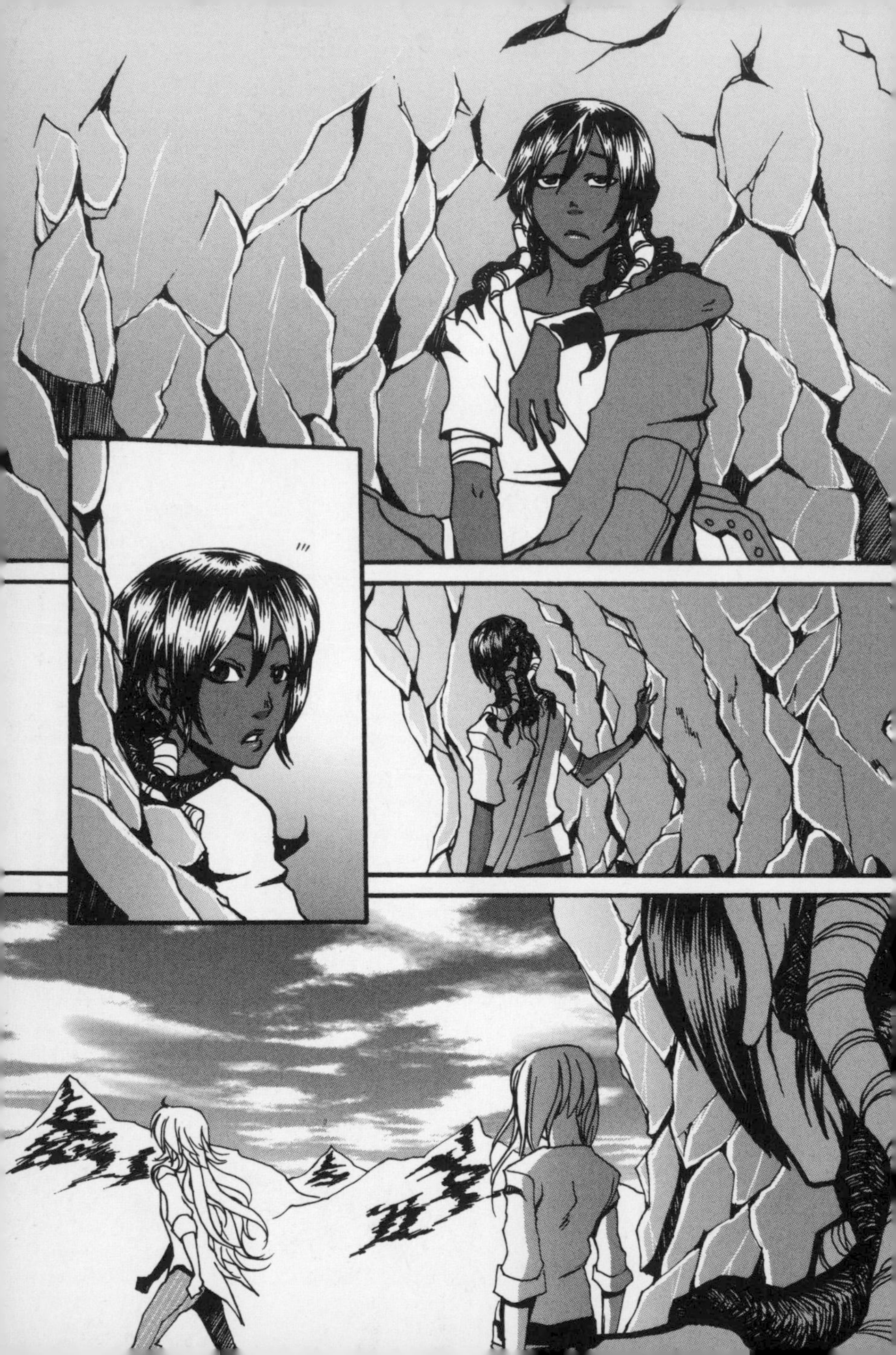

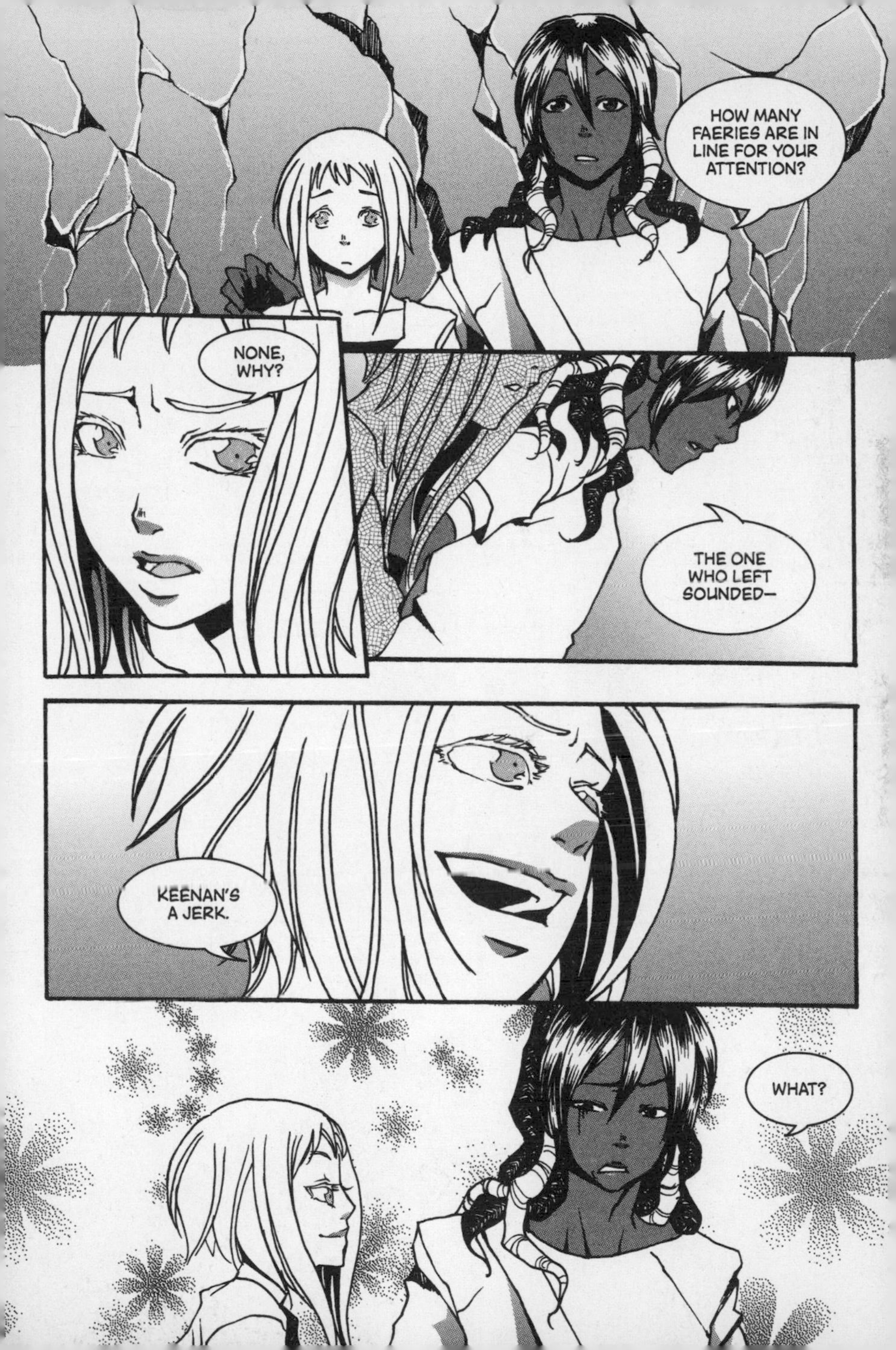
HOW MANY FAERIES ARE IN LINE FOR YOUR ATTENTION?
NONE, WHY?
THE ONE WHO LEFT SOUNDED—
KEENAN'S A JERK.
WHAT?

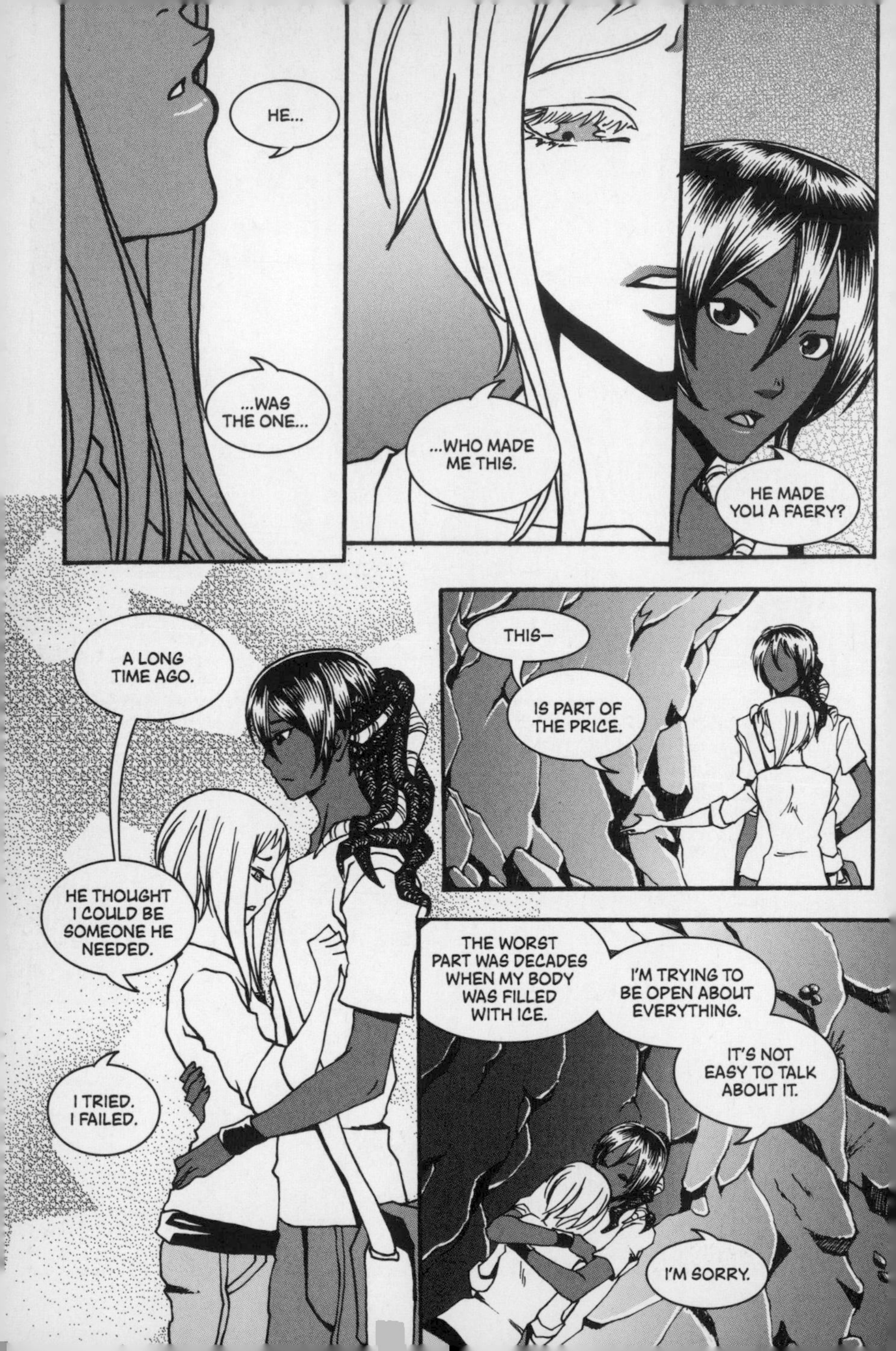
HE...
...WAS THE ONE...
...WHO MADE ME THIS.
HE MADE YOU A FAERY?
A LONG TIME AGO.
HE THOUGHT I COULD BE SOMEONE HE NEEDED.
I TRIED. I FAILED.
THIS—
IS PART OF THE PRICE.
THE WORST PART WAS DECADES WHEN MY BODY WAS FILLED WITH ICE.
I'M TRYING TO BE OPEN ABOUT EVERYTHING.
IT'S NOT EASY TO TALK ABOUT IT.
I'M SORRY.

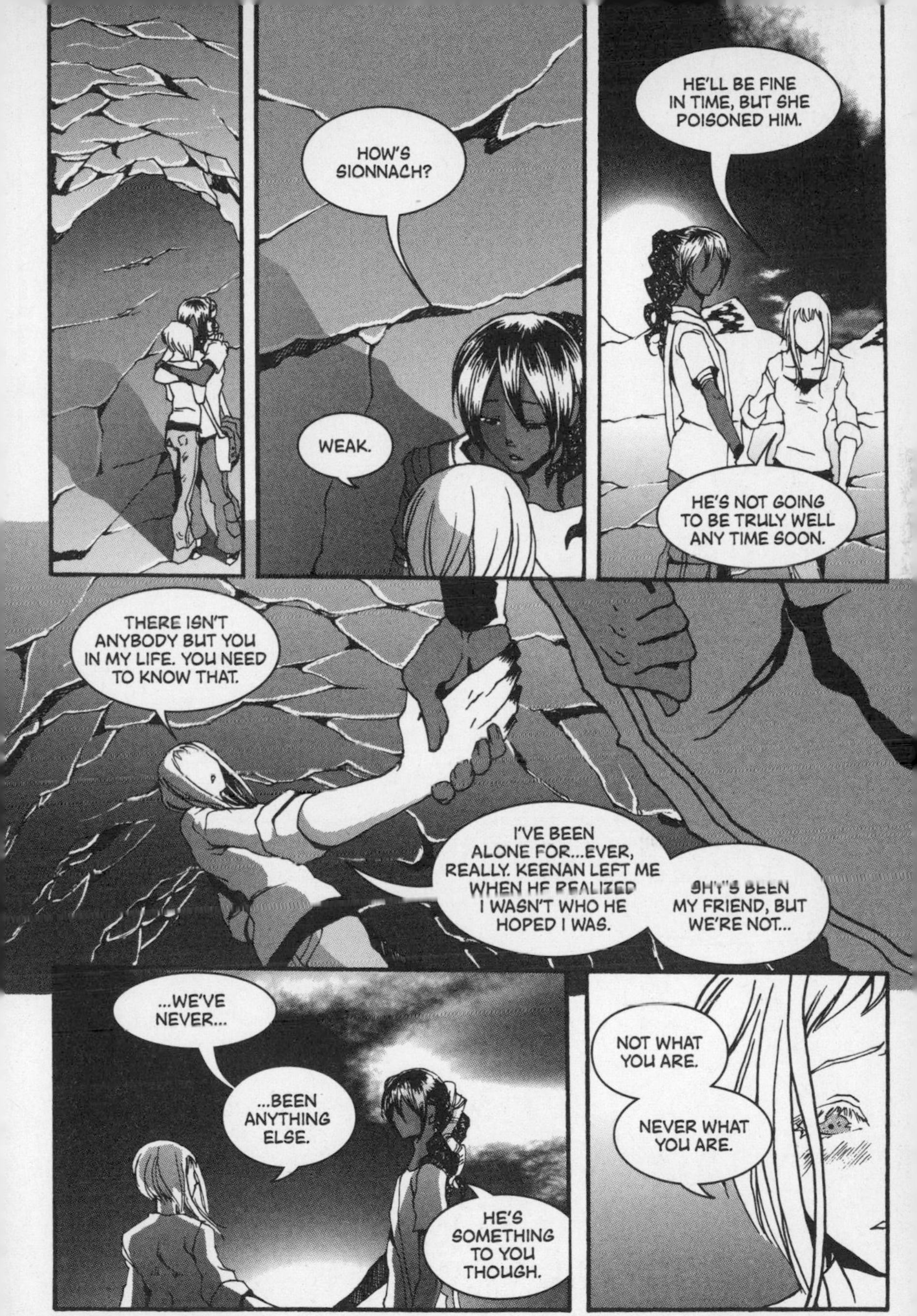
HOW'S SIONNACH?
WEAK.
HE'LL BE FINE IN TIME, BUT SHE POISONED HIM.
HE'S NOT GOING TO BE TRULY WELL ANY TIME SOON.
THERE ISN'T ANYBODY BUT YOU IN MY LIFE. YOU NEED TO KNOW THAT.
I'VE BEEN ALONE FOR...EVER, REALLY. KEENAN LEFT ME WHEN HE REALIZED I WASN'T WHO HE HOPED I WAS.
SHE'S BEEN MY FRIEND, BUT WE'RE NOT...
...WE'VE NEVER...
...BEEN ANYTHING ELSE.
HE'S SOMETHING TO YOU THOUGH.
NOT WHAT YOU ARE.
NEVER WHAT YOU ARE.

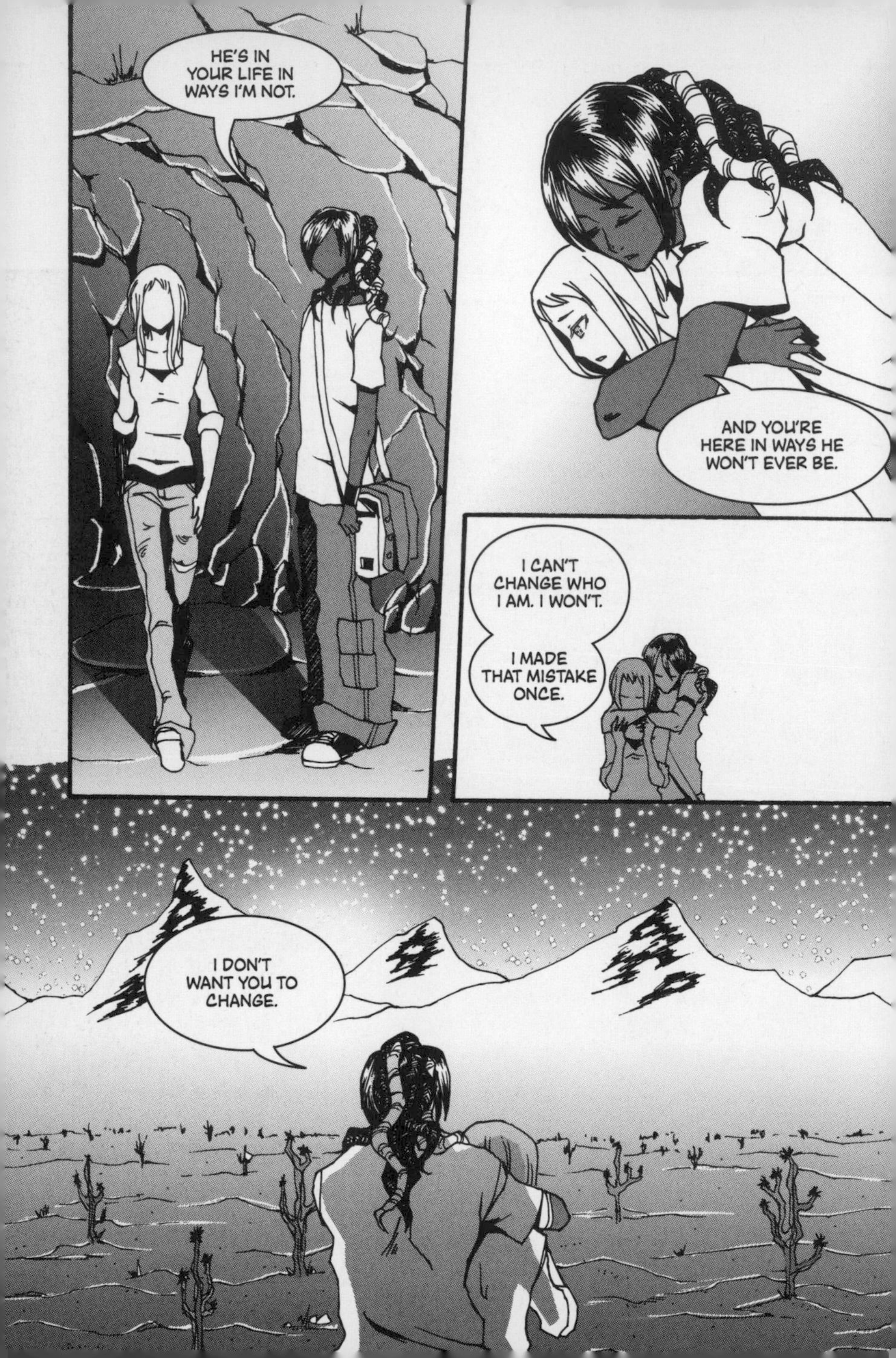
HE'S IN YOUR LIFE IN WAYS I'M NOT.
AND YOU'RE HERE IN WAYS HE WON'T EVER BE.
I CAN'T CHANGE WHO I AM. I WON'T.
I MADE THAT MISTAKE ONCE.
I DON'T WANT YOU TO CHANGE.

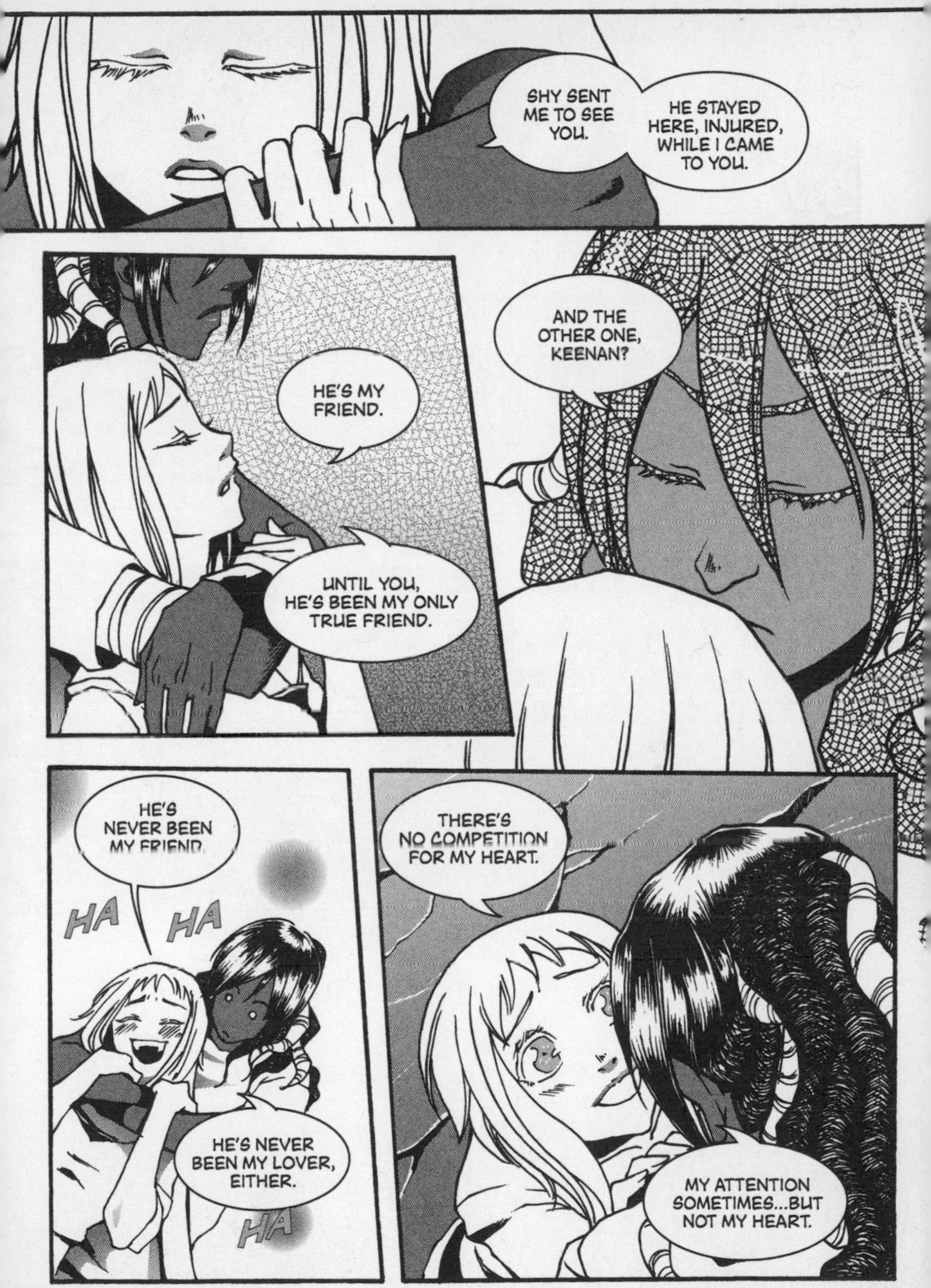
SHY SENT ME TO SEE YOU.
HE STAYED HERE, INJURED, WHILE I CAME TO YOU.
AND THE OTHER ONE, KEENAN?
HE'S MY FRIEND.
UNTIL YOU, HE'S BEEN MY ONLY TRUE FRIEND.
THERE'S NO COMPETITION FOR MY HEART.
MY ATTENTION SOMETIMES...BUT NOT MY HEART.
HE'S NEVER BEEN MY FRIEND.
HA
HA
HE'S NEVER BEEN MY LOVER, EITHER.
HA

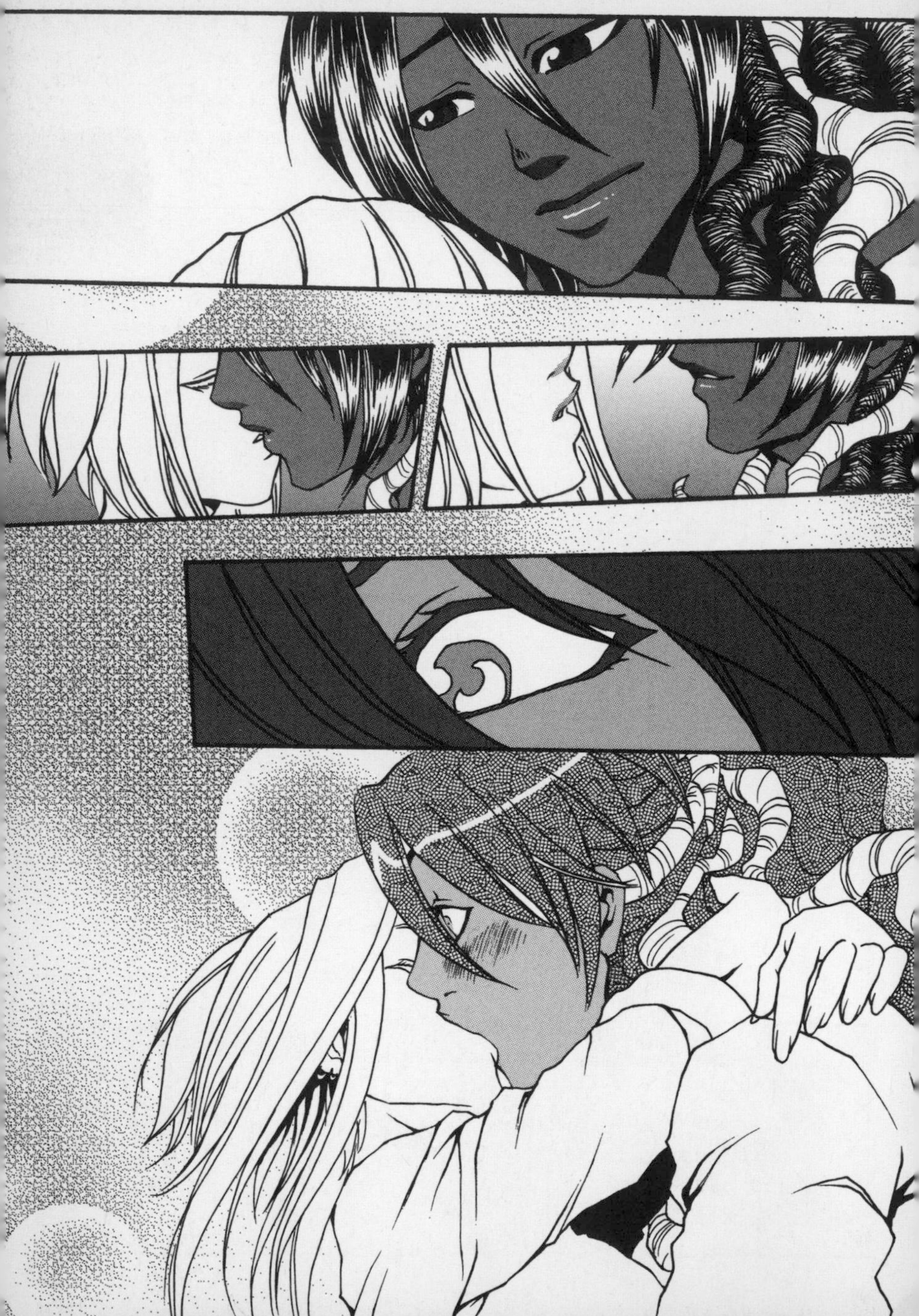

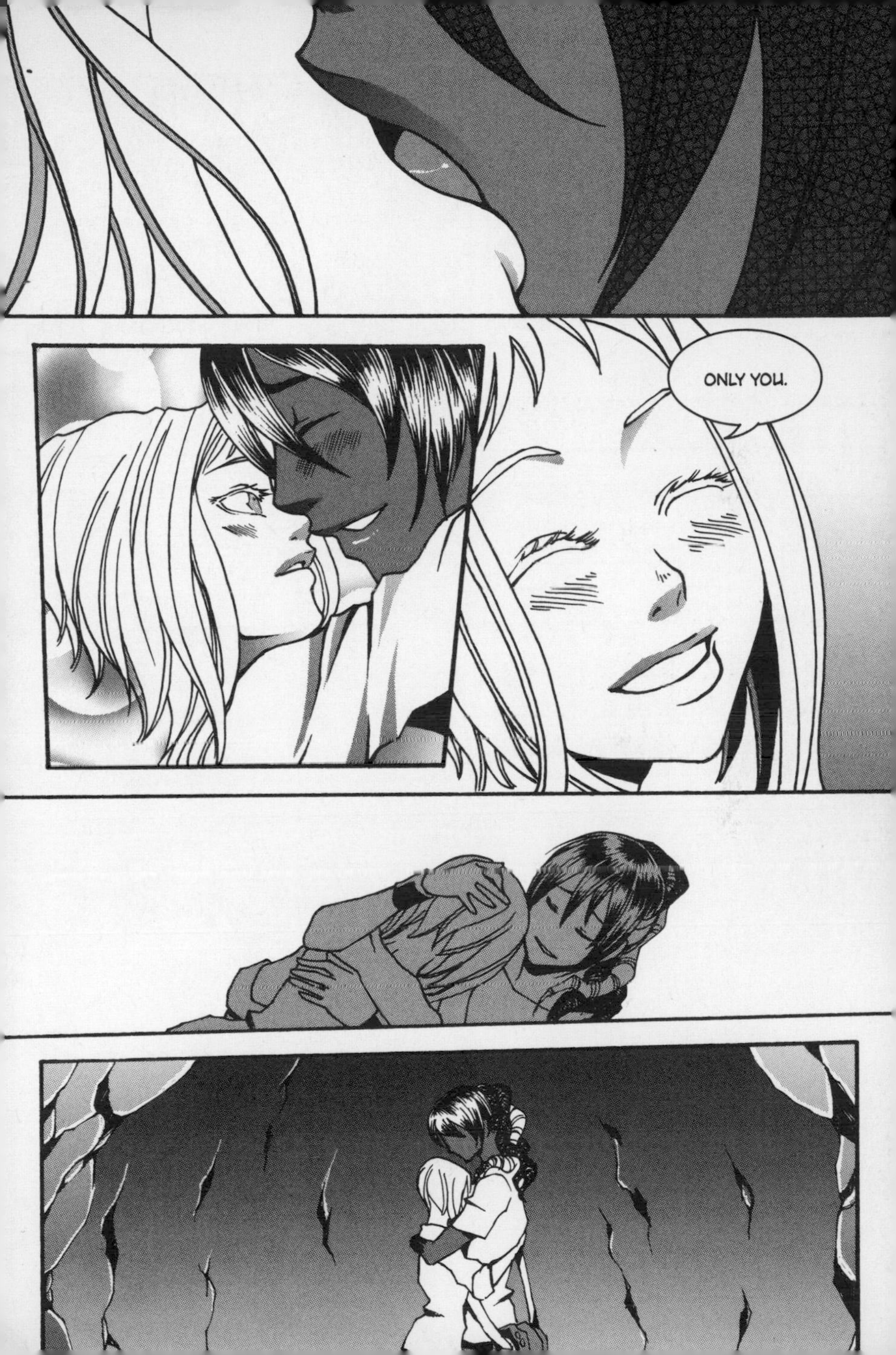
ONLY YOU.

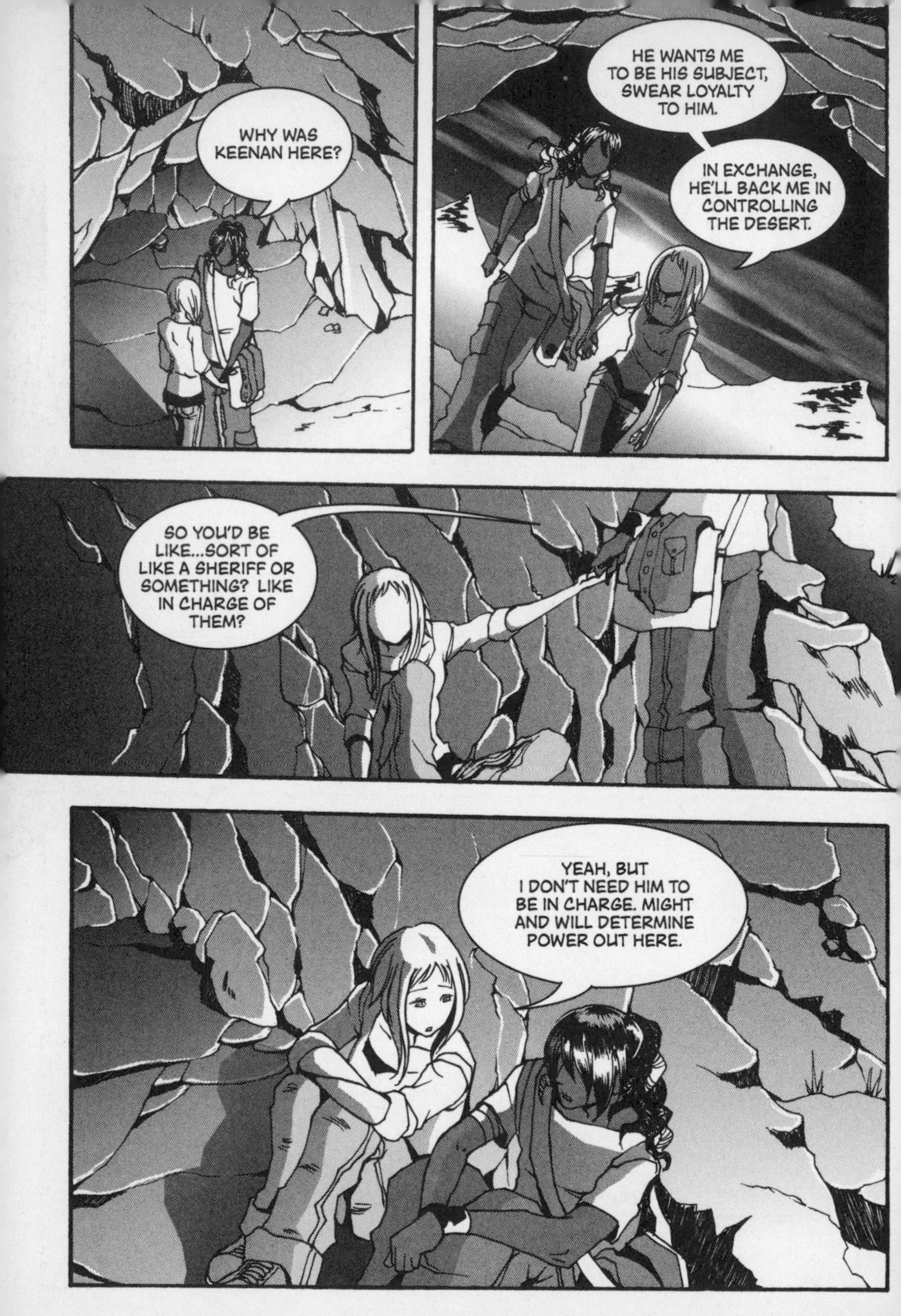
WHY WAS KEENAN HERE?
HE WANTS ME TO BE HIS SUBJECT, SWEAR LOYALTY TO HIM.
IN EXCHANGE, HE'LL BACK ME IN CONTROLLING THE DESERT.
SO YOU'D BE LIKE...SORT OF LIKE A SHERIFF OR SOMETHING? LIKE IN CHARGE OF THEM?
YEAH, BUT I DON'T NEED HIM TO BE IN CHARGE. MIGHT AND WILL DETERMINE POWER OUT HERE.

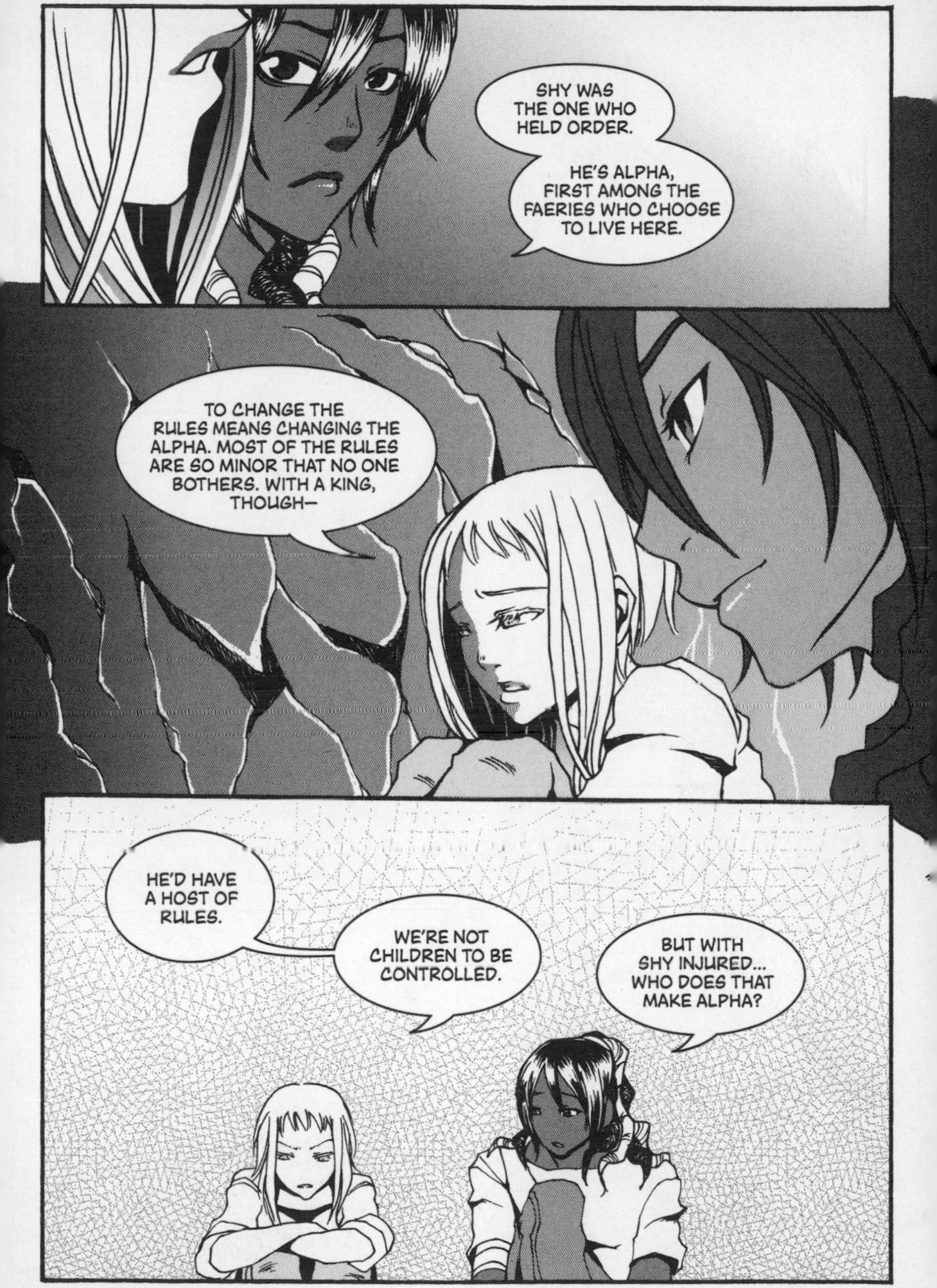
SHY WAS THE ONE WHO HELD ORDER.
HE'S ALPHA, FIRST AMONG THE FAERIES WHO CHOOSE TO LIVE HERE.
TO CHANGE THE RULES MEANS CHANGING THE ALPHA. MOST OF THE RULES ARE SO MINOR THAT NO ONE BOTHERS. WITH A KING, THOUGH—
HE'D HAVE A HOST OF RULES.
WE'RE NOT CHILDREN TO BE CONTROLLED.
BUT WITH SHY INJURED... WHO DOES THAT MAKE ALPHA?

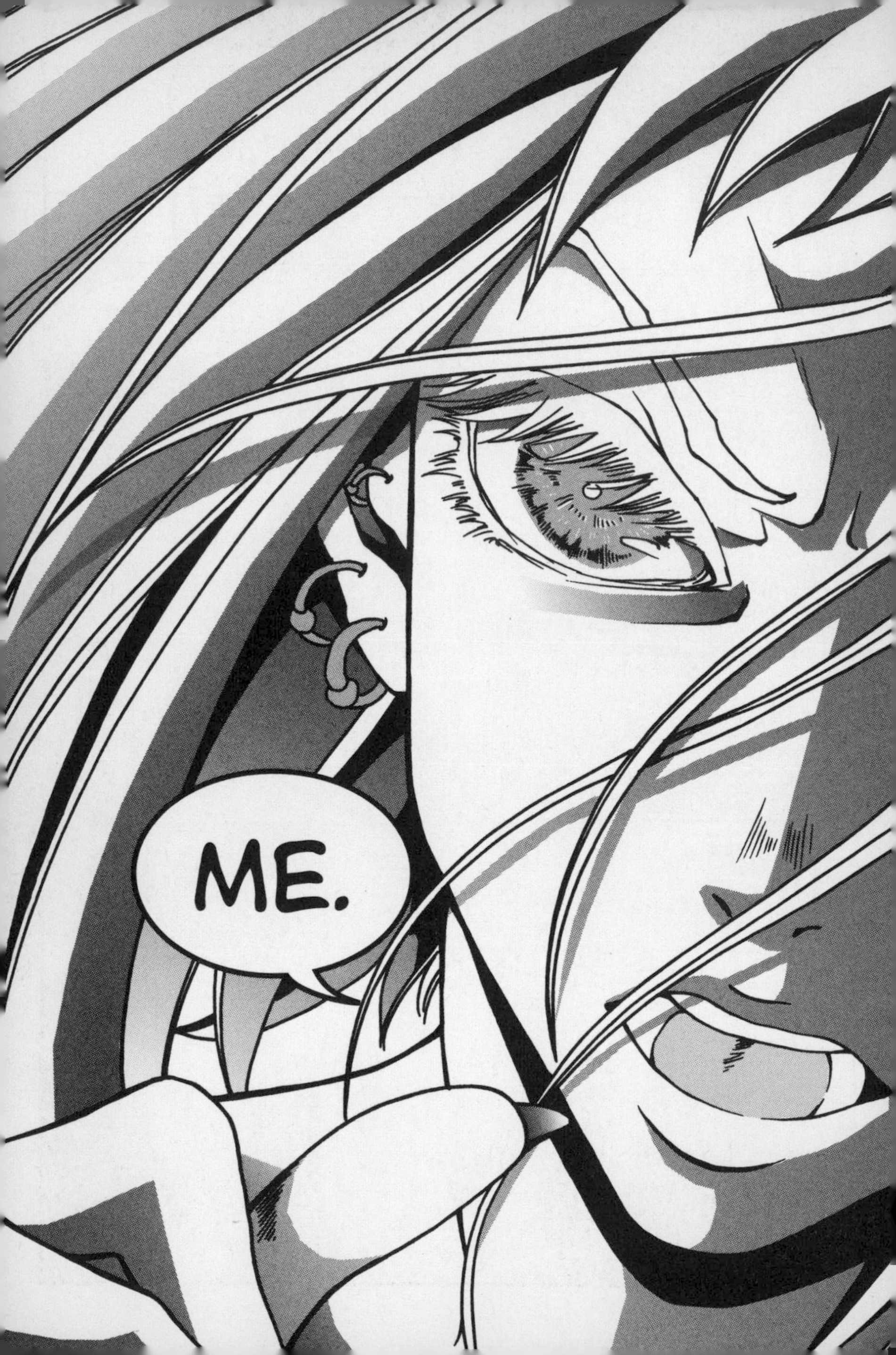
ME.

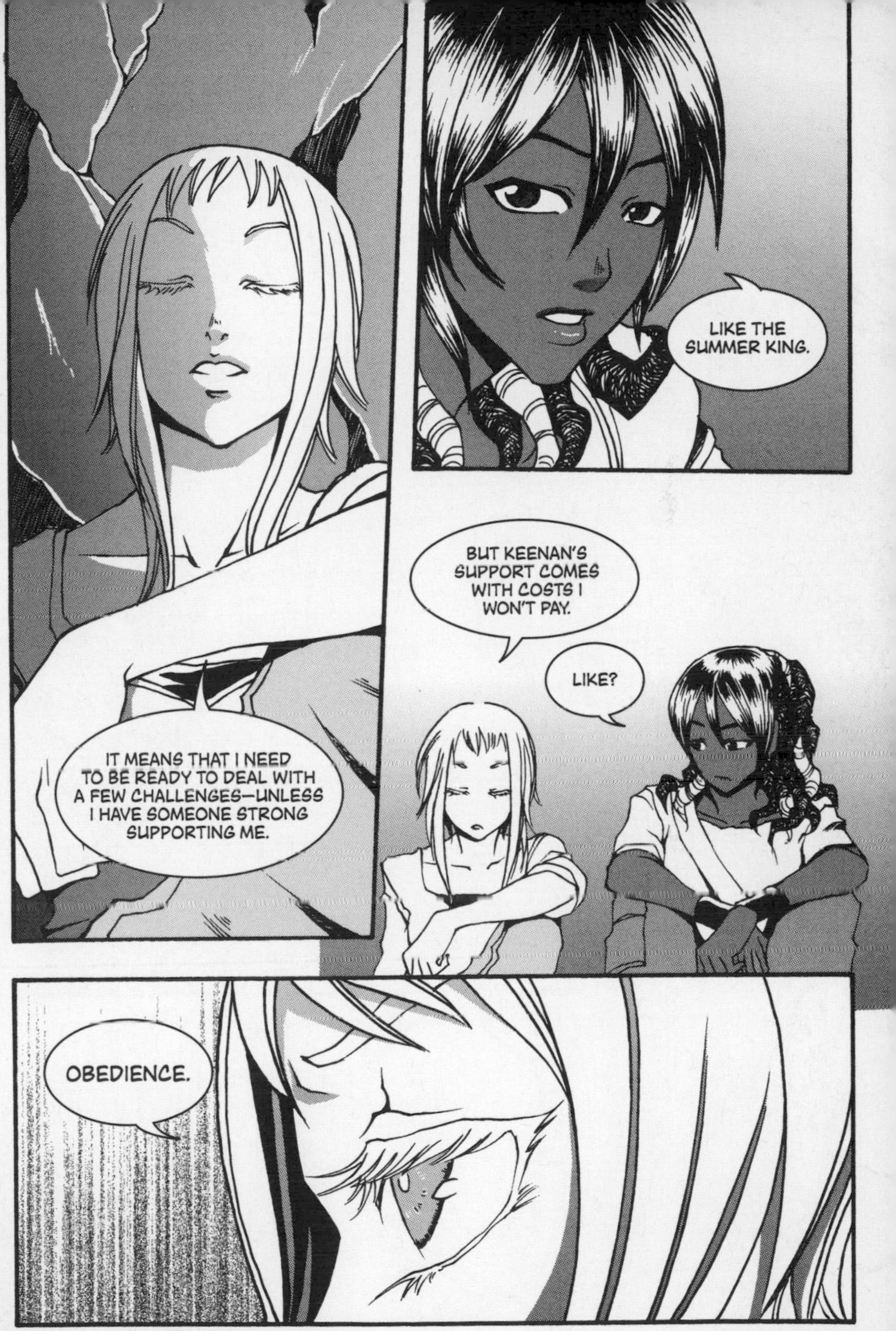
LIKE THE SUMMER KING.
IT MEANS THAT I NEED TO BE READY TO DEAL WITH A FEW CHALLENGES—UNLESS I HAVE SOMEONE STRONG SUPPORTING ME.
BUT KEENAN'S SUPPORT COMES WITH COSTS I WON'T PAY.
LIKE?
OBEDIENCE.

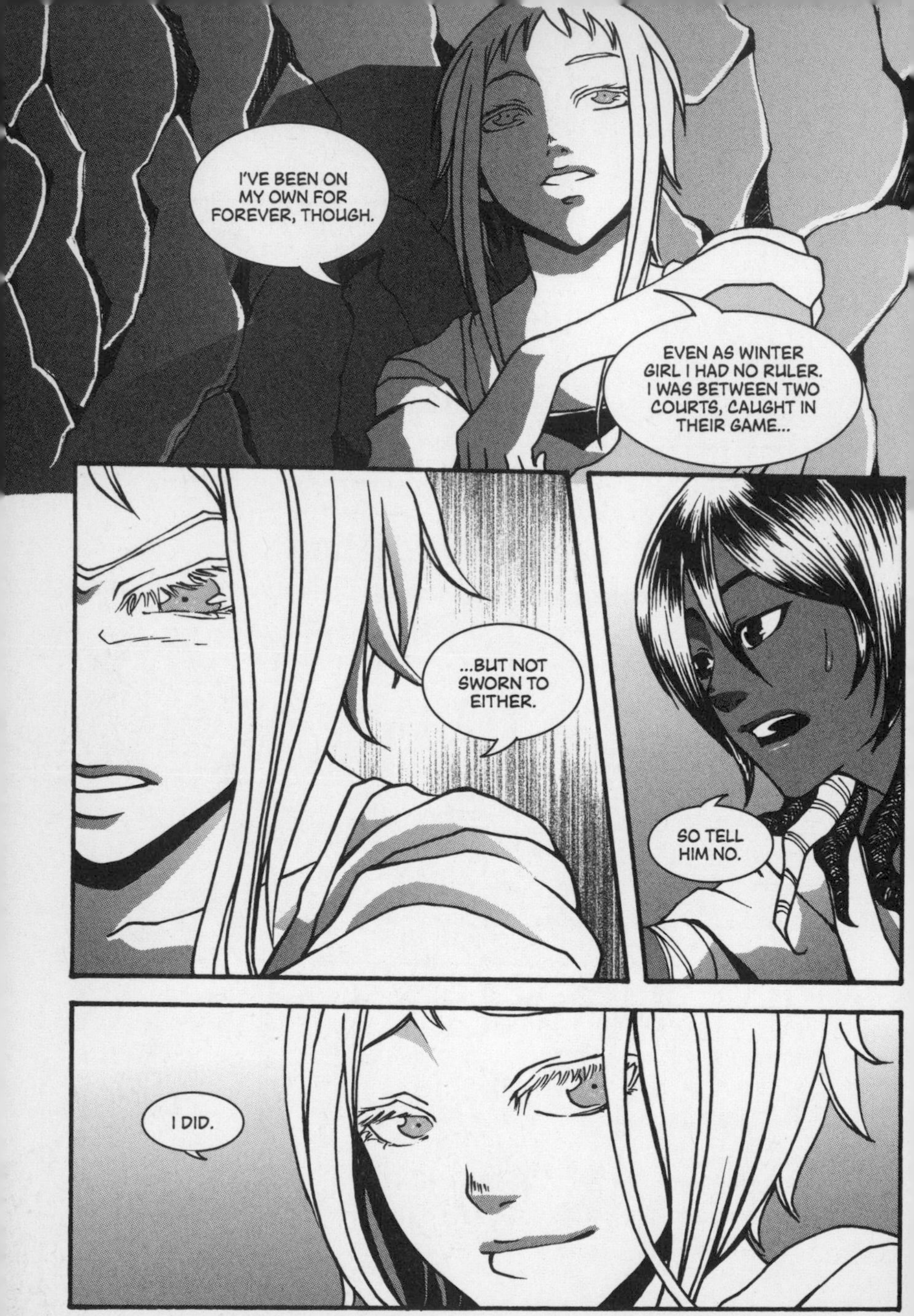
I'VE BEEN ON MY OWN FOR FOREVER, THOUGH.
EVEN AS WINTER GIRL I HAD NO RULER. I WAS BETWEEN TWO COURTS, CAUGHT IN THEIR GAME...
...BUT NOT SWORN TO EITHER.
SO TELL HIM NO.
I DID.

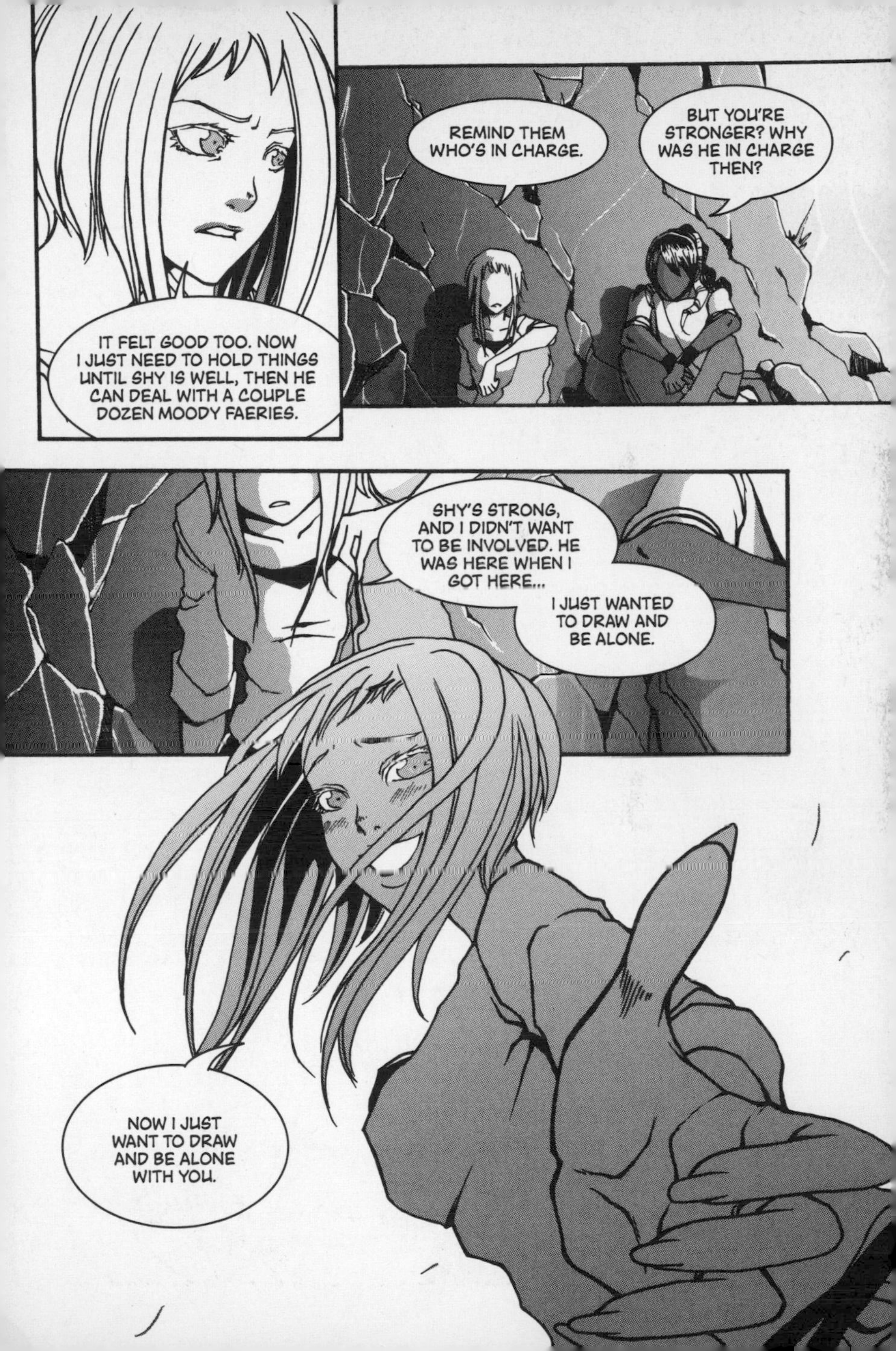
IT FELT GOOD TOO. NOW I JUST NEED TO HOLD THINGS UNTIL SHY IS WELL, THEN HE CAN DEAL WITH A COUPLE DOZEN MOODY FAERIES.
REMIND THEM WHO'S IN CHARGE.
BUT YOU'RE STRONGER? WHY WAS HE IN CHARGE THEN?
SHY'S STRONG, AND I DIDN'T WANT TO BE INVOLVED. HE WAS HERE WHEN I GOT HERE...
I JUST WANTED TO DRAW AND BE ALONE.
NOW I JUST WANT TO DRAW AND BE ALONE WITH YOU.

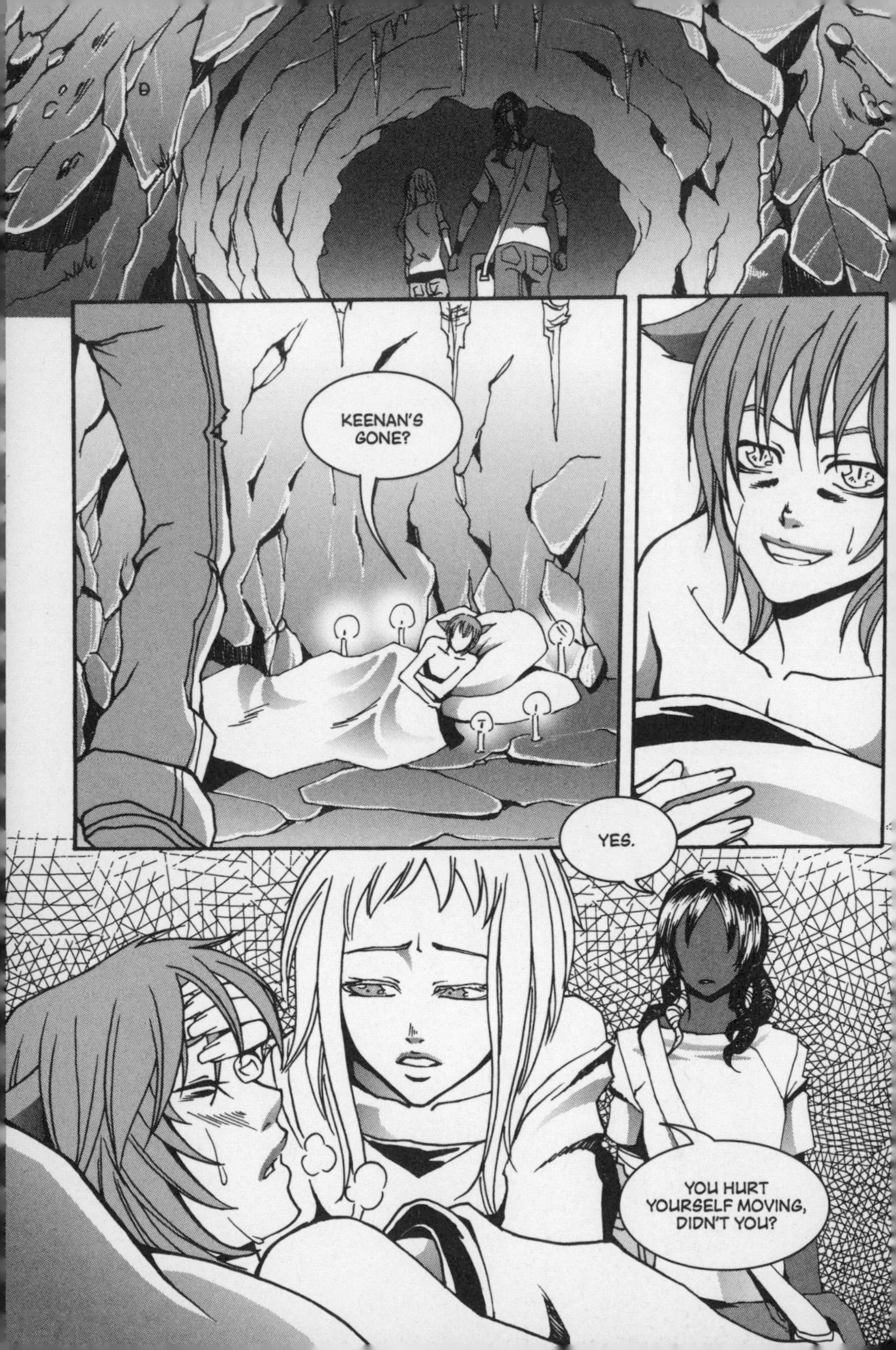
KEENAN'S GONE?
YES.
YOU HURT YOURSELF MOVING, DIDN'T YOU?

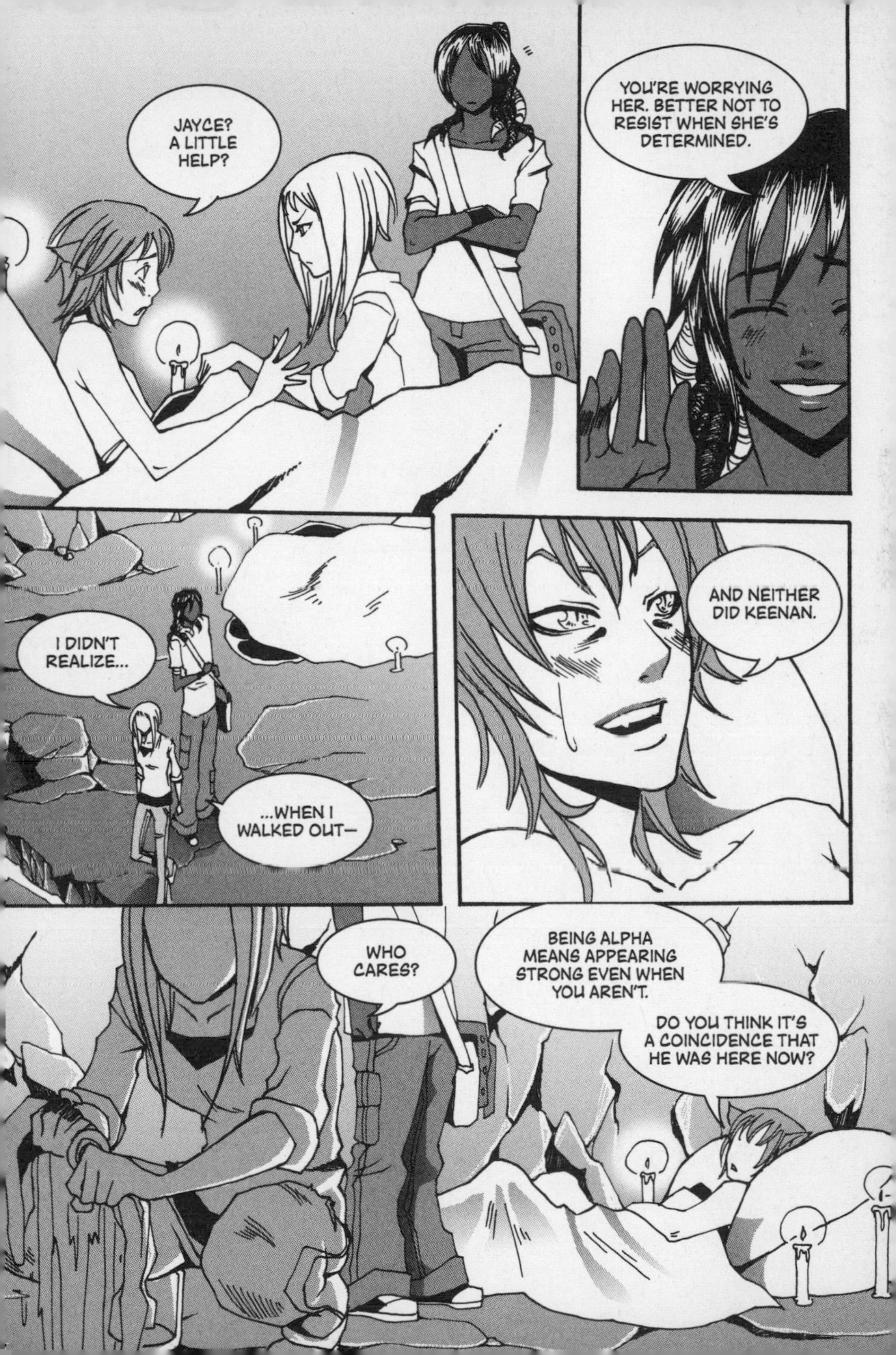
JAYCE? A LITTLE HELP?
YOU'RE WORRYING HER. BETTER NOT TO RESIST WHEN SHE'S DETERMINED.
I DIDN'T REALIZE...
...WHEN I WALKED OUT—
AND NEITHER DID KEENAN.
WHO CARES?
BEING ALPHA MEANS APPEARING STRONG EVEN WHEN YOU AREN'T.
DO YOU THINK IT'S A COINCIDENCE THAT HE WAS HERE NOW?

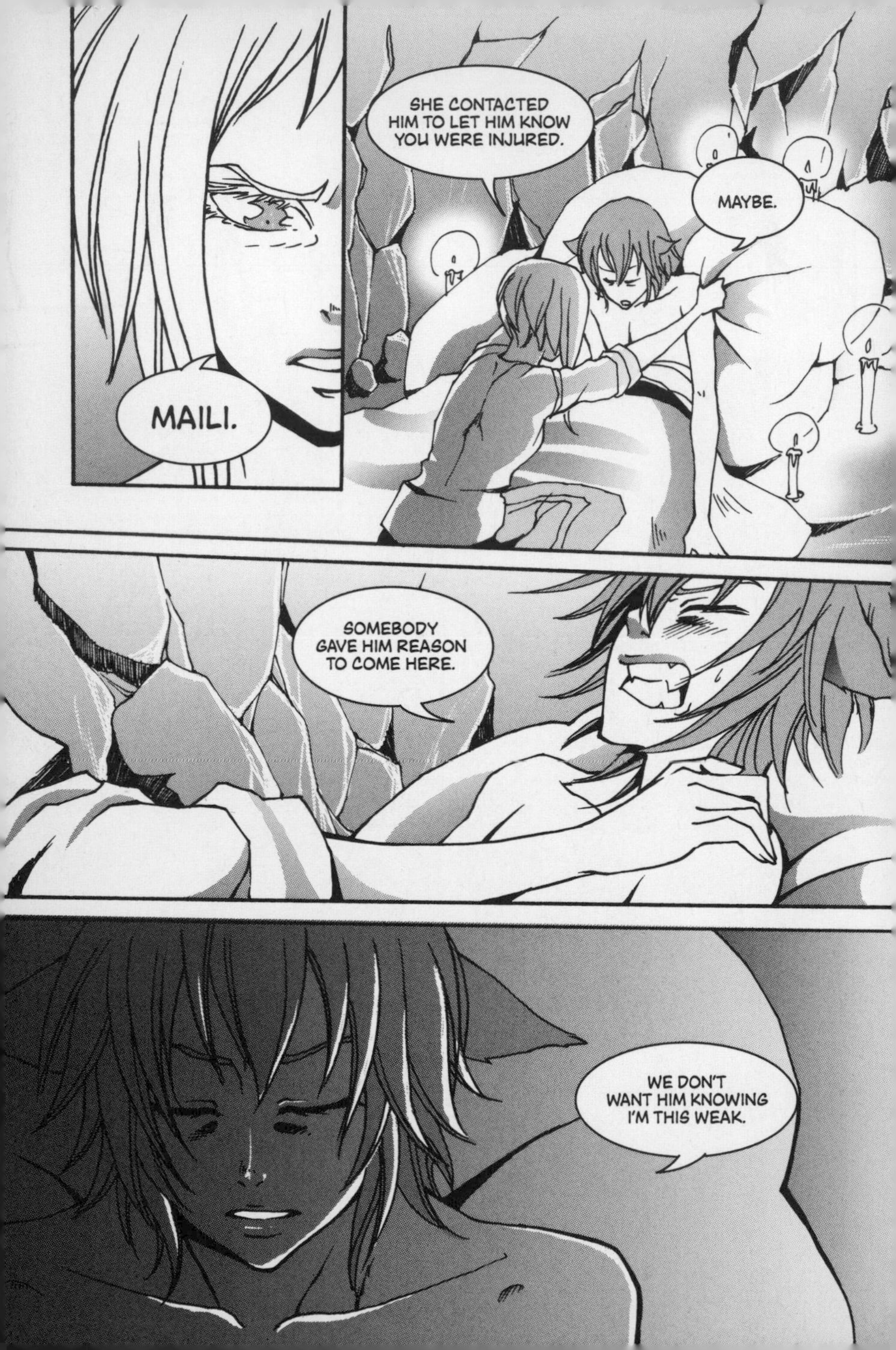
MAILI.
SHE CONTACTED HIM TO LET HIM KNOW YOU WERE INJURED.
MAYBE.
SOMEBODY GAVE HIM REASON TO COME HERE.
WE DON'T WANT HIM KNOWING I'M THIS WEAK.

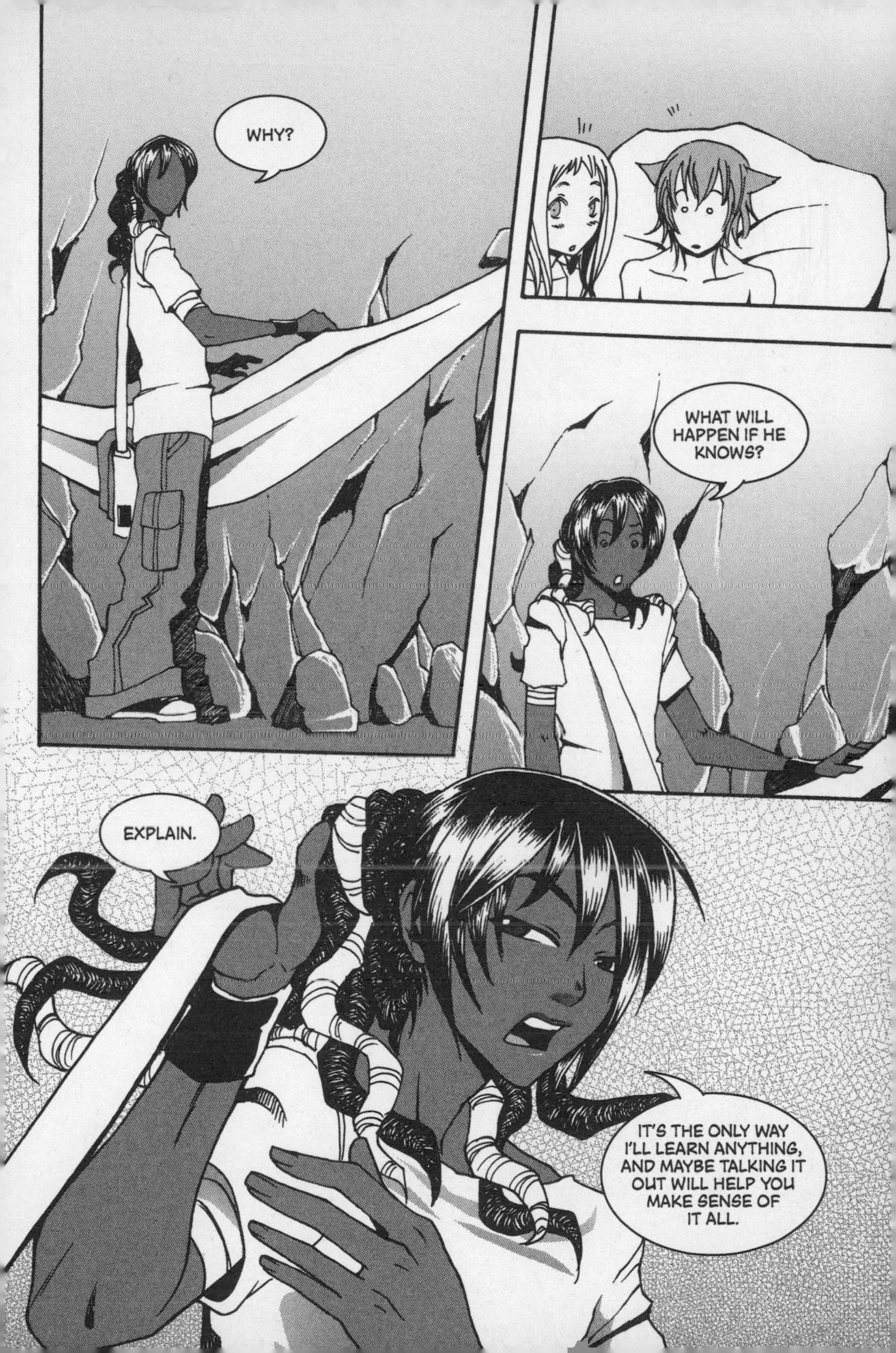
WHY?
WHAT WILL HAPPEN IF HE KNOWS?
EXPLAIN.
IT'S THE ONLY WAY I'LL LEARN ANYTHING, AND MAYBE TALKING IT OUT WILL HELP YOU MAKE SENSE OF IT ALL.

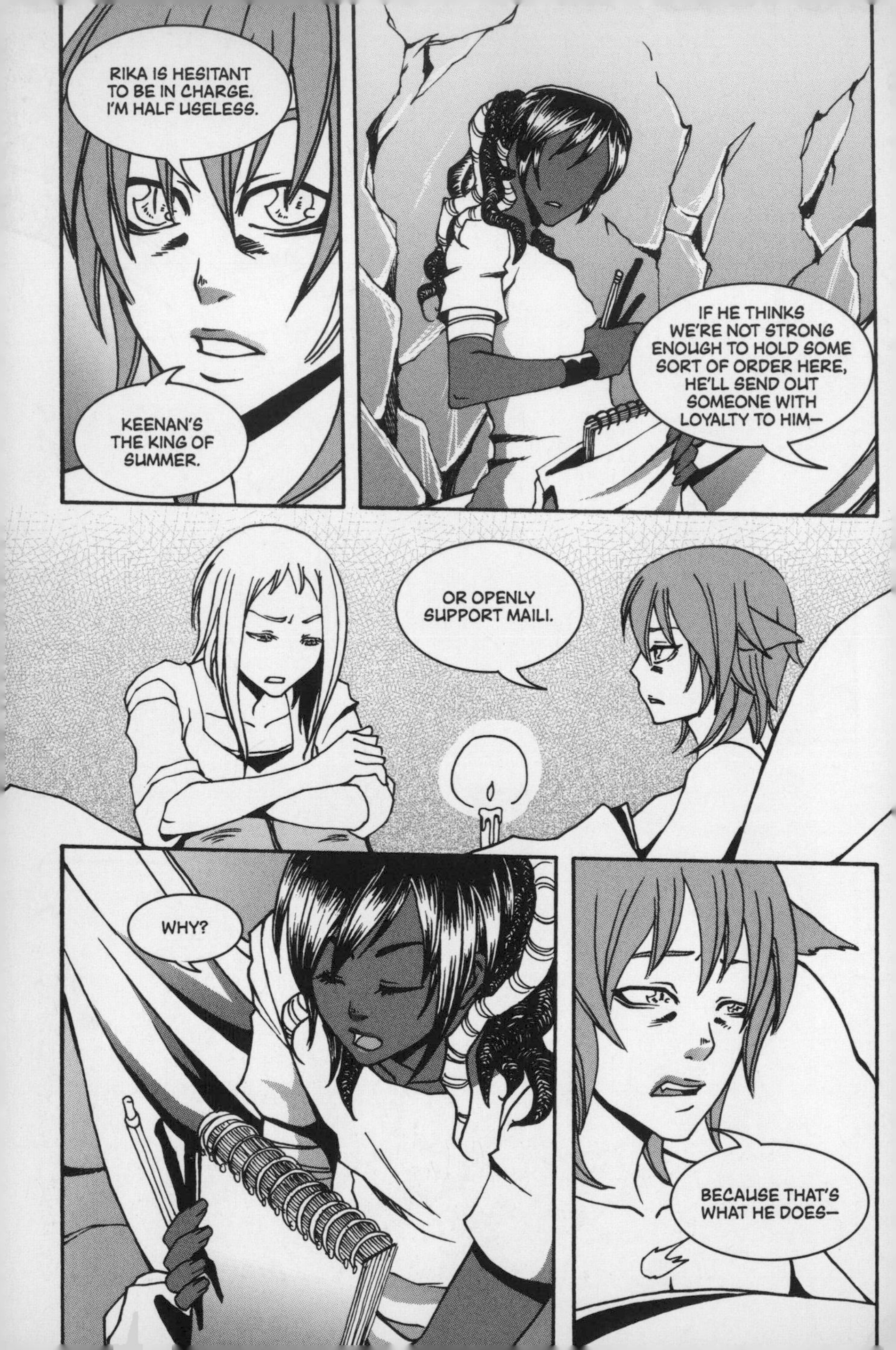
RIKA IS HESITANT TO BE IN CHARGE. I'M HALF USELESS.
KEENAN'S THE KING OF SUMMER.
IF HE THINKS WE'RE NOT STRONG ENOUGH TO HOLD SOME SORT OF ORDER HERE, HE'LL SEND OUT SOMEONE WITH LOYALTY TO HIM—
OR OPENLY SUPPORT MAILI.
WHY?
BECAUSE THAT'S WHAT HE DOES—

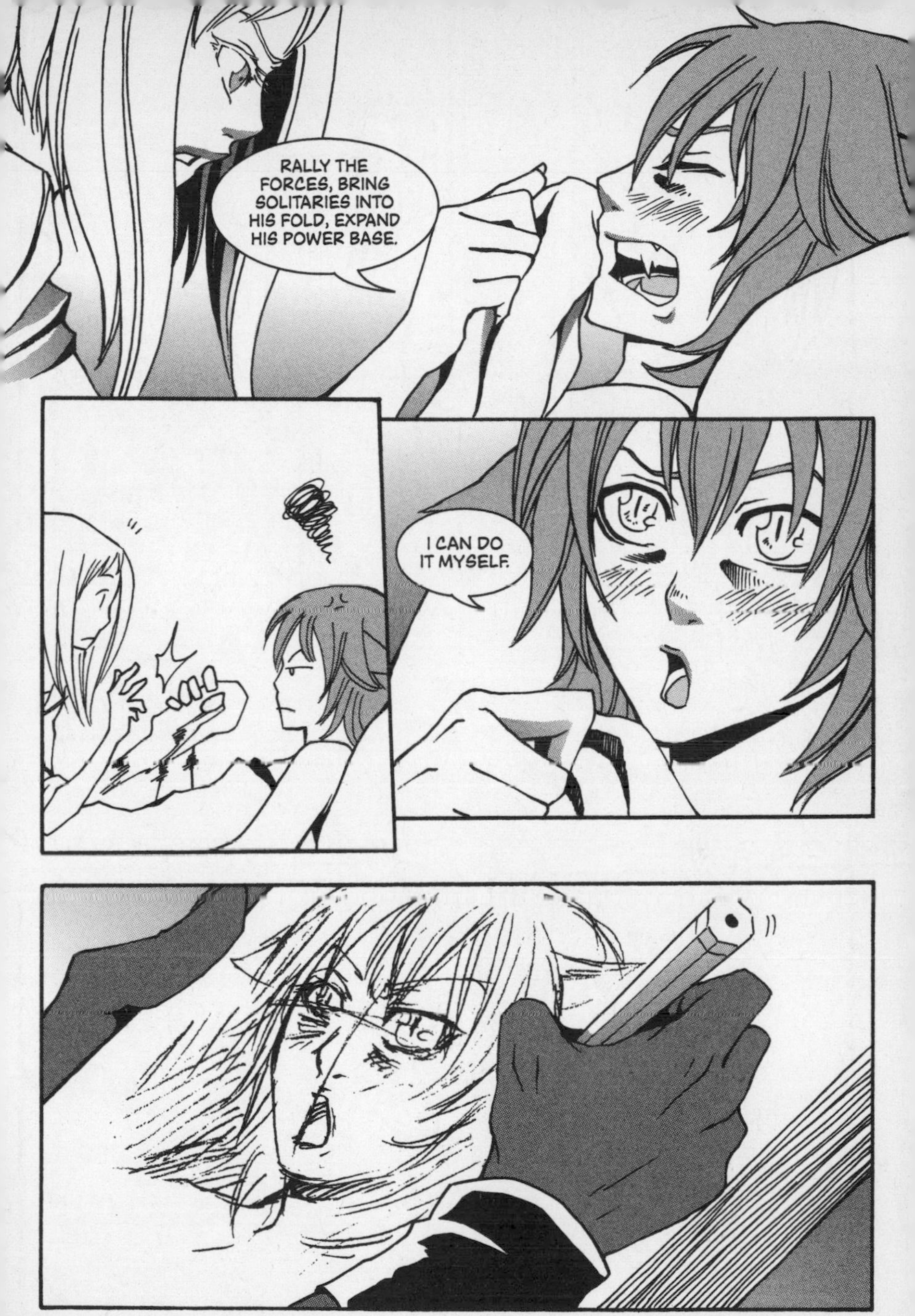
RALLY THE FORCES, BRING SOLITARIES INTO HIS FOLD, EXPAND HIS POWER BASE.
I CAN DO IT MYSELF.

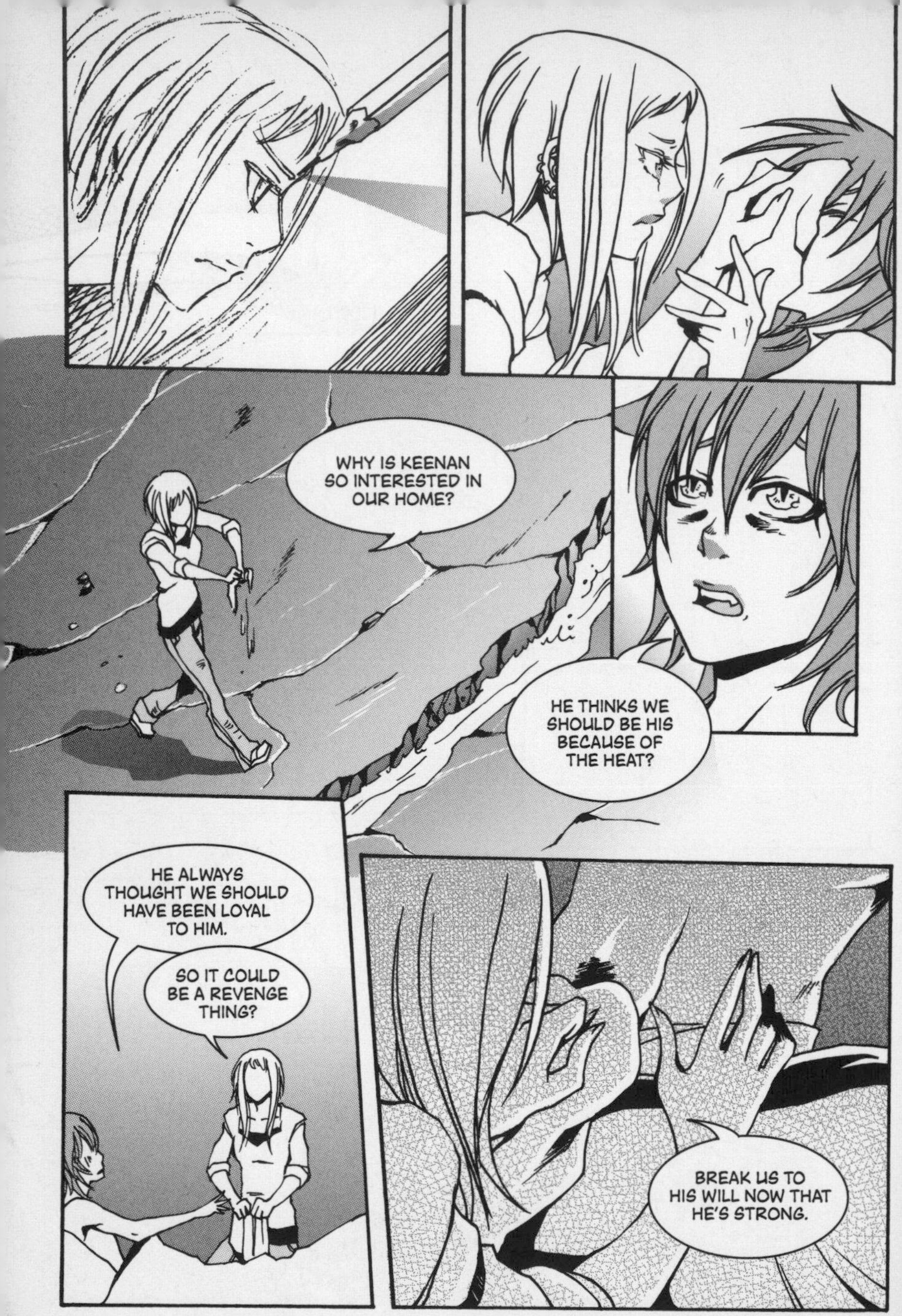
WHY IS KEENAN SO INTERESTED IN OUR HOME?
HE THINKS WE SHOULD BE HIS BECAUSE OF THE HEAT?
HE ALWAYS THOUGHT WE SHOULD HAVE BEEN LOYAL TO HIM.
SO IT COULD BE A REVENGE THING?
BREAK US TO HIS WILL NOW THAT HE'S STRONG.

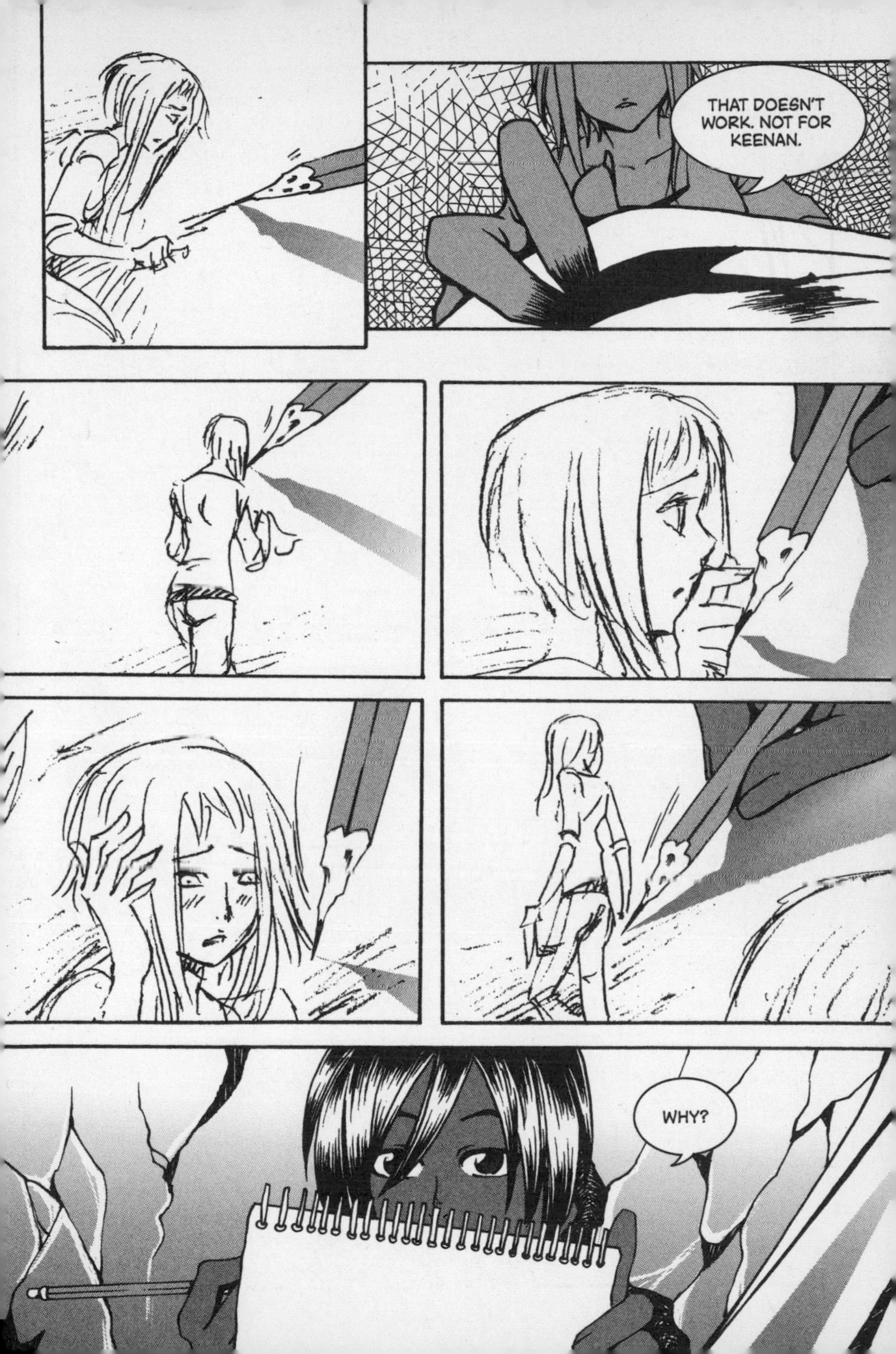
THAT DOESN'T WORK. NOT FOR KEENAN.
WHY?

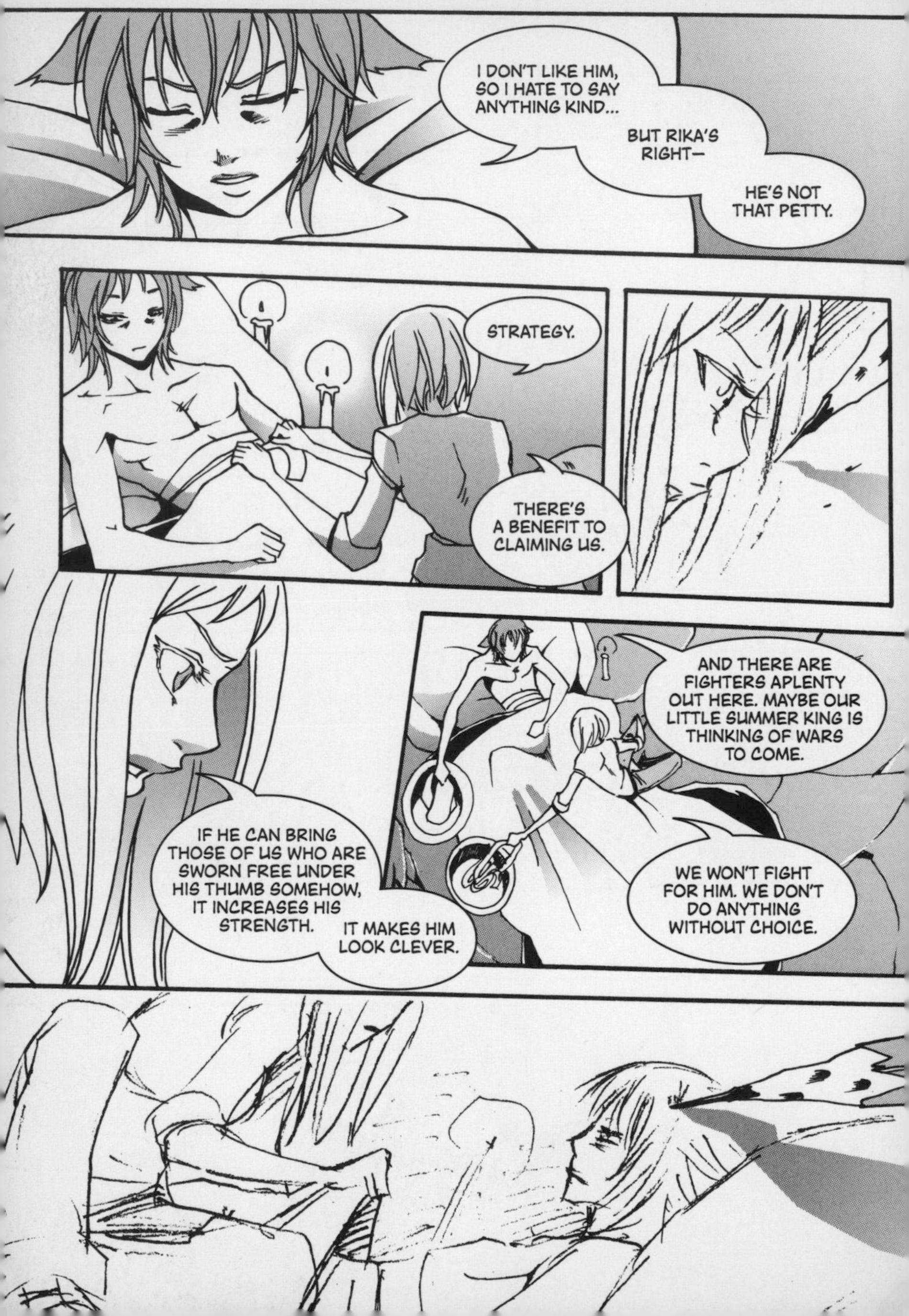
I DON'T LIKE HIM, SO I HATE TO SAY ANYTHING KIND...
BUT RIKA'S RIGHT—
HE'S NOT THAT PETTY.
STRATEGY.
THERE'S A BENEFIT TO CLAIMING US.
IF HE CAN BRING THOSE OF US WHO ARE SWORN FREE UNDER HIS THUMB SOMEHOW, IT INCREASES HIS STRENGTH.
IT MAKES HIM LOOK CLEVER.
AND THERE ARE FIGHTERS APLENTY OUT HERE. MAYBE OUR LITTLE SUMMER KING IS THINKING OF WARS TO COME.
WE WON'T FIGHT FOR HIM. WE DON'T DO ANYTHING WITHOUT CHOICE.

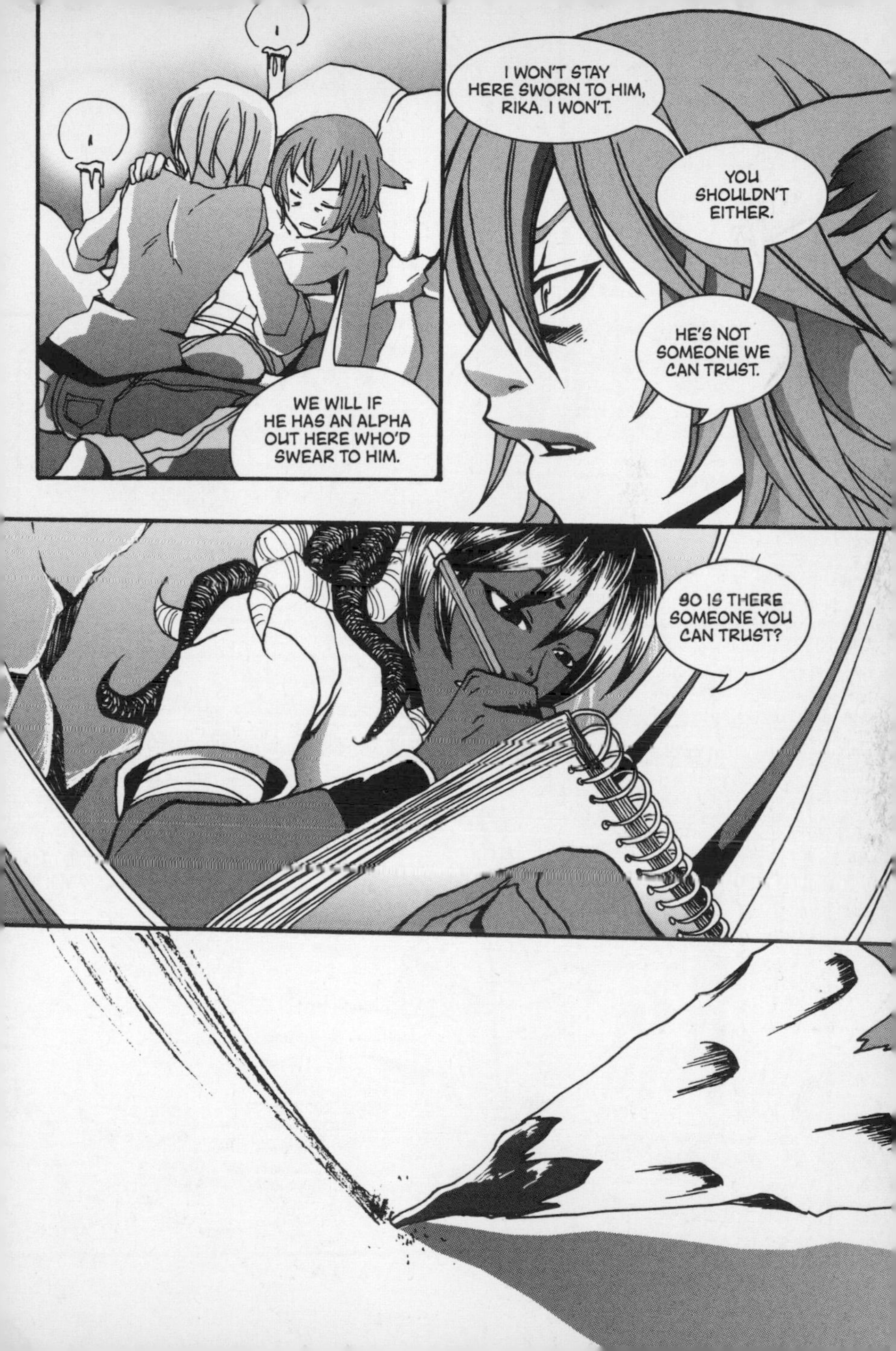
WE WILL IF HE HAS AN ALPHA OUT HERE WHO'D SWEAR TO HIM.
I WON'T STAY HERE SWORN TO HIM, RIKA. I WON'T.
YOU SHOULDN'T EITHER.
HE'S NOT SOMEONE WE CAN TRUST.
SO IS THERE SOMEONE YOU CAN TRUST?

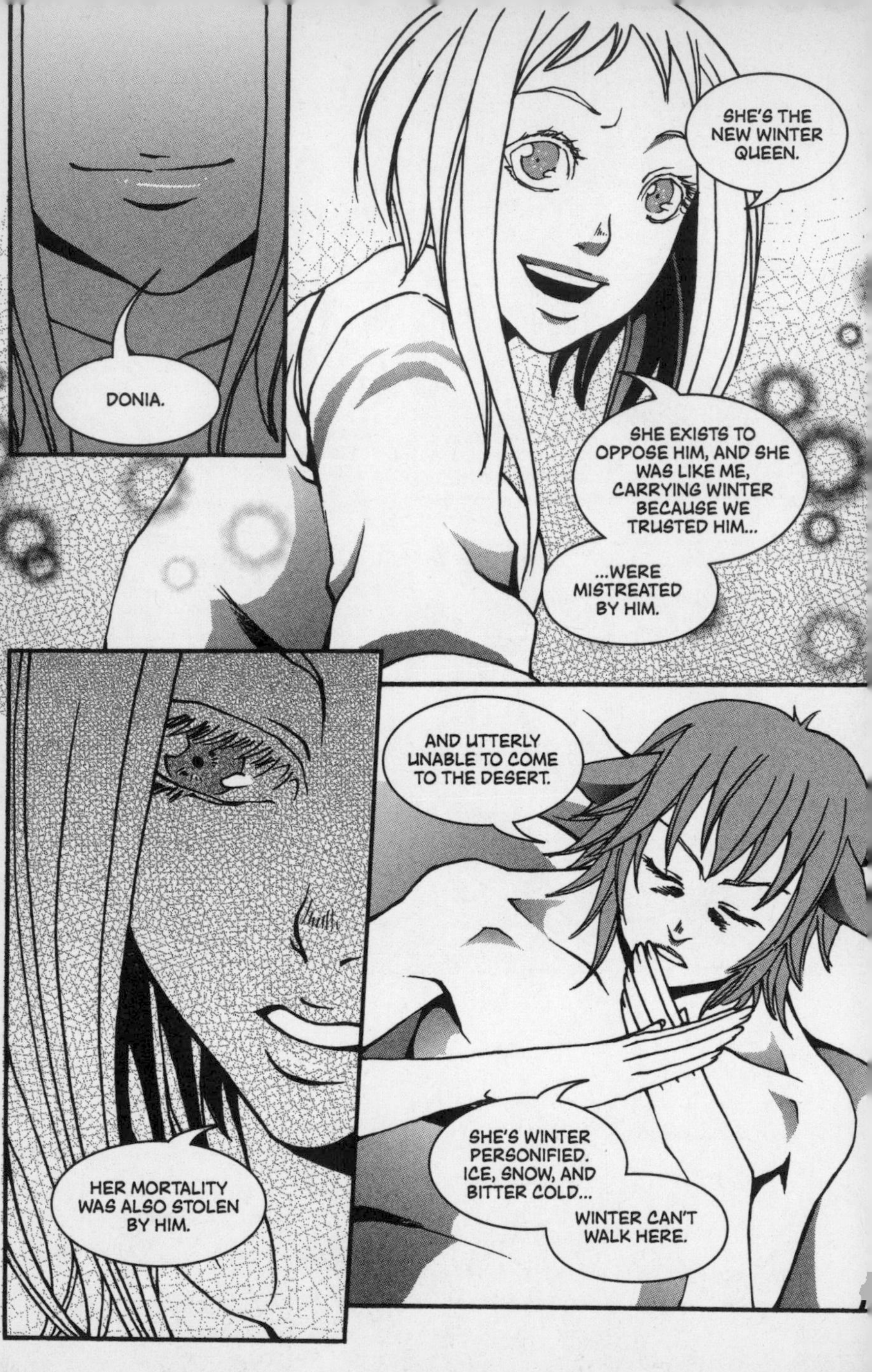
DONIA.
SHE'S THE NEW WINTER QUEEN.
SHE EXISTS TO OPPOSE HIM, AND SHE WAS LIKE ME, CARRYING WINTER BECAUSE WE TRUSTED HIM...
...WERE MISTREATED BY HIM.
HER MORTALITY WAS ALSO STOLEN BY HIM.
AND UTTERLY UNABLE TO COME TO THE DESERT.
SHE'S WINTER PERSONIFIED. ICE, SNOW, AND BITTER COLD...
WINTER CAN'T WALK HERE.

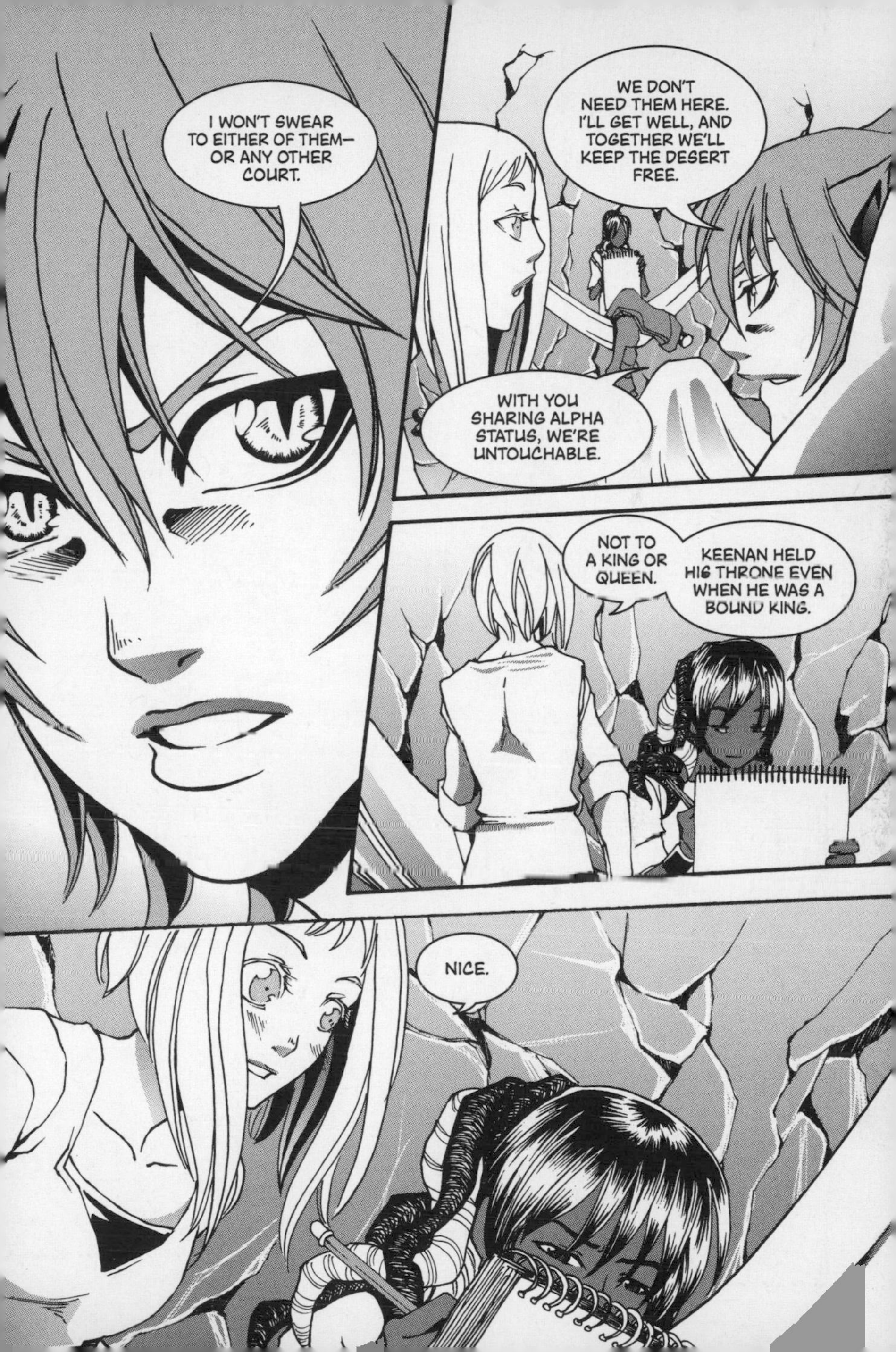
I WON'T SWEAR TO EITHER OF THEM— OR ANY OTHER COURT.
WE DON'T NEED THEM HERE. I'LL GET WELL, AND TOGETHER WE'LL KEEP THE DESERT FREE.
WITH YOU SHARING ALPHA STATUS, WE'RE UNTOUCHABLE.
NOT TO A KING OR QUEEN.
KEENAN HELD HIS THRONE EVEN WHEN HE WAS A BOUND KING.
NICE.

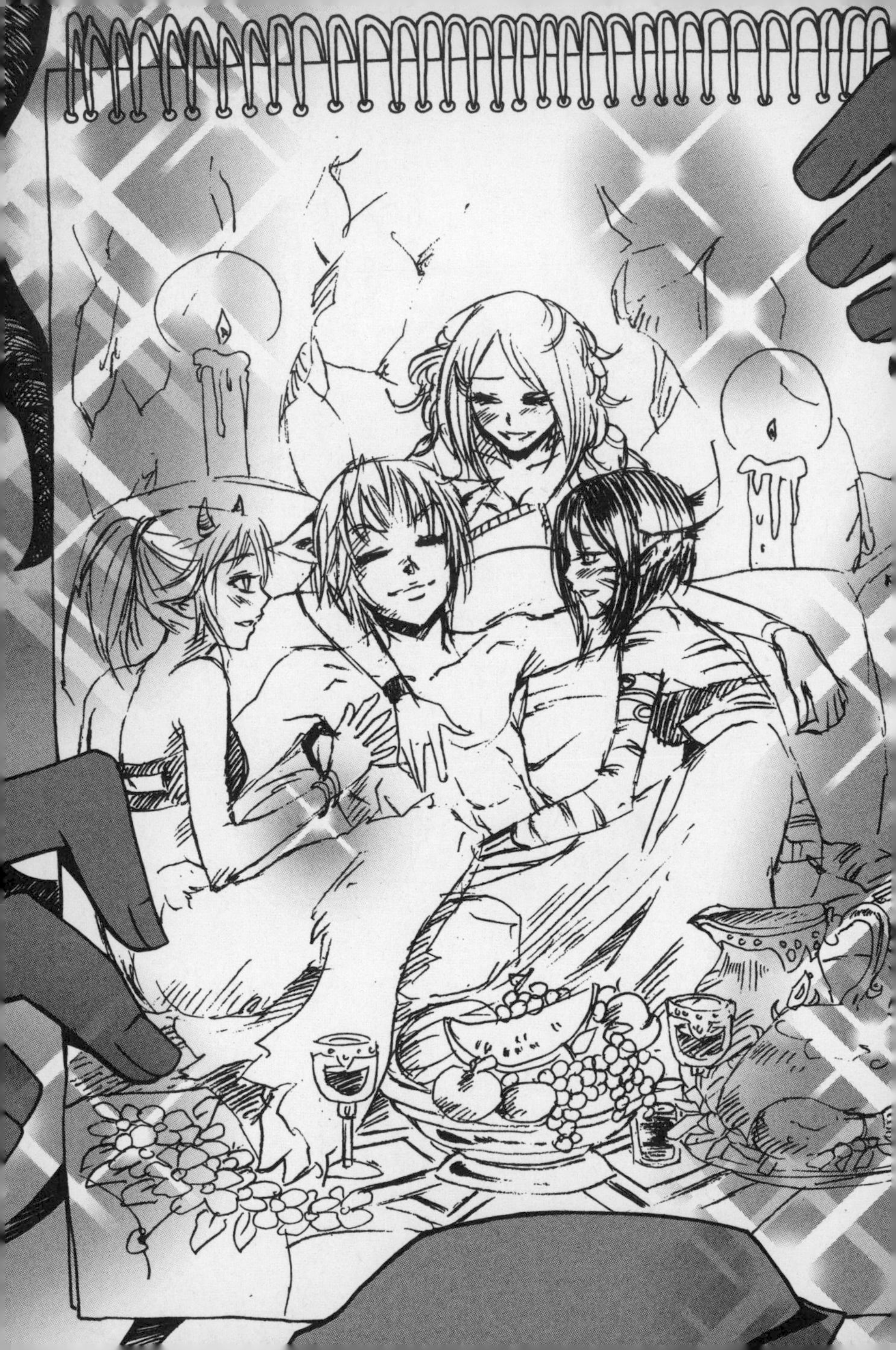

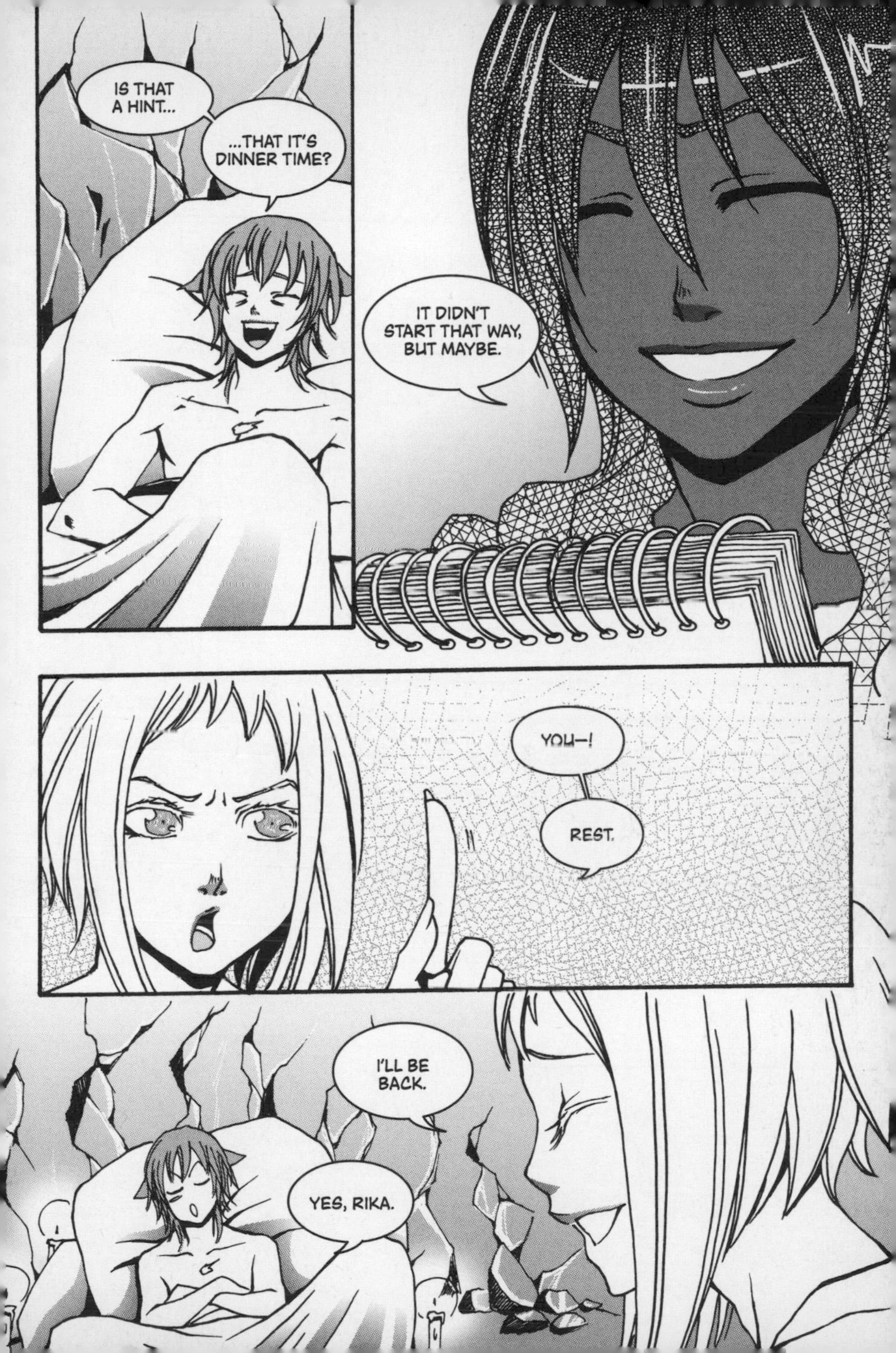
IS THAT A HINT...
...THAT IT'S DINNER TIME?
IT DIDN'T START THAT WAY, BUT MAYBE.
YOU—!
REST.
I'LL BE BACK.
YES, RIKA.

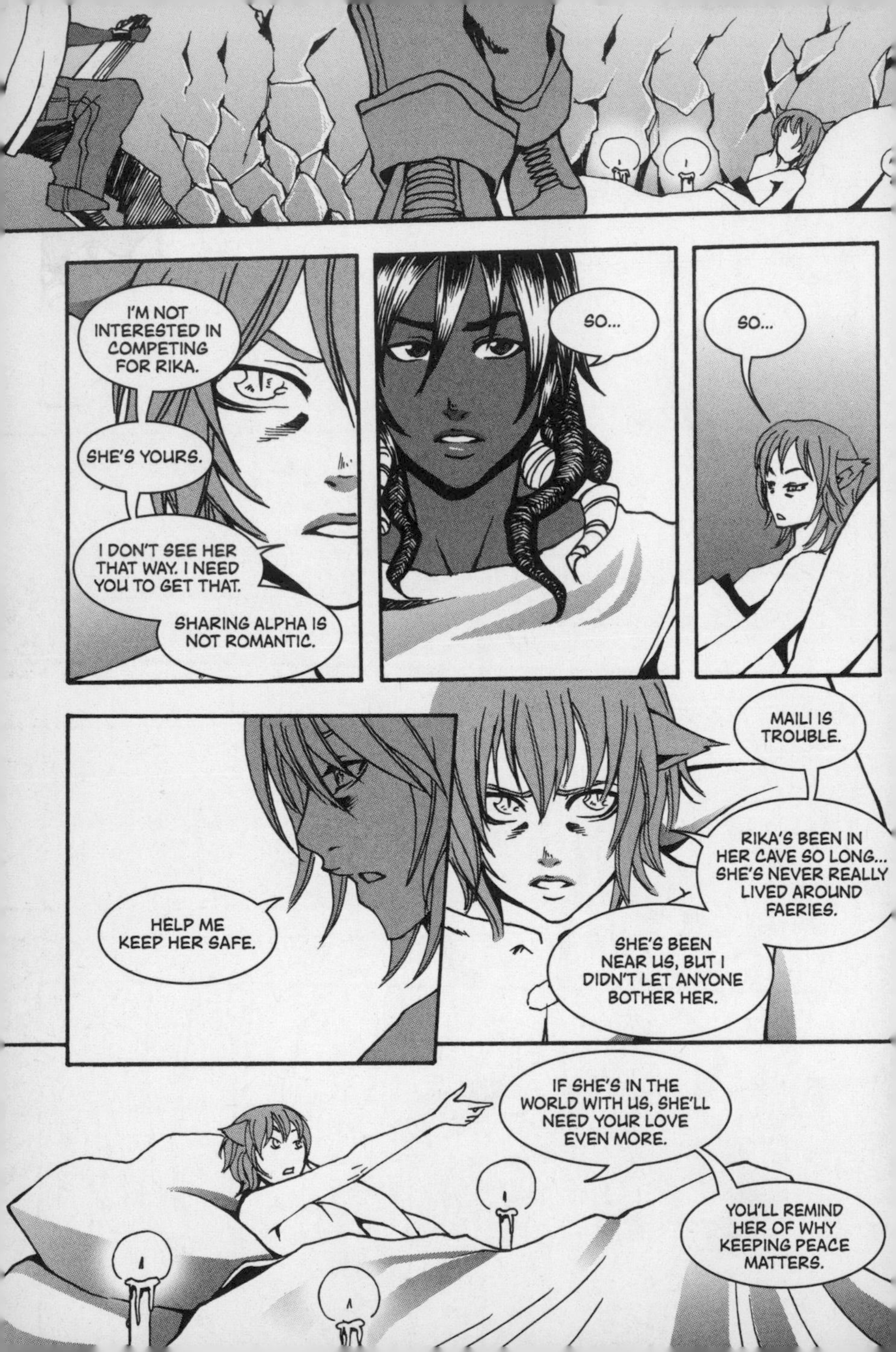

I'M NOT INTERESTED IN COMPETING FOR RIKA.
SHE'S YOURS.
I DON'T SEE HER THAT WAY. I NEED YOU TO GET THAT.
SHARING ALPHA IS NOT ROMANTIC.
SO...
SO...
HELP ME KEEP HER SAFE.
MAILI IS TROUBLE.
RIKA'S BEEN IN HER CAVE SO LONG... SHE'S NEVER REALLY LIVED AROUND FAERIES.
SHE'S BEEN NEAR US, BUT I DIDN'T LET ANYONE BOTHER HER.
IF SHE'S IN THE WORLD WITH US, SHE'LL NEED YOUR LOVE EVEN MORE.
YOU'LL REMIND HER OF WHY KEEPING PEACE MATTERS.

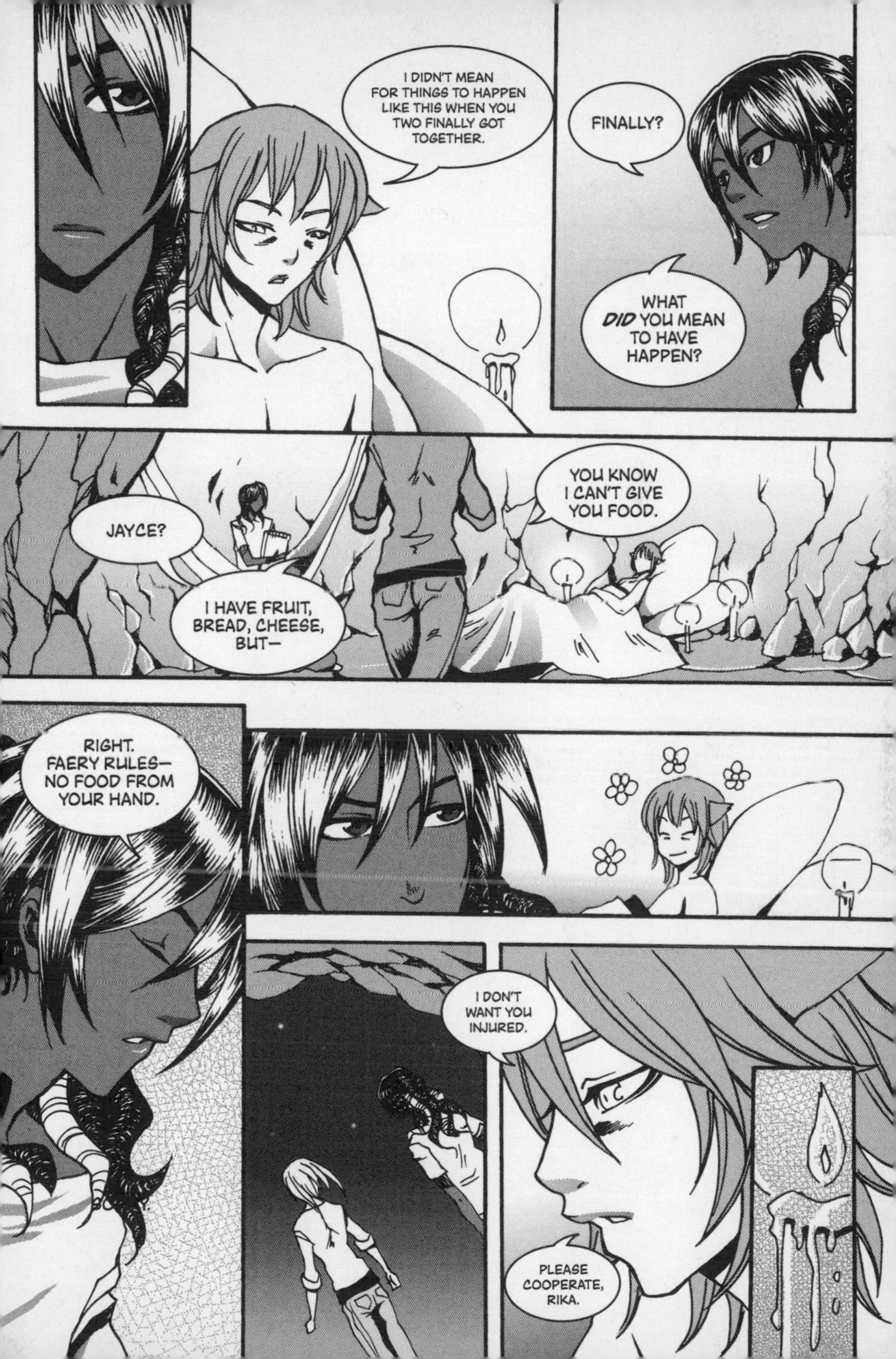
I DIDN'T MEAN FOR THINGS TO HAPPEN LIKE THIS WHEN YOU TWO FINALLY GOT TOGETHER.
FINALLY?
WHAT *DID* YOU MEAN TO HAVE HAPPEN?
JAYCE?
I HAVE FRUIT, BREAD, CHEESE, BUT—
YOU KNOW I CAN'T GIVE YOU FOOD.
RIGHT. FAERY RULES— NO FOOD FROM YOUR HAND.
I DON'T WANT YOU INJURED.
PLEASE COOPERATE, RIKA.

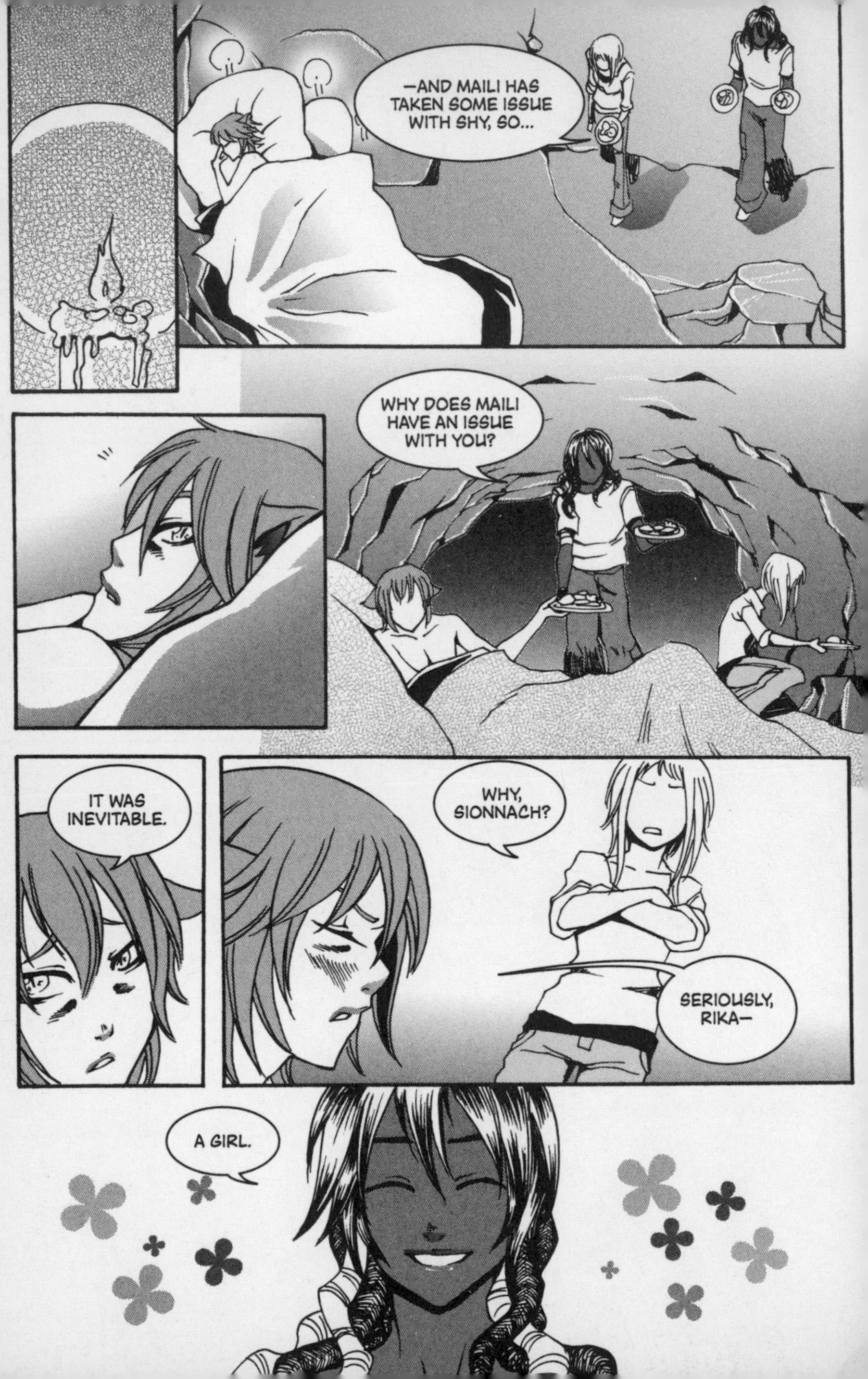
—AND MAILI HAS TAKEN SOME ISSUE WITH SHY, SO...
WHY DOES MAILI HAVE AN ISSUE WITH YOU?
IT WAS INEVITABLE.
WHY, SIONNACH?
SERIOUSLY, RIKA—
A GIRL.

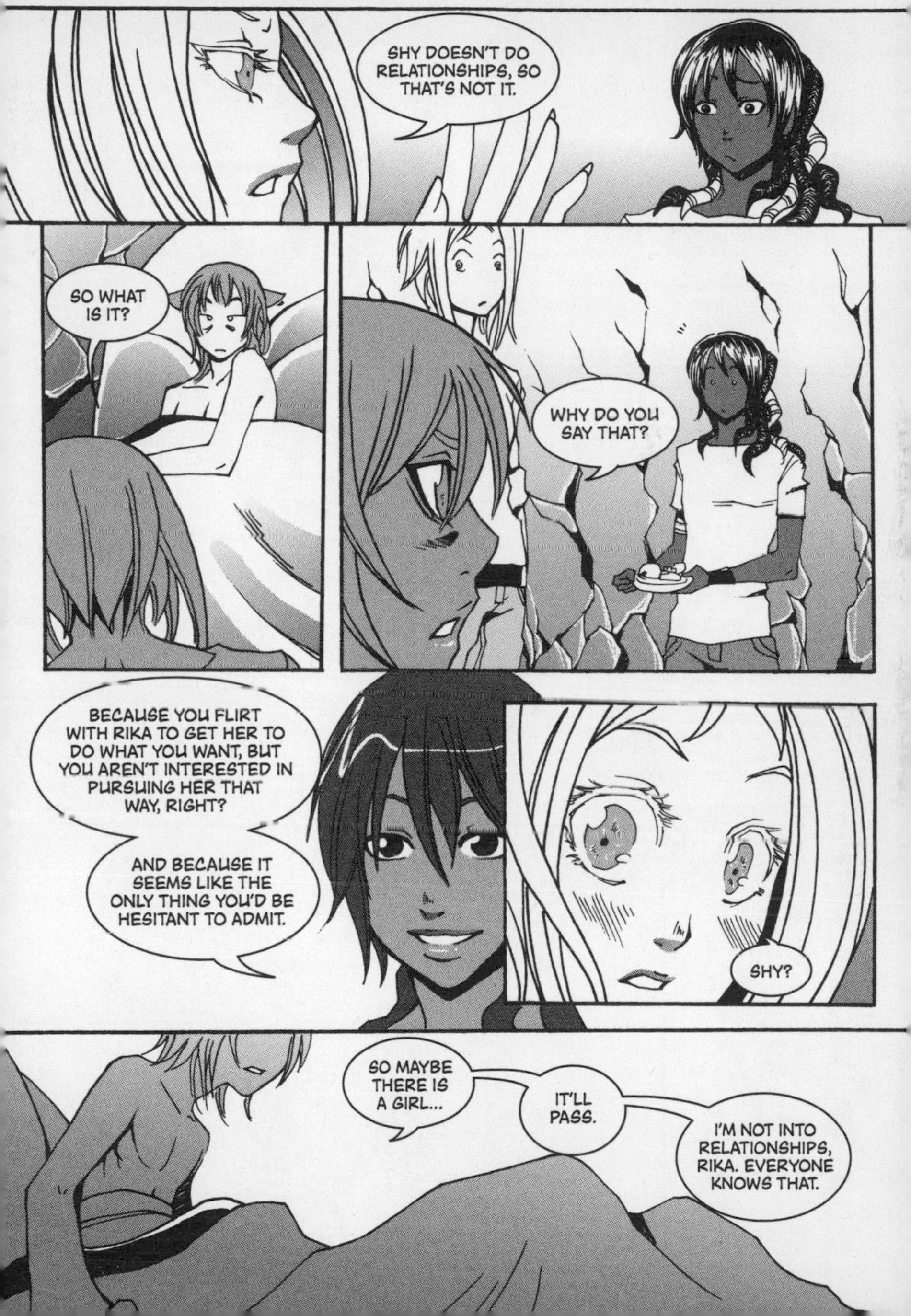
SHY DOESN'T DO RELATIONSHIPS, SO THAT'S NOT IT.
SO WHAT IS IT?
WHY DO YOU SAY THAT?
BECAUSE YOU FLIRT WITH RIKA TO GET HER TO DO WHAT YOU WANT, BUT YOU AREN'T INTERESTED IN PURSUING HER THAT WAY, RIGHT?
AND BECAUSE IT SEEMS LIKE THE ONLY THING YOU'D BE HESITANT TO ADMIT.
SHY?
SO MAYBE THERE IS A GIRL...
IT'LL PASS.
I'M NOT INTO RELATIONSHIPS, RIKA. EVERYONE KNOWS THAT.

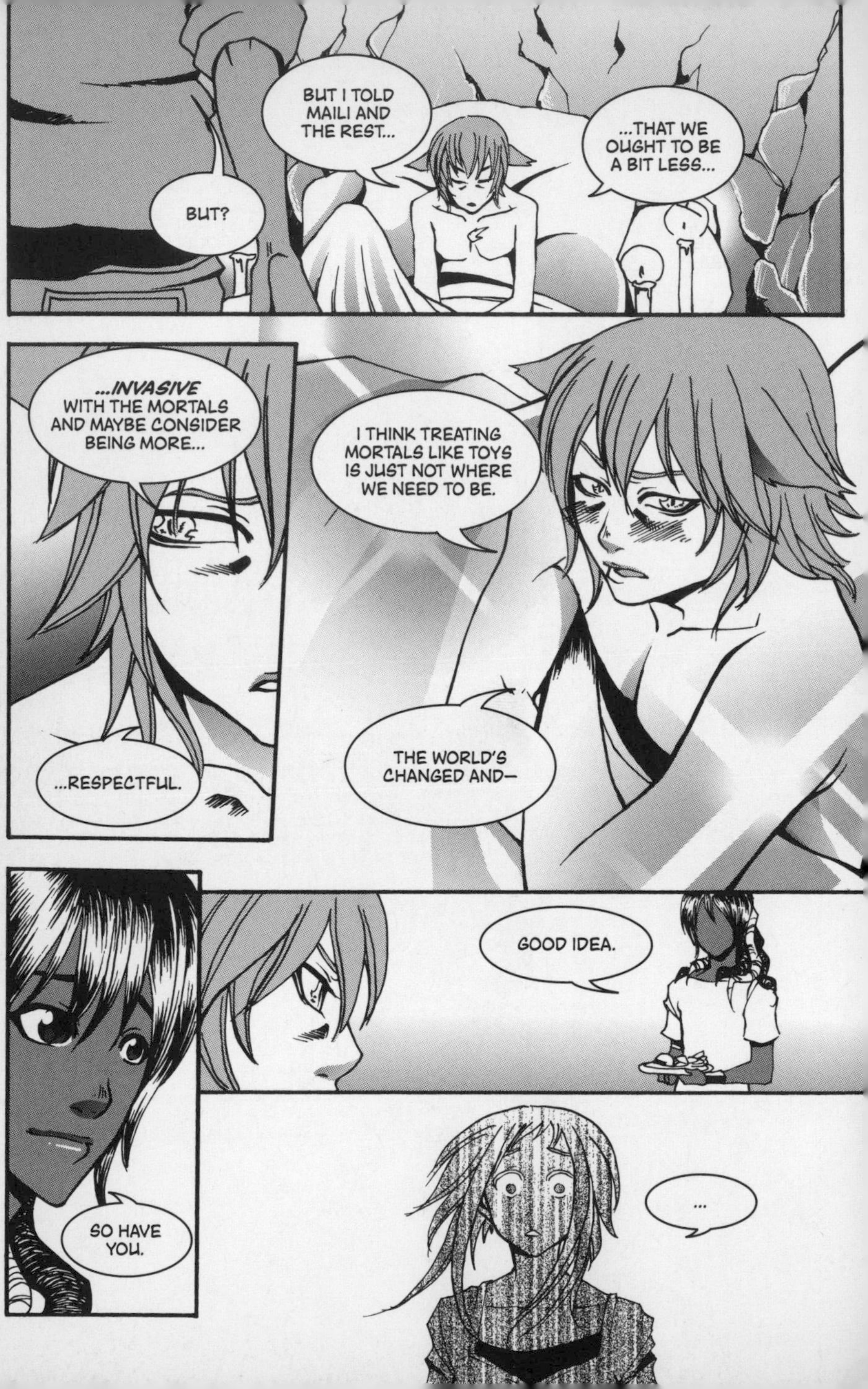
BUT I TOLD MAILI AND THE REST...
BUT?
...THAT WE OUGHT TO BE A BIT LESS...
...*INVASIVE* WITH THE MORTALS AND MAYBE CONSIDER BEING MORE...
...RESPECTFUL.
I THINK TREATING MORTALS LIKE TOYS IS JUST NOT WHERE WE NEED TO BE.
THE WORLD'S CHANGED AND—
SO HAVE YOU.
GOOD IDEA.
...

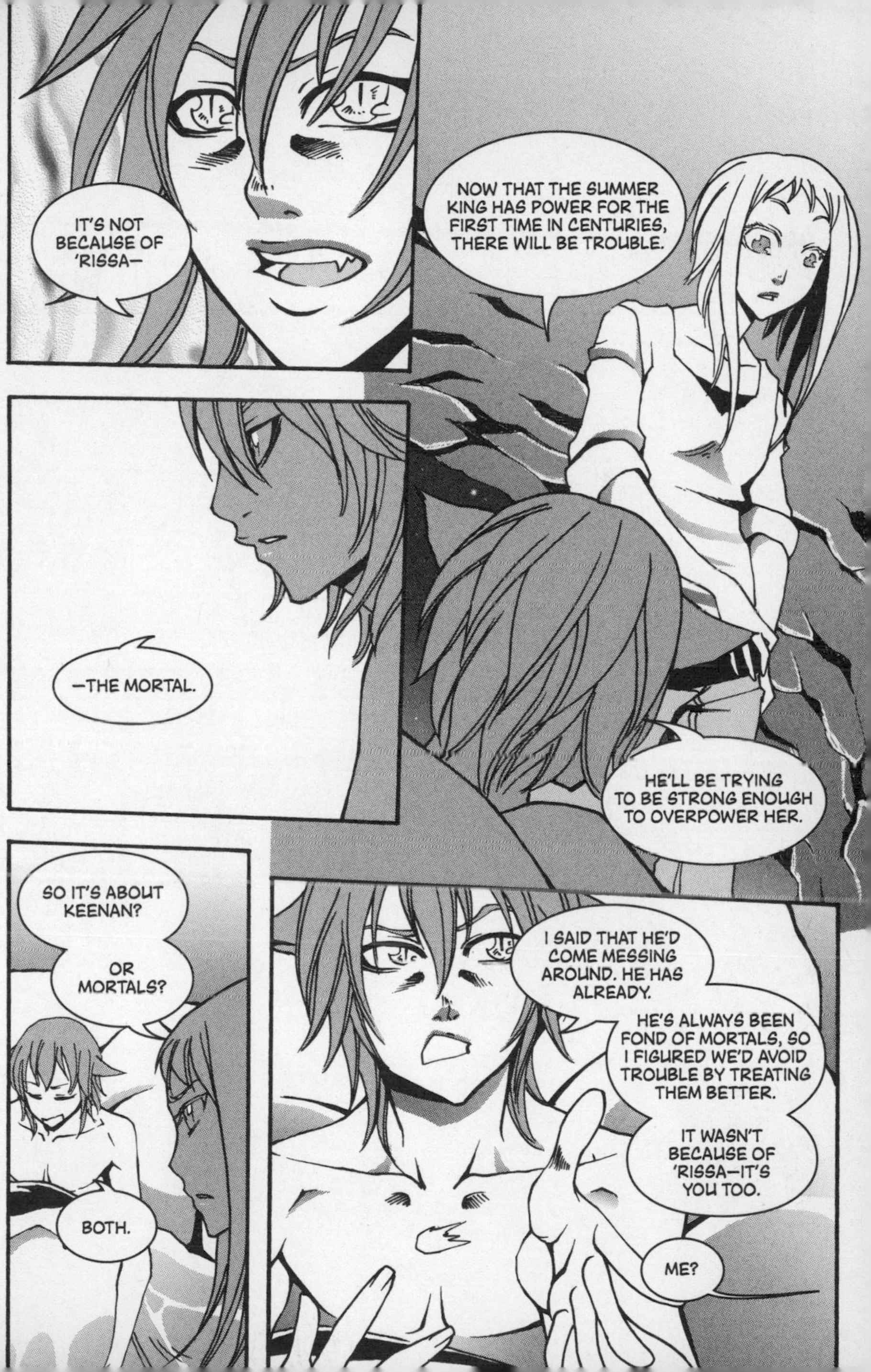
IT'S NOT BECAUSE OF 'RISSA—
—THE MORTAL.
NOW THAT THE SUMMER KING HAS POWER FOR THE FIRST TIME IN CENTURIES, THERE WILL BE TROUBLE.
HE'LL BE TRYING TO BE STRONG ENOUGH TO OVERPOWER HER.
SO IT'S ABOUT KEENAN?
OR MORTALS?
BOTH.
I SAID THAT HE'D COME MESSING AROUND. HE HAS ALREADY.
HE'S ALWAYS BEEN FOND OF MORTALS, SO I FIGURED WE'D AVOID TROUBLE BY TREATING THEM BETTER.
IT WASN'T BECAUSE OF 'RISSA—IT'S YOU TOO.
ME?

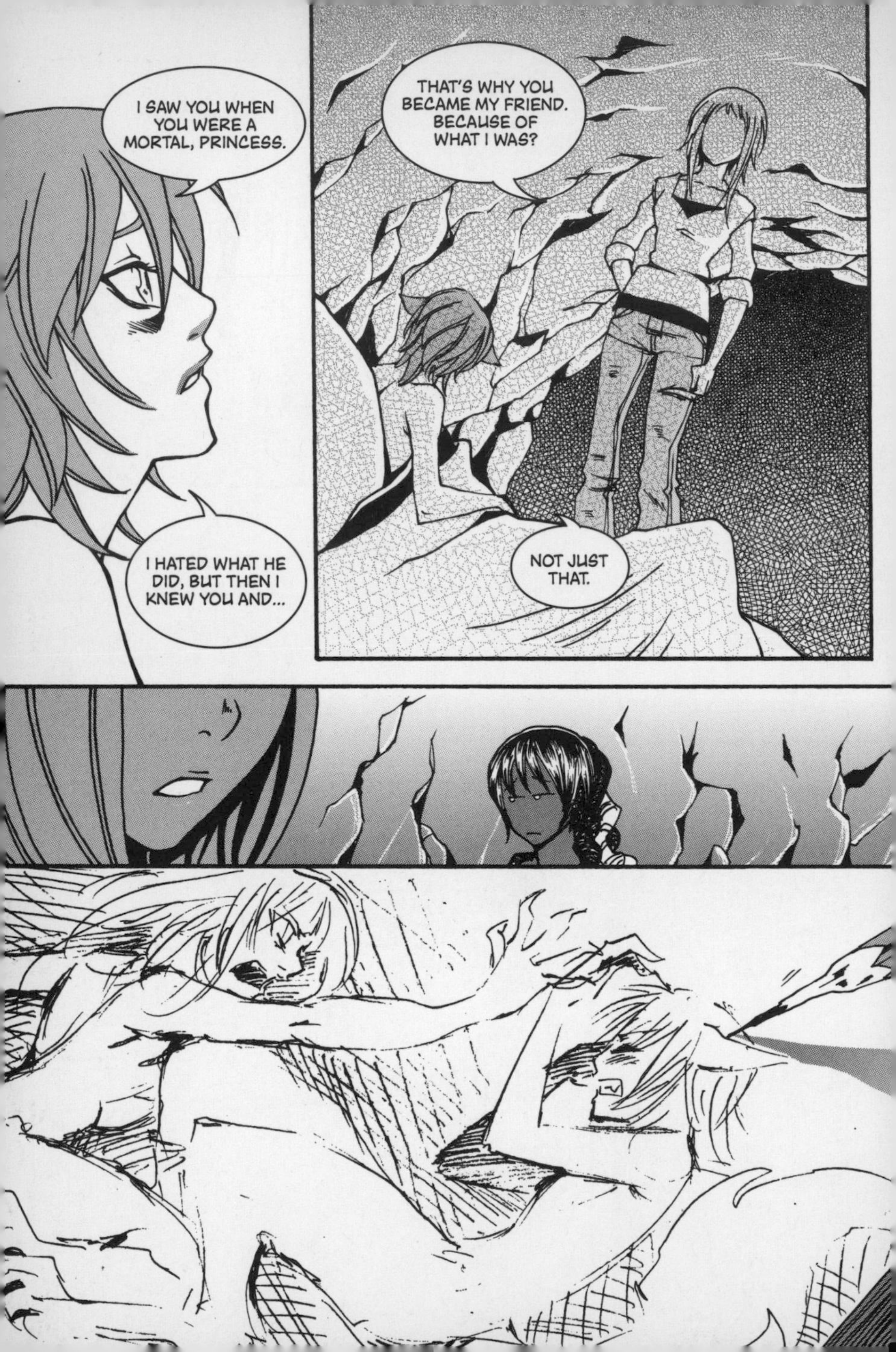
I SAW YOU WHEN YOU WERE A MORTAL, PRINCESS.
I HATED WHAT HE DID, BUT THEN I KNEW YOU AND...
THAT'S WHY YOU BECAME MY FRIEND. BECAUSE OF WHAT I WAS?
NOT JUST THAT.

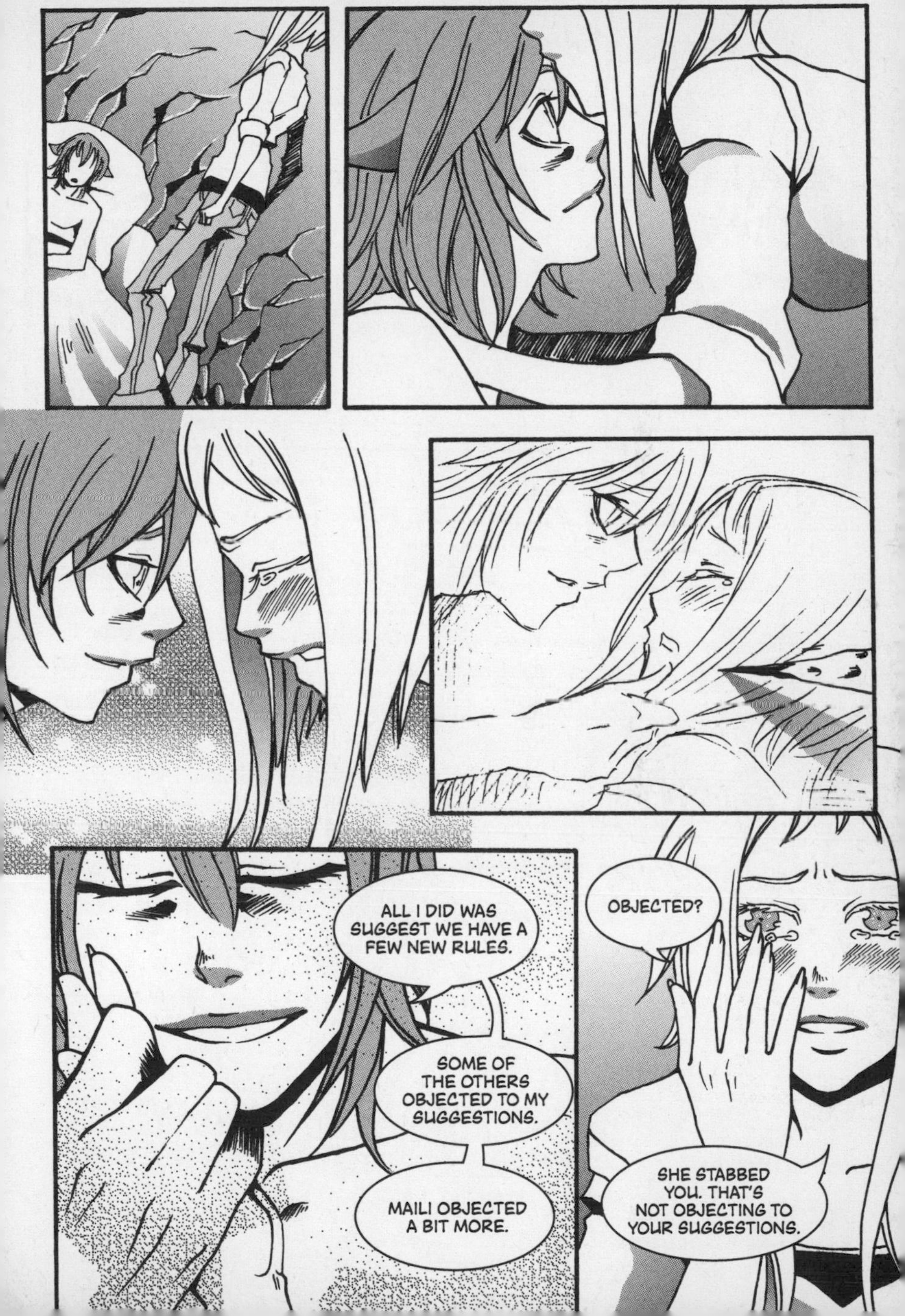
ALL I DID WAS SUGGEST WE HAVE A FEW NEW RULES.
SOME OF THE OTHERS OBJECTED TO MY SUGGESTIONS.
MAILI OBJECTED A BIT MORE.
OBJECTED?
SHE STABBED YOU. THAT'S NOT OBJECTING TO YOUR SUGGESTIONS.

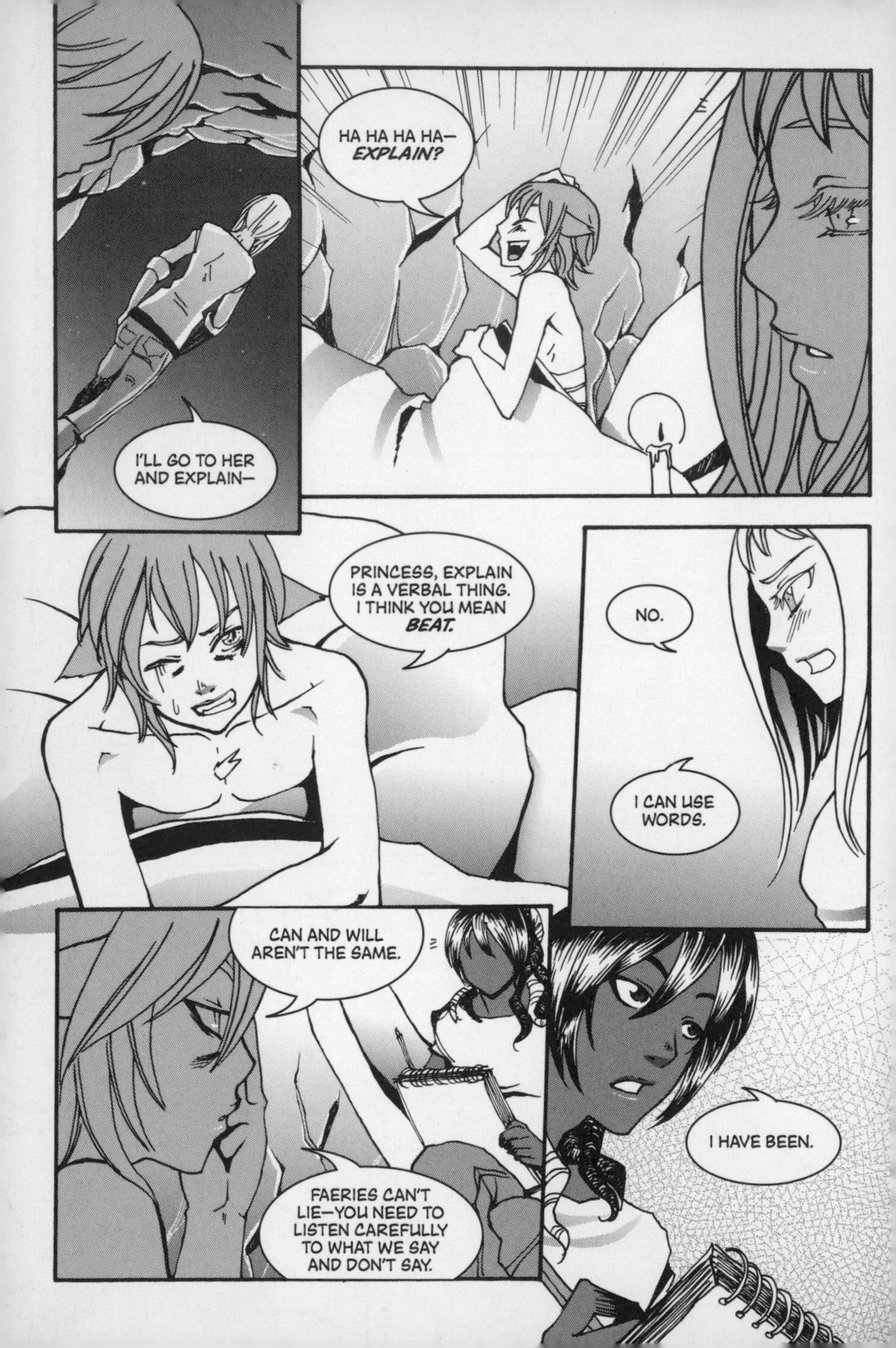
I'LL GO TO HER AND EXPLAIN—
HA HA HA HA— *EXPLAIN?*
PRINCESS, EXPLAIN IS A VERBAL THING. I THINK YOU MEAN *BEAT.*
NO.
I CAN USE WORDS.
CAN AND WILL AREN'T THE SAME.
FAERIES CAN'T LIE—YOU NEED TO LISTEN CAREFULLY TO WHAT WE SAY AND DON'T SAY.
I HAVE BEEN.

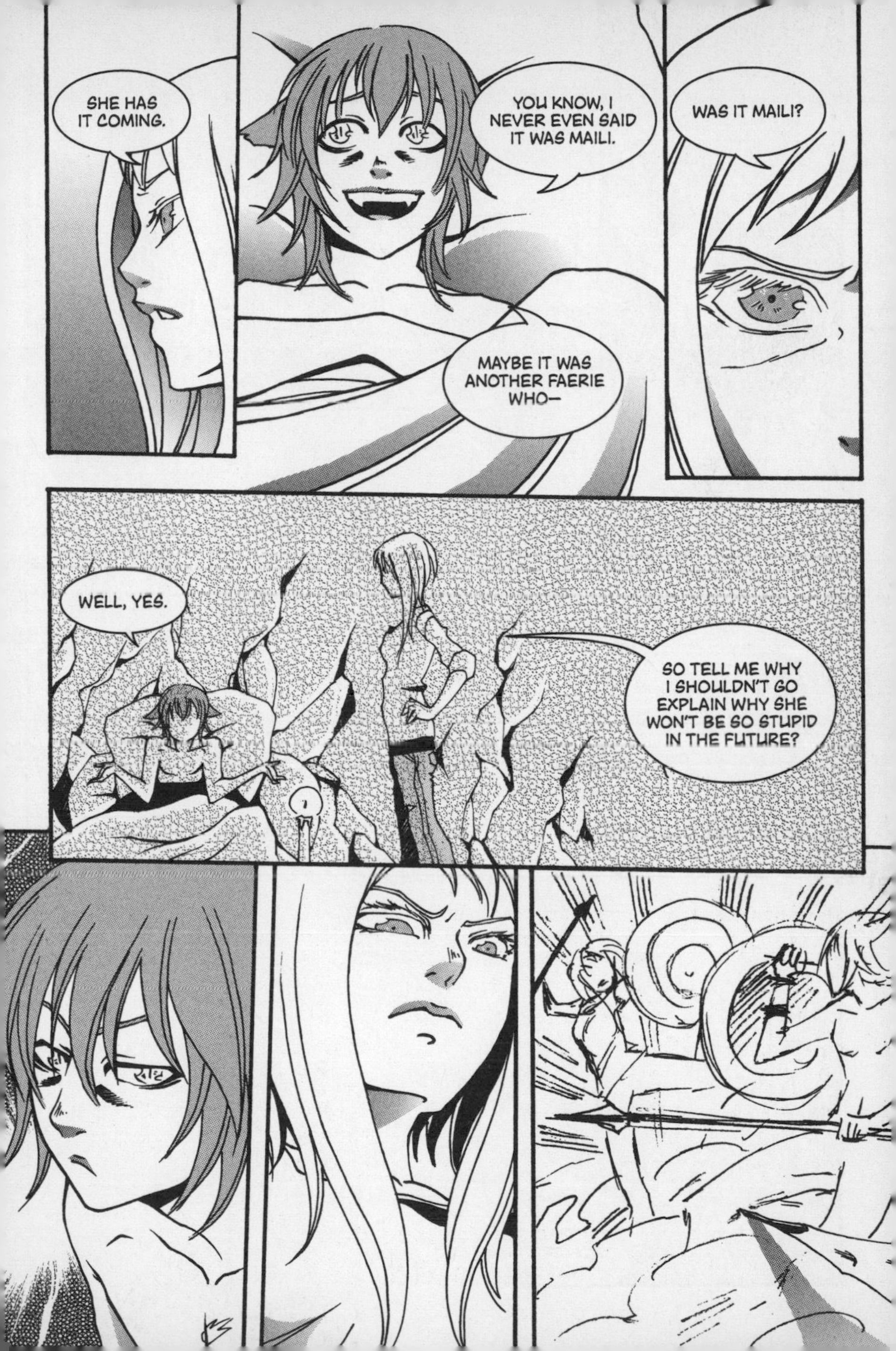
SHE HAS IT COMING.
YOU KNOW, I NEVER EVEN SAID IT WAS MAILI.
MAYBE IT WAS ANOTHER FAERIE WHO—
WAS IT MAILI?
WELL, YES.
SO TELL ME WHY I SHOULDN'T GO EXPLAIN WHY SHE WON'T BE SO STUPID IN THE FUTURE?

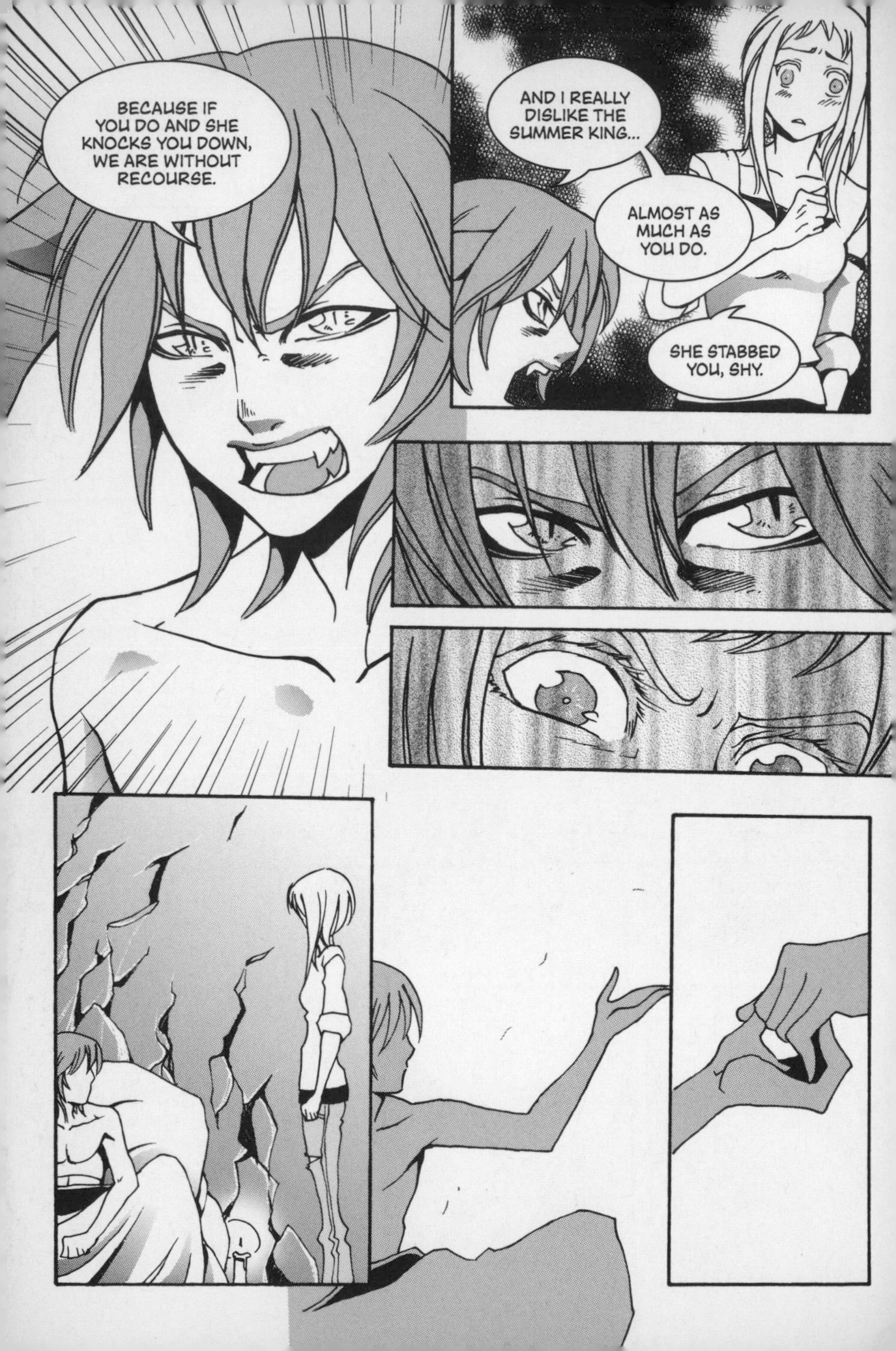
BECAUSE IF YOU DO AND SHE KNOCKS YOU DOWN, WE ARE WITHOUT RECOURSE.
AND I REALLY DISLIKE THE SUMMER KING...
ALMOST AS MUCH AS YOU DO.
SHE STABBED YOU, SHY.

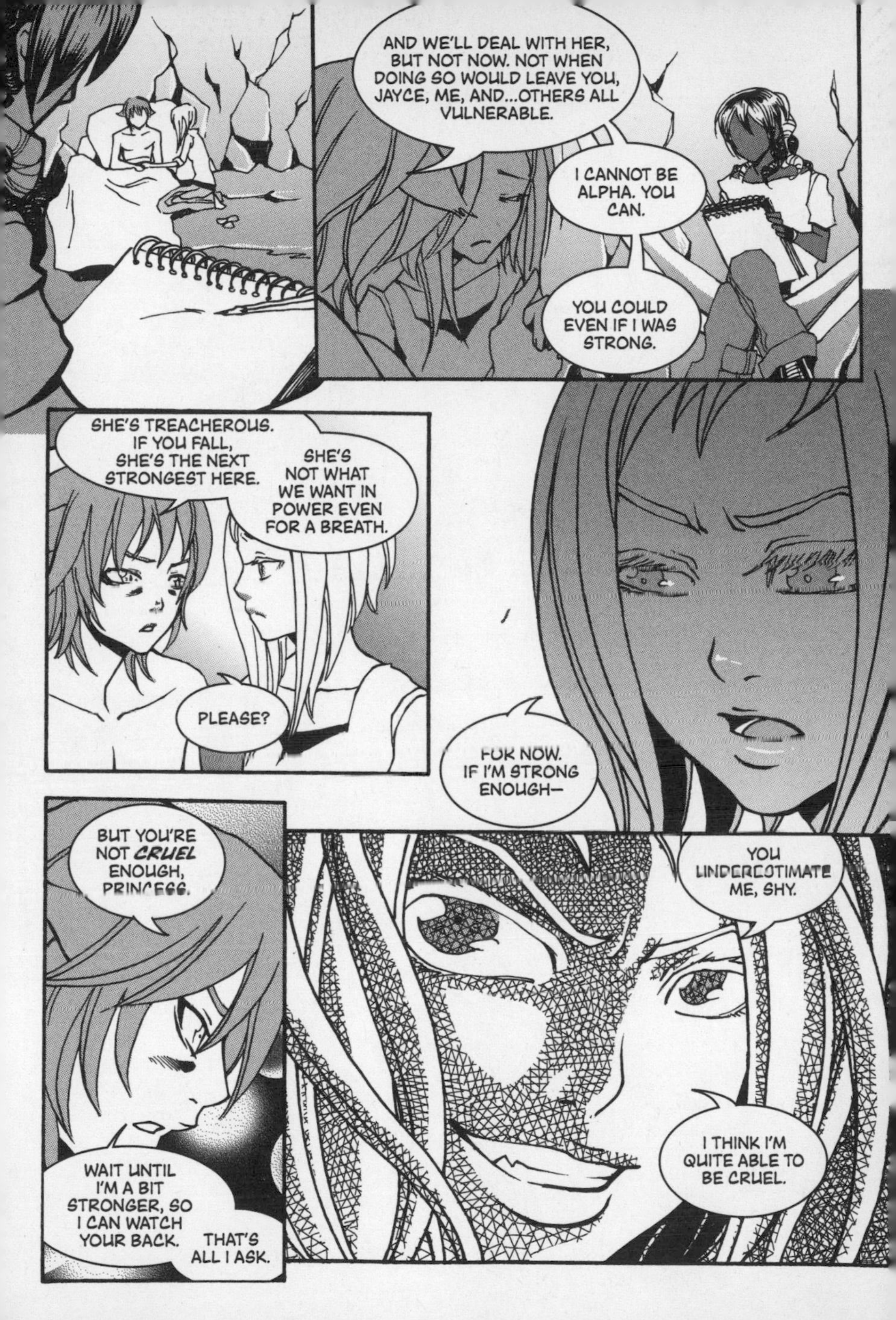
AND WE'LL DEAL WITH HER, BUT NOT NOW. NOT WHEN DOING SO WOULD LEAVE YOU, JAYCE, ME, AND...OTHERS ALL VULNERABLE.
I CANNOT BE ALPHA. YOU CAN.
YOU COULD EVEN IF I WAS STRONG.
SHE'S TREACHEROUS. IF YOU FALL, SHE'S THE NEXT STRONGEST HERE.
SHE'S NOT WHAT WE WANT IN POWER EVEN FOR A BREATH.
PLEASE?
FOR NOW. IF I'M STRONG ENOUGH—
BUT YOU'RE NOT CRUEL ENOUGH, PRINCESS.
WAIT UNTIL I'M A BIT STRONGER, SO I CAN WATCH YOUR BACK.
THAT'S ALL I ASK.
YOU UNDERESTIMATE ME, SHY.
I THINK I'M QUITE ABLE TO BE CRUEL.

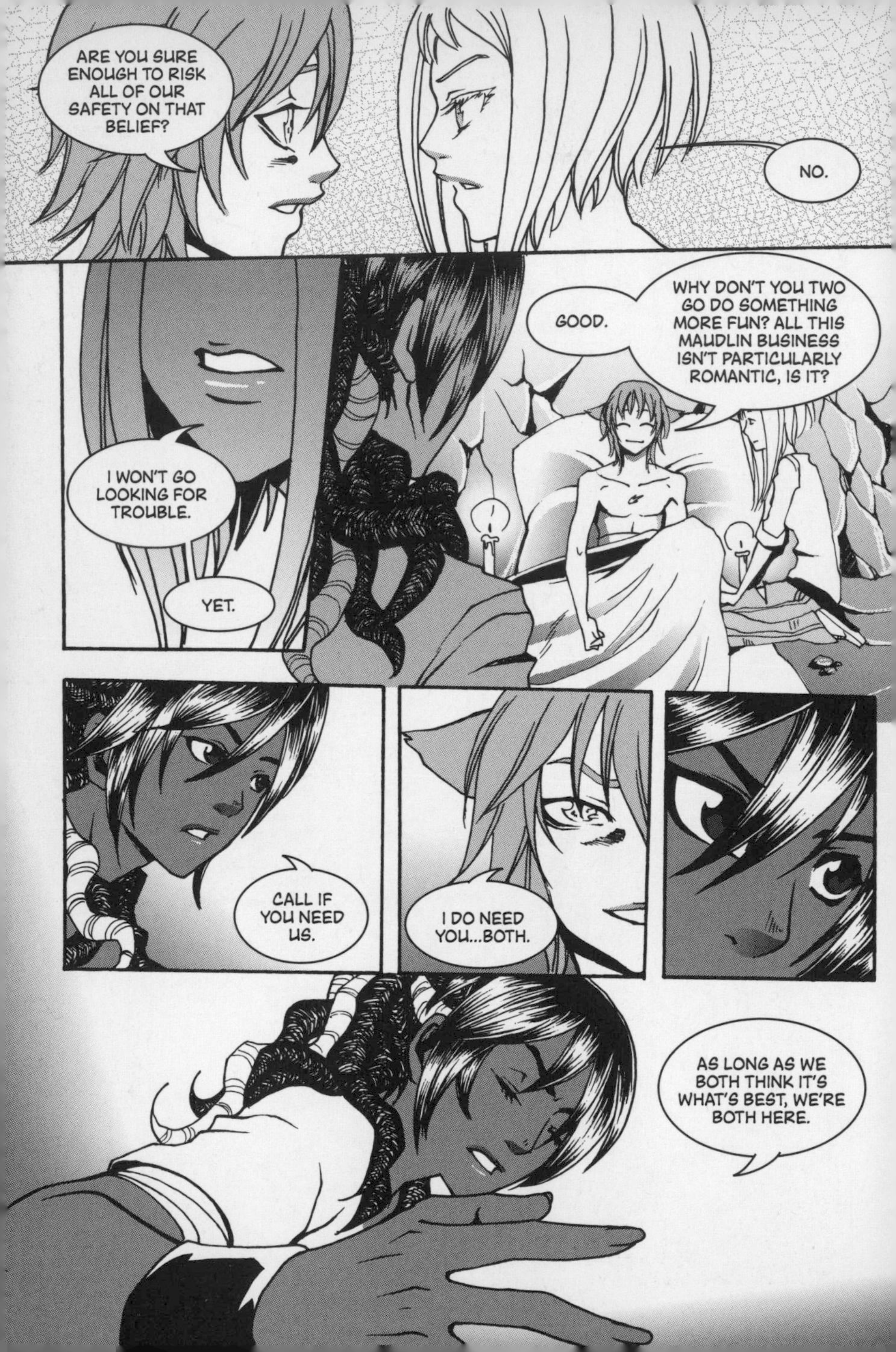
ARE YOU SURE ENOUGH TO RISK ALL OF OUR SAFETY ON THAT BELIEF?
NO.
I WON'T GO LOOKING FOR TROUBLE.
YET.
GOOD.
WHY DON'T YOU TWO GO DO SOMETHING MORE FUN? ALL THIS MAUDLIN BUSINESS ISN'T PARTICULARLY ROMANTIC, IS IT?
CALL IF YOU NEED US.
I DO NEED YOU...BOTH.
AS LONG AS WE BOTH THINK IT'S WHAT'S BEST, WE'RE BOTH HERE.

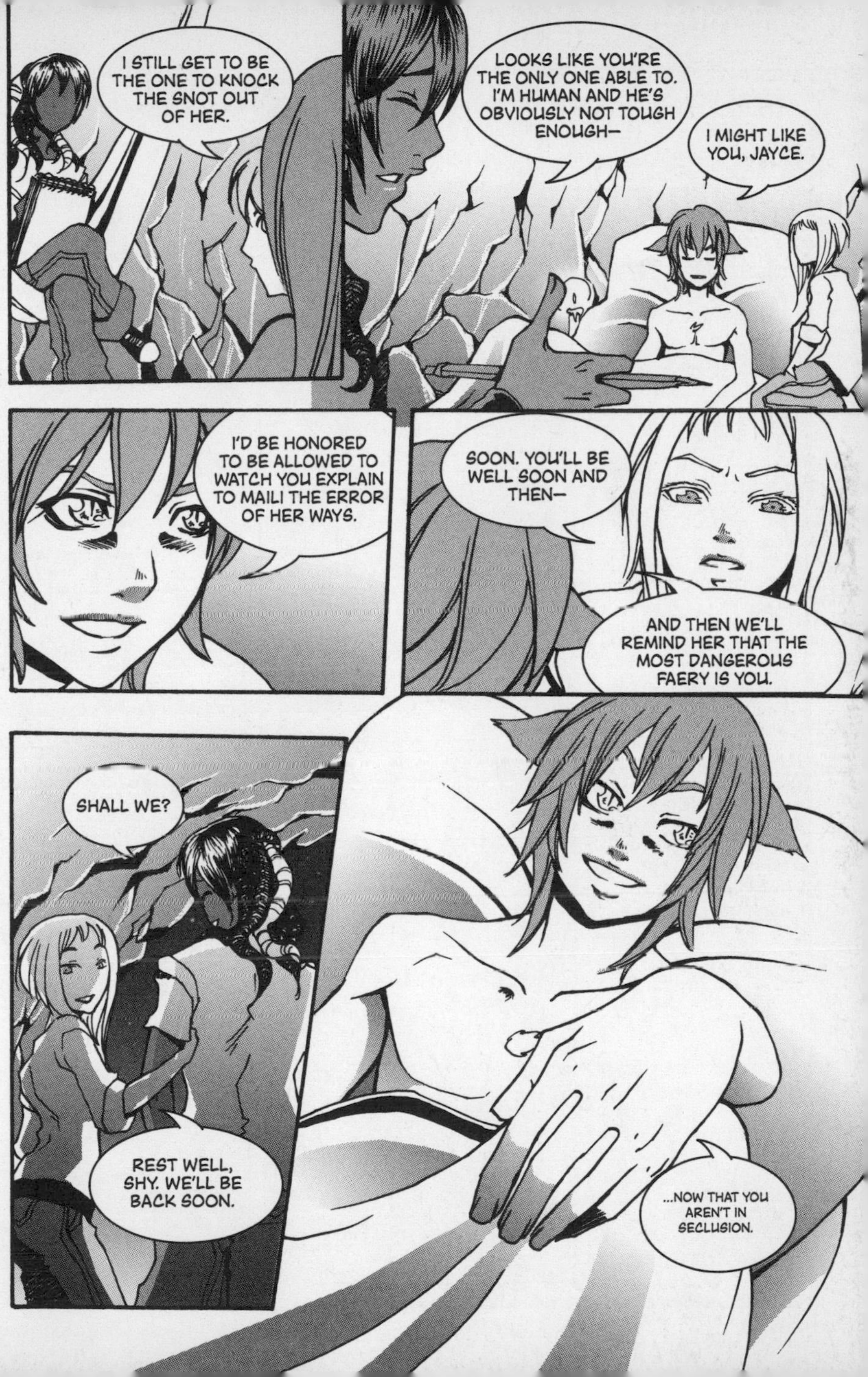
I STILL GET TO BE THE ONE TO KNOCK THE SNOT OUT OF HER.
LOOKS LIKE YOU'RE THE ONLY ONE ABLE TO. I'M HUMAN AND HE'S OBVIOUSLY NOT TOUGH ENOUGH—
I MIGHT LIKE YOU, JAYCE.
I'D BE HONORED TO BE ALLOWED TO WATCH YOU EXPLAIN TO MAILI THE ERROR OF HER WAYS.
SOON. YOU'LL BE WELL SOON AND THEN—
AND THEN WE'LL REMIND HER THAT THE MOST DANGEROUS FAERY IS YOU.
SHALL WE?
REST WELL, SHY. WE'LL BE BACK SOON.
...NOW THAT YOU AREN'T IN SECLUSION.

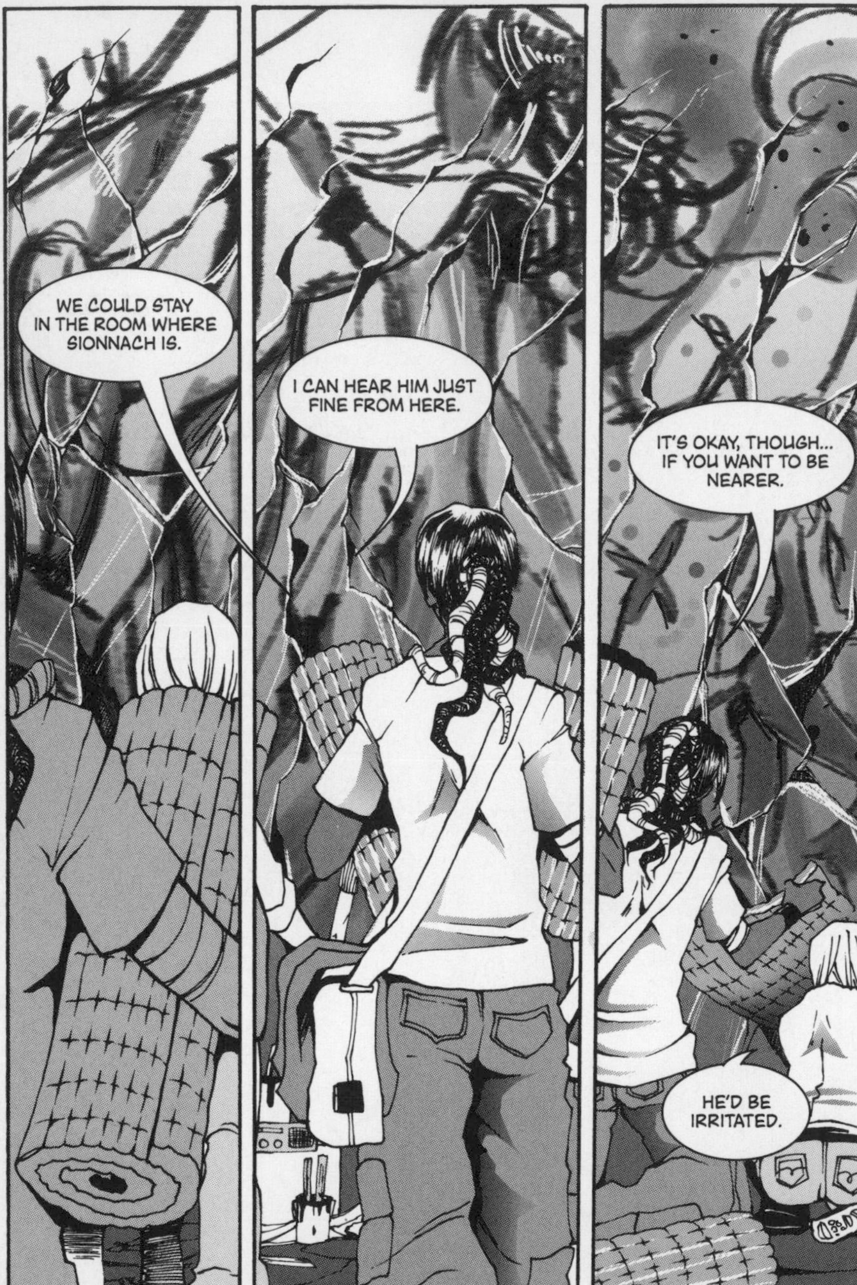
WE COULD STAY IN THE ROOM WHERE SIONNACH IS.
I CAN HEAR HIM JUST FINE FROM HERE.
IT'S OKAY, THOUGH... IF YOU WANT TO BE NEARER.
HE'D BE IRRITATED.

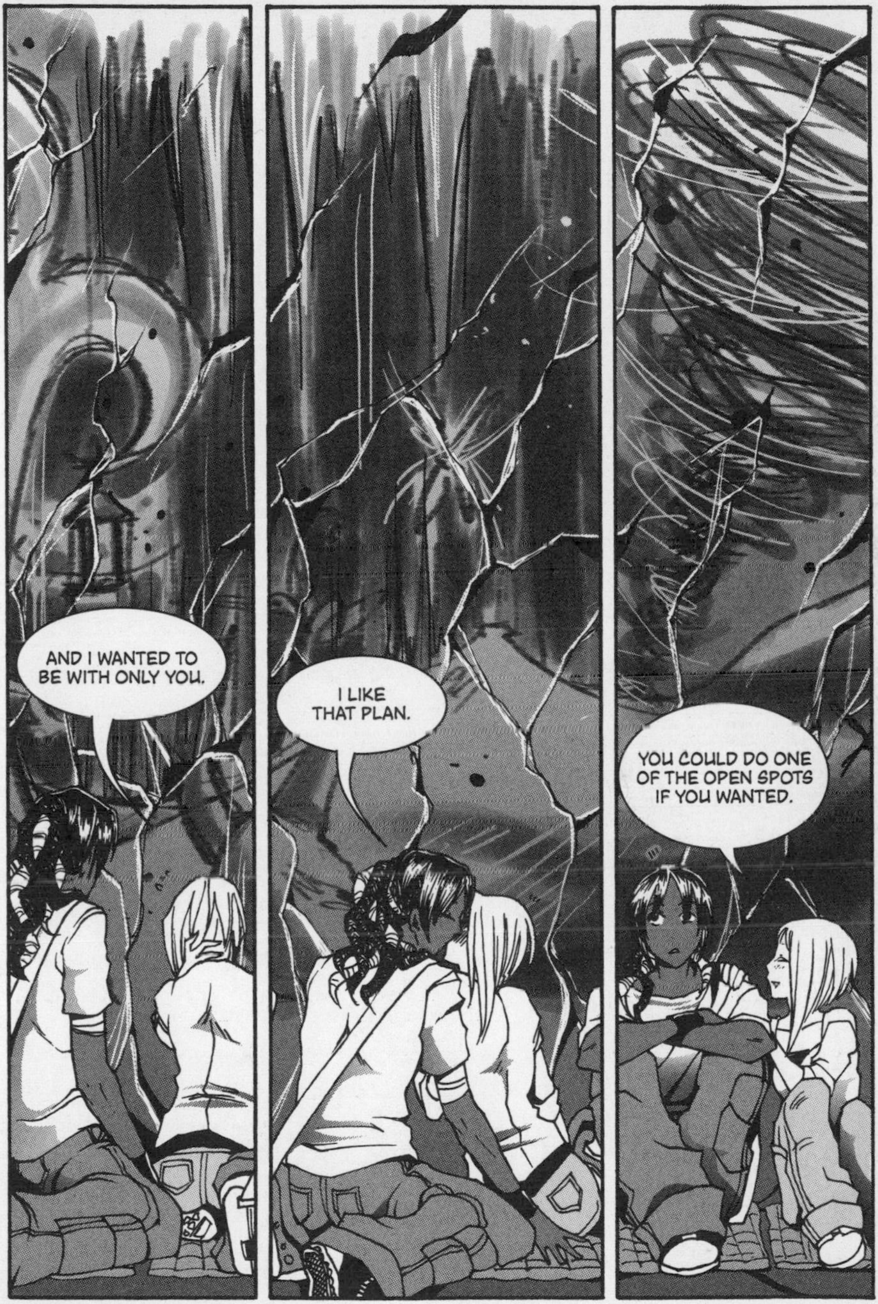
AND I WANTED TO BE WITH ONLY YOU.
I LIKE THAT PLAN.
YOU COULD DO ONE OF THE OPEN SPOTS IF YOU WANTED.

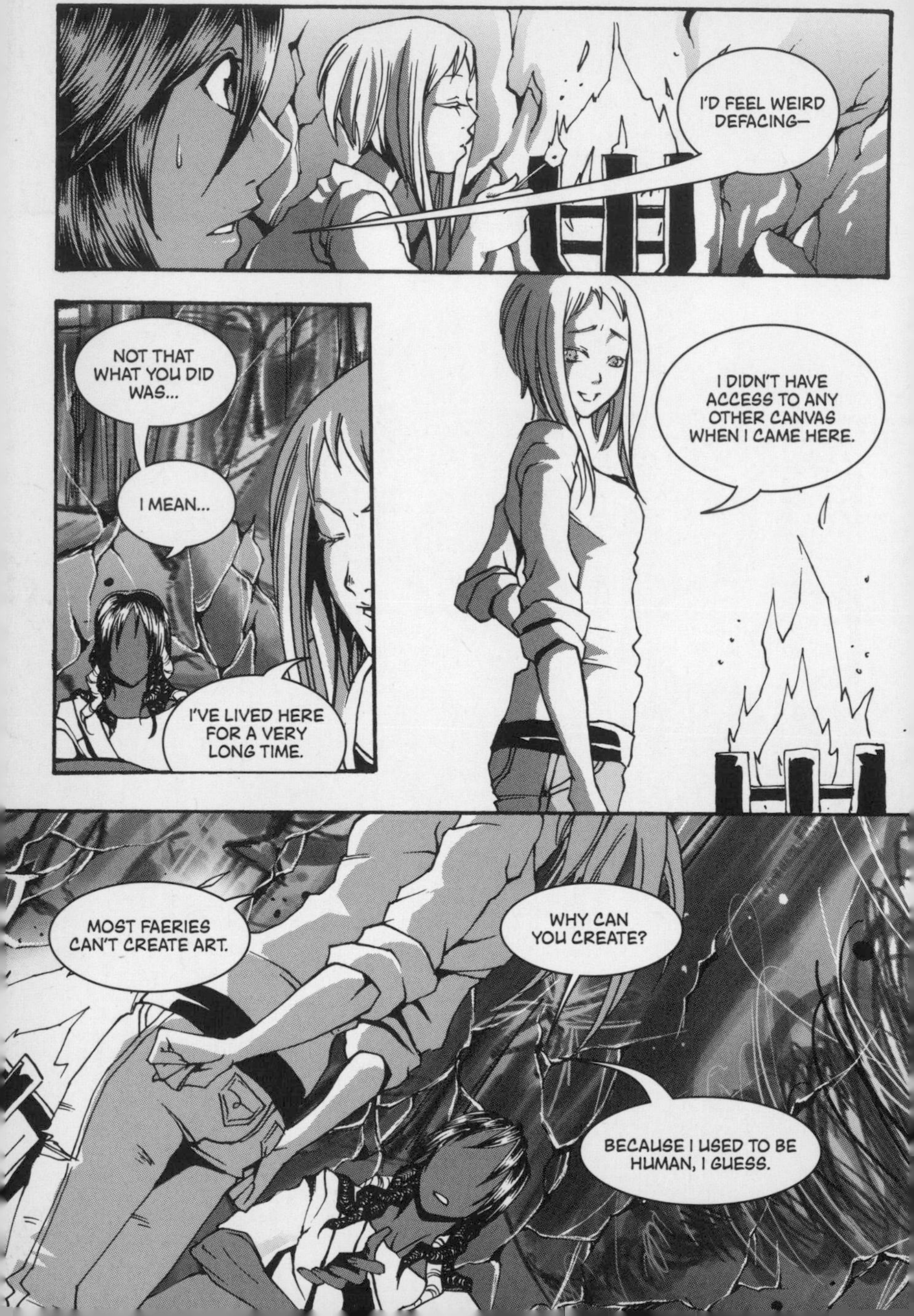
I'D FEEL WEIRD DEFACING—
NOT THAT WHAT YOU DID WAS...
I MEAN...
I'VE LIVED HERE FOR A VERY LONG TIME.
I DIDN'T HAVE ACCESS TO ANY OTHER CANVAS WHEN I CAME HERE.
MOST FAERIES CAN'T CREATE ART.
WHY CAN YOU CREATE?
BECAUSE I USED TO BE HUMAN, I GUESS.

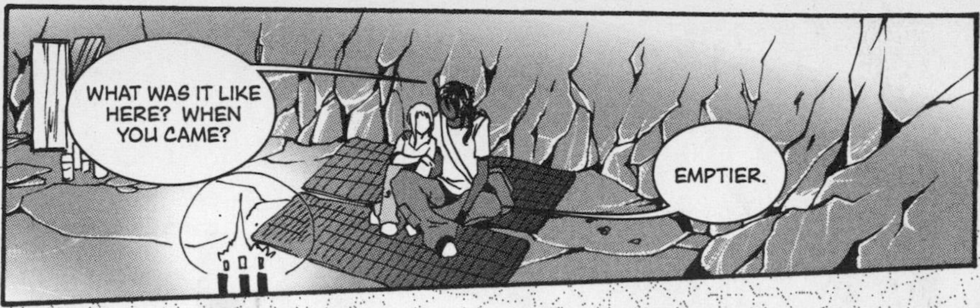
WHAT WAS IT LIKE HERE? WHEN YOU CAME?
EMPTIER.

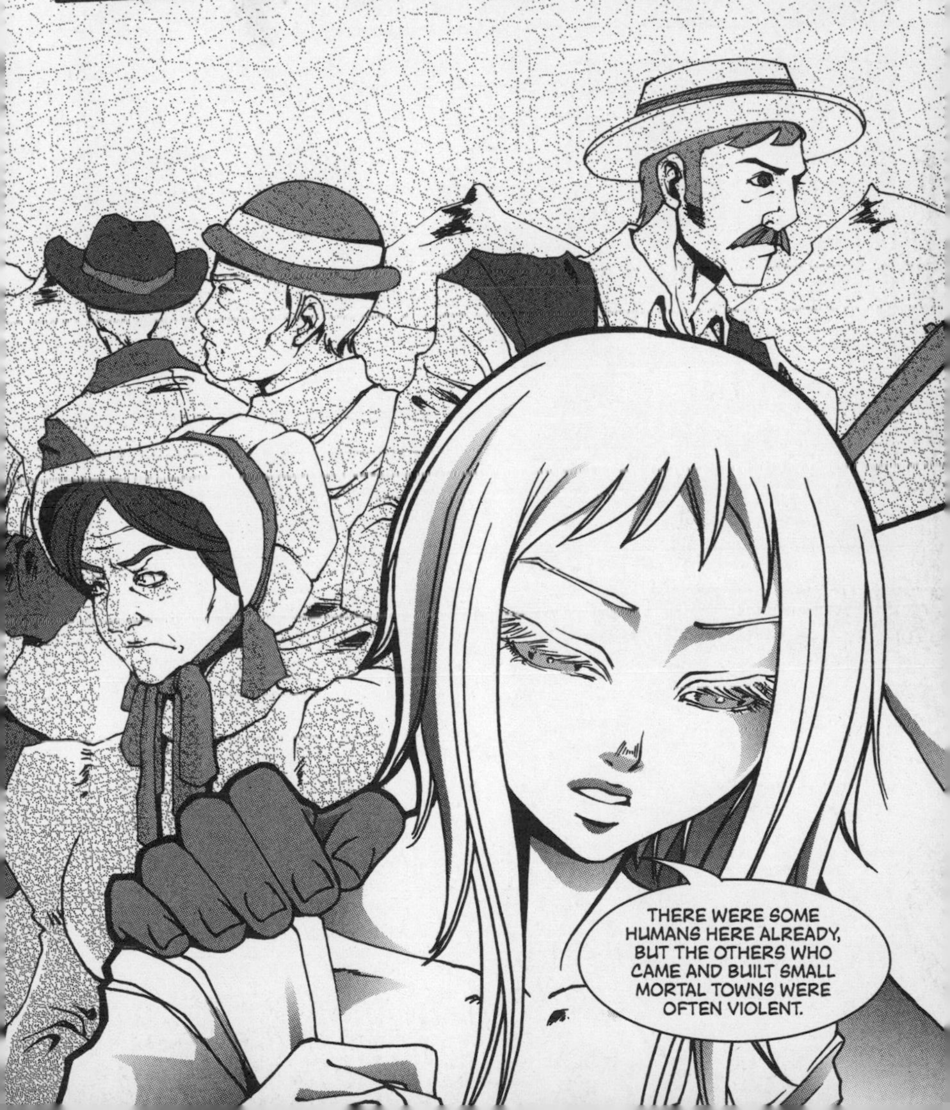
THERE WERE SOME HUMANS HERE ALREADY, BUT THE OTHERS WHO CAME AND BUILT SMALL MORTAL TOWNS WERE OFTEN VIOLENT.

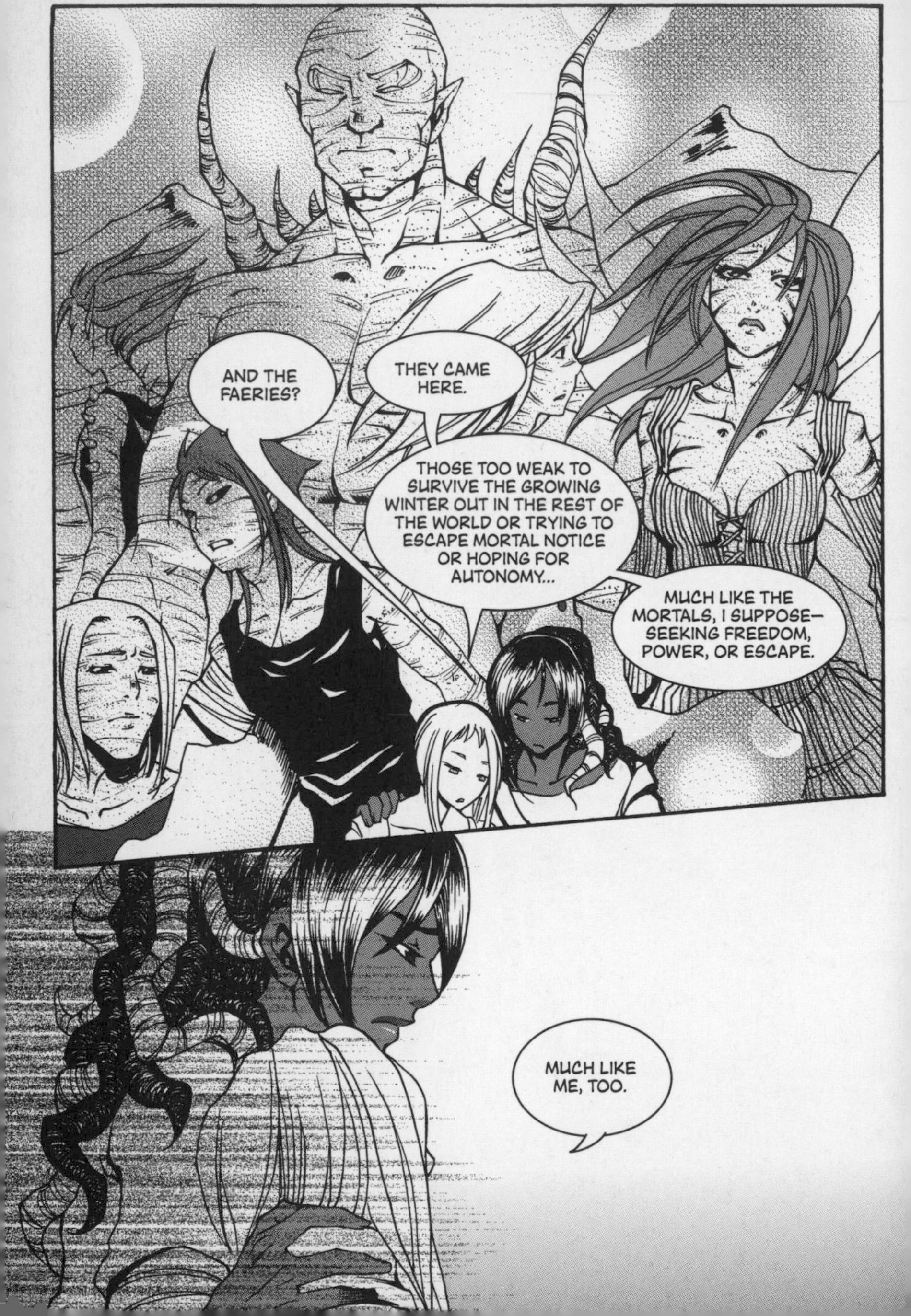
AND THE FAERIES?
THEY CAME HERE.
THOSE TOO WEAK TO SURVIVE THE GROWING WINTER OUT IN THE REST OF THE WORLD OR TRYING TO ESCAPE MORTAL NOTICE OR HOPING FOR AUTONOMY...
MUCH LIKE THE MORTALS, I SUPPOSE— SEEKING FREEDOM, POWER, OR ESCAPE.
MUCH LIKE ME, TOO.

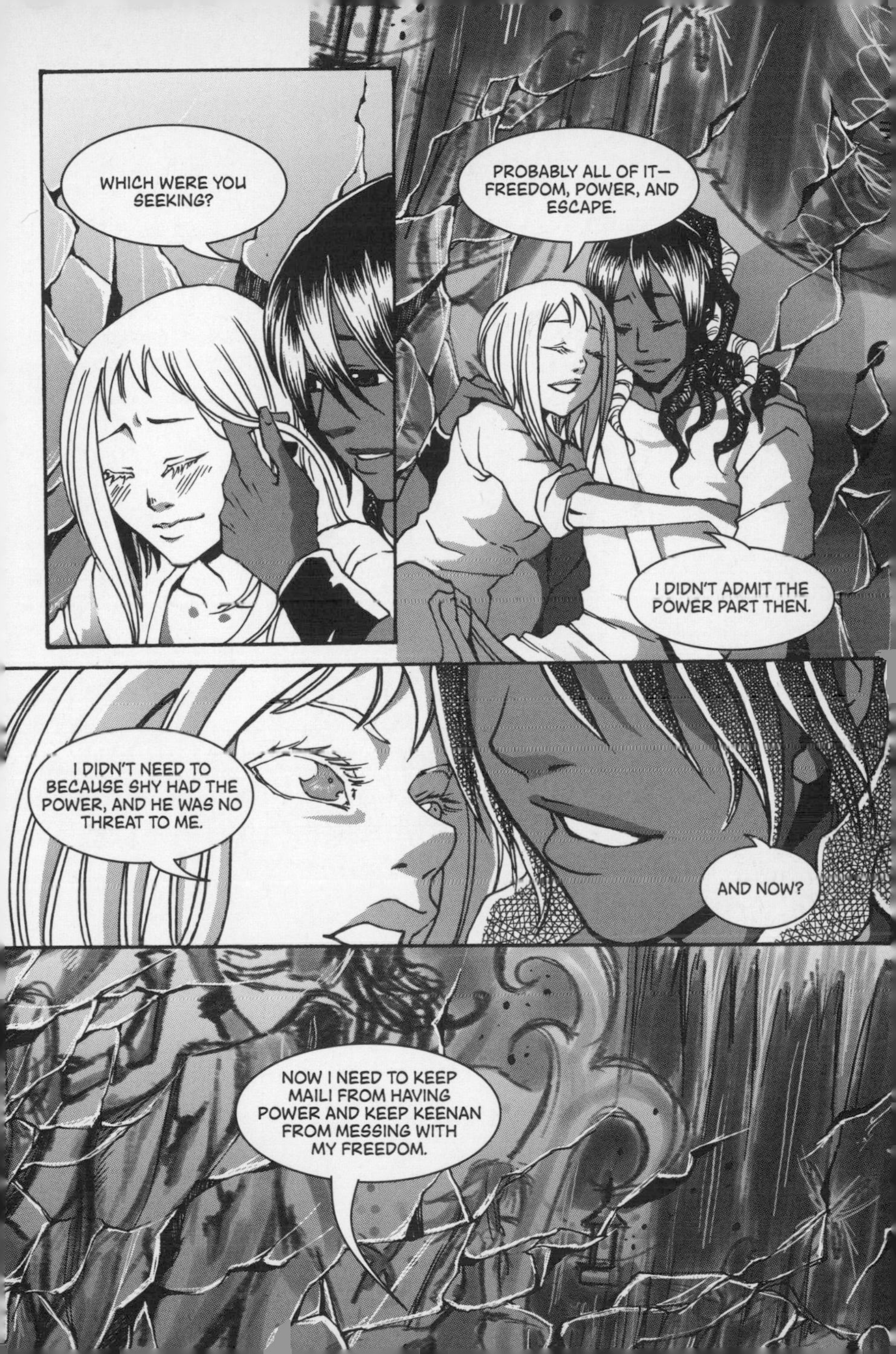
WHICH WERE YOU SEEKING?
PROBABLY ALL OF IT—FREEDOM, POWER, AND ESCAPE.
I DIDN'T ADMIT THE POWER PART THEN.
I DIDN'T NEED TO BECAUSE SHY HAD THE POWER, AND HE WAS NO THREAT TO ME.
AND NOW?
NOW I NEED TO KEEP MAILI FROM HAVING POWER AND KEEP KEENAN FROM MESSING WITH MY FREEDOM.

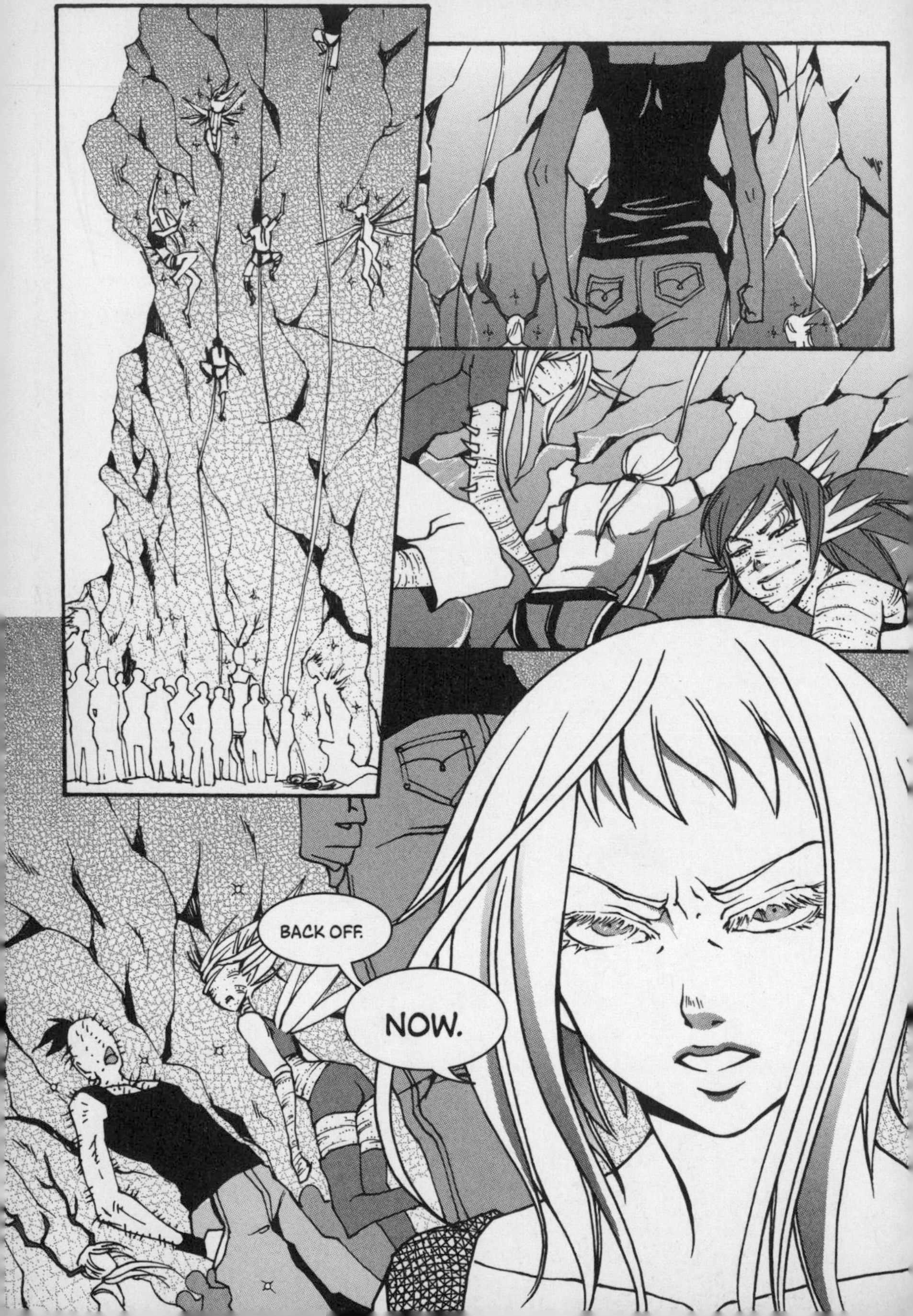
BACK OFF.
NOW.

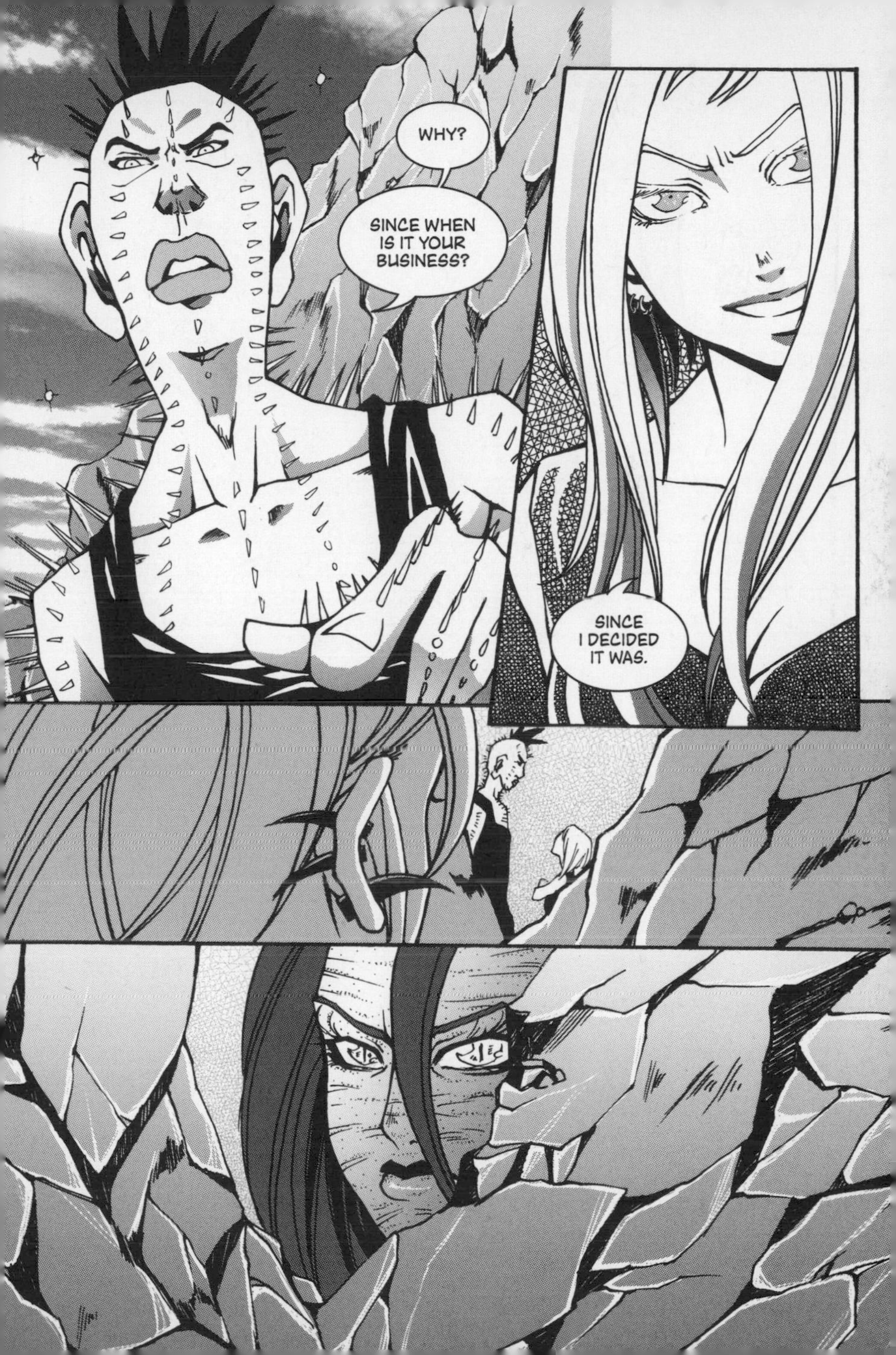
WHY?
SINCE WHEN IS IT YOUR BUSINESS?
SINCE I DECIDED IT WAS.

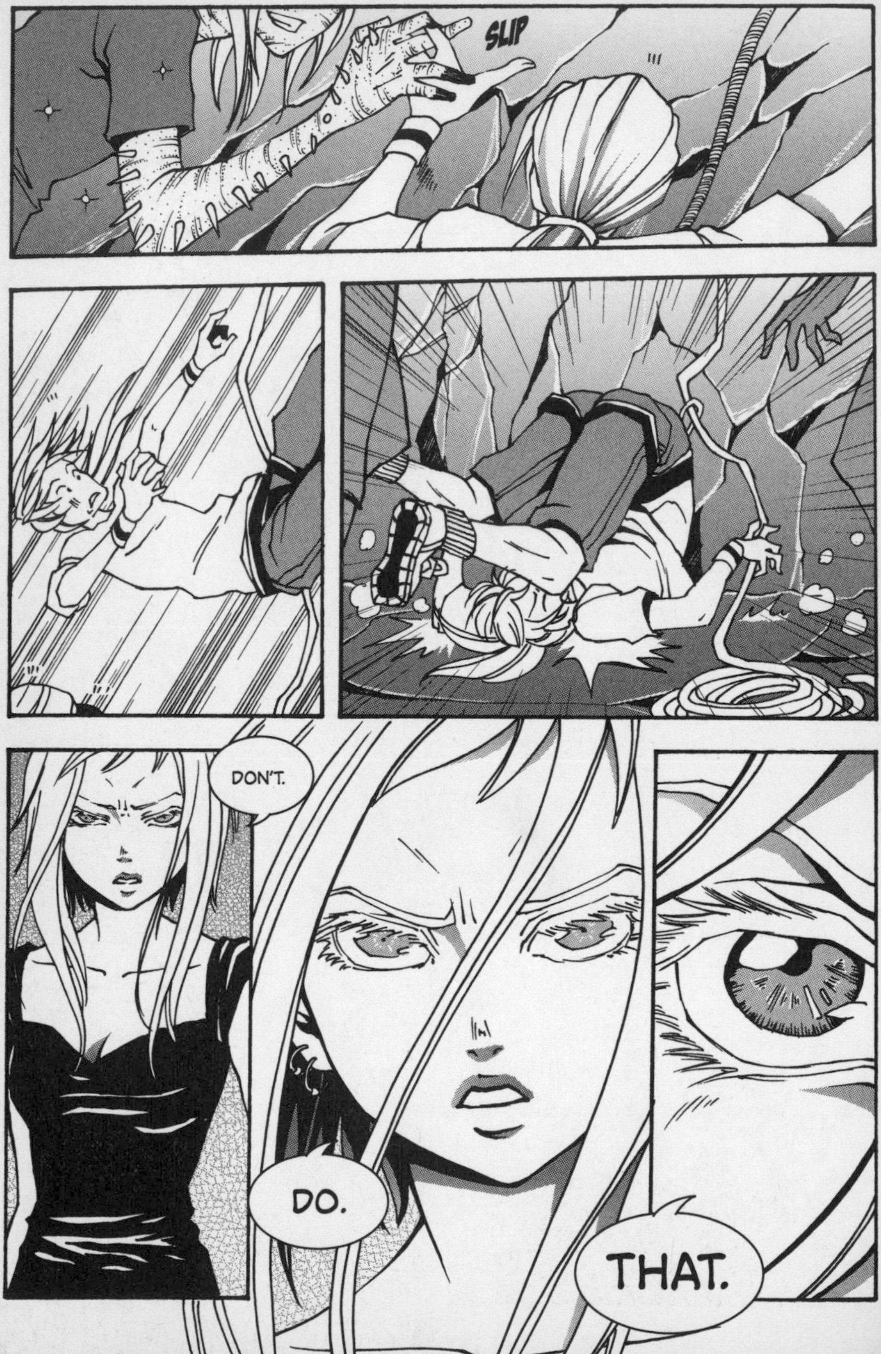
SLIP
DON'T.
DO.
THAT.

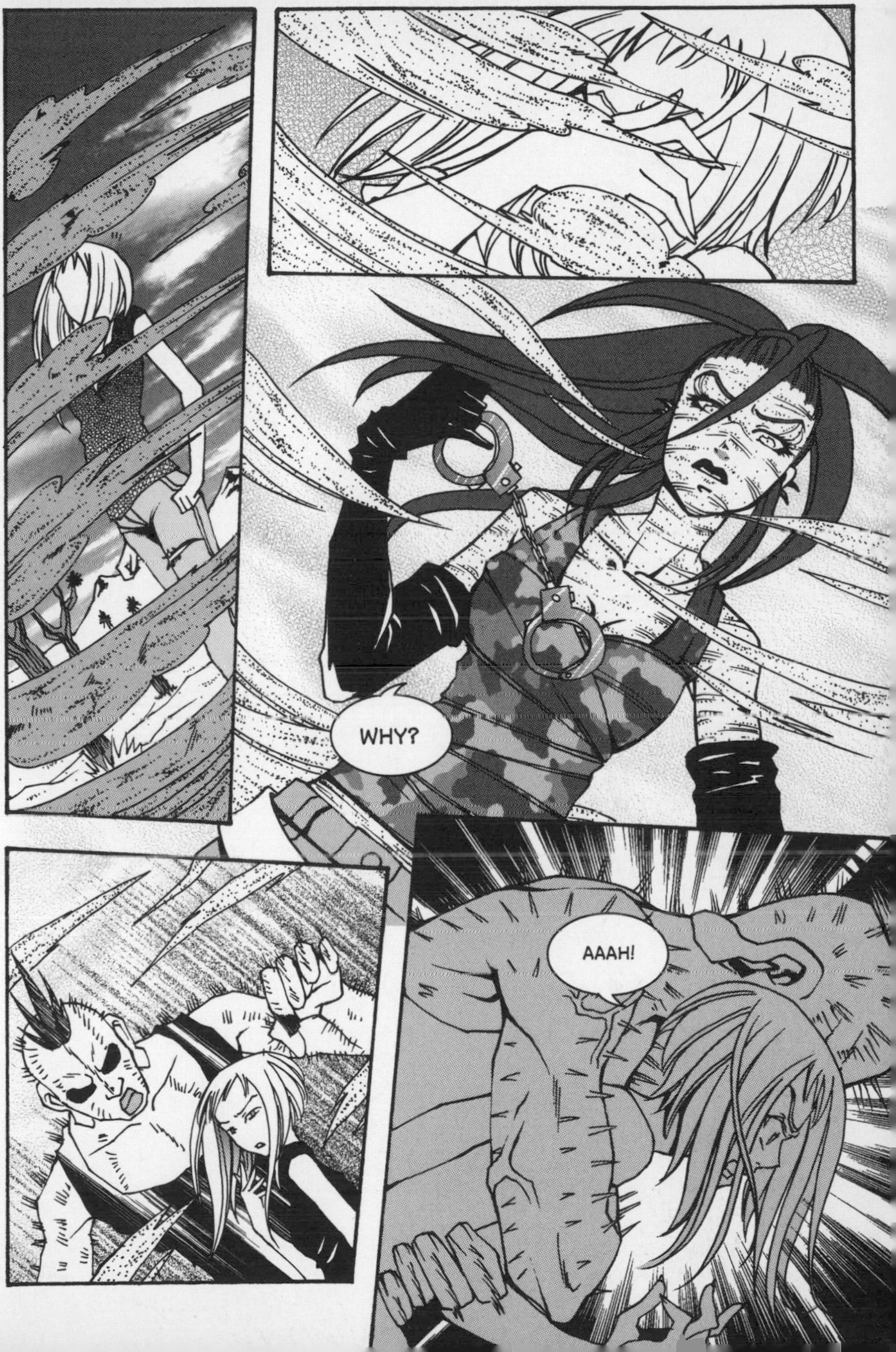
WHY?
AAAH!

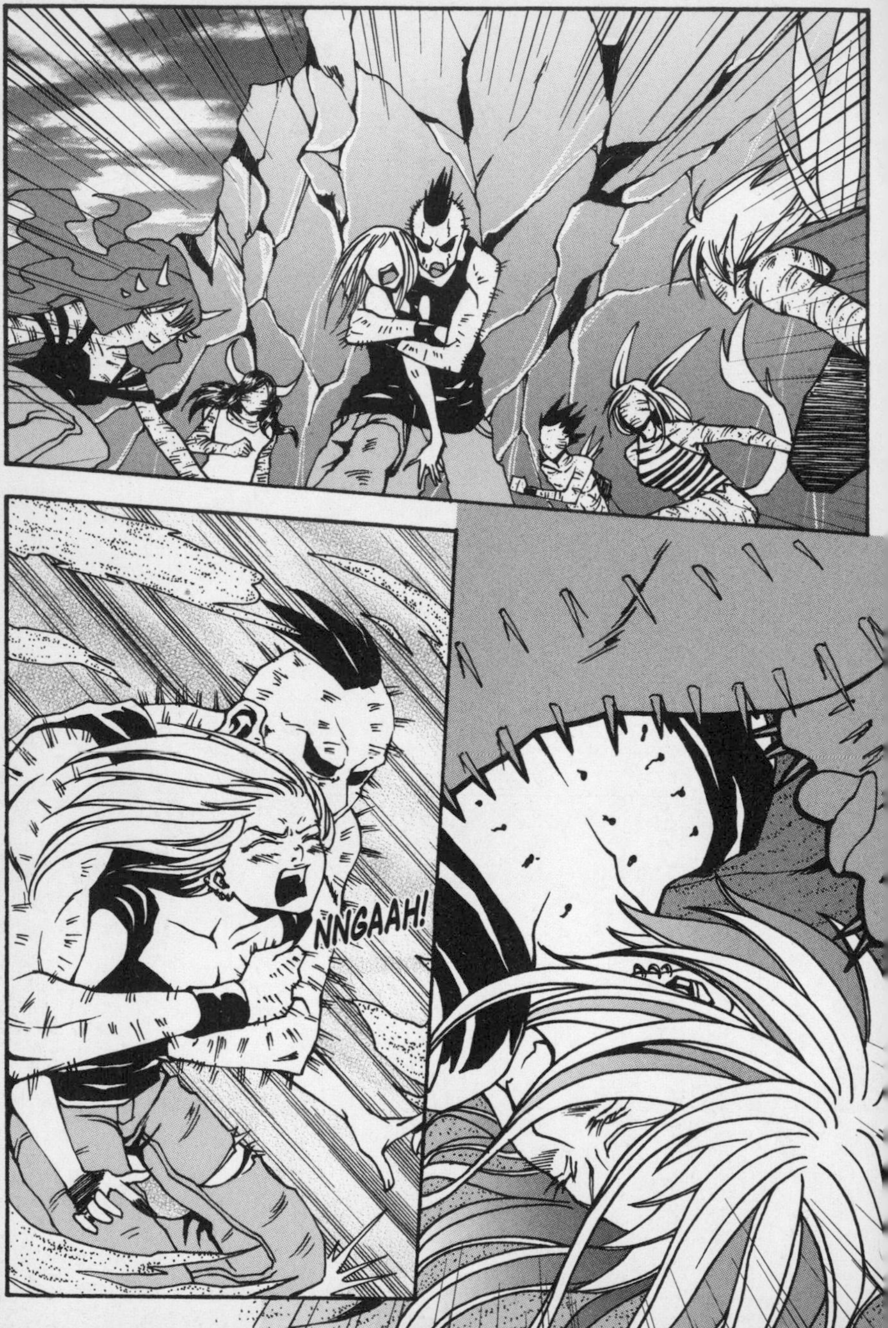
NNGAAH!

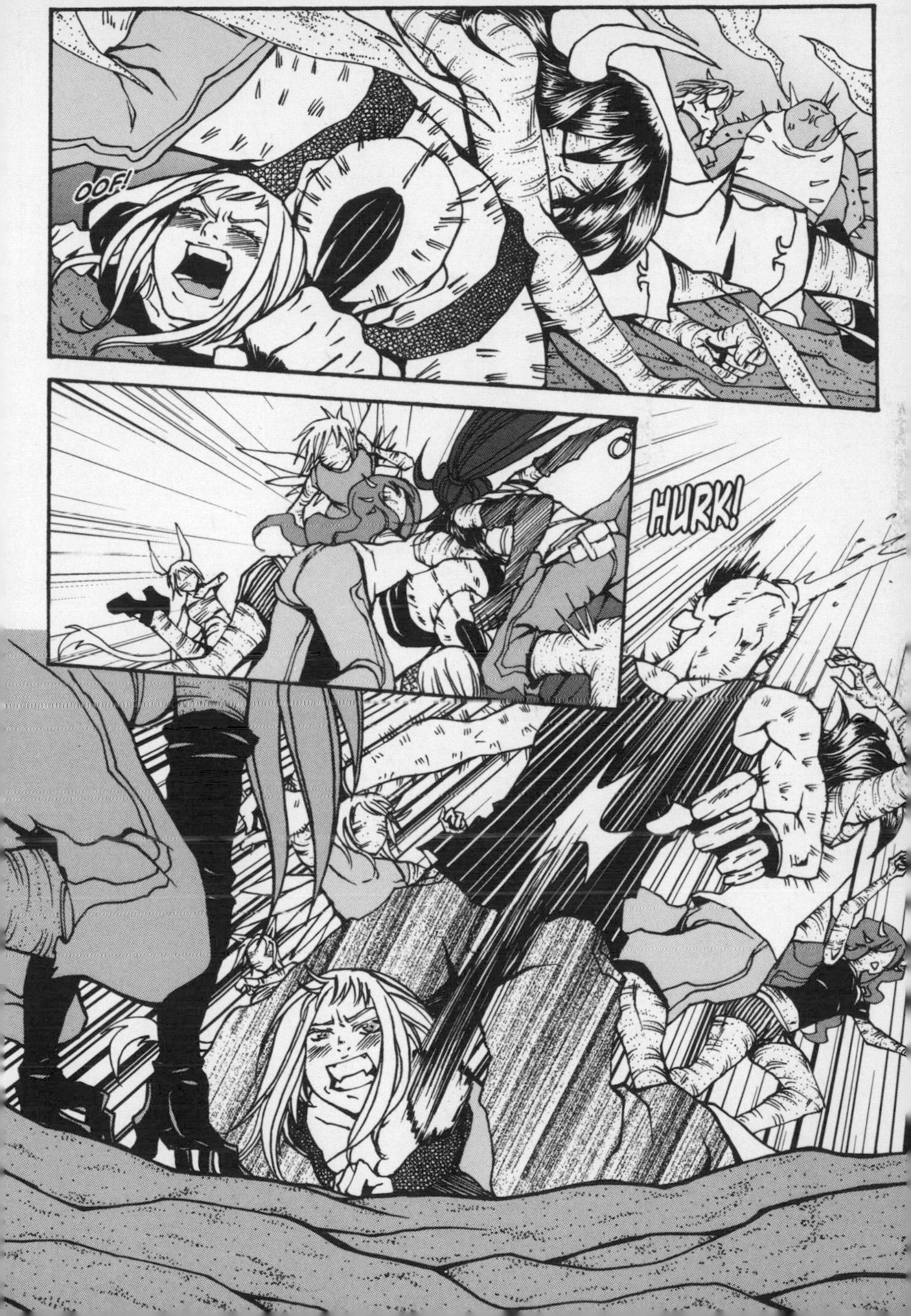
OOF!
HURK!

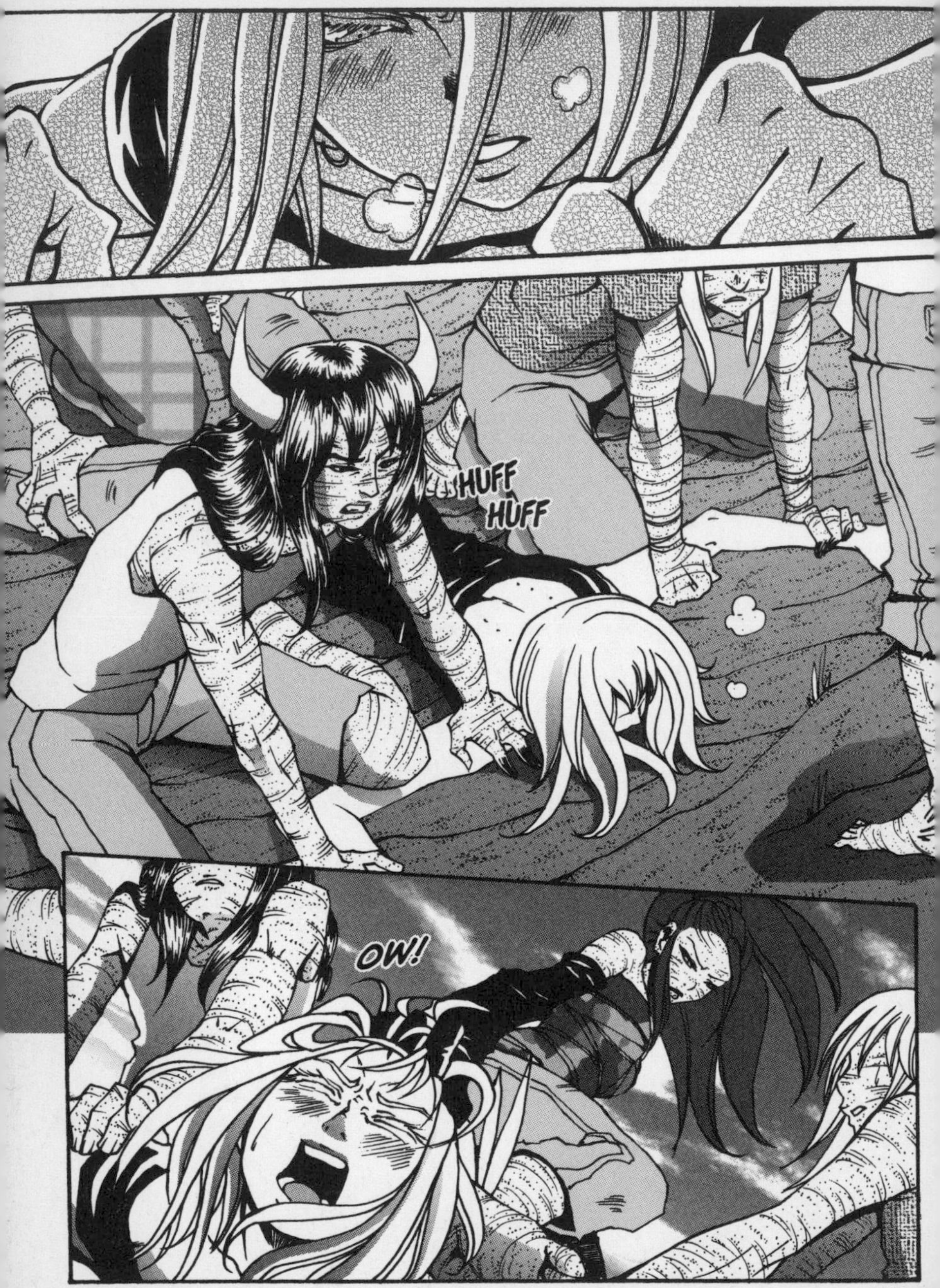
HUFF
HUFF
OW!

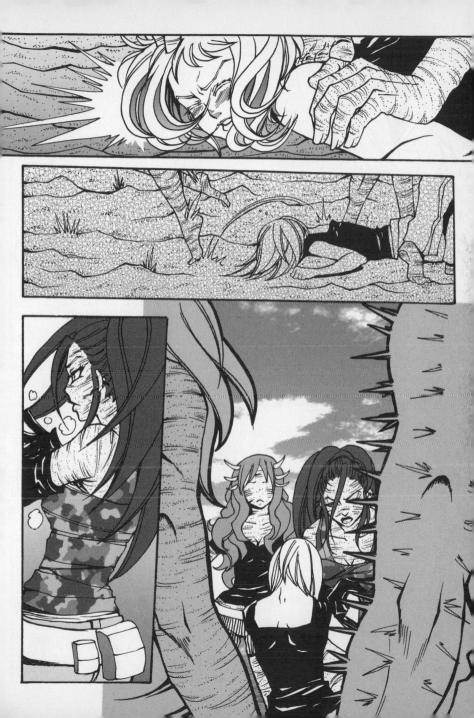

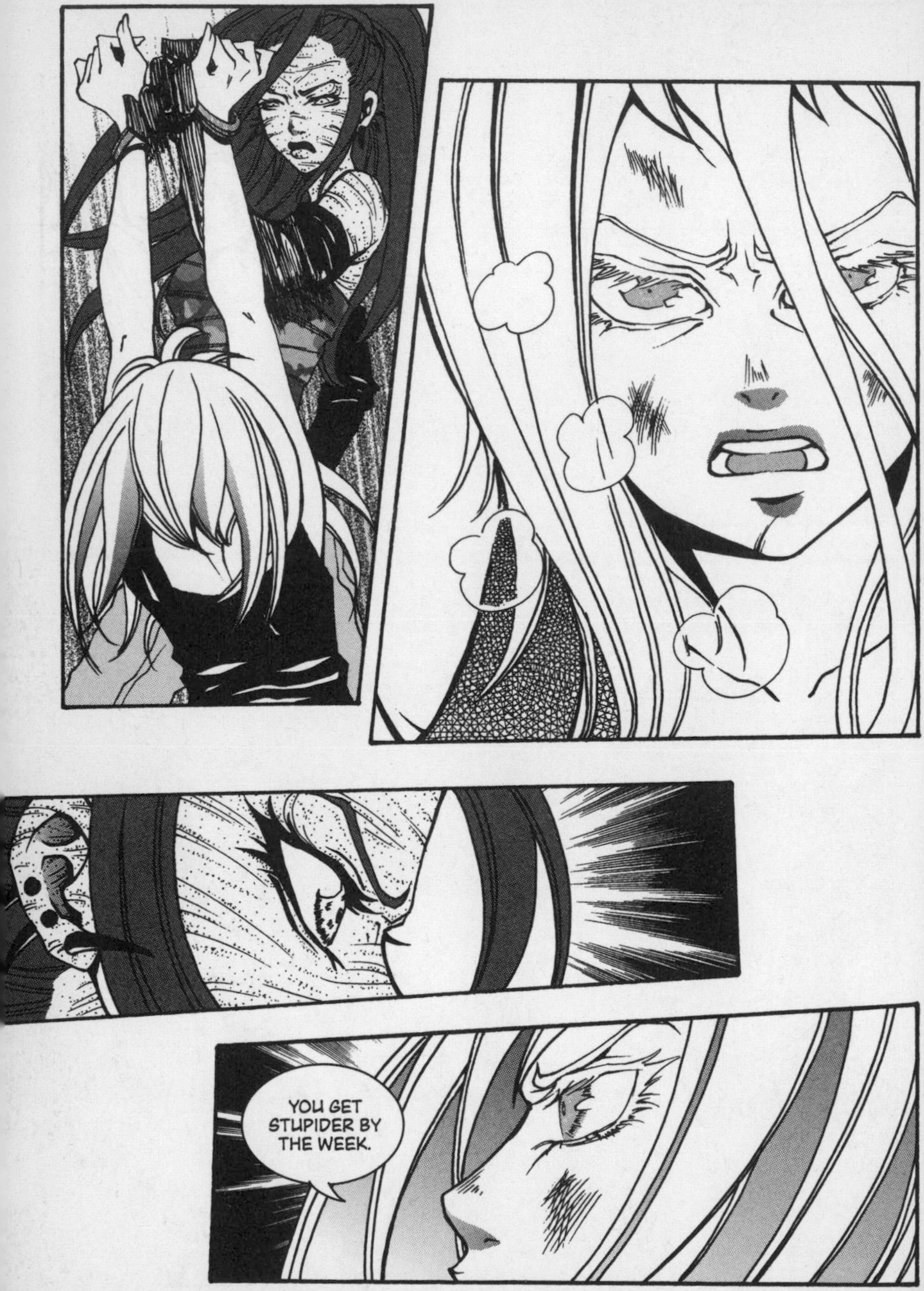
YOU GET STUPIDER BY THE WEEK.

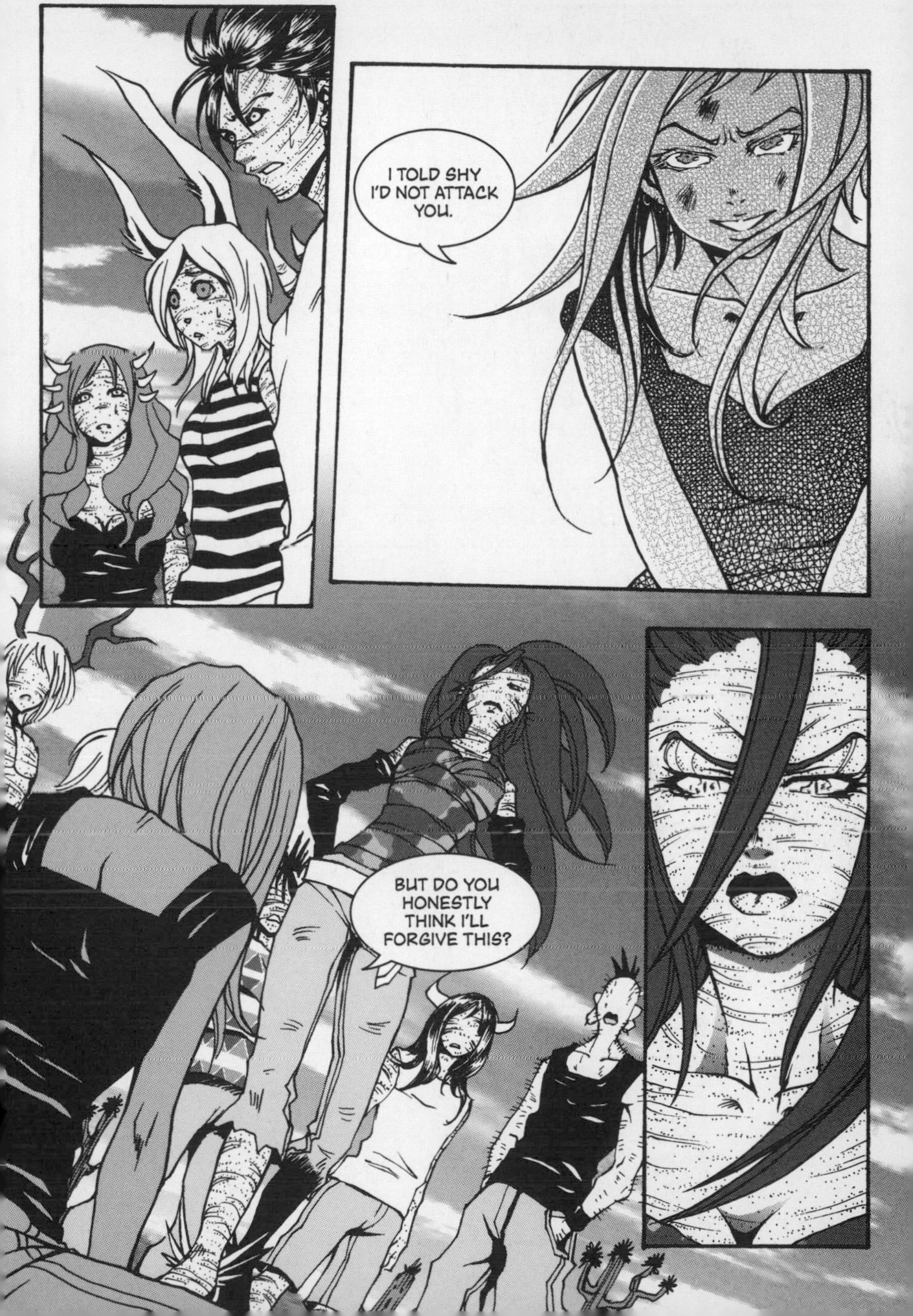
I TOLD SHY I'D NOT ATTACK YOU.
BUT DO YOU HONESTLY THINK I'LL FORGIVE THIS?

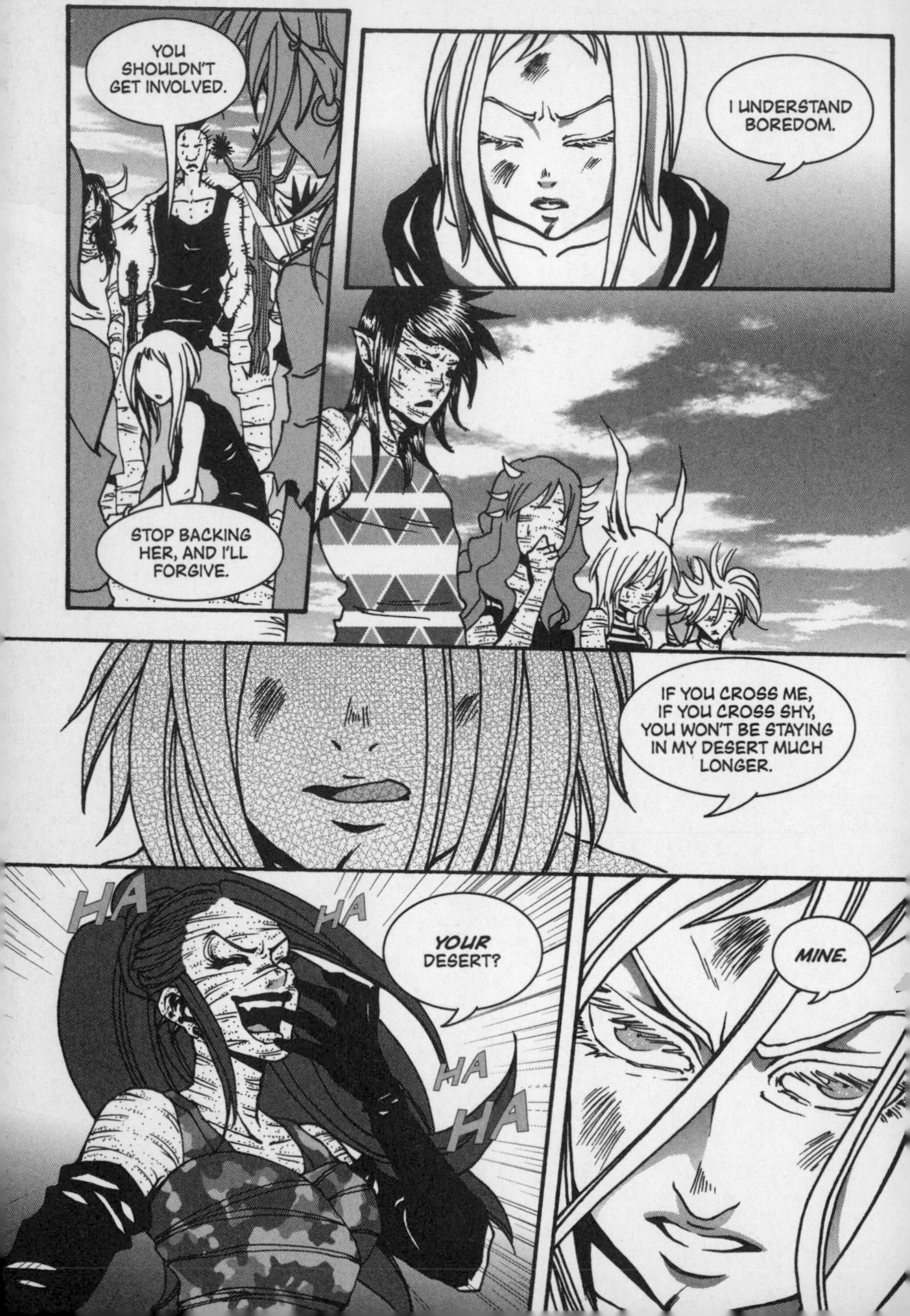
YOU SHOULDN'T GET INVOLVED.
STOP BACKING HER, AND I'LL FORGIVE.
I UNDERSTAND BOREDOM.
IF YOU CROSS ME, IF YOU CROSS SHY, YOU WON'T BE STAYING IN MY DESERT MUCH LONGER.
HA
HA
YOUR DESERT?
HA
HA
MINE.

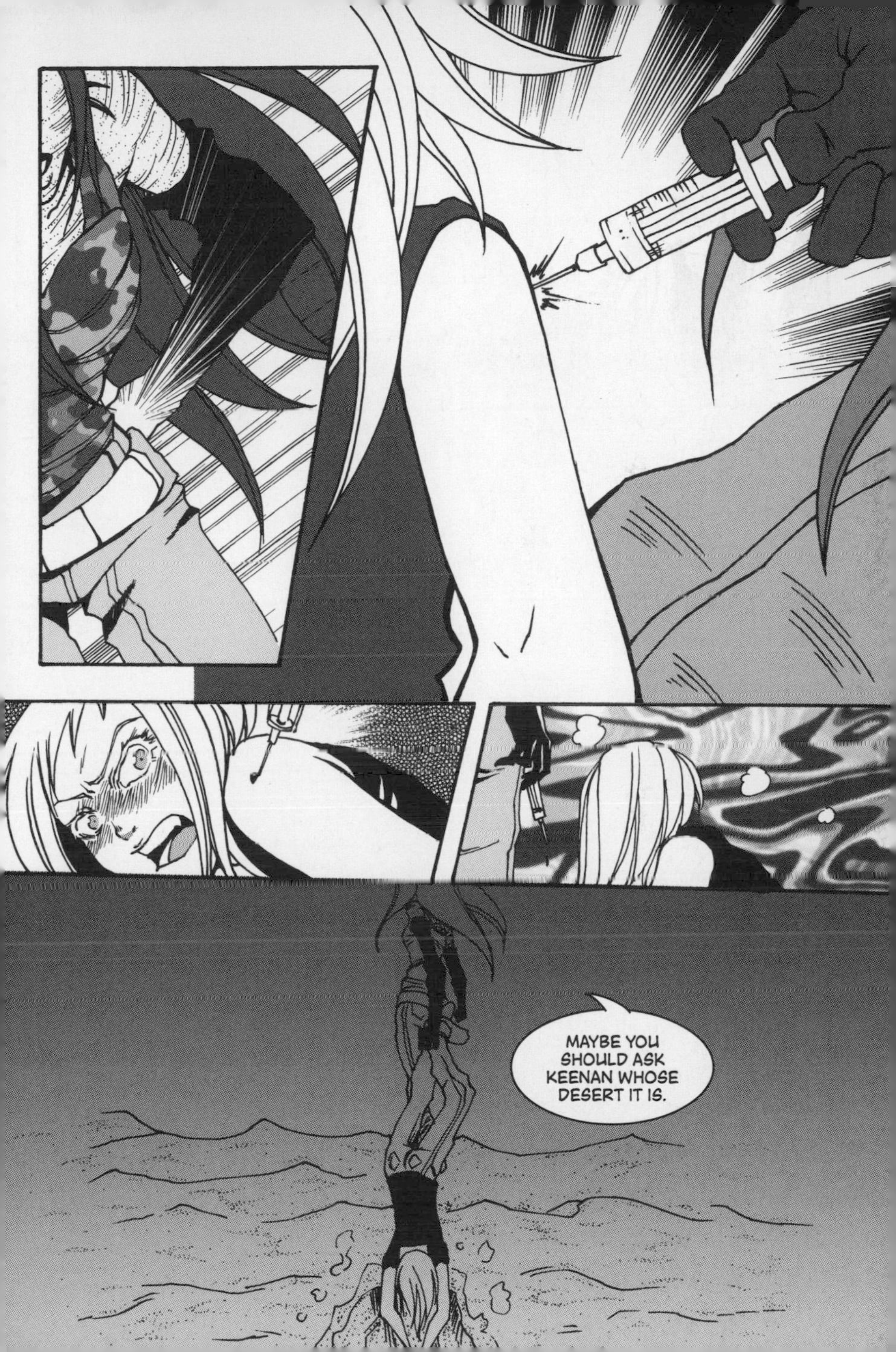
MAYBE YOU SHOULD ASK KEENAN WHOSE DESERT IT IS.

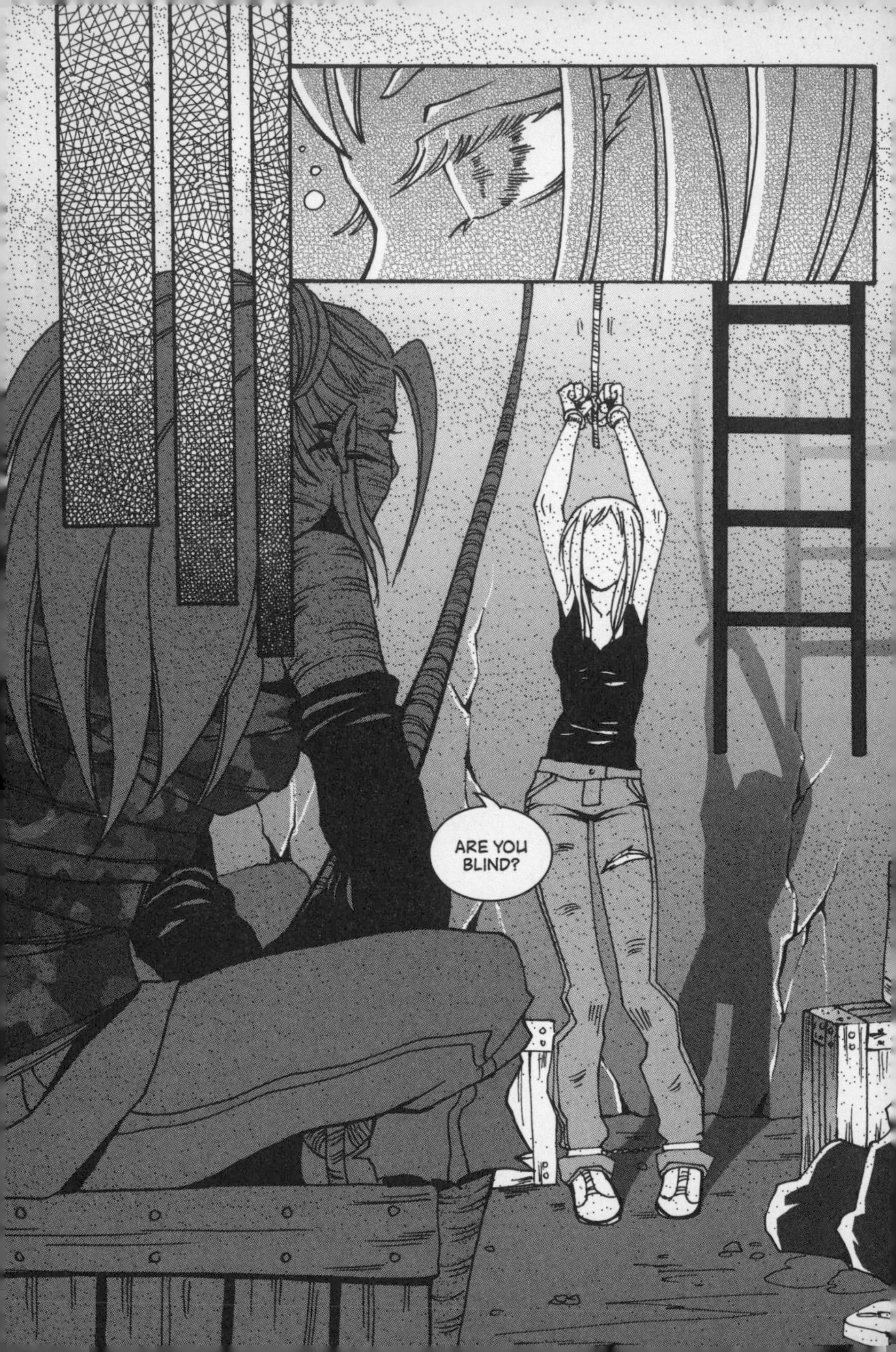
ARE YOU BLIND?

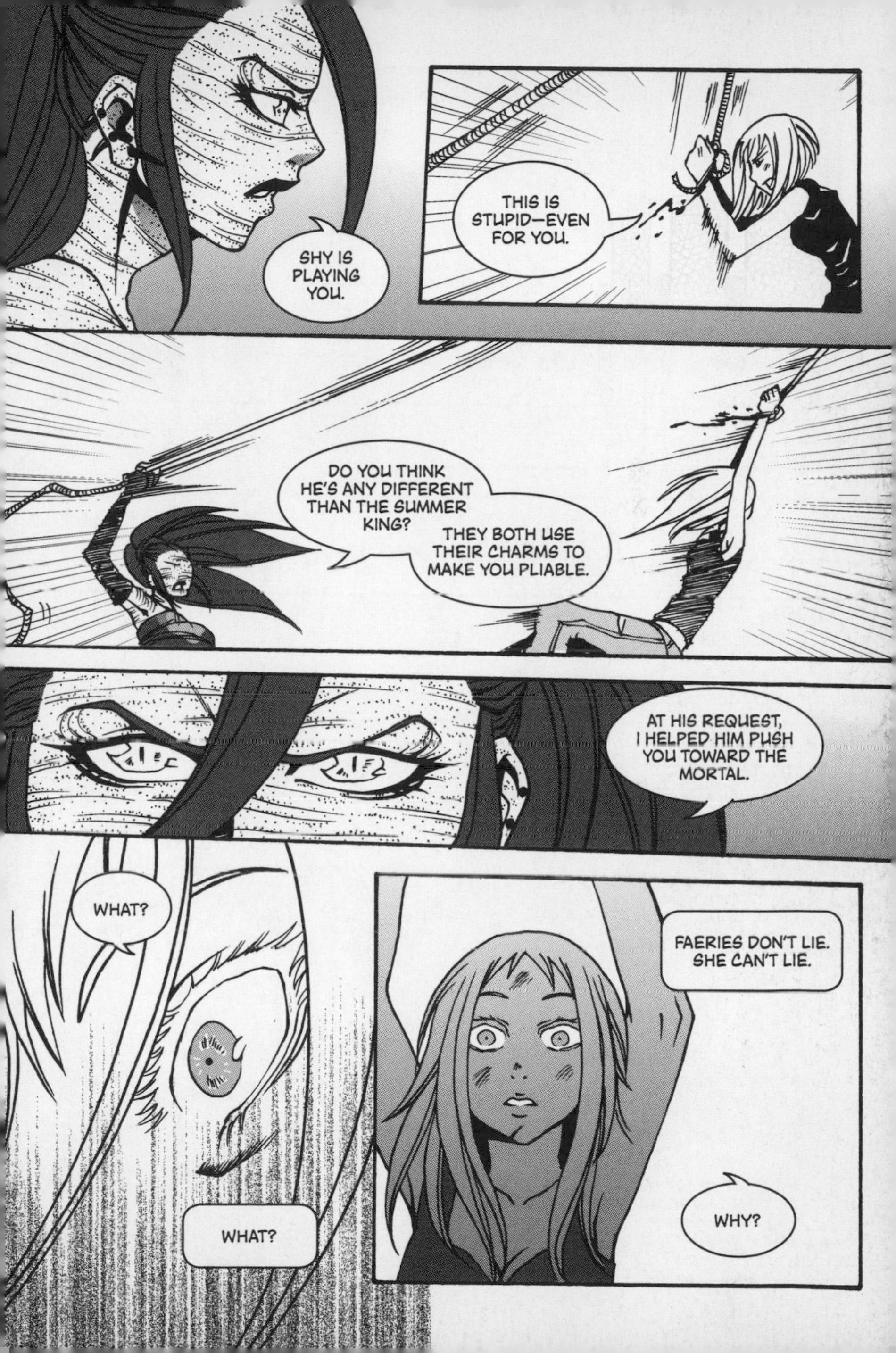
SHY IS PLAYING YOU.
THIS IS STUPID—EVEN FOR YOU.
DO YOU THINK HE'S ANY DIFFERENT THAN THE SUMMER KING?
THEY BOTH USE THEIR CHARMS TO MAKE YOU PLIABLE.
AT HIS REQUEST, I HELPED HIM PUSH YOU TOWARD THE MORTAL.
WHAT?
WHAT?
FAERIES DON'T LIE. SHE CAN'T LIE.
WHY?

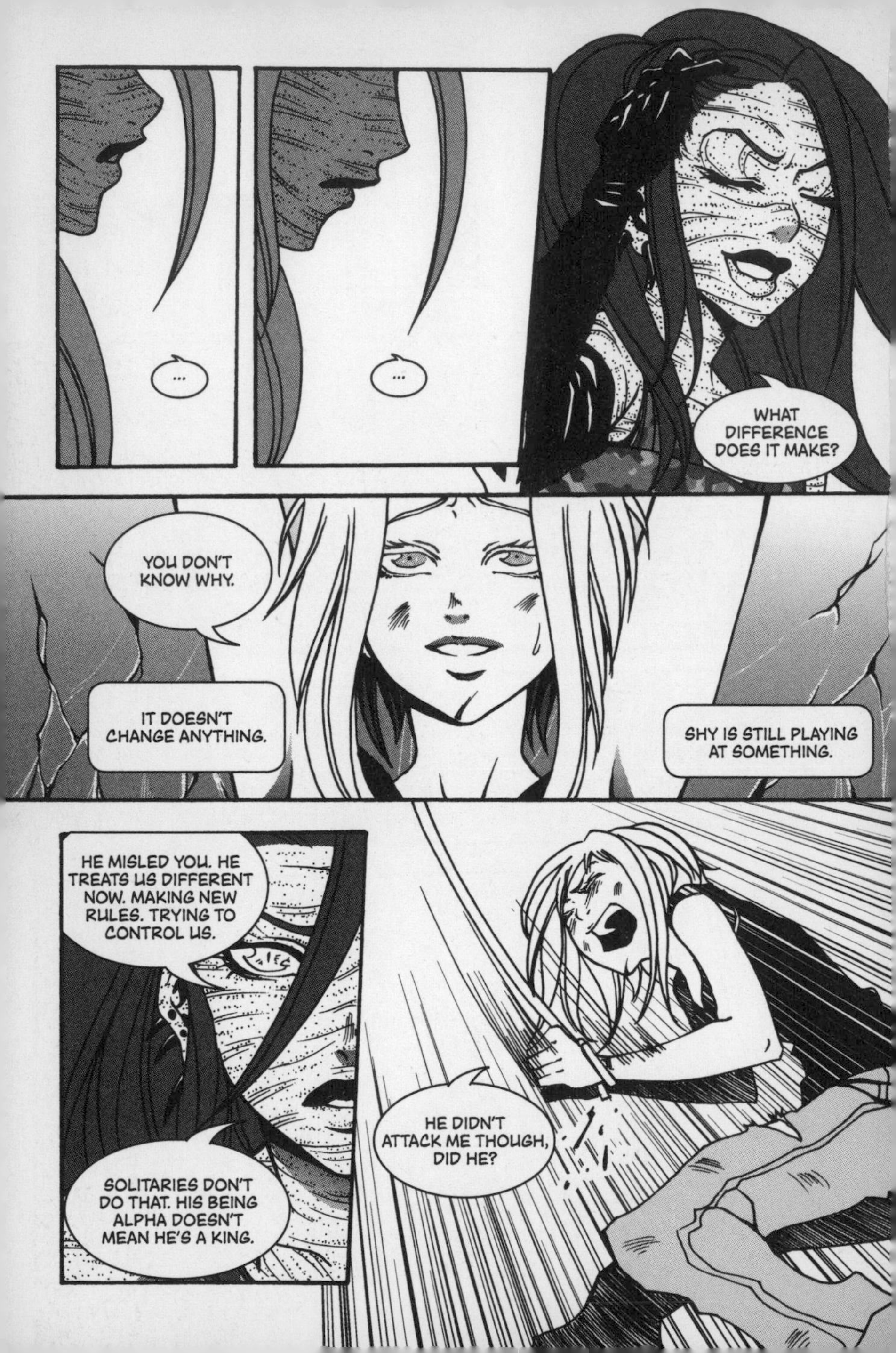
...
...
WHAT DIFFERENCE DOES IT MAKE?
YOU DON'T KNOW WHY.
IT DOESN'T CHANGE ANYTHING.
SHY IS STILL PLAYING AT SOMETHING.
HE MISLED YOU. HE TREATS US DIFFERENT NOW. MAKING NEW RULES. TRYING TO CONTROL US.
SOLITARIES DON'T DO THAT. HIS BEING ALPHA DOESN'T MEAN HE'S A KING.
HE DIDN'T ATTACK ME THOUGH, DID HE?

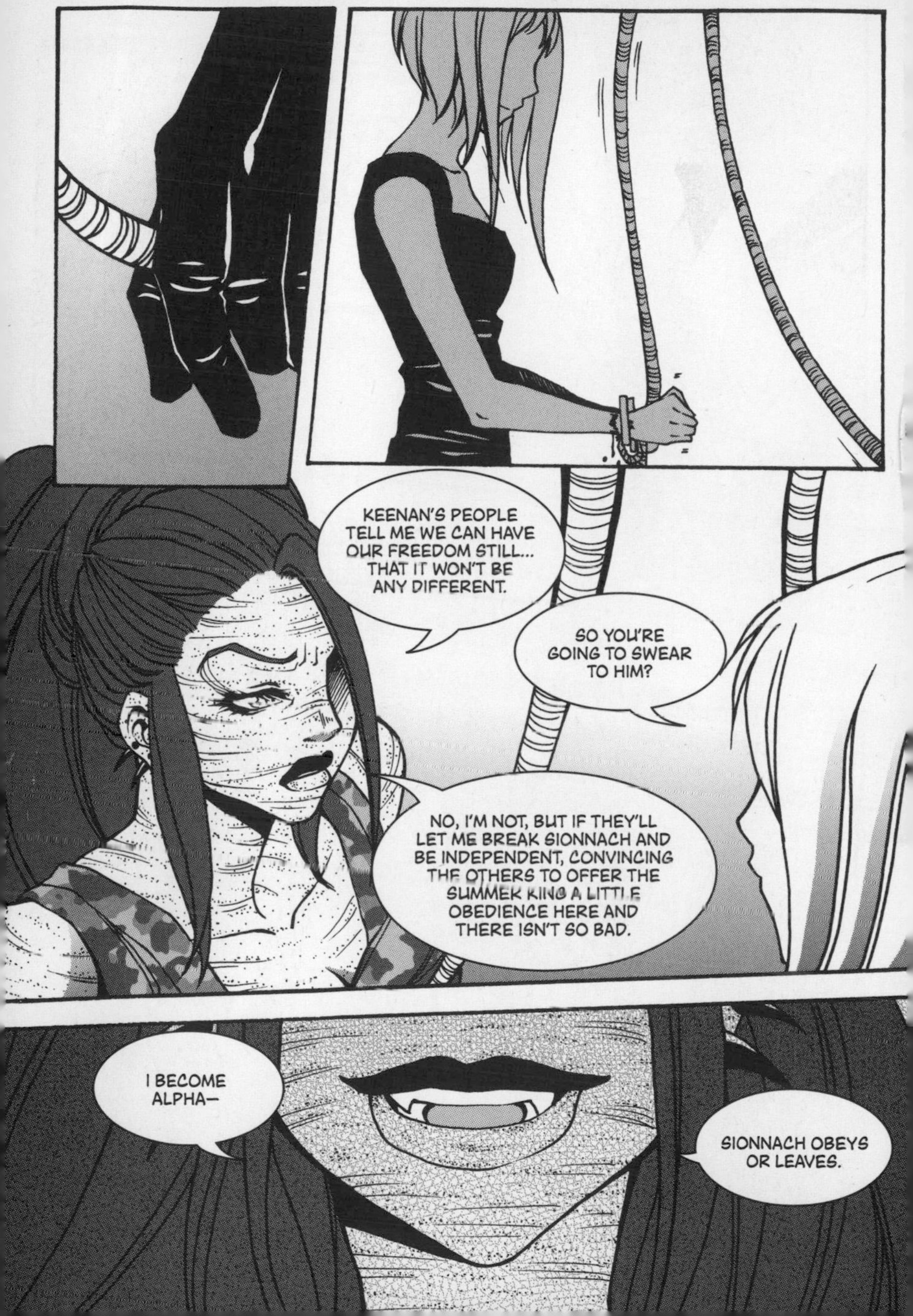
KEENAN'S PEOPLE TELL ME WE CAN HAVE OUR FREEDOM STILL... THAT IT WON'T BE ANY DIFFERENT.
SO YOU'RE GOING TO SWEAR TO HIM?
NO, I'M NOT, BUT IF THEY'LL LET ME BREAK SIONNACH AND BE INDEPENDENT, CONVINCING THE OTHERS TO OFFER THE SUMMER KING A LITTLE OBEDIENCE HERE AND THERE ISN'T SO BAD.
I BECOME ALPHA—
SIONNACH OBEYS OR LEAVES.

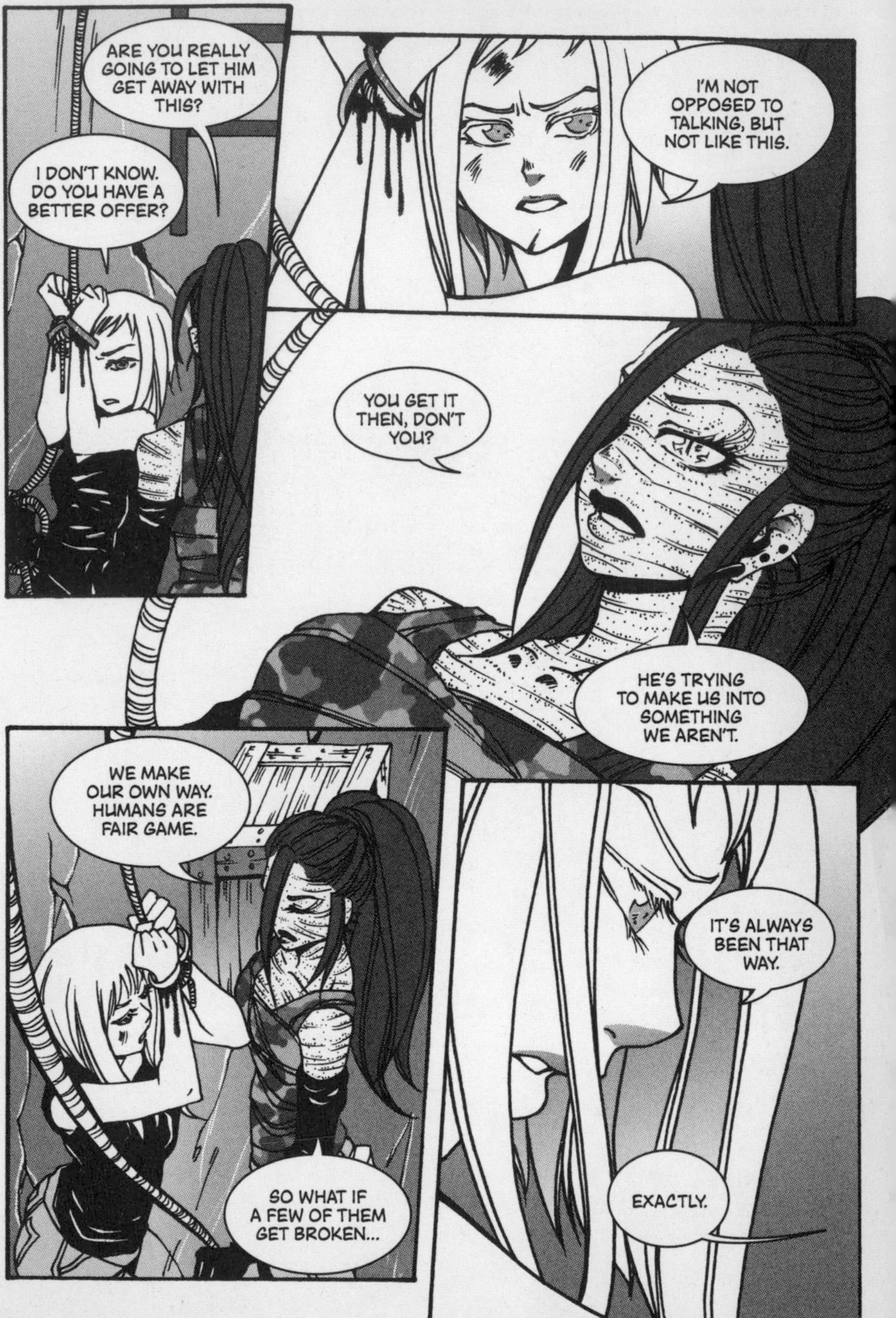
ARE YOU REALLY GOING TO LET HIM GET AWAY WITH THIS?
I DON'T KNOW. DO YOU HAVE A BETTER OFFER?
I'M NOT OPPOSED TO TALKING, BUT NOT LIKE THIS.
YOU GET IT THEN, DON'T YOU?
HE'S TRYING TO MAKE US INTO SOMETHING WE AREN'T.
WE MAKE OUR OWN WAY. HUMANS ARE FAIR GAME.
SO WHAT IF A FEW OF THEM GET BROKEN...
IT'S ALWAYS BEEN THAT WAY.
EXACTLY.

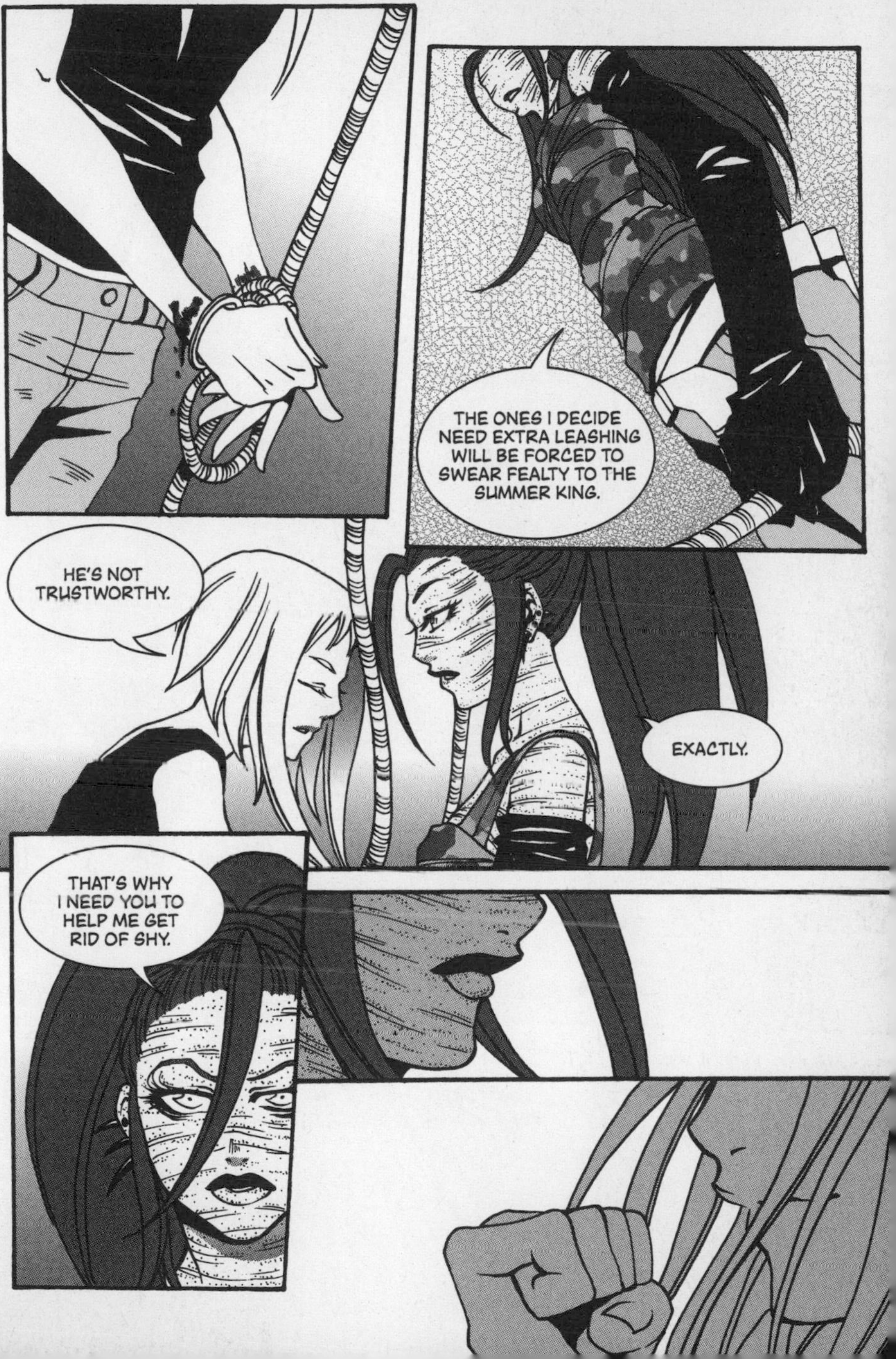
THE ONES I DECIDE NEED EXTRA LEASHING WILL BE FORCED TO SWEAR FEALTY TO THE SUMMER KING.
HE'S NOT TRUSTWORTHY.
EXACTLY.
THAT'S WHY I NEED YOU TO HELP ME GET RID OF SHY.

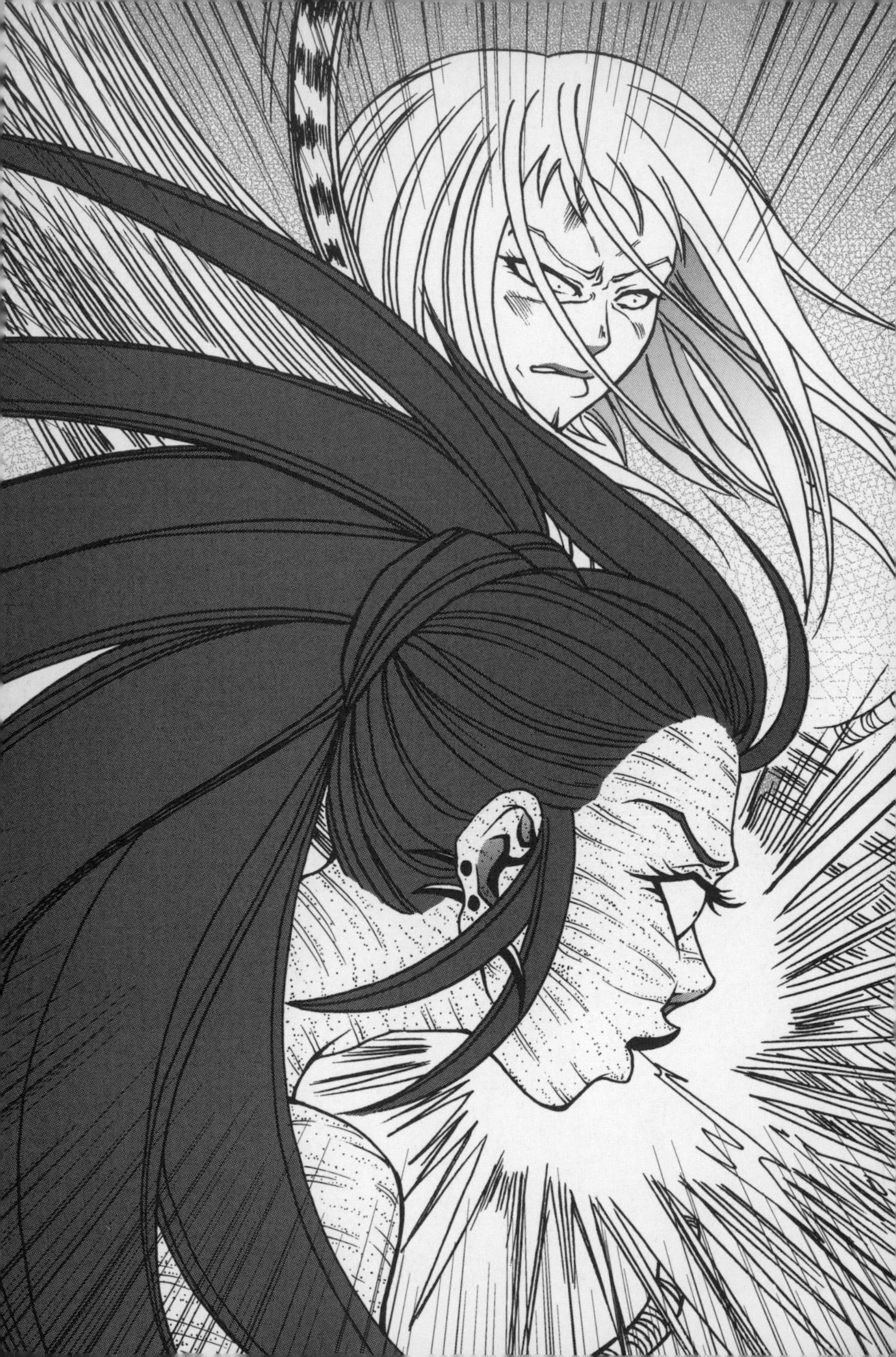

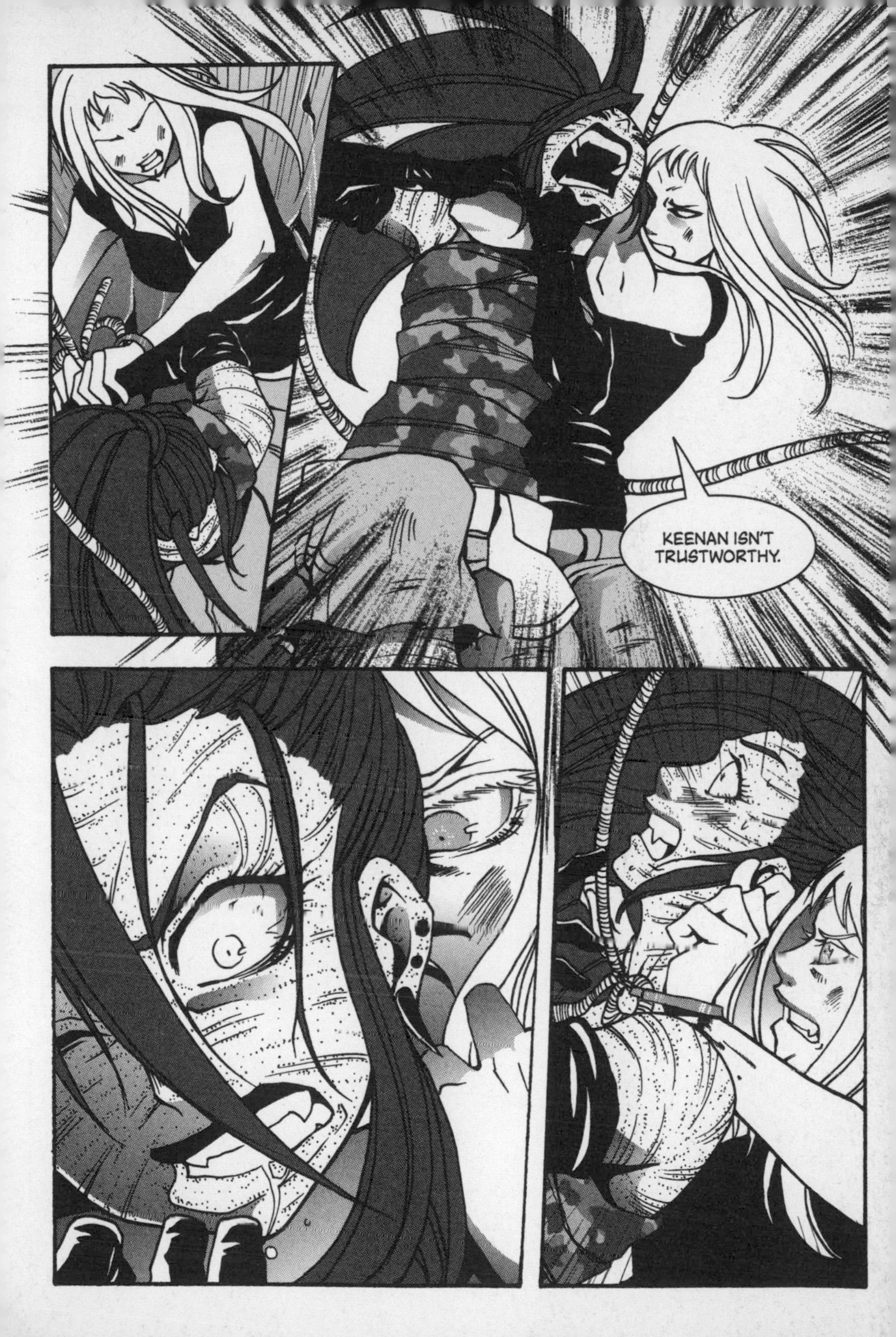
KEENAN ISN'T TRUSTWORTHY.

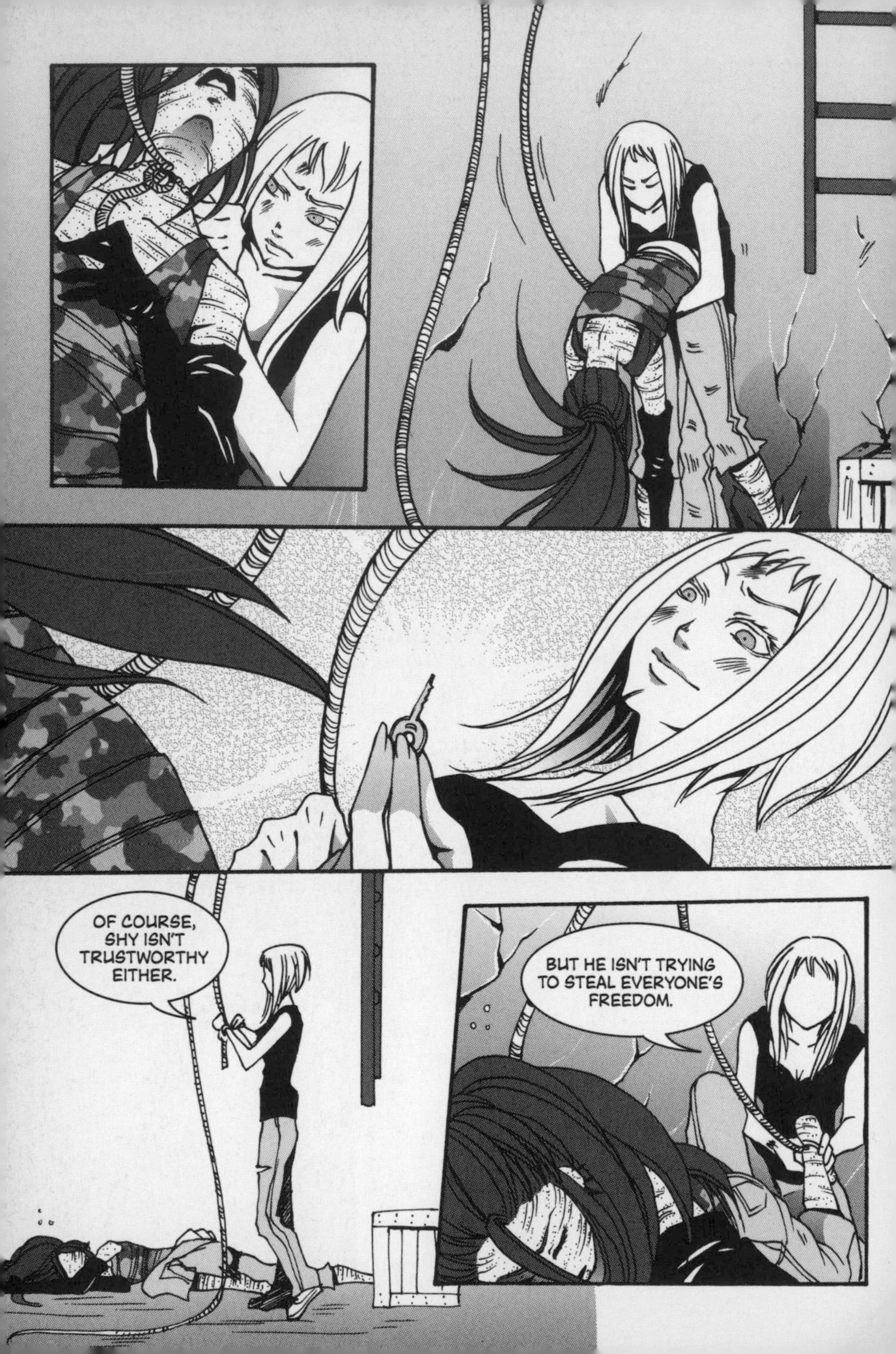
OF COURSE, SHY ISN'T TRUSTWORTHY EITHER.
BUT HE ISN'T TRYING TO STEAL EVERYONE'S FREEDOM.

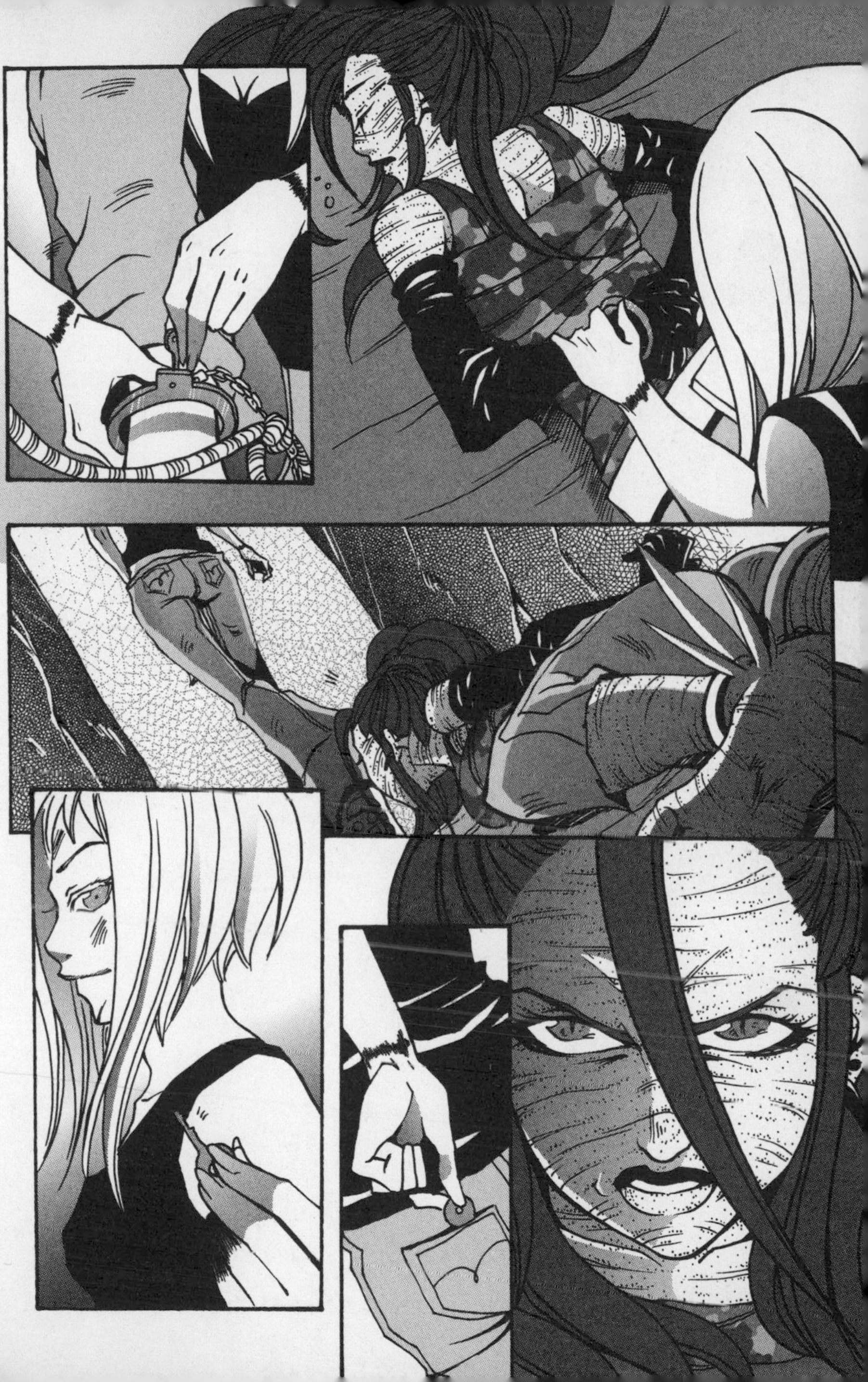

DON'T BE STUPID.
FOLLOWING MAILI OR BELIEVING HER THEORIES ABOUT TRUSTING THE SUMMER KING WOULD BE A BAD IDEA.
MAILI—
IS NOT THE STRONGEST FAERY IN THE DESERT.
NEITHER IS SHY.
I AM.

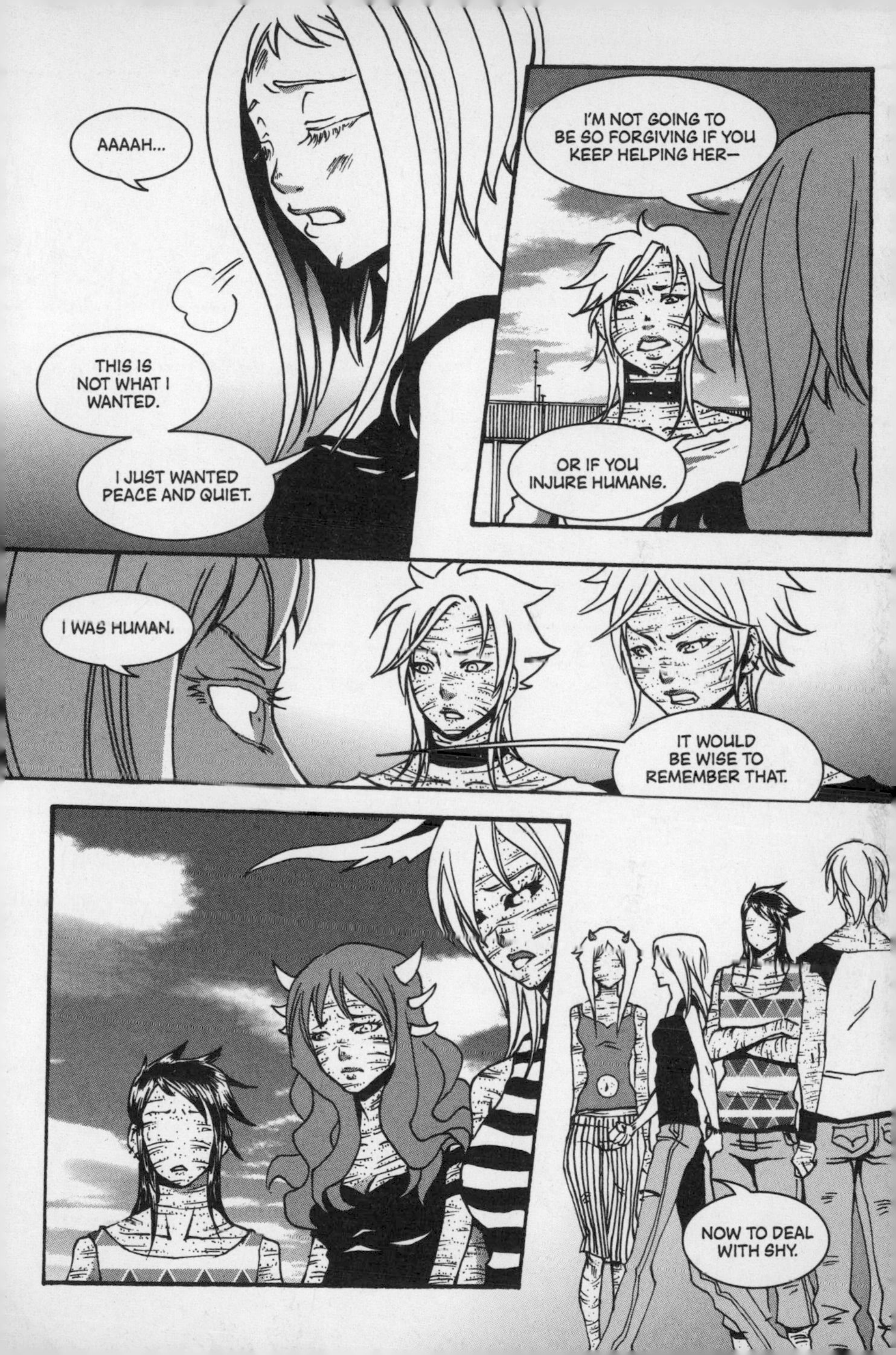
AAAAH...
THIS IS NOT WHAT I WANTED.
I JUST WANTED PEACE AND QUIET.
I'M NOT GOING TO BE SO FORGIVING IF YOU KEEP HELPING HER—
OR IF YOU INJURE HUMANS.
I WAS HUMAN.
IT WOULD BE WISE TO REMEMBER THAT.
NOW TO DEAL WITH SHY.

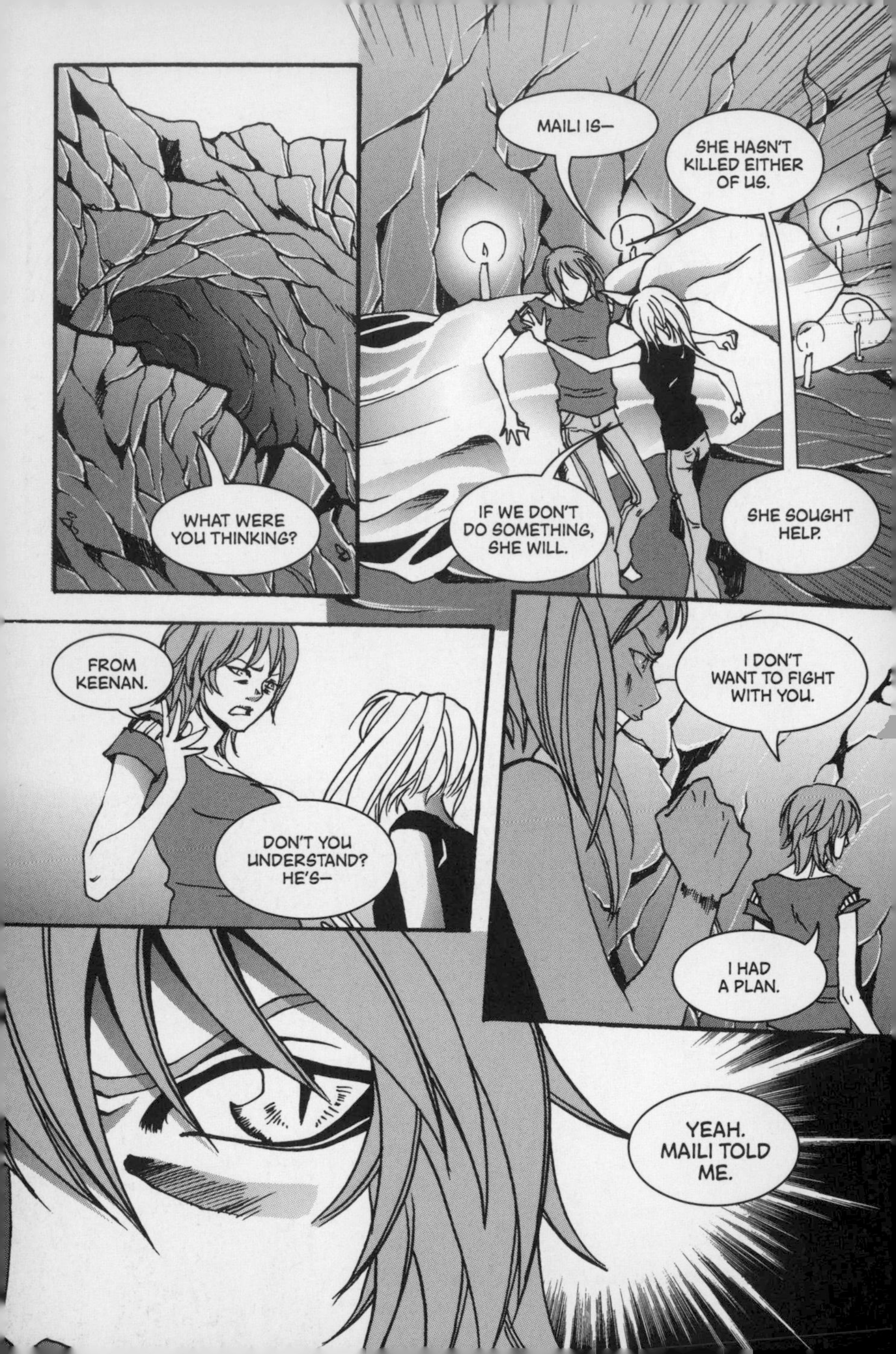
WHAT WERE YOU THINKING?
MAILI IS—
SHE HASN'T KILLED EITHER OF US.
IF WE DON'T DO SOMETHING, SHE WILL.
SHE SOUGHT HELP.
FROM KEENAN.
DON'T YOU UNDERSTAND? HE'S—
I DON'T WANT TO FIGHT WITH YOU.
I HAD A PLAN.
YEAH. MAILI TOLD ME.

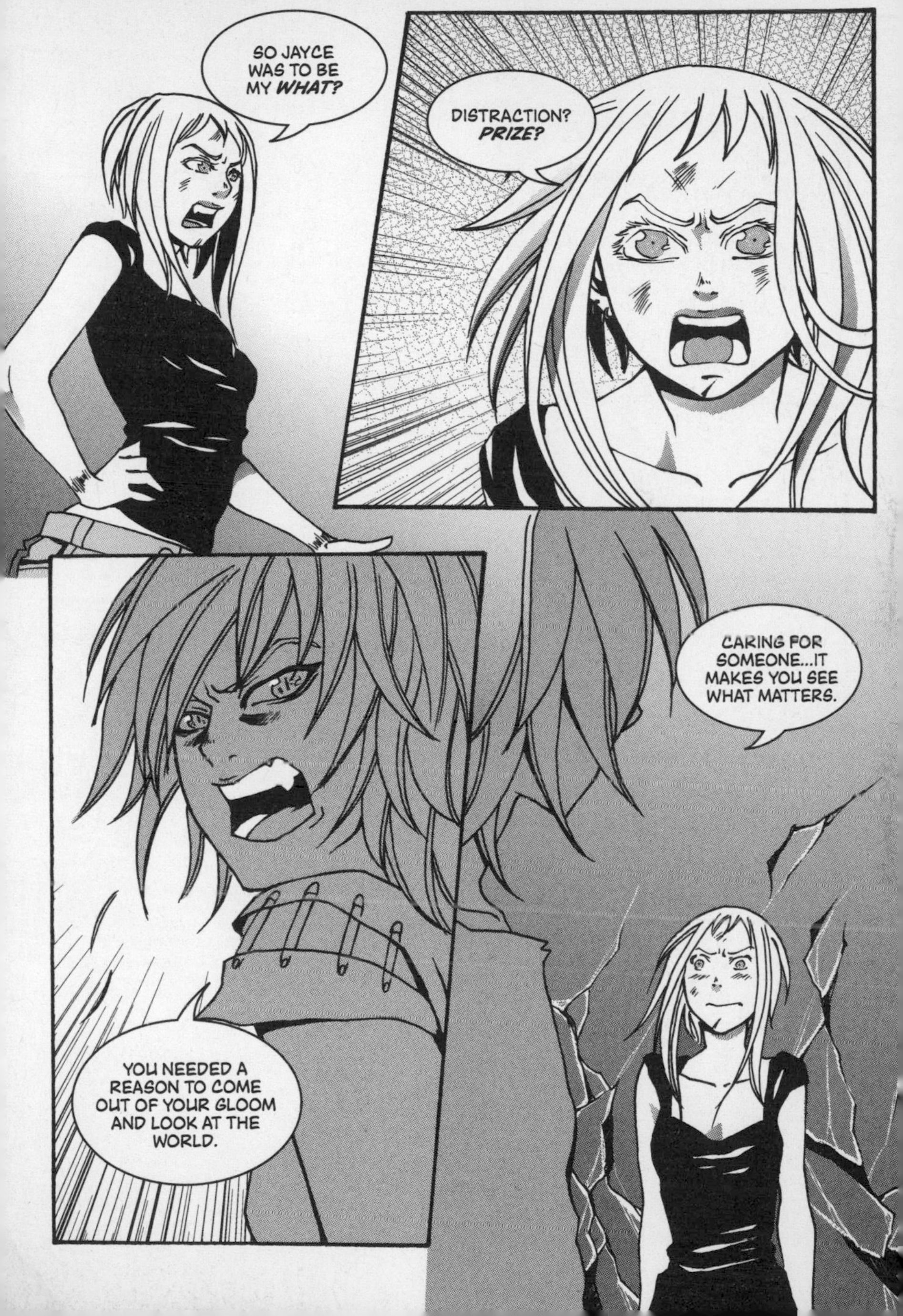
SO JAYCE WAS TO BE MY *WHAT?*
DISTRACTION? *PRIZE?*
YOU NEEDED A REASON TO COME OUT OF YOUR GLOOM AND LOOK AT THE WORLD.
CARING FOR SOMEONE...IT MAKES YOU SEE WHAT MATTERS.

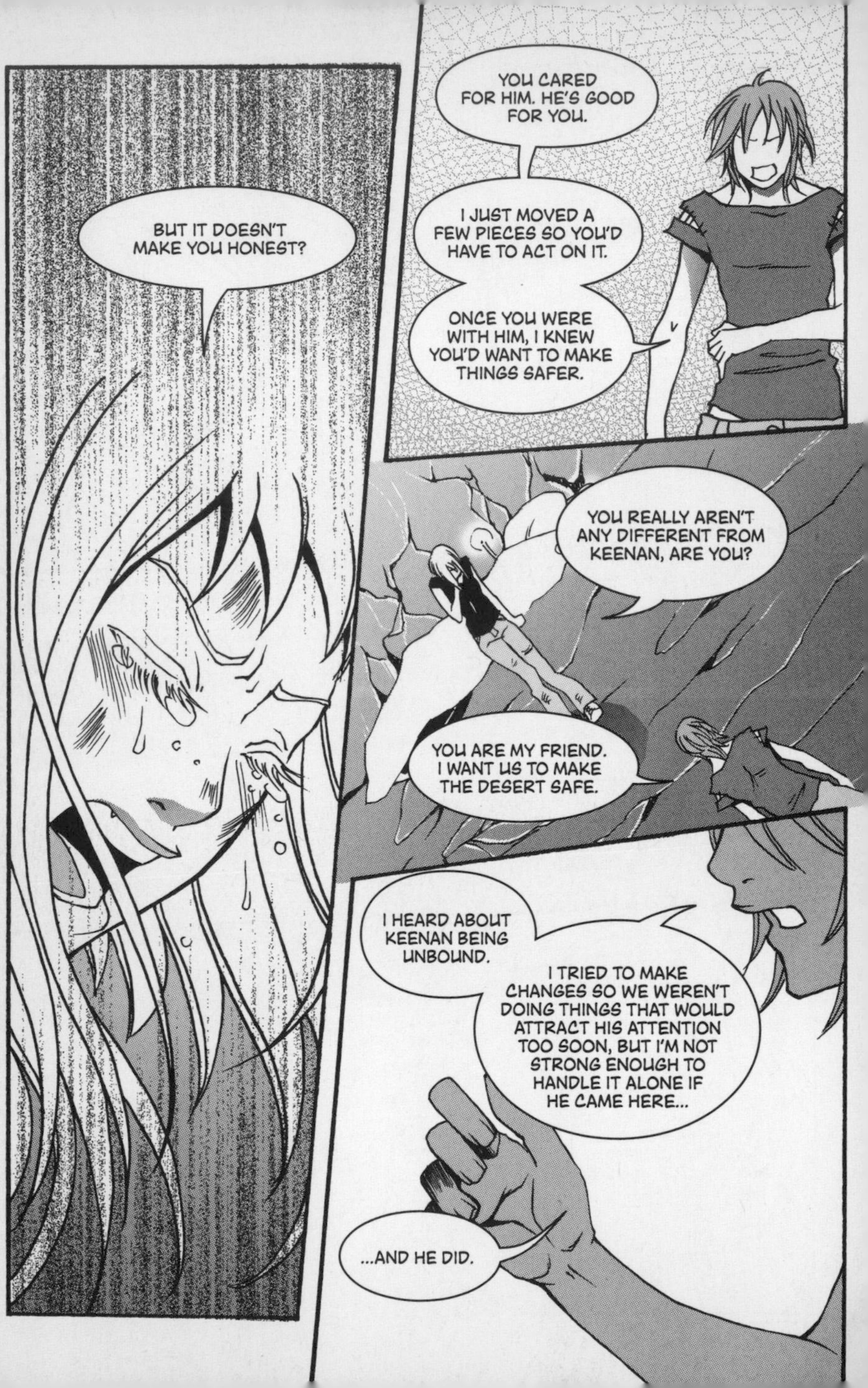
BUT IT DOESN'T MAKE YOU HONEST?
YOU CARED FOR HIM. HE'S GOOD FOR YOU.
I JUST MOVED A FEW PIECES SO YOU'D HAVE TO ACT ON IT.
ONCE YOU WERE WITH HIM, I KNEW YOU'D WANT TO MAKE THINGS SAFER.
YOU REALLY AREN'T ANY DIFFERENT FROM KEENAN, ARE YOU?
YOU ARE MY FRIEND. I WANT US TO MAKE THE DESERT SAFE.
I HEARD ABOUT KEENAN BEING UNBOUND.
I TRIED TO MAKE CHANGES SO WE WEREN'T DOING THINGS THAT WOULD ATTRACT HIS ATTENTION TOO SOON, BUT I'M NOT STRONG ENOUGH TO HANDLE IT ALONE IF HE CAME HERE...
...AND HE DID.

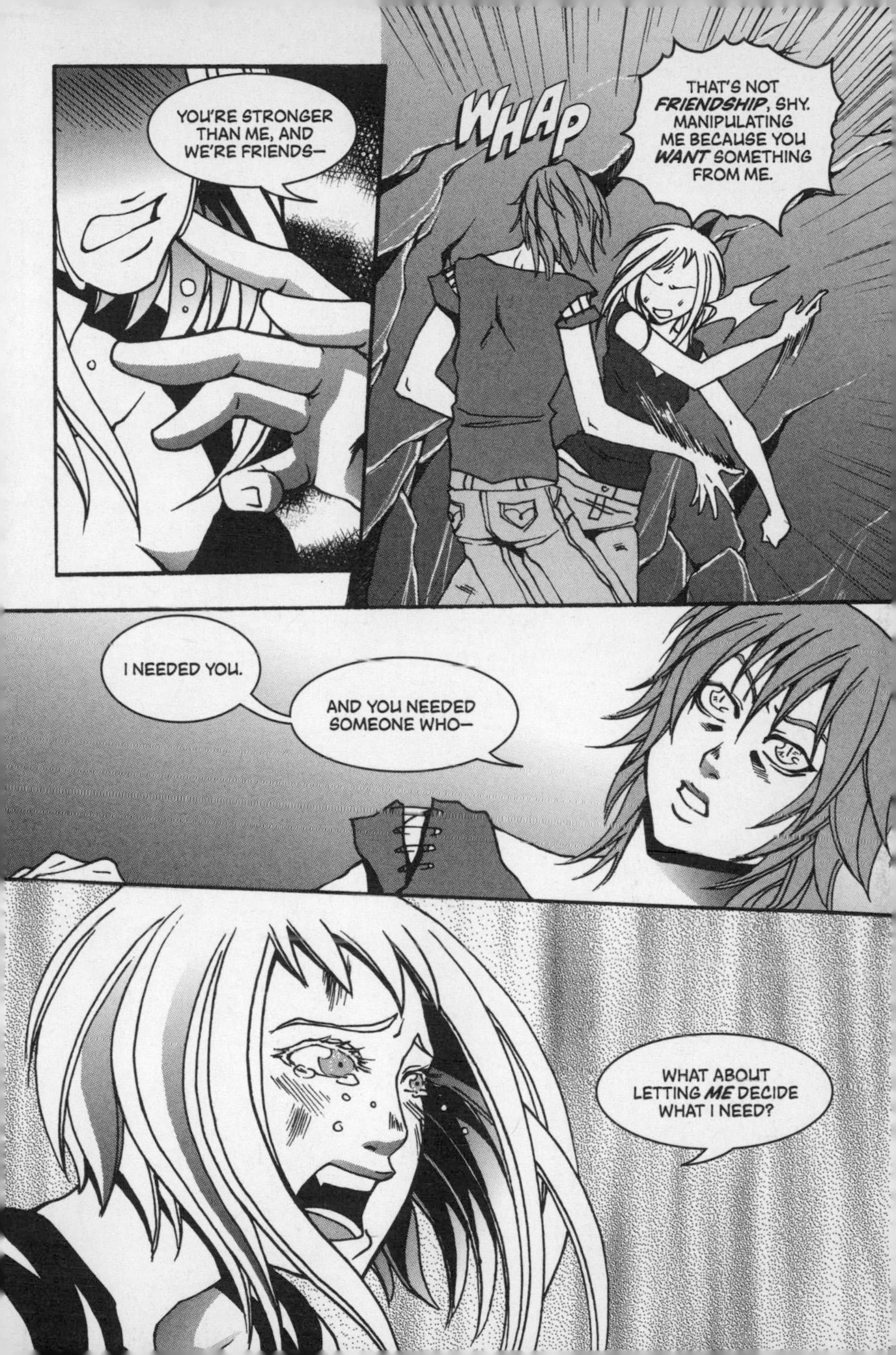
YOU'RE STRONGER THAN ME, AND WE'RE FRIENDS—
WHAP
THAT'S NOT FRIENDSHIP, SHY. MANIPULATING ME BECAUSE YOU WANT SOMETHING FROM ME.
I NEEDED YOU.
AND YOU NEEDED SOMEONE WHO—
WHAT ABOUT LETTING ME DECIDE WHAT I NEED?

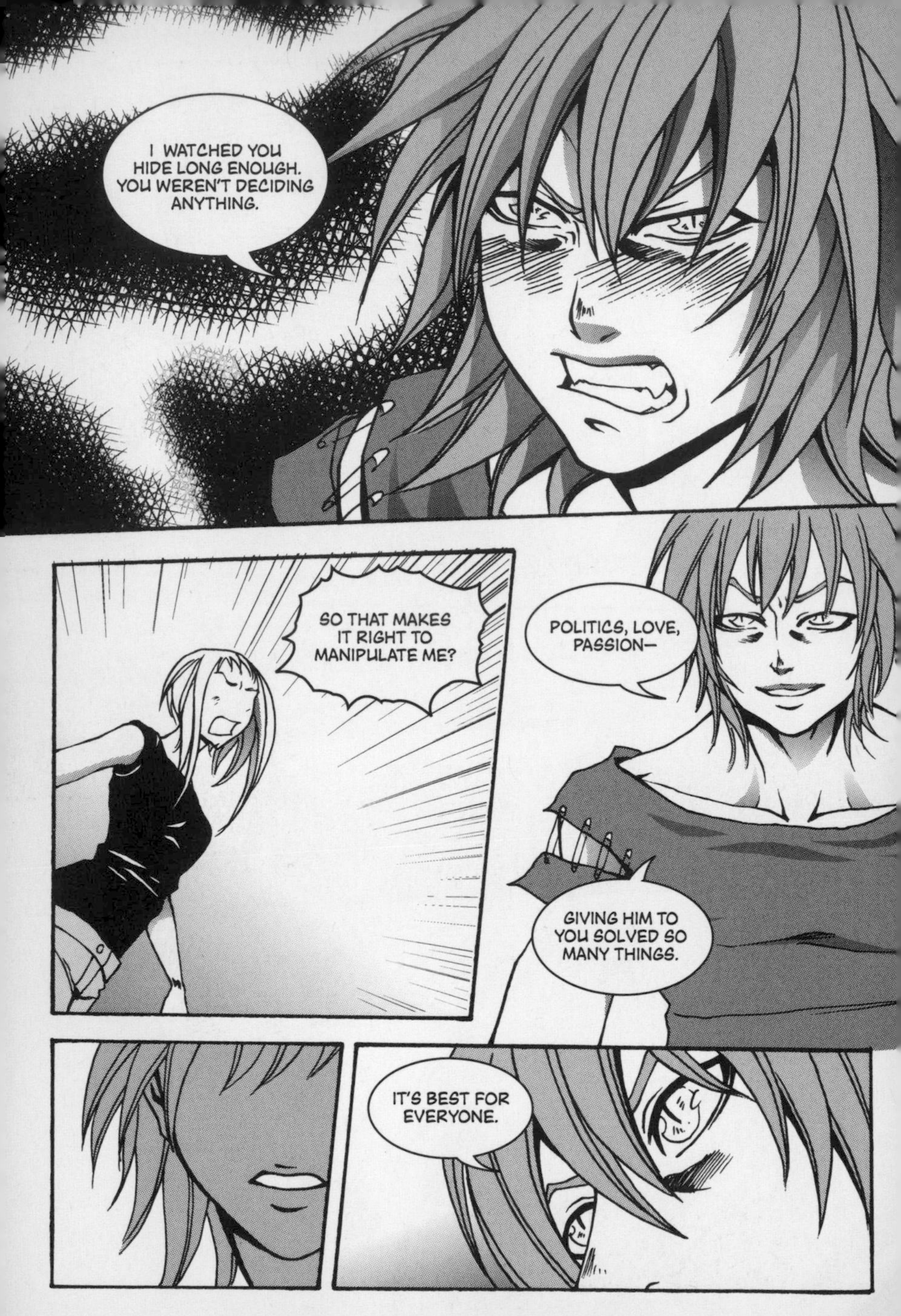
I WATCHED YOU HIDE LONG ENOUGH. YOU WEREN'T DECIDING ANYTHING.
SO THAT MAKES IT RIGHT TO MANIPULATE ME?
POLITICS, LOVE, PASSION—
GIVING HIM TO YOU SOLVED SO MANY THINGS.
IT'S BEST FOR EVERYONE.

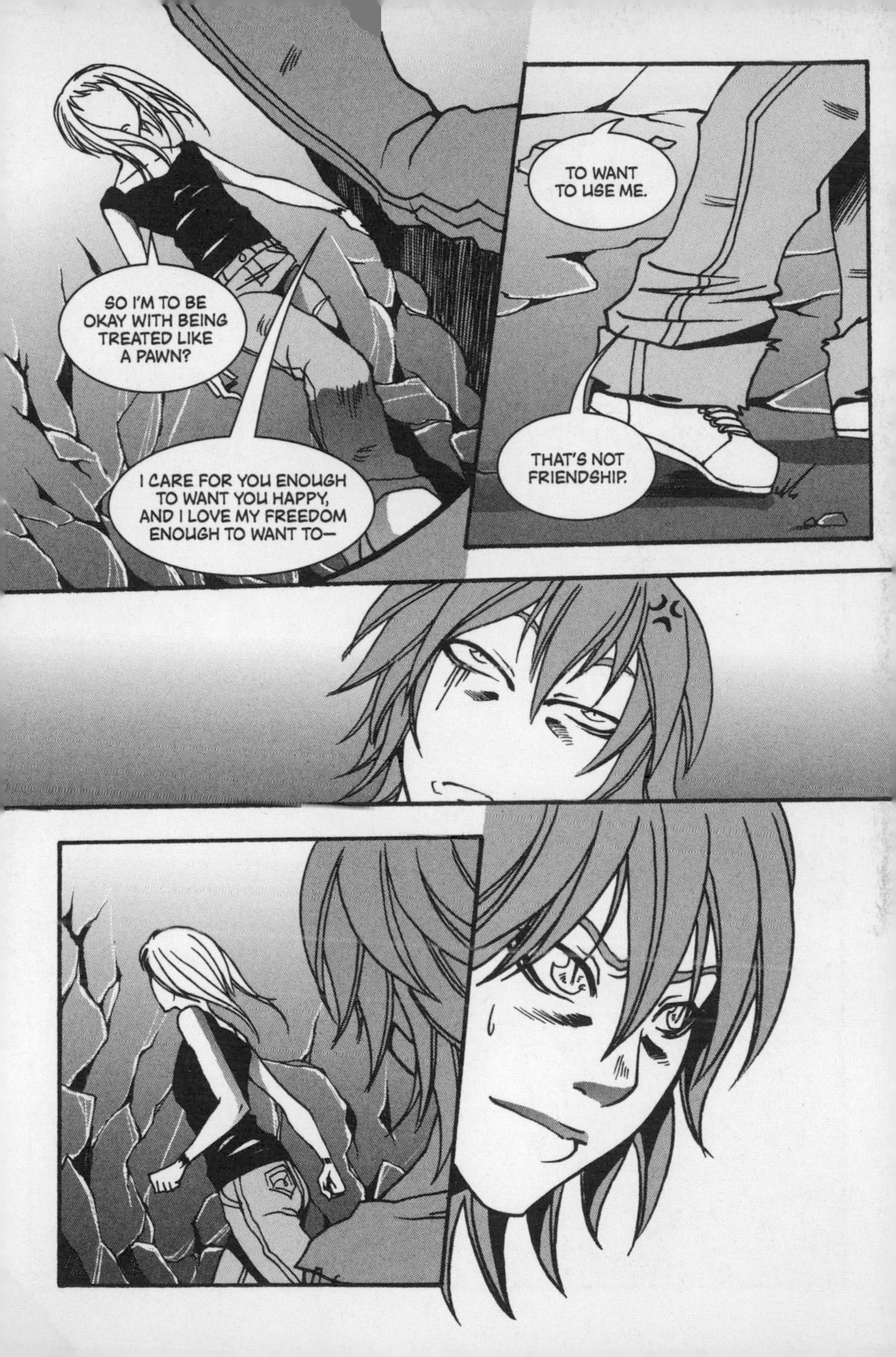
SO I'M TO BE OKAY WITH BEING TREATED LIKE A PAWN?
I CARE FOR YOU ENOUGH TO WANT YOU HAPPY, AND I LOVE MY FREEDOM ENOUGH TO WANT TO—
TO WANT TO USE ME.
THAT'S NOT FRIENDSHIP.

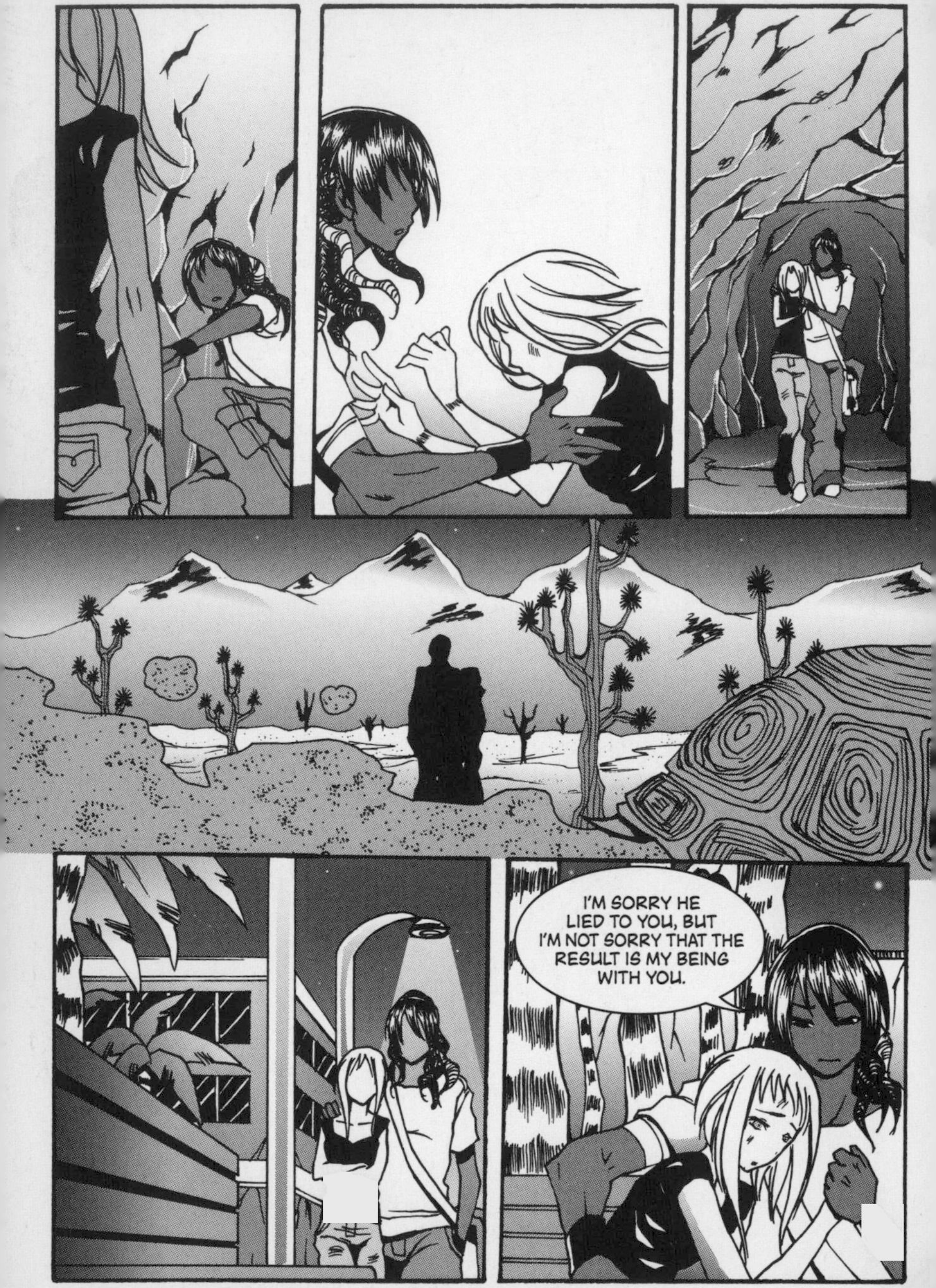
I'M SORRY HE LIED TO YOU, BUT I'M NOT SORRY THAT THE RESULT IS MY BEING WITH YOU.

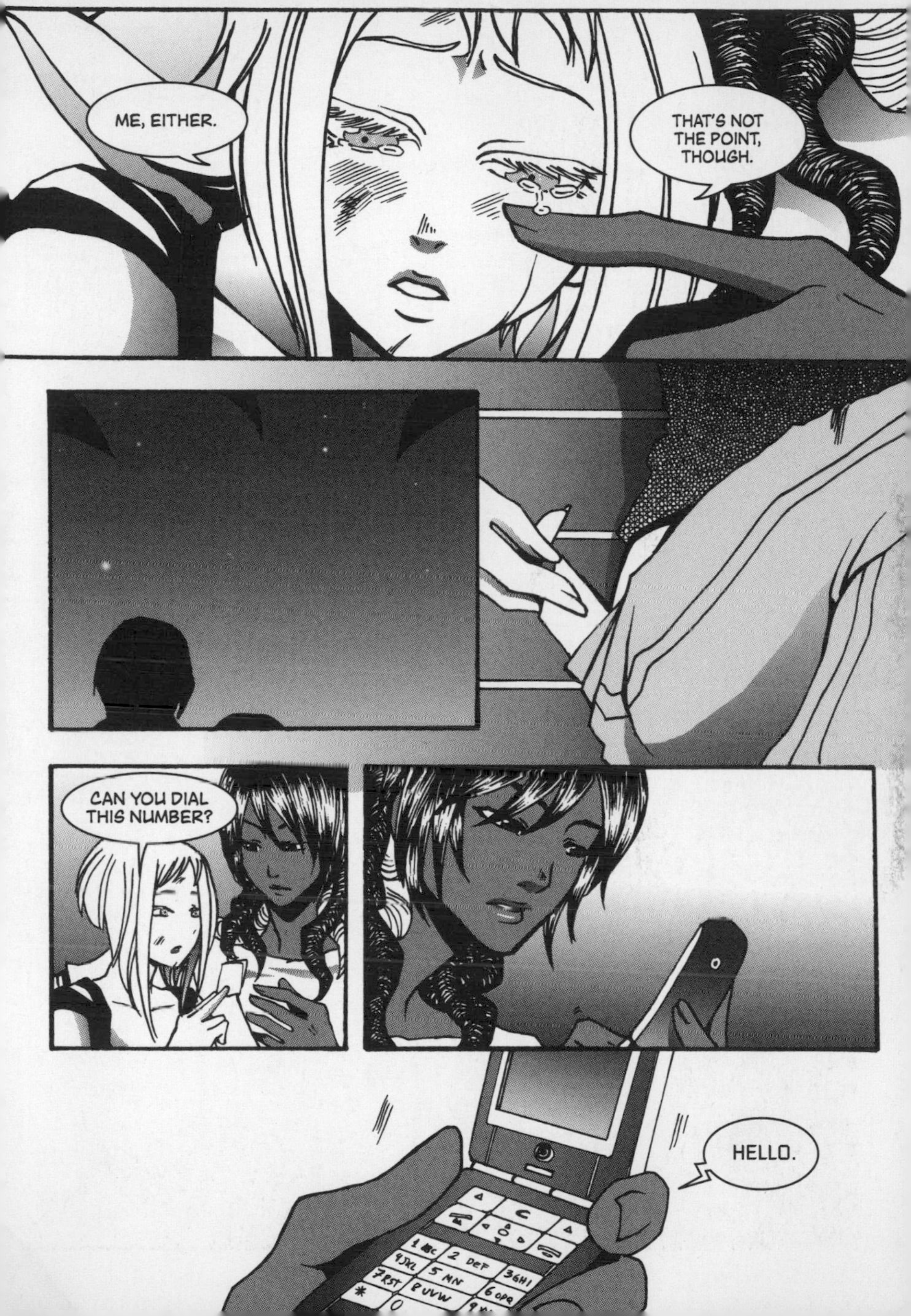
ME, EITHER.
THAT'S NOT THE POINT, THOUGH.
CAN YOU DIAL THIS NUMBER?
HELLO.

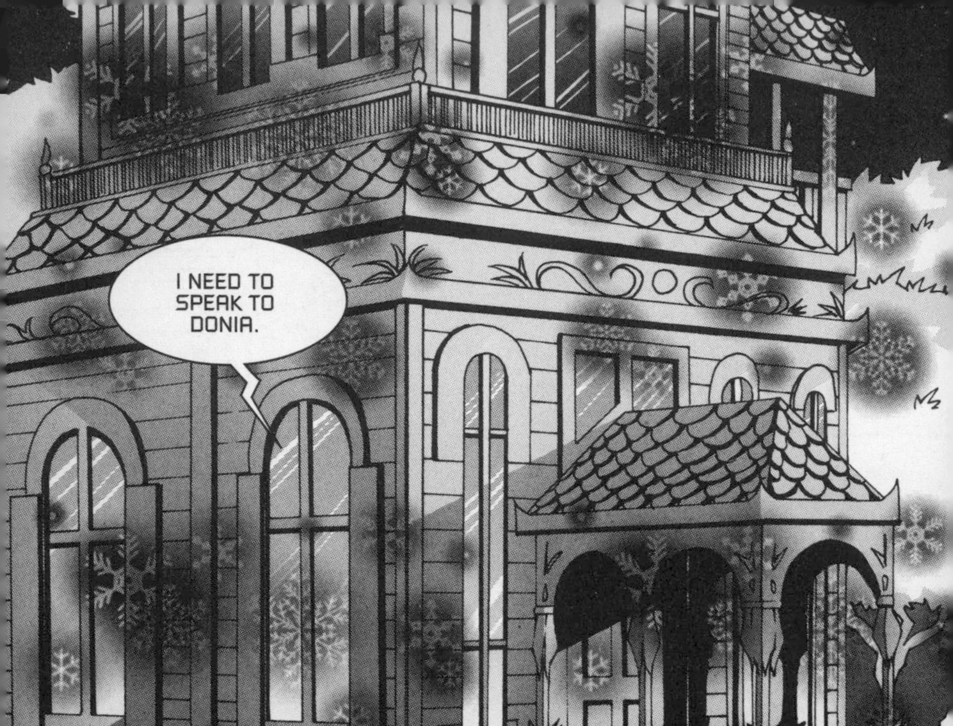
I NEED TO SPEAK TO DONIA.
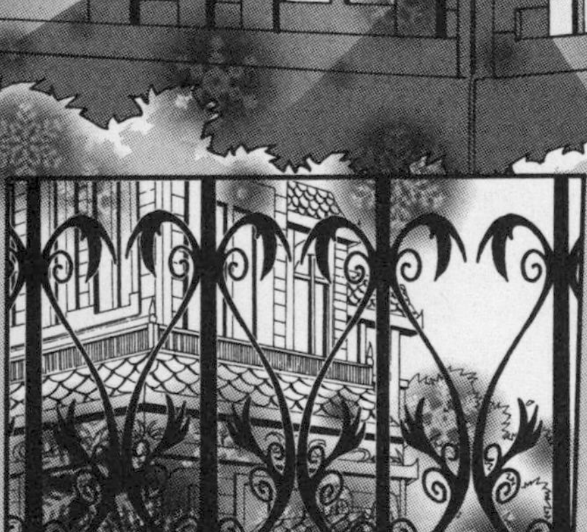
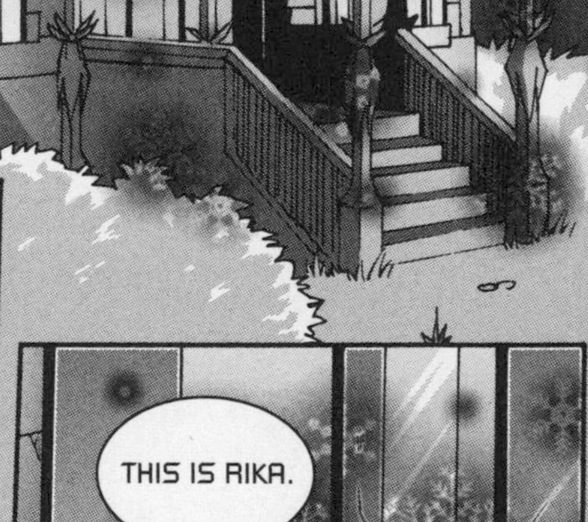
THIS IS RIKA.

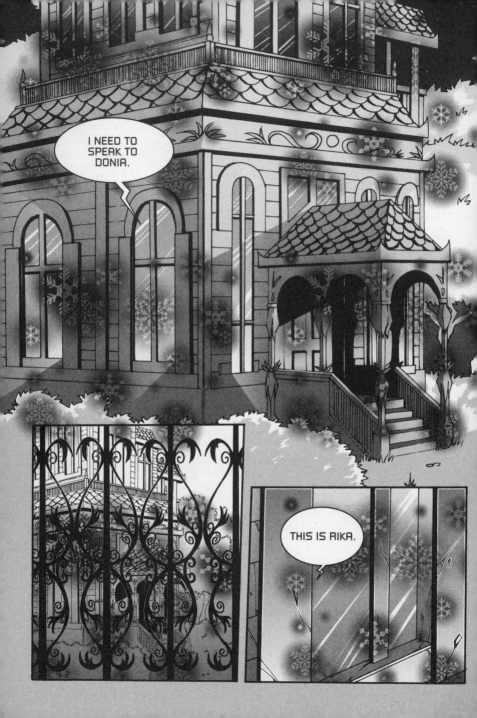

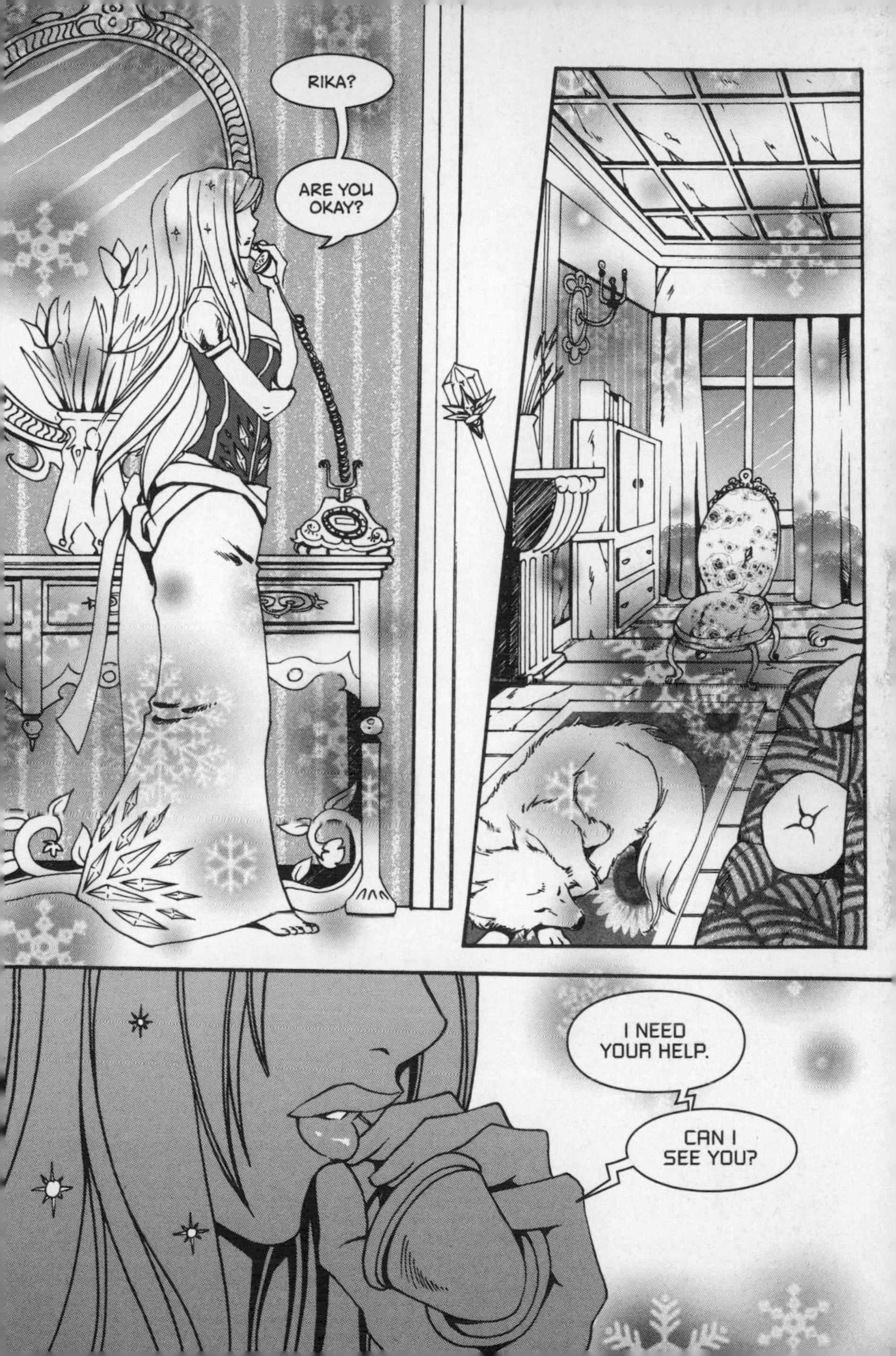
RIKA?
ARE YOU OKAY?
I NEED YOUR HELP.
CAN I SEE YOU?

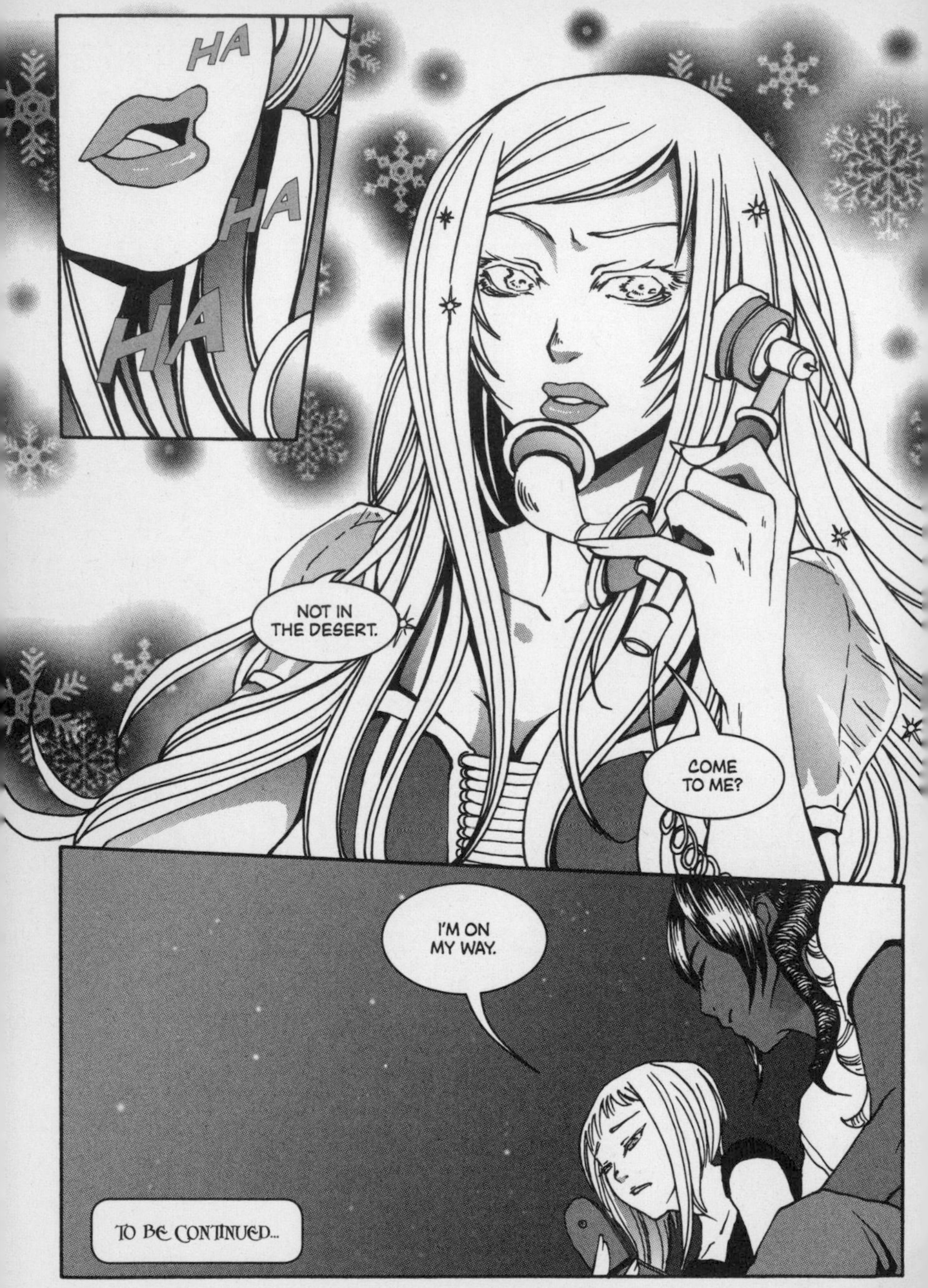
HA
HA
HA
NOT IN THE DESERT.
COME TO ME?
I'M ON MY WAY.
TO BE CONTINUED...

from her. Similarly, her father's attempts at fatherhood veered toward something akin to mortal pretenses. She didn't want a facsimile of a mortal family. She had a family, with Rabbit and Tish, her half-mortal siblings. During the past year when she had been brought to live in the Dark Court, she had hoped for something else: she wanted to be a true part of the Wild Hunt, a full member of her father's pack. That hadn't happened.

The Hound paused his steady motions only long enough to glance at her. "Gabriel's not here either."

"I know. I'm not looking for anyone in particular." Ani came to the stall. "I just like it here."

The Hound looked up and down the open aisle. This early no other Hound was in sight, but there were more than a score of steeds close enough to see them. "Do you need something?"

"Sure." Ani leaned against the wall. It would be an insult not to flirt, even though they both knew action wasn't possible. "A little fun. A little trouble. A ride . . ."

"Get the boss to agree"—the Hound's eyes flashed a vibrant green—"and I'll gladly take you."

She knew her own eyes were shimmering with the same energy that she saw in his. They were both born of the Wild Hunt. They were the creatures that rode the earth, drawing out terror, exacting vengeance, unrestrained by order. They were the teeth and claws of Faerie, living now in the mortal

Read on for a taste of
Melissa Marr's newest tale of Faerie,
RADIANT SHADOWS

Present day

Ani pulled open a side door to the stable. It was as much
a garage as a true stable, and as she walked through the
cavernous building she drew in the mingled scents of diesel
and straw, exhaust and sweat. Most of the creatures kept the
illusion of vehicles when they were outside the building, but
here, in their safe haven, the beasts roamed in whatever form
they chose. One of the steeds crouched on a ledge under
the skylight. It was something between an eagle and a lion;
both feathers and fur covered a massive body. Several other
steeds were lined up in a row of various motorcycles, cars,
and trucks. One anomalous steed was a camel.

A Hound looked up from polishing a matte black Harley
with plenty of chrome. The cloth in his hand was one of the
many swaths of fabric imported from Faerie specifically for
their steeds. "You looking for Chela?"

"No." She stayed in the walkway, not invading his space
or the steed's yet. "Not Chela."

Her father's semiregular mate was a source of comfort,
but Chela wanted to be more maternal than Ani could accept

world, bound to the Dark Court by their Gabriel.

A Gabriel who would chew up anyone who touched his daughter.

"You know he won't give permission," she admitted.

Her father was in charge. His rules meant that only one who could stand against him in a fight was allowed to date her.

Or anything else.

"Hey?"

She looked at the Hound.

"If you weren't *his* daughter, I'd risk it, but crossing Gabe isn't something I'm going to do."

Ani sighed, not in disappointment, but at the futility of ever getting a different answer. "I know."

"Convince him that you're not going to get broken by a little fun, and I'll be in front of the line. Promise." The Hound leaned forward to drop a quick kiss on her lips.

It was no more than a second of affection, but he was ripped away and hurled across the aisle toward the opposite stall. The thud of his body hitting the wooden slats covered most of the curses he was yelling.

"Don't touch my pup." Gabriel stood in the middle of the aisle. He was grinning, but his posture was one of menace. Of course, he was the Hound that controlled the Wild Hunt, so menace was as natural as breathing for him.

The Hound on the floor felt the back of his head as he

leaned on one partition of the wooden stall. "Damn, Gabriel. I didn't touch her."

"Your lips were on hers. That's *touching*," Gabriel growled.

Ani stepped in front of her father and poked him in the chest. "Don't act like it's wrong for them to respond to me."

He glared at her but didn't lift a hand. "I am the Gabriel. I run this pack, and if any of them"—he looked past her to the Hound on the floor—"want to challenge me over you, all they need to do is say the word."

The Hound on the floor spoke up. "I turned her down."

"Not because she lacks anything," Gabriel growled.

"No, no." The Hound held up his hands. "She's perfect, Gabe . . . but you said she was off-limits."

Gabriel held a hand out to the Hound on the floor without looking at him.

The Hound glanced at her. "Sorry . . . I, umm, touched you."

Ani rolled her eyes. "You're a peach."

"Sorry, Gabriel. It won't happen again." The Hound straddled his bike and left with a roar that was more growl than a real Harley's engine could mimic.

For a heartbeat, it was perfectly quiet in the stable. The steeds stayed silent and motionless.

"My perfect pup." Gabriel stepped up and ruffled her hair. "He doesn't deserve you. None of them do."

She shoved him away. "So, you'd rather I'm skin starved?"

Gabriel snorted. "You're not starved."

"I would be if I followed all of your rules," she muttered.

"And I wouldn't have so many rules if I thought you'd follow them all." He threw a punch, which she dodged. It was nice, but not backed by the full force of his strength or weight. He always held back. *That* was insulting. If she were truly a part of the Hunt, he'd fight with her the way he fought with all the rest. He'd train her. *He'd accept me in the pack.*

"You suck at fatherhood, Gabe." She turned away and started down the aisle.

He couldn't taste her feelings, not like the most of the Dark Court. Hounds weren't nourished on the same things, so her emotions were hidden to them. The peculiarity of the Hunt's inability to taste emotions while everyone around them could made them very blunt in their own expressions. It worked out well: Dark Court faeries were nourished by swallowing dark emotions; Hounds required physical touch for sustenance. So the Hunt caused the fear and terror that fed the court, and the court provided the touch the Hounds required. Ani was abnormal in that she needed both.

Which sucks.

"Ani?"

She didn't stop walking. There was no way she was going to let him see the tears building in her eyes. *Just another proof of my weakness.* She gestured over her shoulder. "I get it, *Daddy*. I'm not welcome."

"Ani."

Tears leaked onto her cheeks as she stopped in the doorway, but she didn't turn back.

"Promise to follow the rules while we're out, and you could probably borrow Che's steed again tonight." His voice held the hope he wouldn't say aloud. "*If* she agrees."

Ani turned then and smiled at him. "Yeah?"

"Yeah." He didn't move, didn't comment on the tears on her cheeks, but his voice softened and he added, "And I'm *not* an awful father."

"Maybe."

"I just don't want to think about you wanting . . . things . . . or getting hurt." Gabriel folded the cloth that the Hound had dropped, looking at it rather than at her. "Irial says you're okay though. I ask. I do try."

"I know." She shook her hair back and struggled to be reasonable. That was the worst part sometimes; she *did* know that Gabriel tried. She knew he trusted Irial's judgment, trusted Chela, trusted his pack. He'd never raised a daughter—these past few months that he'd had her around were the sum total of his father-daughter parenting experience. But, she'd never had pack hungers before either. It was a new experience all around.

Later, after she'd secured Chela's consent, gone over the regular stay-close-to-Gabriel rules, and promised to stick with the pack, Ani was back in the stable with her father.

"If Che's steed has anything to say, it'll tell me, and I'll tell you." Gabriel's reminder that she couldn't hear Chela's steed—*that I'll never hear one*—was delivered with an ominous rumble in his voice. He was already feeling the heightened connection to the Hounds who were filling the aisles.

Somewhere in the distance, a howl rose like the scream of wind. Ani knew that only the Hunt heard it, but both mortal and faery *felt* it in the shivers that raced over suddenly chilled skin. To some, it was as if sirens came toward them, as if ambulances and police sped to them carrying words of sudden deaths or horrific accidents.

The Wild Hunt rides.

As Ani looked over the assembling Hounds, the green of their eyes and the clouds of their breath were clear. Wolves filled the room where the steeds were not. They would run between the hooves of the steeds, a roil of fur and teeth. Steed and wolf all waited for their Gabriel's word to begin, to run, to chase those foolish enough to attract their attention. Terror built and filled the air with a prestorm charge. Those not belonging to the Hunt would have to struggle to breathe. Mortals on the nearby streets would cringe, scurry into their dens, or turn into other alleys. If they stayed, they'd not see the true face of the Hunt, but explain it away—*earthquake?*

trains? storms? street fights?—with the willful ignorance mortals clung to so fiercely. They didn't often stay; they ran. It was the order of things: prey runs, and predators pursue.

Her father, her Gabriel, strode through the room assessing them.

Ani felt the stroke of icy fingers on her skin as they prepared to ride. She bit down on her lip to keep from urging her father to sound the call. Her knuckles whitened as she clenched the edge of the wooden wall beside her. She looked at their horrible beauty and shivered.

If they were mine . . . I'd belong.

Then Gabriel was beside her.

"You are my pup, Ani." Gabriel cupped her cheek in his massive hand. "To be worthy of you, any Hound would have to be willing to face me. He'd need to be strong enough to lead them."

"*I* want to lead them," she whispered. "I want to be their Gabrielle."

"You're too mortal to hold control of them." Gabriel's eyes were monstrous. His skin was the touch of terror, of death, of nightmares that were Un-Named. "And too much mine to not be with the Hunt. I'm sorry."

She held his gaze. Something feral inside of her understood that this was why she couldn't live with Rabbit: her brother wasn't as fierce as her father was. Tish wasn't. Ani desperately wanted to be. Like the rest of the Hounds mounting their steeds, Ani knew that Gabriel could kill her if she disobeyed. It was a restraint she needed: it kept her closer to following rules.

"I can't take the Hunt from you"—she flashed her teeth at her father—"yet. Maybe I'll surprise you."

"Makes me proud that you want to," he said.

For a moment, the pride in her father's eyes was the sum of her world. She belonged. For tonight, she was included in the pack. He made it so.

If only I always was.

But there were no unclaimed steeds, and her mortal blood meant she'd never be strong enough to become Gabriel's successor, never be truly Pack.

A taste of belonging . . .

It wasn't enough, not truly, but it was something.

Then a howl unlike anything else in this world or the next came to his lips, and the rest of the pack echoed it. *She* echoed it.

Gabriel tossed her atop Chela's steed and growled, "We ride."

BT 10/21/10